Love
THINE ENEMY

By the same author

Novels

The Bitter Web
The Judas Son
The Walnut Tree
The Luncheon Club

Biography

The Polish Exile

To Jeanette with best wishes

Love
THINE ENEMY

MICHAEL PAKENHAM

Michael Pakenham

AuthorHouse™ UK Ltd.
1663 Liberty Drive
Bloomington, IN 47403 USA
www.authorhouse.co.uk
Phone: 0800.197.4150

This book is a work of fiction. Names, characters and incidents are the product of the author's imagination and are used fictitiously. Any resemblance to actual events, locales, or persons living or dead is coincidental.

© 2014 Michael Pakenham. All rights reserved.

No part of this book may be reproduced, stored in a retrieval system, or transmitted by any means without the written permission of the author.

Published by AuthorHouse 07/08/2014

ISBN: 978-1-4969-8387-9 (sc)
ISBN: 978-1-4969-8402-9 (hc)
ISBN: 978-1-4969-8386-2 (e)

Any people depicted in stock imagery provided by Thinkstock are models, and such images are being used for illustrative purposes only.
Certain stock imagery © Thinkstock.

This book is printed on acid-free paper.

Because of the dynamic nature of the Internet, any web addresses or links contained in this book may have changed since publication and may no longer be valid. The views expressed in this work are solely those of the author and do not necessarily reflect the views of the publisher, and the publisher hereby disclaims any responsibility for them.

As always, to my darling Mrs Bond, with all my love and thanks.

> I love thee with the breath,
> Smiles, tears, of all my life-
> And if God choose
> I shall but love thee better after death.
>
> Elizabeth Barrat Browning

One

1970

Dermot Fitzpatrick was enjoying an all too brief moment of quiet reflection. He eased into a chair on the terrace, loosened his tie and exhaled slowly. It had been another stressful day; violence was simmering all over the brooding city, ready to ignite at a moment's notice.

The light was fading over Lough Neagh and the evening sky was streaked with shades of gold and orange. Mallard circled the glittering waters searching for their favourite landing places. He loved the peace of this place and watched huge, red sun sink slowly like a ship into Belfast's faraway horizon. His mind drifted back to the time when he was a boy, his father, large and red-faced from a few too many whiskies, taking his hand and walking him down to the Lough. They would stand silently listening to the Lough slowly going to sleep; absolute stillness and the drift of the water. They had stood motionless and breathed in the evening air. His father would put a large arm around his shoulders and smile down at him. I still miss him, Dermot thought as he wiped an involuntary tear from the corner of his eye with the back of his hand.

He took a few brief moments thinking about the man who had unintentionally shaped his future. A good father, who he had loved passionately, but as he'd grown up he came to realise that there were those who saw him as an austere, frightening figure – a man who was reluctant to change his bigoted ways in a new order that was threatening his generation's way of life. Dermot gave a rueful laugh. He'd been too young then to understand the underlying feeling of injustice that fermented in the bosom of the Catholic minority. "And now I'm here trying to make up for all your mistakes father," he said out loud.

*

The sound of Jenny's footsteps on the terrace flagstones jolted him from his reverie. He raised his hand behind his head to feel for her. She took it and squeezed it gently before dropping a kiss on his small bald patch. She was relieved to have her husband home alive, living as she did in constant fear that one day he would not walk through the door at the end of his day. She knew he was welded to his job and that she would never be able to prise him away. She tried to keep everyday life as normal as possible for their young son, shielding him from the pressure of danger that they both felt. She supported Dermot wholeheartedly because that was her duty. He called her his 'rock' but most of the time her insides were like jelly.

'It's a beautiful evening', she sighed. "Shall we take our usual walk?"

"Why not? The sounds of the Lough and you by my side are just what I need."

"Tough day?"

"No worse than usual."

"Is it safe to go?"

Dermot reached for her hand. "We've been doing this for years so I'm not stopping now just because things seem to be getting worse again."

Jenny nodded. "Let's go then. I'll tell Eliza where we are going. She is putting Richard to bed. You can read him a story when we get back."

"It's a promise. How is he?"

"He's fine. "Eliza has been telling him silly stories and making him giggle. Richard is so fond of her. She's the best au-pair we've ever had."

"She's pretty too!"

Jenny gave Dermot a playful dig in the ribs. 'Have I got competition, Dermot Fitzpatrick?"

"Absolutely not! You, my darling are in a class of your own."

Dermot slipped out of his uniform jacket and hung it on the back of his chair. He put his heavy bunch of keys on the table and waited for Jenny to return. "There, free from all the shackles of the day," he said as she stepped out onto the terrace. "Let's enjoy a little time of uninterrupted bliss. Where's our faithful old dog?"

"He's right behind you."

"So he is. C'mon Teal old fella, time for a stroll." Dermot bent to stroke the Labrador's greying muzzle.

The three of them walked slowly to the end of the lawn, opened a wicket gate and stepped into the meadow leading down to the Lough side. The ducks had begun their evening patrol of the water. They listened to the splashing and quacking that was all around them. Jenny sighed. "Why can't the whole of Ireland be like this? Why do we have to fight each other, hate each other so much? Why do innocent people have to die, Dermot why?"

It was a question he'd been asked many times by grieving families, the media, and politicians, and he'd never been able to find a satisfactory answer for them. He asked himself the same question day after day and the end result was the same. He shrugged and smiled. "You know I have no answer to that question. One day though perhaps we'll find one." He wrapped his arm round her shoulders and pulled her to his side. "I love you" he whispered.

"And I love you."

The boom of a rifle echoed across the Lough.

The stillness that had filled them with contentment was shattered. The Lough burst alive with frantic noise. Duck and geese took to the sky in panic, squawking nervously. Jenny felt a thud and the weight of Dermot's body against her. He grunted and began sinking slowly from her arms into the reeds. Instinctively she ducked, hunching her shoulders in expectation of another shot. But none came. Then she remembered Dermot once telling her, "These men kill one spouse and leave the other to grieve. It's what they call a slow death."

Michael Pakenham

She stifled a cry and scrambled over to Dermot's side, taking him in her arms, feeling his warm blood soak through her blouse. She didn't have to feel for a pulse, she knew he was dead – the snipers never missed. She started to sob, her tears mingling with Dermot's blood.

*

Patrick Ryan watched through the rifle's scope as his victim fell. The bullet had found its target. The man was dead. He never missed. A smile broke across his face, he blew out his cheeks and wiped the sweat from his brow. A good job had been done. He felt no remorse – the man was his enemy and killing was his occupation. He stood up slowly, stretched, and quietly started to walk back to his car which was hidden a few yards from the road. He'd picked the spot a week earlier when the order went out to get Dermot Fitzpatrick at whatever cost. "He and his wife like to walk alone down to the Lough on a sunny evening, no security, the fools." He'd been informed. He'd sat in his chosen spot for several evenings as dusk settled in over Belfast, patiently waiting for a fine evening.

He tucked the rifle under an arm. He was banking on at least a minimum of half-an-hour before the alarm was raised. The shock of watching her husband die would paralyse Fitzpatrick's wife. Her mind would go numb. It would give him valuable time before she started to run back to the house and alert their body guards. He smiled, relishing the thought of the pain that would be coursing through the widow. Widow! Jesus what pleasure that word gave him! Reaching his car he carefully wiped the rifle with a cloth he'd stuffed into his pocket earlier, and threw the rifle back into the thick undergrowth where he'd hidden it on his visit two days earlier. He didn't want to run the risk of being caught up in a roadside check point. It didn't matter if the army found it – there were hundreds of the same make in the IRA's hands. Tomorrow morning they would claim responsibility for the death of Dermot Fitzpatrick, ex-Chief Constable of the hated RUC.

*

Eliza was getting worried, over an hour had passed since her employees had left the house, longer than usual. Alert to the constant danger they were in, she went to find the protection officers.

*

The alarm had been raised immediately. The helicopter crew found Jenny sitting amongst the reeds with Dermot's head on her knees. She was shivering uncontrollably, Teal sat close by whining. Dermot's second-in-command had to prize Jenny away. She looked up at him, panic radiating from her eyes. Her inertia vanished. "Richard, Richard!" she gasped, leaping to her feet. "Oh dear God, he's in the house!" She started to stagger away. The Deputy Chief Constable grabbed her arm. "Wait!"

"I've left him too long! He's in danger!" Her voice rose to a scream.

He hung onto her arm. "It's alright Jenny, everything is fine. We have checked the house and your son and au-pair are safe. The girl alerted your protection team. They are aware of the situation."

Jenny stared at him through her tears. "But I must go – I must…"

"Of course. It's getting dark. I will get an officer to go with you."

"No, I'll go on my own." She looked down at Dermot – double upped and vomited as she saw the gapping hole in his chest. She felt a hand on her back. "Come on Jenny, there is nothing more you can do here." She tore her eyes away from the body and turned to the Deputy Chief Constable. "You're right." Without another word she started to run, pushing her way through the reeds in panic. The house seemed so far away. Sympathetic eyes followed her until she disappeared into the evening gloom. Every one of the officers on the ground knew how she was suffering – they had been to too many scenes like this.

*

Jenny rushed into the hall and made for the stairs, desperately wiping away her tears. She intended to reach her bedroom and discard her blood-stained clothes before facing her son.

But he was there.

He was standing at the top of the stairs with Eliza, panic slashed across his tiny face. Richard launched himself down the stairs at her. "Where's Daddy?" he screamed, "Where's my Daddy! The sirens and helicopters woke me. I know something terrible has happened." He stopped in his tracks as he took in the horror written on his mother's face and her blood soaked clothing. "It's Daddy, it's Daddy isn't it? Something terrible has happened to him hasn't it?"

Jenny caught him in her arms, feeling his young body tense. She held him tight unable to find the words to tell him that his father had been murdered in cold blood. Her words came in a whisper. "Daddy is dead. I'm so sorry darling."

Eliza gasped.

Richard went limp.

He buried his face in his mother's chest, his shoulders heaving with grief. Then suddenly he reared away, wiping his mouth violently, he could taste his father's blood. Shock hit him like a bolt of lightening, his face contorted in revulsion. He vomited. Making a noise like a wounded animal he fled upstairs to his bedroom and slammed the door. Jenny dashed after him, ripping off her clothes as she ran. She flew into her bedroom and covered herself with a dressing gown before following him.

Eliza stood bewildered, shock waves were still crashing through her body. She ran up the stairs and saw Jenny opening Richard's door. She stopped on the landing, deeming it better not to interfere, she'd wait.

Jenny closed Richard's door behind her, she knew she had to control her grief. Bearing her own pain was one thing, but bearing the pain of her child was something else. She felt helpless. But then reality returned to crush her with an iron hand as she stared at the small naked body sitting on the bed. It was horrible. Richard's wet pyjamas were lying on the floor where he had thrown them. He was holding a photograph of his father to his chest. Henry, his old well-worn teddy, was lying beside him and his face was streaked with tears. He looked up, his eyes confirming his misery. Jenny dropped down beside him, prised the photograph from his hands and pulled him to her. She felt him resist. "It's okay darling." She could feel him shaking, her heart bled for him. She knew there was nothing she could do to alleviate his pain, only time could do that. She began to tell him how his father had died, desperately trying to keep her voice calm. "It was instant; he would have felt no pain." When she'd finished she was drained of all emotion and had drawn on an inner strength she had no idea she possessed. She eased him away from her body and held him at arms length, staring into his eyes. She pulled him close again, running one hand through his damp hair. Finally, after what seemed an age, Richard moved his head so that he could look up at his mother. He put a hand on her cheek and felt the wetness. Then in a voice cracking with emotion he whispered, "I'll miss Daddy so much." They wept together.

Eventually, Jenny felt him relax in her arms and his breathing steady. She didn't bother to find fresh pyjamas, just laid him back on the bed and carefully covered him with the duvet. Exhaustion had come to the rescue. She picked up the photo of Dermot from the end of the bed and placed it on the bedside table, tucking the faithful Henry into bed beside him, she quietly left the room.

Eliza was standing by Richard's door and she saw Jenny sway. "You need coffee."

Jenny nodded and allowed Eliza to take her by the arm and lead her downstairs to the kitchen. She collapsed onto a chair and rested her elbows on the table, staring at Eliza as she made the coffee, she hadn't the strength to talk.

The coffee was black and strong and Jenny drank greedily, her eyes darting to the ceiling every now and then, listening for any sounds from Richard's room. Once her cup was empty she stood up. "I must go and see if Richard's alright."

"Okay," Eliza agreed, then adding, "but then you must rest. You'll have a stressful day tomorrow. I'll sleep with Richard tonight and I will call you if he wakes and asks for you."

Jenny didn't argue. She and Eliza moved back upstairs and quietly opened Richard's door, she heard his regular breathing. "He's asleep," she whispered.

"Good, now you try to do the same."

Jenny touched the girl's face and walked towards her room. Once the door was closed behind her she threw herself onto the bed. She buried her head in Dermot's pillow and thought of the man she'd lost. He had been the only man she had ever really loved, no-one had ever touched her heart like he had and now he was gone – torn away too soon, so violently, but in the way she had so often feared. She felt lost and terribly alone. She thought of her father's words of caution over her marrying a policeman and an officer in the Royal Ulster Constabulary (the RUC) to boot. "But I'm in love Daddy," she'd said. She'd never once regretted her decision; she rolled over on the bed and stared at the ceiling. A cobweb swayed gently from the overhead light, reminding her to wipe it away tomorrow. She dropped a hand over the side and felt Teal's wet nose, patting the bed encouragingly the old dog struggled to jump up. She rested a hand on his neck and buried her face in his fur. He whimpered. She loved his smell and the warmth of his body gave her comfort as she closed her eyes. Very soon there would be friends telling her that everything would work out alright in the end. "The pain will die and life will get back onto an even keel." But she doubted that would ever be the case. She would have to conceal her feelings for the sake of Richard, he must be her priority. She rubbed Teal's ears and the old dog licked her face, sensing, as dogs do, that something was not right.

Two

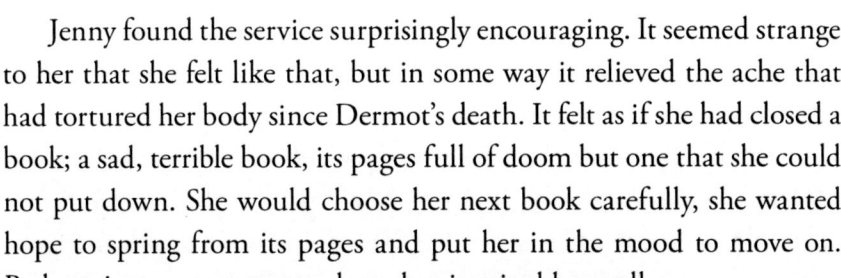

Jenny found the service surprisingly encouraging. It seemed strange to her that she felt like that, but in some way it relieved the ache that had tortured her body since Dermot's death. It felt as if she had closed a book; a sad, terrible book, its pages full of doom but one that she could not put down. She would choose her next book carefully, she wanted hope to spring from its pages and put her in the mood to move on. Perhaps it was a strange analogy, but it suited her well.

They had sung three of Dermot's favourite hymns and listened to a glowing address by a fellow RUC officer. Now, as she walked out of the church gripping Richard's tiny hand and headed for the grave that had been dug several days earlier, she felt as if a great weight was being lifted off her shoulders. This was the final parting – no counting the days to the funeral – no more frantic organisation. Just memories, helped by all the wonderful letters that people had sent her. As well as letters from friends there were letters from people she had never met who had in one way or the other been touched by Dermot's understanding. "A good and decent man," was a much repeated phrase. She would cherish every letter for the rest of her life. To her it meant that he had not died in vain, a small comfort, but something worthwhile to hang on to.

Mourning had to end, she knew it would not be easy but for Richard's sake she would give it her best shot. They reached the grave and stared into the dark rather frightening hole. Richard had stood beside her in the front pew of the little church, solemn, but dry eyed. Now, watching his father being lowered into the ground proved too much and his courage deserted him. Jenny held him tight as he sobbed. She took off her wedding ring and dropped it on top of the coffin and she turned away. Dermot was at peace now, laying in the Gartree Church Yard next to his father and mother and several other Fitzpatricks. It was time to get Richard away, she was very proud of him. "You've been so brave," she congratulated him as they got into their car. He looked up into her eyes and managed a smile. "Daddy would have been very cross if I'd cried all the time."

Jenny lovingly ruffled his hair, lost for a reply.

*

Half-an-hour later the house was packed with people, there was only just enough time for Jenny to catch her breath and make sure Richard was happy to be with Eliza. She didn't want to put any more pressure on him by keeping him by her side. He'd had enough for one day. Looking round the drawing room she reckoned she only knew fifty percent of the gathered company. But she was touched that so many of Dermot's colleagues had come to say goodbye, she voiced this opinion to an officer who had just shaken her hand.

"He was greatly respected you know and his fairness admired, not many of us have admirers in these violent times, but Dermot did." He replied.

By the time the last guest had gone Jenny's nerves were frayed, she was exhausted and a little light-headed from a few too many glasses of wine. Richard was asleep in Eliza's room. She was alone at last. She poured herself a glass of white wine from a half-empty bottle standing on a table – probably a bad idea but what the hell - and flopped onto a sofa. She looked round the large rather austere drawing room, Dermot's ancestors glaring at her from every wall. She'd always longed to pull them down. "They're so depressing," she'd said to Dermot the day after they had moved into the house. He'd put an arm around her and said, "I'm afraid they stay." And that had been the beginning of a growing dislike of the house and Ireland. "I hate you!" she shouted at the room. "You depress me, you haunt me and I will never be welcome here!"

At that moment her father Jack strode into the room, a concerned look on his face, having heard her shouting. He was a handsome man, soft blue eyes, loving and always aware that his daughter had to plough her own way in the world. Even when Edwina, his beloved wife, had died six years earlier he had never once tried to interfere in Jenny's life and she loved him all the more for this.

"You alright Jenny"?

She shook her head. "Not really Dad. Come and sit with me, I'm exhausted."

"Darling you did really well. You were amazingly calm, I'm so proud of you."

"I was hurting so much inside."

"I'm sure you were. And Richard – well he was a star wasn't he?"

"He's got a lot of his father in him – it's called balls I think."

Jack sat on the sofa. "It may be too early to ask this question, but having overheard you just now I feel I can raise the subject. Have you any idea what you will do now?"

"How do you mean?"

"Are you staying in Ireland?"

Jenny whipped off her hat and threw it across the room, her long auburn hair cascading down her face. "To be honest Dad I can't wait to leave. It's an easy decision." Jenny filled up her wine glass, and offered a glass to Jack, who refused. "I'll say it now and again and again if anyone wants to hear. I hate this place – I'm away just as soon as I can sell it."

Jack nodded. "I thought that might be your decision."

"I suspect it's a bit selfish but I'll never settle here now that Dermot is dead. The house has always seemed a bit like a morgue to me – too much history attached to it and most of it sad. The rooms are large and gloomy, made worse by all these awful paintings of Dermot's ancestors. The only redeeming feature is the garden and the view. But I can't live outside and I don't ever want to walk down to the Lough again. Also,

I can't go anywhere without a bodyguard – although I suppose that might change now."

Jack nodded his understanding. Jenny continued. "It'll be like living in a prison. And that's about it Dad, it sends out all the wrong vibes and it makes me desperately sad. But in spite of everything I've had some very happy years with Dermot and Richard was born here, but we've never been able to live a normal life. Countless times I've longed for England and a more secure living and this is the moment to take it. I'm free to make my own decisions – Dermot's parents are dead and there are no other relatives to jump out of an Irish bog and make a scene. So I'll cut my ties and return to England as soon as I can. To some it will seem like I'm running scared and they aren't far wrong. And no doubt others will think it's wrong to sell a home that has been in the family for five generations but it's my life I have to think of now."

Jack wrapped an arm round Jenny's shoulders. He understood completely how she felt and was rather relieved at her decision. He certainly wouldn't be putting any obstacles in her way. "I won't try and stop you darling but if you had decided to stay, I hope you know I would have supported you in any way I could."

"I know you would Dad." She tucked her long legs underneath her and reached for Jack's hand. She could almost feel the love seeping out of him, while he was alive she knew she would never be alone.

*

"I think we have a buyer," said the young man from the estate agents, smiling broadly at Jenny. She felt a surge of excitement; the house and the farm had only been on the market for two months and this came as a great relief. Who in their right mind was going to be prepared to shell out a load of money on a large house with a six hundred acre farm when bombs and killings were every day events?

"Who?" she asked.

"An aviation company."

"A what!"

"It makes sense Mrs Fitzpatrick. You're not far from Aldergrove airport – the land is flat, and the farm buildings could be used for storing small aircraft."

"And the house?"

"The young man didn't look her in the eye. "I think it will be demolished."

Jenny looked at him in amazement. "Demolish it, can they do that?"

"They can."

Jenny took a deep breath to try and control her rapid heart rate. It might well be the only offer she got. But to destroy the house! Dermot would turn in his grave. She looked at the young man standing nervously infront of her. "I can't give you an answer right away. Can I ring you tomorrow?"

"I doubt if there is any hurry Mrs Fitzpatrick, this looks as if it might be the only offer we get for some time. This isn't the sort of property that will sell easily – too remote."

"I realise that. I'll ring you tomorrow."

Jenny immediately rang her father and told him the news. She explained her dilemma. "What shall I do Dad?"

Jack didn't need to think for long. He said firmly, "I'll tell you exactly what you do. You think about yourself for once, you're unhappy there. Sell it Jenny, and if you have any doubts about how Dermot would feel, let me say this, Dermot isn't here darling – you must do what you feel is right for you. I'll fly over tomorrow and not leave until you've got the contract in your hand."

It was all Jenny needed to hear.

*

The house was an empty shell. The contents on their way into storage in London until Jenny could find a house. She sat in the back of the car with Eliza and Richard. Jack drove, judging that Jenny and Eliza had their hands full trying to console Richard. He'd hardly stopped crying since she'd broken the news of the sale to him. He glanced in the rear view mirror at the sullen face and Jack's heart went out to him, but Richard was young, he would recover. He started the engine. "Ready?" he asked.

"Ready," said Jenny and was rewarded with a kick from Richard.

No one spoke on the way to Larne. Richard was wrapped in his own thoughts, wondering if he'd ever speak to his mother again. How could she walk away from his home, daddy's grave, the Lough which he loved? He'd been so happy. His mother was a monster. Looking out of the window at the familiar landscape he made a vow – one day when he was grown up and his monster of a mother could no longer tell him what to do he'd return. He glanced at his mother, indifferent to her tears. *I hate you.*

*

In a pub in the Shanklin Road there was a near riot; voices were raised shaking the rafters of the pub, glasses were held high, drinks were on the house. Patrick Ryan was standing by the bar flushed by all the congratulations. He felt good. Why shouldn't he when he was the hero of the hour? Fitzpatrick dead and now his widow was running back to England, her tail between her legs. Slaps on his back told him what a great man he was – a man frightened of nothing; a man who could put the fear of God into the security forces. When the next history of Ireland was written Patrick felt sure he'd feature in it.

At the back of the crowd, nursing a pint of orange juice, a seventeen year old by the name of Seamus Flanagan stood aloof from the gathered company. He was slowly shaking his head, Ryan was a fucking fool drawing attention to himself, bravado would prove his undoing. He would soon be dead and then he, Seamus Flanagan, would one day be top of the pile. He'd earn respect and he'd be feared. He had no doubt of it. He turned away from the noise and left the pub as quietly as he'd arrived. He had no time for idiots.

Three

2010

The Belfast Chronicle July 14th.

Northern Ireland Riots.

Belfast witnessed serious riots this week as trouble flared over the Orange Orders annual July marches, which mark the victory of the protestant William of Orange over the Catholic King James ll. The riots began on Sunday night after police tried to separate the nationalists in the Broadway area from those attending loyalist Eleventh night bonfires in the nearby Donegal Road. Officers came under attack from nationalists throwing petrol bombs, stones and bottles. Three officers received wounds from shotgun pellets. There were further disturbances across the province on Monday and Tuesday. The worst violence was in the Ardoyne area of north Belfast, where police lines came under frenzied attack and deployed water cannons against nationalist rioters. Gunshots were fired and one rioter attacked a policewoman by dropping a concrete block on her head. The Chief Constable condemned the violence, as did Sinn Fein. Is this the beginning of the unrest the dissidents have been threatening, this paper asks?

    Yes, it is, thought Seamus Flanagan as he sat at his usual table in the café on Lurgan Street, Belfast. He folded the Belfast Chronicle and placed it on the table, reaching for his half-drunk cup of black coffee, now growing cold. He banged a clenched fist on the top of the table and allowed himself a satisfied smile. His rhetoric had proved decisive, tipped the balance and persuaded the doubters. It might be several years since the peace accord but men like him would never give up. The fight back had begun. He rose slowly from the table, his leg hurting from a blow of a policeman's baton and limped towards the café door. There was work to be done.

Four

November.

Even though the threat of violence was in the air, the car bomb shocked the people who lived in Kingsway Road, resting in a quiet suburb of Belfast. Ever since the July riots there had been the odd incident that made the headlines and a few disappearances that were never explained. The day had started like any normal weekday, people hurrying to work, the growing noise of traffic, a few voices raised in argument – a baby crying. Then at 09:50 a family's life was shattered.

A blue, slightly battered Mazda MX5 sat innocently outside Megan Cassidy's family home. Megan parked it there every evening when she returned from the Mater Hospital where she worked as a nurse. She threw open the door of the small semi, juggling with her car keys – late as usual - blew a kiss to her mother, who was waving from the front room window, and ran down the short garden path to the road. She flicked the lock and pulling open the driver's door she jumped in and put the key in the ignition. She turned it and was blown to pieces. The force of the explosion shattered windows in a wide area and blew Megan's mother across her front room, her face lacerated by the flying glass.

Megan's crime was to love a young, protestant boy. Evil men had meted out the punishment. Men who would never accept the peace – never accept religious harmony. Men who would fight, kill and maim with impunity; their sole purpose to stir up hatred so that the peace accord would collapse under the violence.

*

Mary Keogh heard the explosion and then a few minutes later the sirens. She smiled at the floor, not wanting her mother, Eileen, to see. Mary was sitting in the small front room of her home, combing her long black hair and thinking how lucky she was that it was her day off from working at Brascome Manor, as a receptionist. Her mother sat opposite her, nervously sipping a mug of tea wondering what her no-good husband was up to. He'd not returned the night before and to her mind that meant one of two things. Either he'd been too drunk to get home – a common occurrence - or he was getting up to no good with his old comrades in the IRA, which he'd promised her, once the peace agreement had been signed, he'd never do again. But Conor Keogh was a born liar, he'd deny it, but that would just be another lie. Eileen knew that although to all intents and purposes the IRA had been disbanded he was a staunch supporter of the hard-line Republican movement, known as 'Freedom For Ireland' who she knew were a lethal group determined to destabilise the political process working towards peace – a peace she'd prayed for every Sunday since the age of ten. Violence repulsed her, actually if she was honest with herself, Conor repulsed her as well. Long ago he'd swapped their relationship for the whisky bottle and violence. Violence was ingrained in his heart, hatred for the British lay deep in his soul, nurtured by his late father an IRA commander. Peace meant nothing to him. He would never accept it – *never*. Only a united Ireland would make him think twice about revoking violence. But as he told his closest mates, "There will always be a protestant to kill in Ireland." She acknowledged that she should have walked out on him years ago, but women didn't walk out on men like Conor unless you were so tired of the drinking and beatings that you felt death was a better option.

Eileen threw a furtive look across the room at her daughter and was not surprised to see the lack of concern written across her beautiful, slightly freckled, face. Was that even the beginnings of a smile? Eileen was scared. Mary was spectacular - had the beauty to make something of her life. Men gave her more than a passing look. It was her hair, her eyes, her face, smile, and figure. She was stunning. "Nice men, good men admire her. She'll have a great future," Eileen said, trying to convince her friends. They knew she didn't believe her own words. Mary was already shunned by good men sick of sectarian division and resulting violence. Conor's influence over his daughter was overpowering, threatening to eat into her soul. Eileen had already feared the worse for her daughter. There would be no modelling contract, no growing into a famous pop star. She loved her daughter with an intensity that sometimes frightened her, but she was beginning to fear that her love was no longer reciprocated. It was ripping a great hole in her heart. She'd had such hopes and they were crumbling into dust. She had hoped that when Mary had taken the job at Brascome Manor, at Fivemiletown in county Fermanagh, a good hour's drive from Belfast, the company she would be keeping might weaken the influence of her father and drain her growing extreme views from her heart. It seemed not to have been the case. Looking at her daughter she felt the urge to cry. How much better her life would have been if Conor, the fat, fucking layabout, hadn't been intent on killing as many British soldiers as he could. Come to think of it she'd have been better off if a bullet had thumped into his hairy chest years ago. She vigorously crossed herself at such a wicked thought. Had he ever taken his role as a husband and father seriously? Had he just! Always short of a bob or two, because Conor never could hold a job down, they had struggled and would probably have been close to starving at times if she hadn't taken menial jobs for people better off than herself. Conor just drank any spare cash away. Where had her devotion and love got her? She was old at forty-four, bitter and beaten into the ground. Sometimes she wished she had the courage to bury a kitchen knife into Conor's rotten heart.

Eileen's mug of tea slipped from her shaking hands, leaving another stain on the already well-worn carpet. "Holy mother of God what was that?" she exclaimed, although she already knew.

Mary stopped combing her hair long enough to look at her mother. A woman she was struggling to respect because of her meek acceptance of the status quo, and her unswerving belief that God would put everything right in the end. What a load of shit. Conor had long ago persuaded Mary that only the bombs, the rifles and the brave men who were loyal to The Cause could do that. The Good Friday agreement was the work of traitors and if her father had anything to do with it soon to be discarded in the dustbin of false hopes that had plagued Ireland for so many years. "Sounds like a car bomb," Mary said. "Another one of those *kiss the Brits arses* blown to pieces I expect."

Eileen sucked in her breath – wiped away a tear, fearful of looking Mary in the eye, for she suspected that Mary probably knew the target. She would never ask, she didn't want to know.

Mary guessed what was on her mother's mind so she spat, "of course I don't know who the target is. Why would I?"

It was a lie, but like her father she was able to tell a convincing one. Mary knew Megan Cassidy very well, they had been childhood friends. It was Megan who had first introduced her to boys, make-up and lager. Eileen had worried but Conor had just shrugged, he didn't really care what mischief his daughter got up to. Then a year back Megan had fallen for a protestant boy. Mary warned her – begged her to drop him – told her she was putting her life in danger, but to no avail. "It's not like that anymore," Megan replied. So Mary dropped her as a friend. You just didn't fraternise with a protestant in this part of Belfast, let alone sleep with him. Silly fucking cow. But there was no way she was going to tell her mother that her father had hinted the day before that the demise of Miss Megan Cassidy was close.

Eileen had made it quite clear that if she ever again found out that Conor was connected in anyway to violence she would shop him to the police. Something she should have had the guts to do years ago. Fear that she, Eileen, might be killed in revenge, leaving her child an orphan stopped her. She had no such worries now her child was grown up and she had made Conor well aware of this. "In fact I might relish seeing you on a murder charge," she'd said to him. He'd walked away laughing.

Unconvinced, Eileen forced a smile at her daughter's denial. Mary smiled back and began to comb her hair again. She had learnt that when you tell a lie it is better to keep it short – do not elaborate. Eileen felt, as she often did, a stab of pity for her daughter. Conor was continuously brain washing her, filling her with his hatred and telling her to ignore her mother's advice. Conor put his case well.

Mary rose from her chair, smoothing down her short black dress over her slim body. She might well look alluring, with her clear complexion, and long black hair but her dark green eyes, set deep in her face, radiated the anger that festered within her. Her small wardrobe was nearly all black. When anyone asked why, she would reply, "I'm in mourning for all those who died for a just cause." It didn't matter to her that there were a growing number of people who were shocked by this answer and told her so. In her eyes anyone who supported the peace agreement was a traitor. "I'm off out to see what's happened. Won't be long." Eileen made no attempt to stop her.

By the time she'd walked the short distance to Megan's house, the ambulance was just leaving. There were several police cars and army vehicles parked in the road and the bombed scarred house was surrounded by men in uniform. A fire engine was blocking the path and smoke was still rising from the ruined car. Mary saw her friend Sinead and waved. When she got closer she saw that she was crying, Mary was quick to pull out a handkerchief and wipe the smile off her face. "Oh God, what's happened, what's happened Sinead?"

"It's Megan," Sinead managed to say between sobs. "She's dead, blown to pieces Mary. Her mother's badly injured. Her father's okay though – he'd left for work just before Megan. Poor man. Who would do such a thing?"

Mary knew exactly who would do such a thing, and Sinead was a bigger fool than she thought if she didn't know the answer as well. She was putting her arms around her when she spotted her father in the crowd. He saw her and she smiled over her friend's shoulder Conor raised a fist towards his daughter and turned away. A lump formed in Mary's throat and she wasn't quite sure whether it was because of the death of her erstwhile friend or pride for her father. Surely not for Megan, but...feeling slightly perplexed Mary held Sinead's hand a little longer than she'd planned and shook her head. "I think we both know who would do such a thing Sinead; Megan was warned." Sinead pulled her hand away and stared at Mary. It was on the tip of her tongue to ask who had warned her, but thought better of it. She shuddered. "I must go," she said abruptly, thinking a dangerous thought. It was time to distance herself from Mary.

Mary was not slow to note the change in Sinead's attitude, but fuck it, what did she care. She half-raised a hand in farewell and turned away, another friend gone and for the best. It was time for her to leave home, she knew where she would go – she had an open invitation, and Seamus Flanagan would be pleased to see her for more reasons than one.

*

Conor pushed his way through the crowd and felt a surge of pride. His father, God rest his whisky sodden soul, would have smiled at him and said, "Job well done boy." Then he'd have offered him a large Bushmills. Pity he wasn't around to witness his son's latest "adventure," as he used to call them. But you took life as a bonus when serving the IRA and dad's luck had finally run out on a wet night in the Shanklin Road, when he was throwing Molotov cocktails at the armoured vehicles. The RUC, asking no questions had shot him down. Bastards! To be fair he had been getting careless, in his younger days he would never have so blatantly shown his face, knowing that the army and the RUC had been after him for years. Conor swore that he wouldn't be so foolish, but like his father the drink was making him careless. Unaware that he was already as good as dead he smiled with satisfaction as he walked back to his house, wondering what his next target would be. The fight back had begun and those bastards who had betrayed The Cause had better not sleep too well in their beds from now on. He pushed open the door of his house, feeling elated, in spite of the fury that would erupt from Eileen's mouth.

"Eileen!" he shouted as he made for the kitchen, licking his lips at the thought of the first taste of the soft, brown liquid that would caress his parched throat. He swaggered into the kitchen bracing himself for his wife's verbal onslaught, but it wasn't Eileen who greeted him. It was two men holding her at gun point. They made no attempt to hide their faces. He recognised one, a new neighbour who had moved in several months earlier, his mouth fell open and the two men looked at each other. One man, feet apart, arms extended, his 9mm Walther p38 steady in both his hands as he pulled the trigger. The recoil kicked up the barrel and the soft nosed 9mm bullet tore a hole in Conor's chest. It was a man stopper. Conor's eyes widened in surprise and then he dropped dead, Eileen screamed. One of the men glanced at the other. "Got to do it?" he asked.

"No, she's innocent."

"She's recognised me."

The other man crossed the room to Eileen, now staring at Conor's body. He touched her on the shoulder, she jumped and turned to stare at him. "Go on," she said in a tired voice. "I know what you have to do."

The man shook his head. "No! We know all about you Eileen Keogh, we know your views. We know you're no threat, we've no argument with you. It's was your husband we wanted. Give us ten minutes and then ring the police. You've not recognised either of us, right?"

Eileen's mouth sagged in surprise but she said nothing, just nodded, watched the two men put their weapons into their coats and walk towards the door. They turned and left without another word.

Too shocked to move Eileen stood over her dead husband, watching his blood soak into the carpet, her heart was thumping against her ribs. She let out a long sigh and much to her horror felt a strong urge to cry out with joy. "I won't miss you," she whispered through trembling lips and vowed to go to confession the next day.

Five

She felt the comforting warmth of Richard's body, it was a warmth she treasured every day. She rubbed her nose against his back and felt him stir. She moved a hand to ruffle his auburn hair and smiled into the dark. She had good cause to feel such happiness, no guilt at feeling that she was owed it. Years of anxiety as she supported him through his political career and his obsession trying to find a peaceful solution to the Irish problem had taken its toll on them both. Never had Rachel Fitzpatrick felt so relieved when his party had lost the election and his job as Secretary of State for Northern Ireland had been wrenched from his grasp. No longer did she break into a sweat when he was away, imagining that the IRA had carried out their threat to kill him, nor did she jump every time the telephone rang, or put up with security men invading their privacy, nor the constant worry that if the IRA couldn't get to Richard they would target James, their son. The riots in Belfast in July had re-kindled her old fear and experience had told her that one riot almost always led to further trouble. The night before Richard had told her that even an attack on home soil could not be ruled out. Was it possible that once again Richard had become a target?

Richard rolled over; arms outstretched, and drew her body to him. He kissed her lightly on her forehead and sighed, having time for Rachel was the only plus at not having the job he'd set his heart on a year after he'd woken and heard the boom of the rifle that had sent a bullet straight as a die into his father's heart. It had taken many years for him to reach his goal and then, because of the twists and turns of politics, the electorate had decided to punish his party. Almost overnight someone else had stepped into his shoes and successfully completed the job he'd begun. It had wounded him. He knew it was irrational, Rachel told him he was being selfish and should only be pleased that his successor had done so well. He acknowledged she was probably right, but there were not many jobs you lost over night just as you were about to complete a momentous deal. "That's politics," his friends consoled him. "If you can't accept that you should never have become an MP, let alone take a job in cabinet." But he felt unfulfilled, always would do. No good moaning to Rachel poor darling about it – he knew she was happy. He'd put huge strain on their relationship and considered himself lucky to still have her beside him. He owed it to her to settle down and lead a quiet and safe life and he had worked at it with an intensity that surprised him, giving up his seat in the Commons and eagerly throwing himself into running his late mother's farm, Thornbury in Gloucestshire, which she'd bought from the proceeds of the Irish sale.

Six

"I'm dying," Jenny told her son, in her usual matter-of-fact way; "pancreatic cancer." Richard gasped. It made little difference that his mother had warned him some time ago that she was very ill. He put an arm round her shoulders and was appalled to realise it was the first time since that dreadful day she'd dragged him away from Ireland that he had shown her any affection. Their relationship had never recovered from the day they boarded the ferry at Larne. "The day you took me away from my home," as he'd constantly told her as a boy. They had both tried, especially his mother, but the damage was done and Richard was always waiting for her to let him down again. And then he'd entered politics. "Why?" his mother had asked.

"I have a dream," he'd answered. They both knew what that dream was, and it had sent shockwaves of fear coursing through her body.

But he didn't care how his mother felt. He was aware of her distress as he moved up the political ladder, ignoring her pleas to refuse the job of Secretary of State for Northern Ireland, but the old resentment went too deep.

Now it was too late to say sorry – she wouldn't believe him anyway. He dropped down beside her and kissed her. She pulled away, looking surprised. "Do I have to be dying for you to show me affection?" she asked sadly.

There was no answer to that so he kissed her again. This time she moved into the kiss. "This is how it should have been," she said, stroking Richard's face.

"I know."

"But nothing can be done about it now."

Richard shook his head. "Nothing mother."

"Tell me Richard, do you love me? No lies please."

"I have always loved you, but I can't forgive."

"I had to move."

"I know."

Jenny nodded. "Well that is some comfort at least. And do you still have that wish to return to Ireland?"

"It's still on my mind, but the house has gone."

"Good."

He didn't bother to argue, it would only open the old wound. He stayed by her bed that night. Six months later he was beside her bed again and watched her die.

*

And here he was, years on, no nearer his goal of moving back to Ireland to live. In fact he knew he would never return, there was no longer a home to go to. Besides he loved Thornbury – loved Rachel and knew she was happy. Why risk ruining something so special for a worthless property? Okay, he missed not being able to visit his father's grave as much as he would have liked to, and he missed the Lough – its sounds, its beauty, but did he really want it all that much? A demolished house and the noise of aircraft constantly flying over head? Once it had excited him, but not now. He ran a finger down Rachel's bare back and felt her shiver. Desire stirred and he moved his other hand across her stomach. Time didn't matter any longer, no one would disturb them and maybe he should be thankful for that.

*

In a small two bed roomed flat in Haringey a young man stirred, rubbed his green eyes, and slowly rolled out of bed. James Fitzpatrick was lean and fit, a keen squash player and weekend cricketer. *The scarecrow* his journalist friends called him. He had a slightly effeminate face, accentuated by his shoulder length hair, the same colour as his father's and fair skin. But there was nothing effeminate about him, far from it. Like his father he was mentally tough, oblivious to danger and dared to tread where many other journalists feared to go. He was thirty four, free and content; he worked hard and played hard. He loved his job and had a string of girlfriends, none of them lasted long. Life had been good until a few days earlier when his request to cover the riots in Belfast had been turned down by his editor.

"You're not going James and that's that," had been the editor's reply. "Your family are not universally loved over there and I don't want to be mourning the death of one of my best reporters."

"But I go over there regularly every November to shoot woodcock and I'm still alive. Also I bet I know more about the political situation then any other person on this paper. I'm in no danger – let me go."

"No! Going on holiday is very different to sniffing around for a story."

James had turned out of the editor's office and slammed the door.

Now, as he looked at himself in the mirror, his face covered in shaving cream, he understood the editor's concern. He shrugged, there would be other challenging stories to cover, he wasn't going to allow his disappointment to ruin his day. He had a game of squash planned before going to the office and a deadline for his latest report. He hoped his editor would find it interesting reading. He shaved, wiped the excess cream off his face and made his way down to his first cup of coffee; he'd take no prisoners on the squash court this morning.

*

Mary Keogh kicked at a stone on the pavement and walked slowly towards her home, the streets were almost deserted, most people deciding it was prudent to stay indoors. She was wondering where her life would take her now that she'd decided to live with Seamus Flanagan, it gave her a thrill to think she was consorting with such a dangerous man. She knew what people thought of him, called him an animal and other uncomplimentary names, but she was blind to his cruelty. He was just fighting for a cause he believed in, he was powerful and he had chosen *her*.

A hundred yards from home Mary stopped, she could feel her heartbeat crashing in her chest. A police car and ambulance were parked outside her house, blue lights flashing. A small, ghoulish crowd had gathered round the front gate and a policeman was trying to move them back. She stood still unable to take another step, her legs were like lead. Instinctively she knew what had happened. She sucked in a gulp of air – her chest so tight that she could hardly breathe. She forced herself to quicken her step and pushed her way through the growing crowd. A constable blocked her path. "Get away, fuck off!" she screamed. "This is my home!" She pushed past him and ran down the front path. A stretcher was being carried out, she recognised the bulk of her father covered completely with a blanket, her ashen faced mother following, blood splattered across her floral apron. Their eyes met, no words were necessary. Her Dad was dead, her mother had been spared, uncharacteristically she threw herself into her mother's arms. She felt like a small child again – safe and she realised it was the first time she'd hugged her mother in years.

Seven

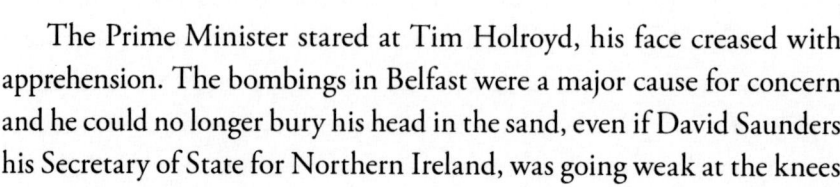

The Prime Minister stared at Tim Holroyd, his face creased with apprehension. The bombings in Belfast were a major cause for concern and he could no longer bury his head in the sand, even if David Saunders his Secretary of State for Northern Ireland, was going weak at the knees listening to Holroyd.

"I put it to you Prime Minister that it is time to act, or unrest will spread. We need a small force to put some of the more violent dissidents out of action, especially a certain character called Seamus Flanagan. His rhetoric is very persuasive and he has a strong following. I know this is a very difficult decision for you, but I need an urgent reply."

The Prime Minister knew Holroyd as a decisive man but a man not always on his wavelength. He knew of his record in various countries. If the public knew of all the clandestine operations he'd carried out they would be horrified, but his actions had saved lives, he was tempted to give Holroyd a free hand; he was to be trusted.

Tim Holroyd rubbed his leg, it was hurting more than usual probably because of the damp London weather, he was paying for his reckless youth on a much-loved motor bike. He was in his mid-forties but up close he looked older – a career in M16 had taken its toll. His black hair was cut military style, his brown eyes were intense and active. Some said he was built like a brick shithouse, he was a fit man, standing five foot ten. He leant across the table and waited patiently for the Prime Minister's decision.

"Some times Holroyd I wish people like you did not exist," the Prime Minister complained. "Then I would not have to deal with you.

Sadly, in this violent world we live in, we need men like you. I admire you, but I can't like you."

"I don't expect you to like me Prime Minister."

The Prime Minister gave him a troubled look. "I would say that the minister and I need time, but I know this is urgent. My answer therefore is you have my support, move quickly Holroyd and wipe out this nest of vipers."

Holroyd heard a sharp intake of breath from the Secretary of State. Liberal appeaser, he thought and stood up. "Thank you gentlemen, I'll keep you posted."

"Only the three of us in this room have had this conversation Holroyd. It will go no further, and if your little escapade goes belly up don't expect any support from me. You will be on your own as always. Understood?"

"Perfectly. No more than I would expect."

"Good." The Prime Minister held out a hand, Tim took it. The Secretary of State made no move to do the same; he thought Holroyd was no better than the men he was going to pursue.

Eight

George Russell took his wife's petite hand as they walked out of the Europa Hotel into Belfast's Great Victoria Street. Rose looked up at him, warming to his touch. At first she had been reluctant to take a holiday in Northern Ireland; it would not have been her first choice, but she'd felt it was churlish to refuse. They had spent so little time of their marriage together that to go anywhere with him was a bonus, and she knew he was keen to show her where he'd spent much of his time while working, as he called it. "It's going to be a lovely day," she said as they walked out into the street.

"Spring is in the air," George confirmed, looking down at the woman he had married thirty years ago. It constantly surprised him that he still loved her as much as the day he'd married her. It had been an afternoon to remember, her thick red hair tumbling down to her shoulders, gleaming in the warm summer sunlight, her striking green eyes full of wit looking up at him with excitement. A crowd of their friends gathered behind them all cheering, their parents, alas dead now, standing to the side of them proud smiles on their faces. It was what they had both wanted since their school days. She looked fragile, rather like a china doll whilst he was over six foot and heavily built. She had worn well, still able to turn an admiring eye and not ashamed for George to see her naked.

"I love you," he said as they moved towards their hire car.

Rose stood on tip toes and kissed him. "Likewise," she replied, the familiar feeling of sheer joy coursing through her veins. What a pity they had never had enough time together since their marriage. It would always be a regret, but then George had earned good money and there had been no time to grow bored with each other. She had quickly grown used to his time away from home, which was shrouded in mystery. The hard part was the weeks, sometimes even months of no contact. It was at times like these that she'd wished she could have had children. He'd been very secretive about his job and she knew he'd never speak of it, she would go to her grave ignorant. She'd guessed he was in danger, but never asked. After all she'd been aware of all this before they had married – so no good moaning. But now, she could savour every second of their time together. Memories would be precious and there was so much to do. What did it matter what George had been up to? He was alive, retired at fifty-three and had a good pension, as she squeezed his hand she thought she was a very lucky woman.

George wrapped an arm around her thin waste and his brown eyes twinkled with joy. He still loved to touch her, he had never thought of himself as a tactile creature, but with Rose it was different. He owed her so much, never pushing him for information that he couldn't give – never once complaining. He knew she suffered when he was away and for that he felt guilty, but enough was enough and when he'd been offered early retirement he'd grabbed the opportunity with both hands. "There is a limit to the risks a man can take, and by God I've taken some for you," he'd told Tim Holroyd on the day he'd retired. He blew out his cheeks, it was good not to smell danger permeating his nostrils. He was looking forward to spending time in the little bungalow that he and Rose had bought a year back at Bexhill-on-Sea. They both loved the sea – the sound of the waves – watching the seagulls battling against the wind. They enjoyed walking, going to the pub on a Saturday night after taking in a film, things that so many couples took for granted but which they had seldom been able to do; life, he told himself was just beginning. He opened the passenger door of the hired Ford – bowed with a smile as Rose made herself comfortable, and then moved round to the driver's side. "Right here we go darling. Our first day, let's make it memorable."

As they drew opposite the Royal Victoria Hospital George began to get worried by a black Range Rover that had been driving very close since they had left the hotel. All his old survival instincts clicked in, he braked and the Rover made no attempt to pass or flash its lights; something was wrong.

His hands became clammy, alarm bells rang in his brain. Deciding not to voice his concerns to Rose he made a decision, at the next turn left he swung the car into the road and jammed his foot down on the accelerator. "Hold tight," he shouted at Rose. For a brief moment he thought the Range Rover had overshot the turning, but no such luck, it was back on his tail. He realised he'd made a mistake – the road was almost empty – no cars in front, none coming towards him.

"George, what's up?" Rose screamed, as she was thrown against her door. "Why so fast?"

George was about to shout, "get down Rose" when the Range Rover drew level. For a split second George saw a man grinning out of the passenger window holding a gun. Instinctively he ducked. The man fired. The bullet shaved George's head and hit its intended target on the side of her face. Rose's pretty face was pretty no more. The Range Rover roared away, no traffic to impede its escape, no one to see the kill. George hit the curb- slammed on his brakes and stalled the engine. He fell across his wife, he could see she was dead, her face had gone. Tears cascaded down his cheeks – he felt he was suffocating. His first thought was that he had killed his wife as sure as if he'd pulled the trigger; he should never have come to Ireland. He had underestimated the enemy and committed the cardinal sin of forgetting that most terrorists have long memories, and no one would have a longer memory than Seamus Flanagan. He had good cause to administer pain on him, what better way to make a man suffer than to kill the one closest to him?

*

The next six months was a living hell for George, he couldn't forgive himself for Rose's death. How could he have been so bloody stupid to have taken her to Northern Ireland? He felt sick with grief, sedatives and too much booze. He felt he couldn't carry on without her and suicide wasn't far from his mind. The only thing that stopped him reaching for the pills was a burning rage that ate at his insides; he would find Flanagan and make him pay.

"You look awful," said Arthur, an old friend who knew how George was suffering, handing him his second tankard of beer. "When did you last eat? Let me order something from the bar."

"I don't want to eat," snapped George. "I'm too terrified to sleep. The nightmares are so real. I keep seeing the gun pointing out of that car window and seeing Flanagan's leering face as he pulled the trigger. I see Rose bleeding beside me - sometimes her ruined face smiling at me. I scream, and if I hadn't ducked, Arthur, I would be dead and Rose would be alive today."

Arthur said, "Listen up George. Patterns in life and events are only visible in retrospect. There is no point putting yourself through more misery, telling me what might have been. I know it's easy for me to say but it's time you looked forward. Rose wouldn't want you beating yourself up like this – would she?"

George said, "No, she wouldn't. Thanks Arthur for trying to put me straight, but it's fallen on deaf ears. I will mourn her for ever."

*

Tim Holroyd made the telephone call an hour after he'd left the Prime Minister. He knew the man he wanted, George Russell, even though he was still in mourning for his wife. He'd come out of retirement, he'd jump at the chance of leading a team to Ireland. He had a score to settle.

The conversation was brief and the outcome was just as Tim had hoped. A meeting was arranged and Tim's plan was on the move. A team would be selected, it was agreed that three men would be enough. "And I know the men I want," George stated.

"Your choice George," Tim agreed.

Nine

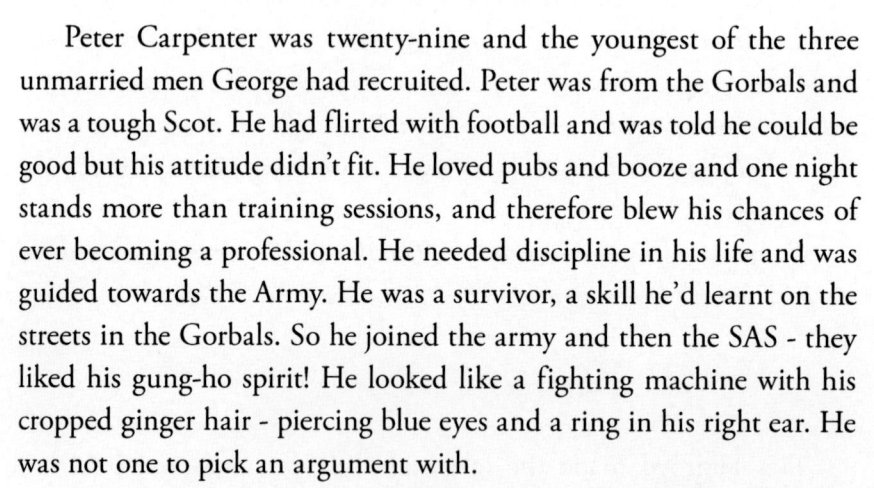

Peter Carpenter was twenty-nine and the youngest of the three unmarried men George had recruited. Peter was from the Gorbals and was a tough Scot. He had flirted with football and was told he could be good but his attitude didn't fit. He loved pubs and booze and one night stands more than training sessions, and therefore blew his chances of ever becoming a professional. He needed discipline in his life and was guided towards the Army. He was a survivor, a skill he'd learnt on the streets in the Gorbals. So he joined the army and then the SAS - they liked his gung-ho spirit! He looked like a fighting machine with his cropped ginger hair - piercing blue eyes and a ring in his right ear. He was not one to pick an argument with.

Phil Dashwood was the opposite of Carpenter, well-spoken with plenty of money behind him. The others teased him and called him 'Toff' and couldn't really understand why he was in the SAS. But Phil loved excitement and the tedium of working in his father's business didn't appeal to him. Carpenter recognised him as a brave soldier and good mate. If it wasn't for Phil, Peter Carpenter would be history; in Iraq Dashwood had shot a sniper who was training his rifle on him and for that Peter was eternally grateful.

"You're my buddy for life you are. I owe you," Carpenter often reminded Phil in his Scottish drawl after a few too many whiskeys, but it wasn't the drink talking - he meant it.

The third man was Dan O'Connor, an Irishman and the oldest of the three. He'd been born in Belfast and had been brought up in the divided city and had grown to hate the constant killings and bigotry, so the army had seemed a good way out. Like Carpenter, his hair was cropped short, true army style - his blue eyes twinkled with good humour. However it was a mistake to take that as a weakness.

All three had served together in Iraq and Afghanistan -they were hardened men, and they were like brothers. They trusted each other implicitly and their respect for each other was second to none. They loved each other, although none of them would ever have admitted to such a frailty. After Afghanistan they'd had a shot at Civvy Street thinking they could live normal, less hectic lives. But danger was in their blood and they soon became bored. They were thinking of putting themselves out for hire when George's telephone call had come, the chance to work together had been too tempting to turn down.

They had moved quietly into the community - found jobs, drank in pubs, chatted up the local talent like any blue-blooded bachelors would. They were accepted as middle-aged men just trying to make a decent living after leaving the army. George had slipped into Belfast once the word had come back that they were ready to go. They were still fit, though a little fatter round the waist than when they had come back from Afghanistan. They knew their lives were at risk but there was nothing new about that. They didn't question the morals of the task, they simply had a professional job to do – seek out the enemy and destroy it. Once the job was over they would be well paid and then slip away back to Blighty as quietly as they had arrived.

Ten

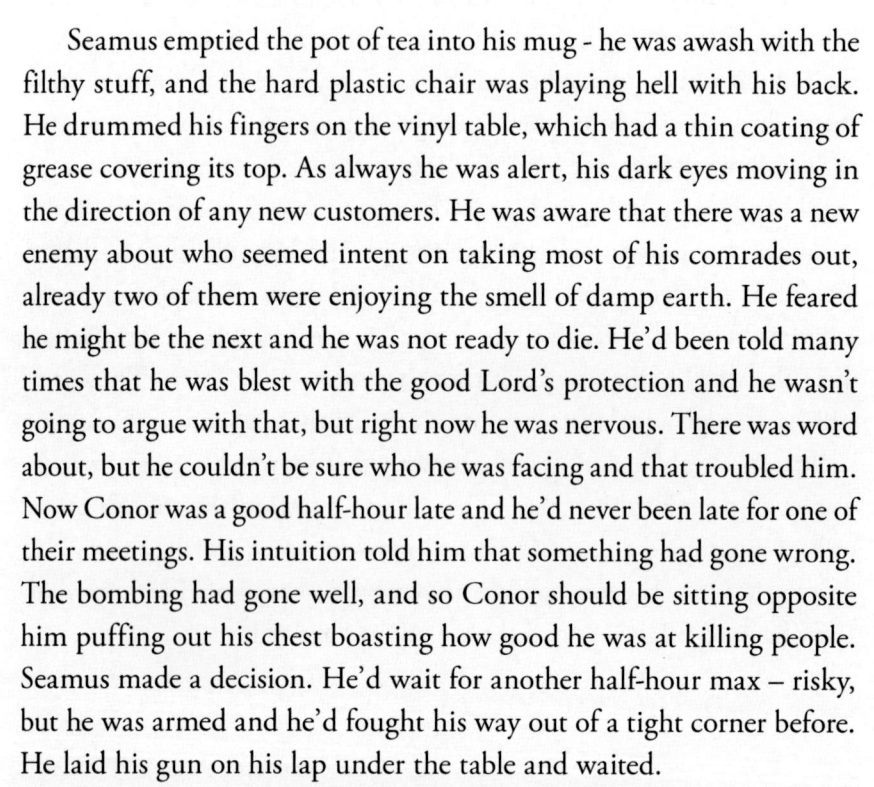

Seamus emptied the pot of tea into his mug - he was awash with the filthy stuff, and the hard plastic chair was playing hell with his back. He drummed his fingers on the vinyl table, which had a thin coating of grease covering its top. As always he was alert, his dark eyes moving in the direction of any new customers. He was aware that there was a new enemy about who seemed intent on taking most of his comrades out, already two of them were enjoying the smell of damp earth. He feared he might be the next and he was not ready to die. He'd been told many times that he was blest with the good Lord's protection and he wasn't going to argue with that, but right now he was nervous. There was word about, but he couldn't be sure who he was facing and that troubled him. Now Conor was a good half-hour late and he'd never been late for one of their meetings. His intuition told him that something had gone wrong. The bombing had gone well, and so Conor should be sitting opposite him puffing out his chest boasting how good he was at killing people. Seamus made a decision. He'd wait for another half-hour max – risky, but he was armed and he'd fought his way out of a tight corner before. He laid his gun on his lap under the table and waited.

Five minutes later Mary hurried into the café and her tear-stained face told him that his intuition had been correct - something had gone badly wrong – no Conor. He smelt trouble. "Where's Conor," he asked, not wasting time on any sympathy – he didn't do sympathy, not even for the young woman who periodically shared his bed. He heaved his six-foot rangy frame off the plastic chair as Mary hurried towards him. She stopped in front of him, ignoring the urge to throw herself into his hairy arms. He would only push her away. "Trouble?" he asked, already irritated by her tears.

"Big trouble," Mary choked, trying to pull her shattered nerves together. She looked up into his eyes, cold, cruel eyes radiating anger. Seamus was always angry. "Dad's been topped, right in front of Mum. Jesus Seamus, she watched them pump two shots into him. Is this the work of the protestant para-military?"

Seamus took her firmly by the arm and guided her to his table, waving to the waitress for another pot of tea. He shook his head. "Not them."

"How can you be sure?"

"As you know there have been two unexplained killings recently, now Conor makes a third. No one has claimed responsibility – most unlike the protestant para-military. I fear this is something more sinister."

"What do you mean," Mary questioned, giving the waitress a weak smile as she put the pot of tea on the table.

"Our information is that there is a small active group from the mainland hunting us down. Ex SAS."

"And they are targeting 'Freedom for Ireland'?"

"It seems so. If this is the case we are up against some very professional men who know who we are. They're a real threat to our organisation, we need to fight back but it's difficult to fight an invisible enemy."

Mary nodded and took a sip of her tea, her hands still shaking. "So Dad would have been a marked man? But how could they know he planted the bomb?"

"I doubt if they did. I expect the hit was already planned, your dad was living on borrowed time."

"And you Seamus, are you living on borrowed time as well?"

Seamus nodded. "I've been on borrowed time for years. But I'm a little more careful where I drink my Bushmills. Heavy drinking in the wrong place can be fatal – has proved fatal. I suspect your father paid the price of not being able to hold his drink and never knew when to keep that fucking mouth of his shut. Always boasting he was. He would have been high on their list."

"Jesus Seamus, I've had a terrible thought."

"Tell me."

Mary hesitated, looked down at the table. She slowly lifted her head and stared at Seamus. "Mum. Do you think she might be tempted to give these people your name? She might be tempted to tell them a few things now that dad is no threat to her. He would tell her everything, especially when drunk." Immediately she saw the rage boil in Seamus – she drew in her breath realising she'd made a terrible mistake.

Seamus crashed a fist down on the table, the tea pot shook and Mary grabbed it. A couple at a nearby table swung round, and then quickly averted their eyes. He looked absolutely demonic, like someone from a horror movie. Somehow he managed to control his rage. His dark eyes flashed dangerously, he sucked in his breath. "She wouldn't," he gasped.

She would, Mary thought, immediately knowing she was evil. She felt a heavy hand rest on her shoulders – she silently wept for her mother. She'd probably condemned her to death.

Eleven

The sun was peeping over Belfast rooftops, as if frightened to show itself on such a day. There was stillness in Chapel Lane as two coffins were taken out of the hearse, a wreath of roses lay on top of each coffin; they had cost Mary a fortune. A small crowd gathered as news of the funeral spread in the neighbourhood, Mary stared at them angrily. *Ghouls.* She turned away to follow the coffins inside and was surprised by the large congregation. She knew few would have come to say goodbye to Conor – his comrades would keep a low profile and there were many others who would probably say, "Good riddance." No, they were there for her mother. Eileen had been christened in St Mary's, married there, and christened her daughter there. Every Sunday she had worshipped there and from the congregation had come her friends. Tears flowed as the coffins were placed in front of the altar. Mary slipped into the front pew, nodding at her two aunts who mouthed, "We are so sorry." She acknowledged their sympathy with a weak smile. Her guilt was threatening to suffocate her and she turned to look at Seamus, who was sitting behind her. The sight of his dark suit and black tie made her cringe - the two faced fucking bastard. He would not be mourning her mother's demise; she should walk away from him now. But she was under his spell and to her shame she was attached to him like an umbilical cord. She loved him - believed in him – shared his views. The bond would be hard to break. The proof was that not even the death of her mother had broken it. She was loathsome; she deserved a man like Seamus. She fed off his power. She had watched him stare a man into submission with his deep set dark eyes. His power to control someone was awesome and it acted like an aphrodisiac on her. She crossed herself and asked God for forgiveness. After all, her mother was always telling her that God forgave everyone, however horrendous their crimes. Well she needed His forgiveness now. She had instigated a heinous crime, however unwittingly and she would have to live with that for the rest of her days. Her mother had done nothing to deserve death – it had been a precautionary killing and Seamus had pulled the trigger. She took out a small white handkerchief from her bag, bought especially for the occasion – wrong word but she couldn't think of another. She had been useless at English. Come to think of it she'd been fuck-all good at anything. She wiped her tears and stared at the coffins. Maybe it was as well that Mum was dead. She'd be horrified to know the depths that she'd sunk to under the influence of Seamus. No doubt about it, Mum would be happier with her God.

*

The funeral was over. Mary would have liked to have had a guard of honour dressed in black, their faces covered by balaclavas, their rifles raised in defiance. But she knew Father Paul would frown on such sectarian antics, as would her Mum. So she'd kept her mouth shut. Her parents were buried in separate graves – they would have hated to be together in death, just as much as they had hated being together in life. At last the mourners had gone. It was time to head home, get in touch with an estate agent and finally she'd be able to shut the door on what she called the first miserable chapter of her life. What the future held she didn't bother to consider.

*

Liam Murphy was a concierge at the Lansdowne Hotel, which was three miles from the centre of Belfast. Its advertising leaflets described its spectacular views over Belfast Lough. The hotel provided ideal

Love Thine Enemy

cover for his more lucrative activity. Murphy had an unmemorable wrinkled face and he was as tiny as an Irish leprhecorn. He looked several years older than sixty. At the Hotel he was charming to its guests but outside he was an introverted loner, there was no room in his life for a wife. He didn't much care for women. His needs were simple and a gossiping, nagging woman keeping tabs on him would jeopardise his main purpose in life, a grubby, but well paid little sideline, passing information to the British and the IRA. A double agent he called himself. The Belfast pubs were where he picked up most of his information, gladly given in exchange for a few pints of beer. He liked the thrill of it but he knew one careless slip would cost him his life. How he'd survived so far and not had his mutilated body found in a skip in the city was a mystery to him. But now with this 'foking damned peace' his cash flow was diminishing.

The mystery death of two ex IRA men and now Conor Keogh had raised his hopes. Seamus Flanagan was not a man to see his comrade's death go unavenged. For sure he'd be planning retaliation in some form. So to celebrate the fact that he might soon be onto a good little earner he dropped by his favourite café in Lurgan Street, sat himself down by a window overlooking the street and treated himself to a large English breakfast, damn his cholesterol. He was just stuffing the last morsel into his mouth when who should he see walking past the café but Flanagan and his right-hand man Declan Ryan, a murderous thug known for his violence and love of killing people. Murphy felt like a dwarf in his presence. His hands were huge, his eyes set deep behind bushy eyebrows and he was not known to laugh. Murphy guessed that he'd be feeling vulnerable right now, there was danger lurking for men like Flanagan and Ryan. To see them together raised his hopes even higher. Were they plotting something? Murphy wiped his lips with a green paper napkin and vowed to have a little chat with Ryan in his favourite pub. Ryan was fool enough to think Murphy was a friend, drink loosened his tongue and Ryan knew how to drink. Murphy had a feeling that if he played his cards right his impecunious state might be about to end.

Michael Pakenham

*

Mary had been in the house for over four hours. She had hoped that Seamus might have stopped by and given her a hand, but he hadn't shown, no doubt nervous that the house might be under surveillance. It was very creepy knowing that someone might be watching. Her work was nearly done, the removers had stripped the rooms of carpets and furniture – rubbish was dumped in the bin at the back of the house – crockery, pots and pans and any items she didn't need to take with her were piled on the kitchen worktops to be collected by Father Paul later in the day. The furniture and carpets would be delivered to him; it was her gesture of good will. It did nothing to dispel her feeling that she was damned. What Father Paul did with the junk, because that's what most of it was, she didn't care a fuck. She moved reluctantly up to her bedroom – quickly threw a picture of her parents into the waste bin – the thought of her mother's eyes following her around the room petrified her. She pulled out two suitcases from the wardrobe and started to fill them with her items – jeans that she seldom wore, preferring short skirts that showed off her shapely legs. Though who the Christ admired them she wasn't sure. There wasn't a man around who dared to challenge Seamus to his right to own her. She threw in her underwear, all her shoes – four pairs badly scuffed, two pairs for better occasions. Not many of those! On the cupboard floor lay two rather weather-beaten teddies, given to her by her mother on her sixth birthday, she smiled at them, picking them up hugging them to her chest. With a sigh she consigned them to the rubbish bin; too many memories. Humping the suitcases down the stairs she took one last glance into the front room, looking even tattier now that it was devoid of any furniture. She had been happy here once, playing cards with her mother, helping her clean up, learning how to cook but not for long. Her father had a way of wrecking everything and once she'd jumped into his camp any resemblance of family bliss flew out of the window. She wouldn't miss her home, which anyway she suspected was about to be repossessed. To her knowledge Conor hadn't paid the mortgage for at least a year.

She opened the front door and locked it behind her. She put the key under a flower pot for Father Paul. Then she turned her back on the house without the slightest feeling of loss. To her surprise Seamus was sitting in his car half way through a cigarette, the usual frown on his face. He got out and took her suitcases without a word.

"Thanks for coming Seamus – bit of a risk?"

"Every where I go I'm at risk," he mumbled.

"Monosyllabic as usual," she laughed.

He grunted – she smiled and jumped into the car. The point was he'd come at considerable risk to himself. Maybe the second chapter of her life would not be as miserable as the first.

Twelve

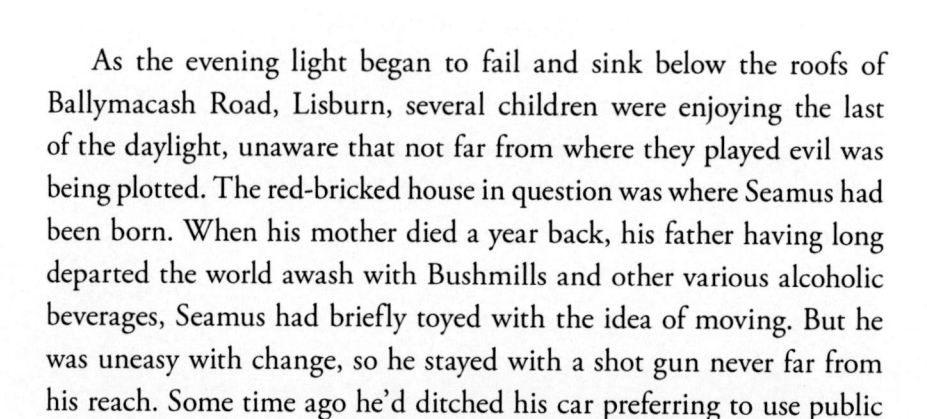

As the evening light began to fail and sink below the roofs of Ballymacash Road, Lisburn, several children were enjoying the last of the daylight, unaware that not far from where they played evil was being plotted. The red-bricked house in question was where Seamus had been born. When his mother died a year back, his father having long departed the world awash with Bushmills and other various alcoholic beverages, Seamus had briefly toyed with the idea of moving. But he was uneasy with change, so he stayed with a shot gun never far from his reach. Some time ago he'd ditched his car preferring to use public transport or walk; if he needed a car he stole one. He reckoned he was as safe as a man of his notoriety could be.

Now, six men sat round his large wooden table in the kitchen, a little stained by endless cups of tea being spilt. They were drinking Bushmills out of half-pint glasses, which were continually filled by Mary. Cigarette smoke drifted up to the ceiling. Their clothes smelt of cigarettes and sweat, their breath stank of whisky. All of them were desperate to work out a strategy to counteract the growing effectiveness of the invisible men and they reckoned they hadn't got long. They had hoped the July riots had posted their intention, but the swift counter-attack had taken them by surprise. Three of their comrades were dead. That was not how it had been planned. Belfast was meant to be on its knees, to re-gain the initiative was imperative. Seamus banged the table with his fist and called the meeting to order.

They cursed at the invisible men – swore revenge – drank more whisky and raised their glasses to their dead comrades. They even began to think they were invincible, they were men used to having their own way. "A minor setback," they muttered amongst them selves. It would not stop them destabilising the hated peace.

Seamus looked across at his comrades with disgust, they were deluded fools. They were up against a force that would not be easily repelled and he realised that he and Declan Ryan were probably on their own. He could trust Declan. He was dumb and brave and Seamus knew he'd die for him. If he couldn't strike back at these invisible killers he'd have to try and stop them by hitting at the heart of the British government. That just might bring them up short, he rose from the table. It was time to dismiss the four other men. It was late and the whisky was making his head ache. They shook hands, promised to put their minds to work on a plan and come back to Seamus with an idea, hopefully within forty-eight hours. Would they fuck! They'd puff out their chests – swagger home and disappear as fast as their feet could carry them down the nearest bolt hole and not surface until they gauged the danger was over, cowards the lot. He slammed the door as the last man left and turned to Declan. "We're on our own."

And as Mary knew when on his own, Seamus was at his most dangerous.

*

On the other side of the city in a rented flat on Antrim Road, George Russell and his team were discussing their operation. Three strikes, three successes, no foul ups. Good work so far. It was time to go for the big fish. "Watch your back Seamus Flanagan," Dashwood said. "We're coming after you."

This was what George had been waiting for. He'd never thought of himself as a revengeful person but the bullet that had shattered Rose's face had changed him. Much to his horror he could not rid himself of the desire to watch Flanagan die. He looked at the three men and said quietly, "He's mine when we find him."

This was a new George to them. The calm planner, the man they would follow anywhere – the man who had fought by their side. He was special. They hoped his burning hatred wouldn't put them all into danger. But they respected him and would still follow him to their deaths if necessary. "Okay boss," Carpenter agreed. "If we catch him we'll leave him to you."

None of them had much doubt about the outcome.

Thirteen

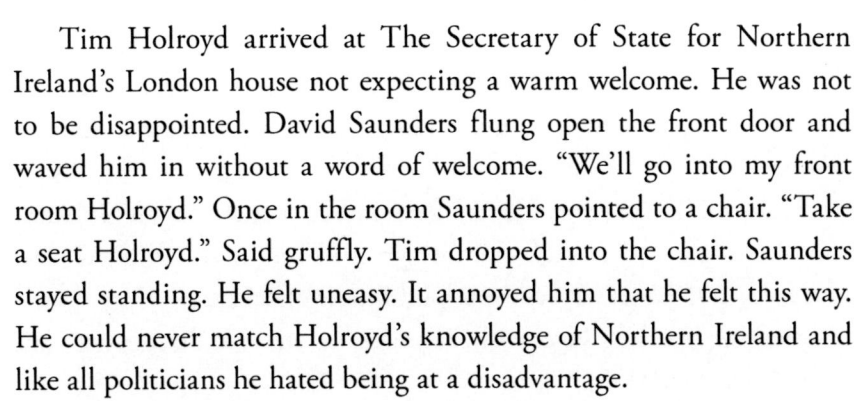

Tim Holroyd arrived at The Secretary of State for Northern Ireland's London house not expecting a warm welcome. He was not to be disappointed. David Saunders flung open the front door and waved him in without a word of welcome. "We'll go into my front room Holroyd." Once in the room Saunders pointed to a chair. "Take a seat Holroyd." Said gruffly. Tim dropped into the chair. Saunders stayed standing. He felt uneasy. It annoyed him that he felt this way. He could never match Holroyd's knowledge of Northern Ireland and like all politicians he hated being at a disadvantage.

Holroyd stared at the minister and decided that his first impression had been right. Saunders was lazy. In politics for a cushy life, relying on his staff to keep him up to speed. Certainly he didn't welcome anything that interfered with his clubby life style. He was overweight, his white hair was receding and he was short. Holroyd rested his hands on his knees and did his best to smile. "You want my report minister?" Holroyd scratched his chin as he stared contemptuously at the man pacing up and down.

"Tell me Holroyd, have you contingency plans if this little expedition fails?"

"It won't fail," Holroyd stated slowly and deliberately. "My men are professionals. However I understand your unease. I accept that this is a high risk operation and not one we want to reach the public domain. But we are good and seldom fail. Success will bring rewards. Already we have eliminated three men from the group 'Freedom for Ireland.' Give us another two weeks and we will be out. Operation done."

Saunders grunted. "You sound very confident Holroyd."

Tim nodded. "I am."

Saunders inclined his head. "Well I can't say I share your optimism." He scratched a mole behind his left ear and stared at Tim, sitting relaxed in the chair. He felt a deep loathing for the man. He couldn't stomach men like him. Confidence oozing from every pore – ruthless - possessing not a jot of compassion. Sign of the times? Maybe, and no doubt he'd saved lives, but he felt disgusted at being in the same room. He wiped the perspiration off his face with a large yellow handkerchief. "Well I think I have heard all I need to. I'm a busy man, as I'm sure are you." Then he couldn't resist adding, "planning another killing no doubt."

Holroyd did not react. He rose from his chair and held out his hand. Saunders took it in a weak clammy grasp. Tim's nose wrinkled – he squeezed, and was rewarded by a loud intake of breath.

Shaking his hand vigorously Saunders asked, "No doubt you want me to brief the PM?"

"Already done," replied Holroyd with some satisfaction.

Saunders swore loudly. "Damn it man that's my job. This is intolerable. I'm deeply offended."

Tim shrugged his shoulders. "Better take it up with the PM then minister. I couldn't refuse when he asked."

"Ha," hissed Saunders his face reddening. "Typical of you public school lot. Always sticking together." Then pointing at the door he said, "On your way Holroyd, I've had enough of your company."

Fourteen

Charlie O'Malley lowered his large frame into his desk chair, running his hands over his thinning hair. His sideburns were flecked with grey. It annoyed him that his hair was falling out, but not half as much as the three files that lay on his desk. His well manicured fingers tapped irritably on the brown covers and he bit his upper lip. Rarely had he felt so impotent and this was bugging him. He knew he was a good copper. One of the best, he'd been told. He possessed a ferocious intelligence, and his affable manner hid a man dedicated to justice, as many a criminal had found out to their cost. You did not underestimate Charlie. He'd never married. When asked why not, by puzzled friends, he'd say rather sadly, "In my job you witness many deaths and the terrible grief these deaths cause wives and relatives. I don't want my family constantly worrying about me or to leave them mourning my passing. So better to stay single."

He'd served in the RUC and was now a Chief Inspector in the new Police Service of Northern Ireland (known as the PSNI) During the Troubles he'd been respected by both sides, a very rare occurrence. Charlie had been an atheist all his life. "I cannot believe in someone floating in the clouds, mapping out our lives – its baloney. As for immaculate conception, well pull the other one mate," was his stock argument when discussing religion. He would continue, if allowed, "and if no one believed in all the religious clap-trap spouted out by priests, mullahs, zealots and their like this God-damned world wouldn't have half as many wars."

No one had ever tried to argue with him, which was just as well, as he would have lectured them on the disastrous decision to give the Jews their own homeland.

If pushed on the subject of religious bigotry and hatred in Northern Ireland Charlie had always chosen his words carefully. He valued his job and his integrity. But the truth was he felt some sympathy for the IRA. Oh he hated them for the killings, but he understood their reasons. They had just gone about their fight for freedom the wrong way. "Violence gets you no where," as he told the kids when he visited schools. "Violence leads to violence until whole communities are at war." So Charlie reckoned he was fair to both sides, for it wasn't only the IRA who killed innocent people. Yes, Charlie had been respected, and that was why he was so frustrated by the random killings that had suddenly bludgeoned on his patch. In spite of a small army of what he thought were loyal contacts no one could give him a lead, either by choice, fear, or because there wasn't word about.

He put aside the two top files which held as much information as his team had been able to collect over the killing of the Keoghs. He had no sympathy for a man like Conor but justice should not be meted out by the gun. As for Conor's wife's death, well that was a puzzle and one he feared would never be solved. He had his own opinion, but no proof. Finally, he turned the pages of the third one. This one intrigued him. Rose Russell. An apparently innocent tourist staying with her husband in Belfast for a week. But ever since he had prised George Russell off his wife's body he had felt there was more to her death than just a mistaken hit. The husband had been evasive from the start, which he could put down to grief. However his explanation of why he and his wife were driving down a quiet street that led to no place that a tourist would want to go filled him with suspicion. Something didn't fit, but he got nowhere with Russell. As there were no witnesses and it was obvious that Russell hadn't killed his wife he had no option but to accept his story and send him on his way back to the mainland with his wife's coffin. He slammed the file shut and stood up. He stretched – stamped his size fourteen feet - fiddled with his moustache and decided he was in need of a very strong black coffee.

Fifteen

Richard Fitzpatrick stretched out his long legs and surveyed his rather worn brown brogues. He wondered about getting a new pair but quickly discarded the idea. The old ones were too comfortable. He looked out of the window at the wintry morning sun playing on the red bricked façade of Thornbury and felt surprisingly content, a moment of being at ease with the world and himself. Today he and Rachel were going to Hampshire to buy some highland cattle from the man who had introduced water cress to nearly every household in Britain. They needed half a dozen more heifers to add to the fold that were grazing in the park in front of the house. His father had bred a prize winning fold and this was one small way of keeping his memory alive, even if the cattle weren't adding anything to the profitability of the farm. He still missed his father. Years that should have been full of family love had been empty. The bond between father and son cruelly cut off. At night, when at times he wasn't able to sleep, his thoughts often turned to the man he'd tried to emulate. He'd been a giant among men. A man with principles, dedicated to trying to help sort out the mess that was Northern Ireland. He'd tried hard to be even handed under great stress and been rewarded with a bullet in his chest.

Richard turned to smile at Rachel as she walked into the library, walls packed high with books – he was an avid reader of everything as diverse as Penny Vincenzi to Shakespeare. She moved across to the chair where he was sitting, reading the paper. In her hand she had a mug of black coffee. "Coffee sir?" she asked, her large green eyes flashing mischievously. He put the paper down and nodded, lightly tapping her bottom as she leant over to put the mug on the small glass table by the chair. He reached out and pulled her down so that her face was level with his. Gently he ran his lips across her mouth. He was rewarded with the faint taste of marmalade as her tongue returned the kiss. He sighed, and ran a hand through her shoulder length blond hair. "I love you Mrs Fitzpatrick," he whispered in her ear.

"And I love you too," she replied. "Now when are we setting off?"

"Just as soon as I've drunk this coffee and finished reading this rather depressing piece on Ireland. So let's say in half-an-hour. Okay with you?"

"That suits me fine, I'll go and ring James and see if he's coming down at the weekend."

"He'll be in Ireland shooting woodcock."

"Of course I forgot. Okay, I'll just finish a letter I'm writing and then I'm all yours for the rest of the day."

Richard watched her move towards the door. *She's worn well.* He admired her long legs and slim body. He eased himself back into the chair and took a sip of coffee. Perhaps it was time he took more trouble with his diet. He rubbed his growing paunch – far too big – must take more exercise, and cut down on what? He laughed. Chocolate of course.

*

The Haringey flat rang with laughter, as it always did when Henry Walters was in full flow. James had once wondered how a man could remember so many bad jokes. When asked, Henry had confessed that he jotted down every joke he heard or read into a little red notebook. "Another one Henry," encouraged one of the four young friends gathered in James's flat in spite of having heard them all at least a dozen times. They were celebrating the onset of two weeks holiday. Two of them were stockbrokers; Henry was a much respected corporate lawyer. The two stockbrokers were looking forward to spending time with their young children. James and Henry had no such burden and were off on their annual visit to Ireland to shoot woodcock. A third bottle of champagne was cracked open and James knew that he was going to have the usual thumping headache in the morning. It was the penalty he paid for this annual get together. He raised his glass to Henry and shouted, "Come on Henry let's have another one of those terrible jokes!"

He woke at seven the following morning and felt the familiar thump at the back of his head. He needed coffee and two panadol. He moved from his bedroom to the kitchen and switched on the kettle. Before waking Henry he'd have a shower in the hope that the panadol and the coffee would clear his head. He could hear Henry snoring in his small office which served as a spare bedroom when anyone came to stay. As he drank his coffee he thought of Henry. Fostered since the age of seven, mother running off with some dreadful man and his father killed racing his sports car. No siblings. James always felt it would have been easy for Henry to have given up on life at an early age, but not Henry. He was made of sterner stuff and done well in life. He was fun to be with and one of the most generous men he'd ever met. Standing only five foot six but large in width, he was known as Bunter to his friends. A fairly substantial waist bulged over his trousers. His hair was already receding, but Henry didn't care. As he told James countless times, "I'm fat but life is for living – you never know when you might be dead." It didn't seem to bother the girls – they loved his happy disposition, his wicked sense of humour and his flashing brown eyes. And they felt safe with him. Maybe it was because Henry had never quite worked out his sexuality. They had been friends since university, partly because James was a good listener. "I miss my father," Henry had confided on their second evening together. "Tell me about him," James had asked, feeling the familiar stab of lose himself.

James heard a grunt and knew that Henry was waking from his champagne induced sleep. It was time to get him a cup of tea. Tea made, sugar liberally added, James moved to the sofa. "Wake up you bugger," he said playfully as he shook Henry's shoulder. "Got to leave for the Stranraer ferry in a couple of hours."

Henry moaned, clasping his head in his hands as he struggled to stand up. "Getting too old for this," he groaned, grinning at James. "Your entire fault – you shouldn't have offered us so much champagne."

James didn't bother to remind him that it was he who had provided the champagne.

Sixteen

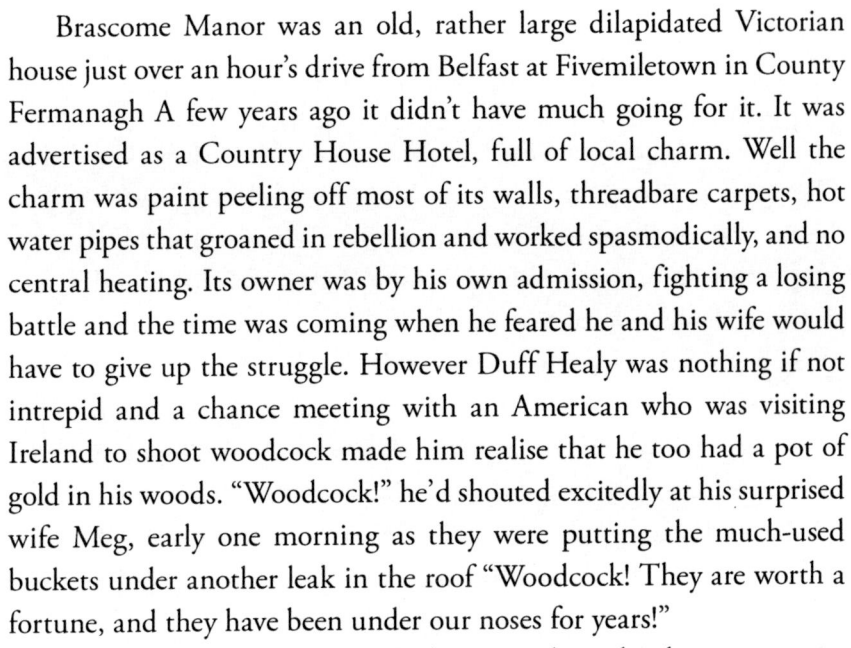

Brascome Manor was an old, rather large dilapidated Victorian house just over an hour's drive from Belfast at Fivemiletown in County Fermanagh A few years ago it didn't have much going for it. It was advertised as a Country House Hotel, full of local charm. Well the charm was paint peeling off most of its walls, threadbare carpets, hot water pipes that groaned in rebellion and worked spasmodically, and no central heating. Its owner was by his own admission, fighting a losing battle and the time was coming when he feared he and his wife would have to give up the struggle. However Duff Healy was nothing if not intrepid and a chance meeting with an American who was visiting Ireland to shoot woodcock made him realise that he too had a pot of gold in his woods. "Woodcock!" he'd shouted excitedly at his surprised wife Meg, early one morning as they were putting the much-used buckets under another leak in the roof "Woodcock! They are worth a fortune, and they have been under our noses for years!"

So the couple slapped on a little paint where the damp was at its worse – bought a few electric heaters – hired two staff for the season and started selling Woodcock shooting. At first business was slow, but then his American acquaintance visited and bookings started to pile in from across the Pond. Word spread that the shooting was the best to be had on the island – even better than the well known woodcock shoots in Cornwall. Now central heating had been installed, the roof leaked a little less and the beds had new mattresses. Three extra staff where employed throughout the shooting season and Meg's cooking was the final touch that made Brascome so popular. Five years had passed since

James and Henry had paid their first annual visit. They had survived the cold, the damp and the tepid baths with good humour. They had trudged the woods with Duff leading them at a ferocious pace. Seen very few woodcock, but consumed a lot of whisky. Perhaps now a little of the character had disappeared but there was no doubt that the comfort was welcome and the woodcock shooting, now managed by a young man not so addicted to whisky at every opportunity, had greatly improved and demand exceeded availability.

*

"It was a stroke of luck," Seamus boasted to Mary. "Luck has followed me all my life." Which Mary couldn't argue with, given the number of times he'd cheated death. He'd seen the advert for a receptionist at Brascome Manor in the Belfast Telegraph and it had immediately started his mind racing. Wealthy people went to Brascome, could be useful to have someone on the inside. "Apply," he'd ordered Mary, which she'd done without a word of dissent, and much to her surprise got the job. What she didn't know was that Meg liked saving young people and having dug into Mary's circumstances thought she filled her criteria perfectly – besides she was very presentable. "A knock out," grinned Duff. "Also a very nice smile," Meg had added, digging her husband in the ribs.

After a day of sulks and just grunts from Mary, Meg felt she might have made an error of judgement.

Mary looked over her cup of coffee at Seamus. "It's a total waste of time working there and I hate it."

"You'll stay there until I tell you," Seamus growled, thinking that his luck might be deserting him.

"Then I better get going," said Mary. I wouldn't want fat Meg thinking she'd made the wrong choice."

*

Love Thine Enemy

Meg smiled her usual 'good morning' to Mary as she hurried through the front door. Mary scowled and headed towards the reception desk without saying a word.

Not for the first time Meg wondered what was going on in Mary's pretty head. Why had she taken the job when she so obviously wanted to be somewhere else? Meg disliked failing and although Duff, in spite of being smitten by her looks, advised her to get rid of Mary, Meg stuck her heels in. "She's a lost soul Duff. Give her a chance."

"Well she's too damned sulky for me. Waste of money," he replied.

"Besides, you old moaner, you wouldn't be of such a sunny disposition if you came from a home where your parents had both been killed," Meg retorted.

Duff blew out his cheeks. "A family where the father had been big in the IRA and the mother no doubt a sympathiser."

Meg hadn't been about to give in. "All the more reason to give the girl a chance. If she wasn't working here she'd probably be on the streets."

Duff had put up his hands in mock surrender - run his fingers through his thick matt of jet black hair and smiled at the woman he'd married thirty years ago. Twenty of them fighting decay in the old house that he'd inherited from an aunt had filled him with admiration for Meg. He'd uprooted her from a comfortable life in rural Surrey where they had livered horses. He was sure that most women would have quit a long time ago. So when Meg gave her point of view on what ever subject that came up Duff seldom argued. "I understand where you're coming from Meg, but it would be nice to get a smile every now and then from the girl."

"I keep trying." Meg had replied, smoothing down her long green skirt – long for two reasons – to keep out the cold and to hide her rather wide girth. She screwed up her weather-beaten face. It had been smooth and glowing when Duff had fallen in love with her, but the years of toil had taken their toll. All that mattered to her was that Duff still told her she was beautiful.

Meg watched Mary pull up her chair behind the desk – open the bookings register – lift the telephone for any messages – Meg and Duff were hopeless at checking their messages. *Weird that, considering they run a hotel.* She looked up as Meg tried again, "Good morning Mary, easy drive in?"

Mary rewarded this renewed effort with a grin. The truth was she was finding it very difficult to dislike Meg. How the fuck this large overweight woman was working her way into her affections she had no idea. But these days she was confused. "Good morning Mrs Healy, sorry I'm a bit late – fucking traffic."

Meg winced. She hated swearing. "Oh that's alright Mary," she said lightly. "You have a long way to come."

You bet I have, and not for the purposes of getting to like you- fatty. Mary laughed silently at her thought and said, "But I will try and do better – don't want to get the fucking sack do I."

"Mary, I really would appreciate it if you didn't swear. Our guests won't like it."

Tough! I'll speak to anyone the way I like and if I want to say fuck I'll say it. "Okay I'll try not to use it. It just comes a bit natural."

"I'm sure." Meg knew her request had fallen on deaf ears, but she wasn't going to make an issue out of it. "Well, must be getting back to the kitchen. You alright here, no problems?"

"None." Mary watched Meg waddle away. How very strange she was finding life at the moment. She'd thought it would be exciting to feel wanted by Seamus for other reasons than sex and at first that had been the case. But now Seamus told her nothing - it was as if he didn't trust her any more, and it hurt. It came as quite a shock to think she was falling out of love. She'd followed him like a puppy – given him her body and loyalty. She'd wanted to be in the action – even dreamt of pulling the trigger on some unsuspecting policeman or soldier. She still hated them. She wanted them out of Ireland. Recently however, she was becoming more of a realist than Seamus. There was peace and she was beginning to think it was here to stay even if Seamus and his comrades refused to believe it. Doubt was invading her senses. "Fuck," she said out loud, remembering her mother's words. "Go with Flanagan, go on. You will regret it." She'd laughed in her mother's face. "I love him, I love him, I love him," she'd taunted Eileen as she'd walked defiantly out of the room, two fingers raised behind her back, knowing that every word she spoke was driving the knife deeper into her mother's heart. Yet now there was little doubt that the bond with Seamus was no longer so strong. She saw no way out. She was tied to him - trapped. She gave an audible sigh. Her life had always been shit. There was no way to climb out of the deep dark pit she had dug for herself. Resignedly she pulled her note book out of her bag, and as she had done ever since coming to Brascome, scribbled down the names of the new arrivals for the week. As usual they meant nothing to her, but they might mean something to Seamus.

*

Warren, Holt, Conrad, Walters, Fitzpatrick. Seamus ran a finger over the names in the note book. His brow creased as he looked at the last name. It sent a shiver down his spine. His face broke into a rare smile. He turned to Declan Ryan as he walked into the house. "Our luck's in, our fucking luck has turned! Look at this!" He threw the notebook at Declan. See the last name?"

Declan turned white. "Fitzpatrick! Holy shit Seamus, this is a gift from God!"

"Indeed it is. If this man's not part of the family I'll give up drink."

Declan nodded. "I'll check if you like. My contact in London will be able to verify if this is a member of that family coming over here."

"Get your arse out of here then. This could be just what we have been waiting for."

Declan flew out of the door and Seamus turned to smile at Mary. "Well done girl. I knew putting you in that hotel might bring a result."

Mary's heart was racing. She remembered her father telling her about the Fitzpatrick family. How stupid of her not to recognise it in the arrivals book. Would she have left it out of her note book – surely not? But she was shocked to think she'd even thought of it. Jesus was she going mad? She dared to ask, "Have you got a plan?"

Seamus tapped his nose. "That I have girl."

"Are you going to share it with me?"

"Not necessary. You'll find out soon enough."

Mary watched him turn away without a word – bastard.

*

Declan parked in a lay-by a mile from Seamus's house – no one ever made a call from the house. He punched a number into his mobile. It was answered immediately. He wasted no time with pleasantries. He asked the question. His contact assured him that within the hour he'd have an answer. That was good enough. He thanked the voice and closed the call. He lit a cigarette, settled down for the return call thinking that at last the tide might be about to turn. Fitzpatrick – a name emblazoned on his memory. He closed his eyes, drawing in deep breaths of nicotine, his mind replaying, as it often did, the night his father left the house and came back a hero.

*

"There's a big job going on tonight," whispered Patrick Ryan to his eleven year old son. "A very, very big job – a killing planned. A dead senior RUC officer before the night is out. You make sure you and Ma stay in tonight – no going out onto the streets shouting at the soldiers do you hear me?" He cuffed Declan lightly on an ear. Declan smiled – he would never disobey his father. He was in awe of him – his hero. He knew he was big in the IRA, with British blood on his hands. The fact that innocent people had died because of his father's vicious ways did not concern him even at such a young age. The end justified the means, and one day it was his dream to be like his father. He smiled at the man and nodded. "I won't go out. Does Ma know?"

Ryan said, "That she does."

Declan watched his father take a long pull from a glass full of Bushmills. Was it to bolster his confidence or just an early celebratory drink? He reckoned it was the latter. His father needed nothing to bolster his confidence – he was brave – a true soldier, ready to die for his beliefs. "Good luck then Dad – hope the bastard dies slowly."

Ryan didn't even blink – it was the way he wanted his son to grow up. For sure as hell there would still be fighting when he was dead, and he wanted his son to be ready for the fight.

*

Declan smiled as he remembered that night. The target had died. The army and the RUC had been hit below the belt – losing one of their own hurt like hell, especially the Chief Constable. Worse, they knew the IRA would be rejoicing at their pain. His father's name became revered by many. Even when he was eventually cut down in a fire-fight in the Shanklin Road he was not forgotten. Declan crossed himself and mumbled, "God rest your soul Dad."

*

As promised, the answer came back within the hour. "I owe you big time mate," Declan said, unable to keep the excitement out of his voice. But the man on the other end of the line knew better than to ask what was up. No names were ever mentioned – no plans ever discussed – mobiles thrown away after every call. It was why the likes of him and Seamus had survived so long.

Declan threw his fag end out onto the lay-by and then having removed the SIM card threw the cell phone far into the bushes – he had four replacements in the glove compartment. He gunned the engine and headed back to the house.

*

An hour later Declan and Seamus were in a state of high excitement. "Jesus fucking Christ," exclaimed Declan, "This is what we need. The ex-Secretary of State's son coming here to shoot woodcock."

Seamus rubbed his hands. "Well Declan my friend, we will be ready for him – make sure he has a warm welcome. We will do this on our own. If any of those lilly-livered bastards are still around they won't have the stomach for what I have in mind."

"What have you in mind?" asked Declan.

"I'll tell you when I'm ready."

Declan didn't press the point. He'd only get a fist in his stomach.

"You'll slap me on the back Declan when I decide to tell you. Get glasses Mary and a full bottle. We will celebrate tonight."

Mary seldom saw Seamus excited these days. He'd become moody of late, black moods – dangerous moods. Fear still kept her tight to him, and when he was in one of his black moods, though black as hell, Mary knew she was the only one who could lift him. She ran to the kitchen for the glasses. A few weeks ago she'd have celebrated with him – not now. She had a feeling that an innocent man was about to be killed and she wasn't too sure she wanted that. She shook her head in bewilderment.

She brought the glasses and the bottle. Seamus patted her arse. "A good job you have done there girl."

Mary rewarded his congratulations with silence.

Seamus glared at her. "Go into the kitchen and get us some food girl, we don't want you here."

Mary quickly turned away – she didn't want Seamus to see her tears. It would only bring back his anger.

Seventeen

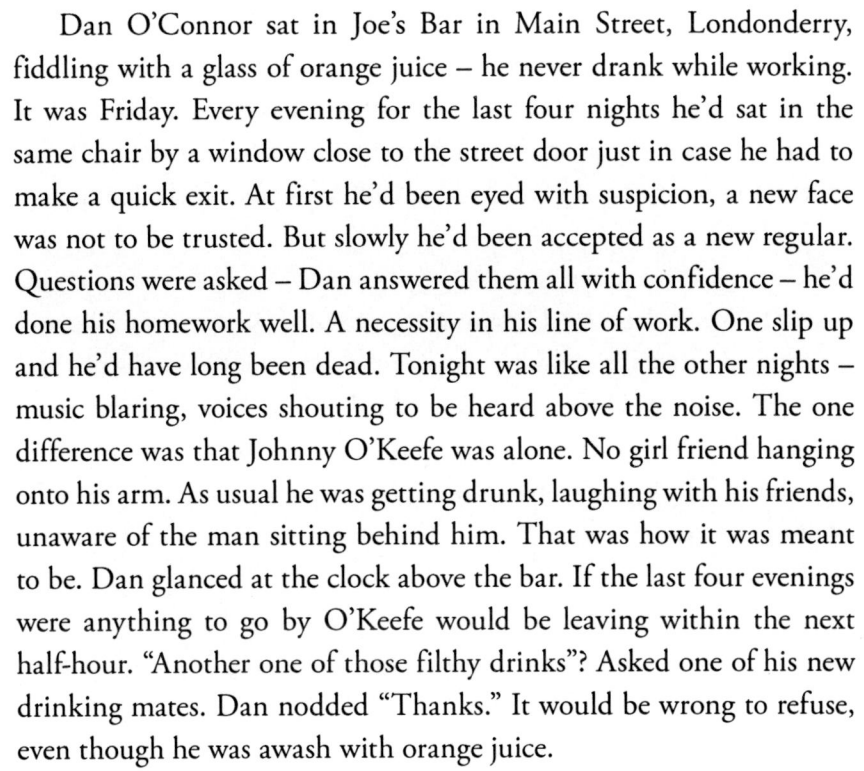

Dan O'Connor sat in Joe's Bar in Main Street, Londonderry, fiddling with a glass of orange juice – he never drank while working. It was Friday. Every evening for the last four nights he'd sat in the same chair by a window close to the street door just in case he had to make a quick exit. At first he'd been eyed with suspicion, a new face was not to be trusted. But slowly he'd been accepted as a new regular. Questions were asked – Dan answered them all with confidence – he'd done his homework well. A necessity in his line of work. One slip up and he'd have long been dead. Tonight was like all the other nights – music blaring, voices shouting to be heard above the noise. The one difference was that Johnny O'Keefe was alone. No girl friend hanging onto his arm. As usual he was getting drunk, laughing with his friends, unaware of the man sitting behind him. That was how it was meant to be. Dan glanced at the clock above the bar. If the last four evenings were anything to go by O'Keefe would be leaving within the next half-hour. "Another one of those filthy drinks"? Asked one of his new drinking mates. Dan nodded "Thanks." It would be wrong to refuse, even though he was awash with orange juice.

"Orange juice for this man and my usual pint for me barman," shouted the man. Once the juice had been put down beside Dan the man lost interest. Thank God, thought Dan. The last thing I want is a half-cut man engaging me in a conversation. He turned his attention back to O'Keefe. He saw his eyes were not focusing – he'd be no trouble.

As if on cue as the clock ticked the half-hour O'Keefe stretched, shook the hands of those around him. "See you Monday," he said, winking at the small crowd. "Got other things to do this weekend." His boast was rewarded by murmurs of, "randy fucking sod," which made O'Keefe feel real good. He thrust out his chest, waved and walked unsteadily towards the street door. Dan waited a few moments to let the crowd settle down and then sauntered towards the door.

Once out in the cold air he watched O'Keefe tuck his head into his coat and weave his way up the street. It was quiet. The job could be done now but Dan chose to wait. He knew O'Keefe's route and had already chosen his spot. Never change a plan unless you have to. He quickened his step and passed O'Keefe – raised a hand and hurried on. Ahead was a junction. O'Keefe would turn left. The road led to a line of houses – no pub – no late night convenience store. Dan walked a few yards into the street and turned just as O'Keefe came off the main road.

Perfect.

Dan made his move.

As O'Keefe drew level he bumped into him. "Sorry mate," he said quietly and drove the eight inch knife up and under O'Keefe's ribs and twisted the blade. O'Keefe's eyes widened in surprise. He came to an abrupt halt – coughed once and sank to his knees, blood running from his mouth, hands desperately pulling at the knife. Dan knew he'd be dead in seconds.

Job done.

He walked back the way he'd come, down past the pub, smiling at several greetings and reached his car. As he drove away he heard the first scream. He drove carefully back to Belfast to report to George Russell that target number four had been dealt with. Things were going to plan.

*

Charlie O'Malley fought to contain his frustration as he was informed of the killing of Johnny O'Keefe in Londonderry– no loss mind you, but still another unexplained death. Well at least to him. His superior officers were only too keen to blame a Protestant break-away group. The cynical view being that someone was doing a bloody good job. But Charlie didn't buy into the Protestant solution. It was too damned simple. Most dissident groups of which ever side they supported loved to claim responsibility – none had done so. To Charlie's way of thinking and most telling, was that not one of his contacts had any idea what was going on. In a place like Belfast that was always teeming with rumours and full of people only too happy to pass on information for a quick tenner or two this increased his feeling that there were sinister moves going on. Even, and this was a thought he knew he had to keep to himself unless he could get proof, a political connection. Charlie shook his head – he'd been reading too many Lee Child and Gerald Seymour thrillers recently. But the nagging feeling that the whole police force was being deliberately kept out of the picture would not go away. He was known as a shrewd copper, his intuition sometimes picking up on a small detail that had been overlooked. And Charlie was in the mood to start sifting through what evidence they had. Somewhere he was certain there had to be a clue.

*

Seamus looked demonic. The devil himself could not have been more frightening in the flesh. Mary thought of him in church sitting beside her, taking Communion, smiling at everyone around him. He had the knack of turning on the charm. No charm right now. A glass smashed against the kitchen wall. "Bastards, fucking bastards," Seamus shouted, sweeping everything on the kitchen table onto the floor and then aiming a kick at one of the chairs. His eyes blazed with fury and his body shook. Mary and Declan stood rooted to the spot. To speak would earn them a fist in the stomach. He stared at Mary and she braced herself for a blow, but he turned away with a shout and ran from the room. Only when she heard the front door open did she dare to breath. She collapsed into a chair. "Jesus!" she said to Declan. "He's mad as hell. Best left alone. Only time will calm him down."

Time ran to an hour. She heard the front door open – held her breath as Seamus walked back into the kitchen. He looked at Declan. "Fucking bastards," he spluttered. "O'Keefe was a good man. He will be missed, but soon we will hold an ace." Then he laughed mirthlessly. "Providing we are not all dead."

*

Dan O'Connor was growing uneasy with killing. Even as he took the congratulations from his comrades he felt no satisfaction. His childhood in Belfast had taught him to loath violence. His father had instilled into him that everyone on earth deserved a chance to live a life whatever their religious beliefs. But he'd justified his chosen career by convincing himself that he was doing a necessary job. Eliminating terrorists was saving lives. To his knowledge he had never killed anyone who beyond any doubt hadn't deserved to die. He felt no remorse for ending their lives. But now he feared he was killing people who were considered a risk – not people who had beyond all doubt committed an atrocity. It did not rest easily on his conscience. As he sipped coffee and briefed George Russell of his successful hit it dawned on him that maybe after all it really was time to quit. Find a girl, buy a house, raise a family and grow roses.

Eighteen

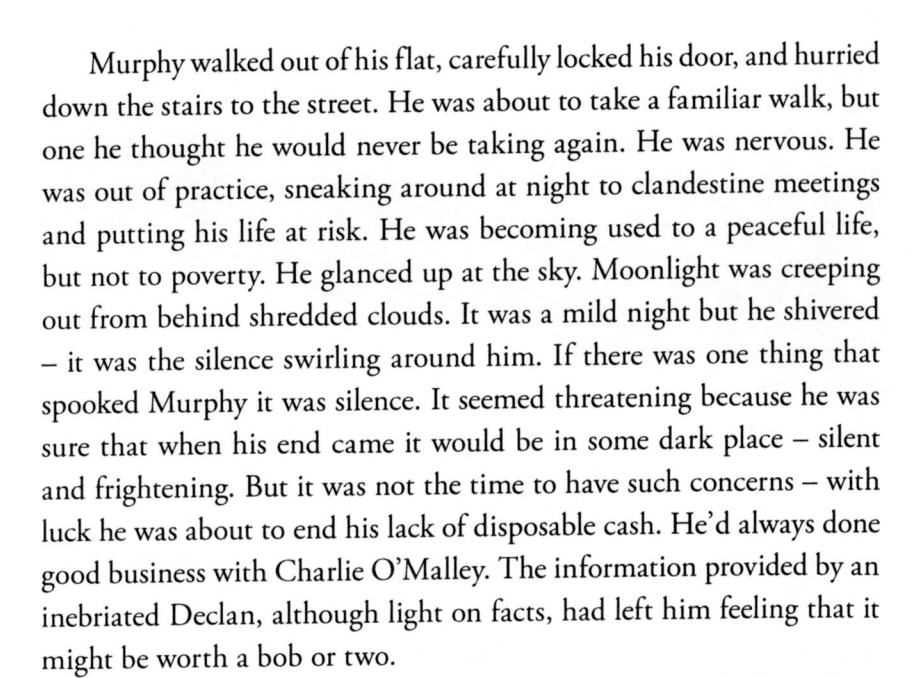

Murphy walked out of his flat, carefully locked his door, and hurried down the stairs to the street. He was about to take a familiar walk, but one he thought he would never be taking again. He was nervous. He was out of practice, sneaking around at night to clandestine meetings and putting his life at risk. He was becoming used to a peaceful life, but not to poverty. He glanced up at the sky. Moonlight was creeping out from behind shredded clouds. It was a mild night but he shivered – it was the silence swirling around him. If there was one thing that spooked Murphy it was silence. It seemed threatening because he was sure that when his end came it would be in some dark place – silent and frightening. But it was not the time to have such concerns – with luck he was about to end his lack of disposable cash. He'd always done good business with Charlie O'Malley. The information provided by an inebriated Declan, although light on facts, had left him feeling that it might be worth a bob or two.

He walked along the street, head low, ears alert. He had a mile to go before he reached the agreed meeting place. He knew the route well – every side street, every empty pub, every broken street light. The area had not changed for the better since the peace accord. No new houses, no repaired pubs and no new shopping centre. Nothing. Just the smell of decay. The recession had not been kind to this part of Belfast. He would have much preferred to have met in a café, but Charlie had always insisted, "The yard as usual Murphy. There are enemies skulking about everywhere with alert eyes and flapping ears and you wouldn't want to have your throat slit would you, you two-timing rogue."

Murphy had understood the sense in that and had not wasted time arguing – Charlie knew best – besides he was the pay master. He hitched up his trousers, now getting loose around his waist, the result of necessary fasting. With luck tonight would change all that. He pulled out a filthy handkerchief and wiped away the snot which was irritatingly running from his nose. He slapped his thighs, this was not the brave cunning Murphy of old - this was a pathetic specimen of a nerve wracked man sliding into old age and past his best. He grunted and shook his head. That was crap. He would not surrender to old age. He was just out of practice. He had never expected to have any worthwhile information once the peace agreement had been signed. So being a strong believer that God worked miracles Murphy had gone to church the day before and thanked his Maker.

*

Charlie was feeling particularly happy, his frustration ebbing. The call from Liam Murphy had raised his spirits. At last he might be about to get some much needed information. Murphy had been his most reliable contact for years, though Charlie knew he'd been dealing with both sides. Murphy was a greedy bastard and he was surprised he'd lived to see the peace. He reached the rusty iron gates of the now deserted factory. The owner had met his end during the Troubles and his family were still squabbling about ownership. The area around had been falling into decay and the houses had long since been deserted. It was a perfect place for a meeting. As had been his practice, he'd parked his car half a mile back and walked. His senses were more alert when he walked. Nothing much seemed to have changed since his last visit. There were no street lights. The area had grown even more desolate since his last visit and the only light came from traffic on the nearby road. Since he'd left his house the moon had become covered by cloud, blowing up from the west. A sure sign that rain would follow soon. The world seemed very dark to him. It was at moments like this that took him back to his childhood in Sandwich, Kent where he'd lived with his divorced mother. One night a great storm had swept up from the bay and plunged huge areas of the county into darkness. He had been terrified. After that he had never quite got over the fear of dark places. He took several deep breaths to control his heart rate before turning on his torch. The sharp ray of light calmed his nerves as it cut through the wall of blackness. He moved slowly, walked through the rusting iron gates, careful not to fall into one of the many pot holes scattered about the concrete yard in front of the factory. A couple of rats, startled by the beam, scurried across the yard making for the protection of the factory walls. There had been an old wooden bench on the left of the large unloading doors, now in danger of collapse as their hinges slowly rusted away. It had been where the factory workers had sat for a moment's relaxation, inhaling nicotine into their lungs before going back to the grind of shifting large bales of wood shavings. He'd lost count of the number of times he'd sat on that bench waiting for his contacts. It was two years since his last visit and he quite expected the bench to have disintegrated. But no, it was still there. He smiled and moved towards it. Once beside it he directed the torch beam on it, noticing it was a little worse for wear and covered in pigeon droppings. He chose a spot not dotted with the glue-like offerings - sat down and waited. The sound of traffic behind the factory was his only companion. He was alone, and if he was honest with himself, just a little scared. Murphy could be playing a double game.

Charlie was well aware he still had enemies with long memories. The little turd would go where there was most money on offer, and that meant he might well be walking into a trap. If his investigation hadn't hit a brick wall he would have told Murphy to jump into Belfast Lough. But when needs must Charlie was prepared to consort even with the Devil.

*

If Charlie was feeling apprehensive it was nothing compared to how Murphy was feeling as he walked through the iron gates. He didn't have the advantage of a torch and his eyes were not what they used to be. The damp atmosphere was beginning to eat into his bones. He cursed himself for not putting on his thick over coat. He screwed up his eyes and scanned the darkness. And there it was, a pinprick of light coming from the walls of the factory. He prayed it was O'Malley. *If not you're dead Murphy old son.* Carefully putting one foot in front of the other he moved towards the light, his heart thumping hard against his ribs. He cursed at not having his flask of brandy with him to bolster his courage. He sucked in his breath as he grew closer to the light. He could make out a figure sitting on the familiar bench. Was it O'Malley? He screwed up his eyes again, but couldn't be sure. "O'Malley," he dared to croak. He was rewarded by a blinding light embracing him in its glare. He threw up his hands to shield his eyes, and swallowed a scream.

"Murphy," came the voice behind the torch.

Murphy's knees went weak. "Thank the Lord Mr O'Malley. I was getting the caterpillars in my stomach that I was."

"Butterflies."

"What?"

"It's butterflies Murphy."

Murphy said nothing.

"Come and sit here Murphy," Charlie said, slapping the wood, which he soon realised was a mistake. The smell coming off Murphy was foul. He pulled out a handkerchief and held it to his nose. "I can tell you're still frightened of soap," he complained.

Murphy said nothing.

Charlie asked, "Now then Murphy what's got you out of retirement eh, or is this a trap?"

"No trap. Would I do that to you Mr O'Malley?"

"Yes."

"That's very hurtful Mr O'Malley. I promise I'm on my own. I have picked up a bit of news that might help my cash flow problems

– interesting news. This peace does a man like Murphy no favours at all. But the shooting of Conor Keogh and several others of the same way of thinking, the Lord bless them, has made one or two people very angry – yes, very angry indeed."

Charlie decided not to say, "And me." Instead he asked, "there's trouble coming is there?"

"Definitely."

"Tell me about it Murphy as briefly as you can. Not one of your long drawn out stories to make me think you're worth more than you are."

Murphy cleared his throat. "I know a man called Declan Ryan. The old IRA men are still willing to tell you, if asked, that his father, Patrick Ryan killed that Chief Constable fellow. Oh shit what was the bastard's name?"

"Dermot Fitzpatrick," Charlie reminded him.

"Yes, that's the one. Well I happen to be on good terms with Declan and in the past he has inadvertently passed useful info to me while under the influence. Did the same a few nights ago."

"And what did he say?"

"That he and a man well known to you were going to give the British Government a fucking great shock."

"The man's name?"

"Seamus Flanagan."

"The devil himself."

Murphy laughed uneasily. Flanagan frightened the shit out of him. If he knew he was sitting on a bench in the middle of the night feeding info to Mr O'Malley he suspected he wouldn't see the year out.

"So Murphy, spill the beans."

"Declan wasn't precise, but he hinted that something big was about to explode. Something that Flanagan hoped would end these killings. They are really getting on his tits."

"Yes, yes, yes Murphy, but what good is that to me?"

"It warns you to be especially vigilant."

"Is that all you have to say?"

"Isn't that enough Mr O'Malley? Ryan and Flanagan do not mess about."

"But what are they planning for Christ sake Murphy?"

A rat scurried across Murphy's feet. He gasped. "Jesus Mr O'Malley did you have to choose this spot. Vermin! I hate vermin."

"Seems they know one when they see one," Charlie couldn't resist saying. "You'll be out of here more quickly if you stop giving me titbits and tell me something worthwhile."

"I've just told you about Ryan and Flanagan," whined Murphy.

"Not enough."

Murphy could see his payoff disappearing. He cleared his throat, lifting his feet onto the bench as a precaution against any more rats and said, "The word about is that they are going to target someone. Identity unknown."

"That's a useless bit of information."

"It might be a kidnap."

"That's better, but only might?"

"That's the best I can do. Lips are zipped Mr O'Malley."

"Even your friend Ryan's?"

"Knowing Flanagan the way I do, I doubt if Ryan knows the details."

Charlie felt frustration growing – it seemed par for the course. He felt flat. He fumbled in his trouser pocket and pulled out a wad of notes. He peeled off five tens and held them out.

Murphy felt peeved. "Fifty – is that all I get for risking my life? I'm a poor man now Mr O'Malley. I'm wasting away."

"I'm being generous Murphy."

Murphy took the money.

Then Charlie waved the rest of the notes in Murphy's face. "Smell these. There's another fifty here. There yours for more information. Sure you haven't forgotten something?"

Murphy took a deep breath. "There's a rumour going about that the target comes from the mainland."

Charlie came alert. "Why didn't you tell me this earlier?"

Love Thine Enemy

"Scared shitless Mr O'Malley. Besides it's only idle talk."

"But the smell of money has overcome your fear. You're a turd Murphy."

"I know that Mr O'Malley. Now can I have the money?"

"No."

"Ah come on Mr O'Malley, have a heart for a poor man. It's not as if it's your money."

"Good night Murphy."

Murphy knew he was beaten. Fifty was better than nothing. "I don't like you Mr O'Malley."

"The feelings mutual Murphy. Now off you crawl. We've spent too much time here."

Murphy wasted no time in moving away. He was pissed off. He grunted, "Good bye," and walked off into the night.

Charlie made no attempt to follow him, he needed time to digest Murphy's news. It was a small morsel, but a very disturbing one. If true how the hell was he going to discover the target? His heart sank. He had no idea where to start. It quickly dawned on him that his task was as good as hopeless. "What changes," he shouted to the dark sky.

*

Murphy sensed something was wrong. The solitary light over the stairs leading to his one-roomed flat was not working – strange, it had been working when he left. He stood at the bottom of the stairs wondering why his internal warning system was glowing red. He flipped at the light switch again – definitely broken. Time to get out. He turned and fled straight into the arms of Seamus.

"In a hurry Murphy?" His voice was low and threatening. "I thought you'd run for it if I took out the light bulb. I can read you like a book you wretched piece of Irish shit. Now what have you been up to talking to the Inspector?" He drove a fist into Murphy's belly. Murphy dropped to the ground, fighting for air. "I told him nothing – fed him rubbish. I was short of cash."

"Not good enough," said Seamus, putting a foot on Murphy's hand.

"You have my word. I was desperate." Murphy knew he was in deep shit. He was buggered. "It was harmless stuff Seamus."

"Show some respect Murphy, my name is Mr Flanagan to you, as I've told you many times." He kicked Murphy again. "Now get up you spineless individual."

Murphy struggled to his feet. "Please don't hit me again," he snivelled.

Seamus laughed. "It has come to my notice that you are up to your old ways again, visiting pubs and sniffing around – very bad news. So don't tell me you gave O'Malley nothing. I've had you watched and here I am. Naughty Murphy."

Murphy said nothing – he was shafted.

"I am very mad Murphy. Your usefulness could be coming to an end but I will spare your life because I know any information you fed to that Inspector would be useless and because I might need you in the future. But no more getting up to your old tricks, do you hear."

"I promise," said Murphy unable to believe his luck.

"I should put a gun to your head and blow those two brain cells of yours to Kingdom Come," growled Seamus. "That will come later."

Murphy said nothing.

"Now fuck off back to your hovel."

Murphy turned and started to walk slowly back to the building relieved of one thing – Declan had obviously said nothing to Flanagan about the meeting in the pub.

"Oh Murphy," called Seamus.

Murphy hunched his shoulders, Declan *had* opened his mouth. He turned. Seamus never shot anyone in the back.

"The money."

"What?"

"Give me the money."

"What money?"

"Don't play games Murphy. The money O'Malley paid you for the useless information. Come on, I'm losing patience." Seamus held out his hand.

Murphy felt like crying as he pulled the notes out of his pocket. You're' a hard man Mr Flanagan."

"And you're a double crossing shit."

Murphy's hand was shaking so badly as he held out the notes that he nearly dropped them.

"Thank you Murphy, glad your saw reason."

Murphy scowled and turned away.

"Oh Murphy."

Murphy swung round to face Seamus. This time he really was going to die.

"Scared you didn't I," laughed Seamus, holding out the light bulb.

Murphy wet himself.

Nineteen

Richard smiled at his son as he walked into the room. He waved at a chair opposite him. "Sit down James I want to talk to you."

James sat. All ears.

His father settled himself down in his favourite armchair – worn, showing signs of its age - rubbed his chin, which James knew was a sign that he had something serious to say.

"I was eleven when your grandfather was killed. Already he was my best friend. Quite simply I adored him. Of course I was ignorant of the dangers he faced. As I grew up I learnt that he believed strongly that whatever ones religion one had a right to live in peace. He put this into practice in his job. Apparently it was not easy in a Force that was inclined to be anti-catholic. I learnt that he was admired by both factions of the community. It is my belief that is what got him killed. The evil men saw him as a threat to their murderous aspirations. I still remember hearing the shot. That split second, when the bullet was nearing my father's heart, was going to change my life. I was too young to be planning a career, but a politician would certainly have been low on my list. But when I was old enough to know my own mind politics seemed the best way to carry on where your grandfather left off. I know at times you have been puzzled by the relationship between myself and your grandmother, but I can't find it in my soul to completely forgive her for uprooting me from my home. At first I hated her for that, and I have never been able to forgive her. You may well think that I should be enough of a man to forgive and you are probably right. But your grandfather's death and being uprooted from home has left a huge scar. I still feel I have been robbed of a life that would have been so different and far less stressful. I have *never been sure what path that life would have taken. It would certainly not have been politics. But as I have chosen that career it is my ambition to one day return to Ireland to live, when the island is at last at peace with itself. I still have dreams of the times your grandfather took me down to the Lough's edge to watch the sunset over Belfast."*

*

James took a lung full of air and brushed back his hair with a hand. Every time he came to Ireland he thought of that conversation. He was never quite sure why. Maybe it was because he thought he understood why his father had wanted to return. James wrinkled his eyes, feeling the familiar charge of excitement as the lights of Larne appeared across the water. Dawn would soon be breaking, heralding the start of a week he looked forward to every year. He sighed – dropped his half-smoked camel cigarette over the side of the ferry and turned to see Henry Walters walking towards him, dishevelled. It only took Henry a few hours to shrug off his smart blue suit that he wore most working days to his office or court and turn into a totally different character. On holiday Henry did not believe in shaving – come to think of it a bath was rare and his suits and ties were resting in his wardrobe at home. James liked his idiosyncrasies. He smiled and the two men touched hands. "Not long now Henry."

Henry smiled. "I can smell Meg's breakfast already."

James laughed. "Another two hours and you'll be there."

Henry looked at his watch. "That will be nine o'clock. God knows what my stomach will be saying by then."

*

At Brascome Manor Meg Healy was glad of the extra time before her guests arrived. Henry had rung her to say they were running late. Mary had not yet put in an appearance, which was riling her somewhat.

Michael Pakenham

Usually the most placid of people Meg was not prone to showing her displeasure, but this time she decided to have a strong word or two with the girl when she eventually deigned to arrive – lateness was one thing Meg could not tolerate.

*

It took longer than usual to drive off the ferry and head towards Brascome – they were growing impatient and hungry by the time the wheels of the Jeep touched the dock's tarmac. By then Henry's stomach was loudly rumbling. "Put you foot down," he begged James.

"As fast as I can go Henry," James assured him, as he drove onto the A8 heading for the M2. The rain lashed down on the jeep's windscreen – huge drops that sounded like sparks from a fire. "Nothing changes," laughed James as he flipped the wipers into fast mode.

*

Seamus was growing restless. They had been sitting in the stolen Volvo for over an hour hidden by some oak trees a couple of hundred yards from the iron gates leading to Brascome Manor. The jeep should have been here by now. He was beginning to think that Fitzpatrick was not coming, and the silence from Declan's informant at the docks was worrying. Was his great plan about to be sunk in the Irish mud? His anger was beginning to rise. "No news yet?" he asked Declan, making no attempt to hide his frustration.

Declan drew on his cigarette. He'd trust his life to his informant. "He'll ring." Declan was not prone to long sentences.

*

Johnny Cash invaded every part of the jeep. His voice was giving Henry a headache. He couldn't stand the man - so bloody depressing.

Love Thine Enemy

But James raved about him – even had a stupid sticker on the back window announcing to all who cared to read it that he loved Johnny Cash. But as he was driving he had the choice of CD. Henry decided that next year he'd re-negotiate the deal. He looked out of the window –couldn't see much, it was pissing down.

*

Declan's mobile vibrated. Seamus gripped the steering wheel. Mary sat forward in the back seat. A few seconds of silence. Breaths held. Declan nodded and pushed the mobile back into his jacket pocket. "Two of them on their way. Confirmed as James Fitzpatrick. Other man is a Henry Walters. Blue Cherokee Jeep, Reg number HK07VMG."

"Thank the good Lord!" said Seamus, wondering why he'd ever doubted Declan.

Mary sat back in her seat and wondered what she had let herself in for. Ripping open a packet of mint chewing gum she offered the packet to the two men. Declan took it. They had another hour to wait. Seamus opened his door and urinated by the side of the Volvo – Declan followed suit. How easy for men, thought Mary curling up in her seat. To her surprise she felt no excitement as her sweaty hand closed on the baseball bat. For years she'd waited for a moment like this, when she would be part of the action. But now… the adrenaline was not pumping. Her bewilderment was growing.

*

James was now singing along tunelessly to Johnny Cash.

"You'll never make the choir," joked Henry, putting his hands over his ears. There was only about a mile to go and then the agony would be over and they'd be sitting at Meg's large kitchen table, covered in a floral table cloth, a plate of fried eggs, bacon, black pudding and large pieces of fried bread in front of them, her round happy face smiling at him and James.

James passed the Volvo without giving it a second glance.

Seamus saw the two men in the front – read the number plate. He gunned the engine, excitement flowing through his veins. In the next few minutes the first step to giving London the shits. The British Government would be shaken to the core. He drove a fist into Declan's arm, heard him wince and laughed. "Ready?" he asked.

No less excited Declan stroked the sawn-off shotgun resting on his lap. "Ready," he croaked.

"And you Mary?"

"Ready."

Seamus pulled out into the lane. He knew he only had a few minutes to stop the Jeep. He had reconnoitred the lane several times – it was not ideal for the manoeuvre that he had in mind. But he could do it – had to. There was only one spot he could get past the Jeep and force it to stop. A lay-by just before the iron gates on the right. It all depended on precise timing. It would not be easy but the other alternative was to blow the back tyres out and that might alert the occupants to the danger – they might just have time to get through the gates. Seamus might catch them, he might not, and he had never been one to take unnecessary risks. He swung the wheel – Mary toppled to her left – Declan was pushed against his door. For a second Seamus fought the wheel – the lay-by was feet away. He pushed his foot hard down on the accelerator and as he swerved into the lay-by he drew level with the Jeep. He swung the wheel hard to the left forcing the Jeep to brake violently. He heard the scrap of metal on metal and then he was passed. He braked – the Jeep hit the rear of the Volvo. Both cars came to a juddering halt. Declan leapt out of the Volvo, Mary followed. Seamus turned off the ignition and slowly exited the car. It was Declan's job to do the dirty work.

Declan moved quickly. He tore open the driver's door waving his shotgun in James's face. Mary opened the passenger door and a dazed

Henry fell out, crumpling to the ground. Mary kicked him in the ribs. Henry cried out and didn't move.

"Out," screamed Declan, pushing his shot gun into the side of James's neck.

For a split second James thought of launching himself at Declan. Declan read his thoughts. "Don't try it!" he said through gritted teeth. "I'd love to kill you."

James stepped into a vicious blow to the chin. He fell to the ground unconscious. Declan smiled – he loved hurting people.

It was all over in a matter of minutes.

Declan ran back to the Volvo and pulled out a can of petrol. Seamus went through Fitzpatrick's pockets – found his wallet, rifled through various debit cards before finding the driving licence. He let out a cry of triumph as he stared at the photograph. "Got him!"

Mary looked down at Fitzpatrick and said nothing. She felt no satisfaction. It was not how she was meant to feel.

"Right, let's get them into the Volvo," ordered Seamus. "Hurry up with that fuel Declan. You take Walters and I'll take Fitzpatrick."

Declan reluctantly poured the last drop of petrol onto the Jeep's bonnet – he'd loved playing with fire ever since he was a boy and Declan being Declan had put his love to good use ever since. At the right price he'd burn anything. He fingered the box of matches in his pocket and looked at Seamus.

"No! Bodies in the Volvo first," growled Seamus.

The two men were dumped into the back of the Volvo. "Tie their hands Mary," Seamus ordered. "Now you can torch the Jeep Declan."

Seamus checked the damage to the Volvo – a dented bumper, left hand light glass broken. Bulbs looked in tact. There was nothing to worry about. He jumped behind the wheel – tested the indicators – gunned the engine and laughed triumphantly.

Seamus roared away.

*

Duff shrugged into his Barbour and opened the front door. His terrier bolted out into to the rain. "Just off up the drive to the lane with Scruff," he shouted over his shoulder to Meg.

"Okay," said Meg coming out of the kitchen. "And if you see Mary, tell her to get her arse down here double quick."

Duff jammed his hands into his pockets, hunched his shoulders against the stinging rain and headed up the drive. His mind was on woodcock. This weather was perfect for their migration. He loved this time of the year. The house rang with laughter – he drank copious glasses of malt whisky with his guests and told them his same old stories with more embellishment every year. No one had the heart to yawn. He was shaken out of his reverie by the urgent barking of Scruff. "Hey. Hey, what's the matter little fellow, seen a deer? Don't get ideas, they run faster than you." Duff looked up the drive, squinting his eyes against the rain. "Damn glasses," he complained. He pulled out a handkerchief and vainly tried to wipe the rain off the lenses. He could just make out the shape of a vehicle and hear shouting. The driving rain made it difficult to see more than a few yards. "Sounds like someone's broken down on the lane Scruff. Come on let's go and have a look." He started to run, Scruff snapping at his heels. Duff slowed his pace after a short while. "I'm not built for sprinting," he said to Scruff. He could now just make out two vehicles and angry voices. He decided on a final sprint.

The force of the explosion threw him backwards into the air. He fell heavily on his back, the wind knocked out of him. He lay there for several minutes, stunned, his ears ringing, his glasses gone. He shook his head – felt his body to make sure he was all in one piece. No blood, some pain. He saw his glasses lying beside him, unbroken thank God! He staggered to his feet and looked up the drive. Flames were shooting into the air. He gazed open mouthed at the sight. "Bloody hell," he shouted into the wind. He looked around for Scruff. The dog was nowhere to be seen. He felt panic welling up inside him. For a moment he hesitated, trying desperately to get himself together. Then he turned and started to stagger back to the house. He was soon blowing badly.

His back hurt – there was drumming in his ears. Reaching the front door he sighed with relief and there was Scruff shaking on the doorstep. "Thank God your safe," said Duff breathlessly, patting the dog's wet fur. He threw open the front door and ran towards the kitchen shouting, "Meg, Meg, quickly woman come here."

Meg ran out of the kitchen. "What…" She looked at the sodden and dishevelled figure standing in front of her and immediately knew something was wrong. "What's happened?"

"There's a car burning at the top of the drive – exploded just as I was reaching the end of the drive. Call the emergency services! Fire and ambulance. It looks serious. I have a terrible feeling its James's Jeep and if there was anyone in it when it exploded they are certainly dead."

Never one to flap Meg nodded and ran to the telephone. Two minutes later she put down the receiver and ran to Duff's side. She reached for his hand. "What on earth is going on?"

"No idea."

Meg rushed to where her thick coat was hanging on the back of the front door. "Come on, no point in sweating with fear down here." With a terrible feeling that the day was only going to get worse Duff followed her back out into the rain.

Twenty

Seamus drove fast, aware that he probably had only minutes before the sound of sirens split the air. Once clear of the area he could relax a little. The immediate danger would be passed. There was silence in the car – nerves were jangling, both Mary and Declan aware that the next half-hour was fraught with danger. Mary was biting her nails; Declan was half lying on Henry. James was jammed between the two of them.

Seamus glanced at his watch. He'd been driving for twenty-five minutes. Not far now. He reckoned he was about a mile from the rough track he'd discovered on one of his reconnaissance journeys. There was a field where he could leave the Volvo. He relaxed a little and allowed himself to smile– *lucky I never leave things to chance.* So far so good. "You clever fucking sod," he said quietly. He slowed – didn't want to miss the turning. He was almost opposite the track when he heard the sirens in the distance. *Too fucking late!* He was clear. He slowed, spotted the track on his left and turned down it. It was rough – the tarmac was breaking up. The steering wheel juddered in his hands. He drove on, his eyes searching for the gate into the field. "Got you," he exclaimed and swung the wheel, guiding the car through the gate. He drove a few more yards and stopped. "Out!" he shouted. "This is where we do the switch."

Mary leant forward from the back seat. "Switch?"

Seamus turned and gave her a broad smile. "A switch. Did you think Seamus would try to reach the cottage with a beat-up car? What do you take me for – a fool?"

Mary detected a note of triumph in his voice. She had to admire him. She had never met anyone who planned so meticulously as Seamus.

That was one of the reasons she was with him. "You have another car here?"

"I do."

She couldn't help saying, "Oh you are a clever sod."

"I know."

"So where is it?"

"Behind you, under the hedge."

Both Mary and Declan turned round. A blue Subaru.

"Four wheel drive as well," added Seamus with another smile as he saw Mary looking at the slippery grass.

"Just one question," Mary asked.

"I know what that is. Answer is I have my friends. You don't need to know more. Now, no more time for friendly chat. Let's get these bastards out of this car and into the Subaru. I want to get them home."

Declan needed no encouragement. He dragged Henry out of the car onto the grass. Then he did the same to James. They lay on the ground unable to move. Fear radiated from Henry's eyes – James was semi-conscious. Wasting no time the two men took their prisoners by the legs and dragged them to the Subaru and unceremoniously dumped them on the back seat. "Watch them," ordered Seamus. "I have a phone call to make."

Mary squeezed onto the back seat thinking the two men were in no shape to go anywhere.

*

Two miles away the phone rang in a small farmhouse. A man answered immediately – he'd been waiting for the call. "Okay," he said and broke the connection. He ran out of the house into his farm yard and jumped into his JCB. He drove carefully. It took him just short of forty-five minutes to reach the field. Using the JCB's front loader he picked up the Volvo and took it to a pit he'd dug several days earlier. He dropped it into the pit – covered it with earth – levelled off the ground and was back inside the farm house before Seamus reached his destination. The payment was generous – badly needed – his one man building business was not doing well. The recession had done him no favours. At least he'd now be able to pay the finance company and keep the JCB. There was always the possibility that Seamus might want the use of the JCB again. Cars or bodies, he wasn't fussy. He reached for his bottle of cheap brandy resting, as it always did, on one of the kitchen worktops – he could no longer afford the taste of his favourite malt. He drank Seamus's health. He moved into the small sitting room and dropped into the only chair in the room. He'd sold most of the furniture to exist. He looked at the picture of his late wife above the fire place and raised his glass. Things were about to change.

The bullet smashed the window, drove deep into his flesh. He was dead within seconds. His lifeless hands dropped the glass, and rivulets of whisky spread across the woodlice infested floor.

Seamus trusted few men. Certainly not an impecunious old builder.

*

Murphy jumped into his stolen Renault. He knew he was getting out of his depths and he was scared shitless. He'd never shot a man in cold blood before and he didn't want to do it again. On his run back to the car he'd vomited. He never imagined that Seamus would ask him to be an assassin. Well 'demanded' would be a better choice of word. He'd tried to object – received a cuff around the ear and was asked if he preferred to be dead. He slammed his door shut and began to cry. He was convinced that his time on earth was limited – Seamus left very few loose strings and Murphy reckoned that he now came into that category. He knew too much now and Seamus would see him as a danger. He wiped a tear from his right eye and took stock of his predicament. It really was time to run. Run where? Seamus's tentacles stretched a long way. He imagined the bullet tearing into his flesh. How many days did he have before Seamus came after him? Maybe one! He didn't want to die. *Get a grip or you are a dead man for sure.* Murphy reached for a much needed cigarette –lit it, inhaled deeply and felt a little better. He sat back in his seat and put his mind to work. After ten minutes an idea was forming in his head. It was dangerous, but then a condemned man was short on choices. This might just get him out of death row, and if it didn't, well at least he'd tried. He smiled to himself and gunned the engine. His first priority was to get a long way from the farmhouse. He'd already spent too much time in the locality.

Twenty-One

A headache hammered at James's brain. Tentacles of fear were entwining themselves around his guts. His eyes burnt – his limbs ached – his hands and feet were numb from the tight bindings. He knew he was in a desperate situation. He was lying on a sofa. He tried to change positions and pain coursed through his body. He let out a cry. Immediately he saw a man approach him.

Seamus stood looking down at him, his whisky laden breath washing over him. He spat in his face. "Welcome back to Ireland Fitzpatrick" he said. "Not what you expected eh? No shooting woodcock this time."

James felt the spit run down a cheek – his stomach turned in revulsion. "Who are you?" he managed to ask through parched lips.

Seamus poked a finger into James's stomach. "That's no concern of yours Fitzpatrick. All you need to know is that you are my prisoner – my bargaining ace. I need money and I'm going to exchange you for it. If the government or your daddy don't pay you're a dead man."

Shock slammed into James's guts. He said nothing.

Seamus laughed. "That's shaken you Fitzpatrick. Thinking they won't pay up are you? Sweat on it you piece of shit."

"Where am I?"

"Found your voice have you. Well I'll tell you where you are. You're in a cottage at Gartree Point. Ah that rings a bell doesn't it?"

He was not slow to see the look in James's eyes. "Yes, I bought it when your grand father's estate was sold. Thought it might come in useful one day. Never thought it would be a Fitzpatrick's prison though or his tomb. Rather symbolic don't you think?"

Love Thine Enemy

Seamus's words struck at James's heart - his life hung in the balance. The man staring down at him didn't seem the sort to show mercy. Fighting to keep the fear out of his voice he said, "You're evil." He was rewarded with a blow to his head.

"More talk like that and I'll kill you now," hissed Seamus.

James's voice was weak when he asked, "what of my friend?"

"Ah yes, Mr Henry fucking Walters. London solicitor, Unionist lackey, a good friend of yours – always comes to shoot woodcock with you. He's lying over there on the floor no doubt wishing he'd never come. The fat little bastard is going to be my messenger."

"Messenger?"

"No need to tell you more."

James looked at Seamus and prayed silently for his friend. Seamus moved to walk away but had second thoughts. He bent over James and drove a fist into his stomach. He doubled up in agony and fell off the sofa onto the wooden floor. "You can stay there you piece of British shit," Seamus said.

James lay face down on the floor fighting the pain. With the little strength he had left he managed to roll over so that he was on his back– at least he could breath easier. The wooden floor was hard – unyielding – he wondered how long he'd be left lying like this. He moved his head and looked to his left – he could see chairs and a table – a pair of feet, but no sign of Henry. He looked to his right and let out a moan. Henry was lying a few feet away. His arms and legs bound. But worse was the sack over his head. James turned away – he couldn't bear to see him like that. His eyes filled with tears – he felt utterly defeated.

*

Charlie O'Malley sat in the warmth of the Healy's kitchen, but there was nothing warm about his thoughts. He had picked up on Murphy's hint and spent hours running likely kidnap targets through his brain. The Chief Constable had ordered surveillance of all prominent people in Belfast and alerted the security forces on the mainland. That was all he could do. But from the outset Belfast and London knew it was a hopeless task. No leads, nothing. Sure enough James Fitzpatrick had not come onto the radar. Why should he? The fact was that the kidnappers held all the aces. Charlie looked at a tearful Meg. "There is no doubt that the Jeep was Fitzpatrick's. We've checked. There were no bodies in the burnt out wreckage so I'm afraid it's as I feared."

"Kidnap," gulped Meg.

Charlie nodded.

Duff was puffing on a cigarette, normally frowned upon by Meg, but these were not normal times. "James would have been a prime target for a kidnap," he stated, inhaling the nicotine. "A prime target. How the hell did they know he was coming here?"

Charlie shrugged his shoulders. "They must be better informed than I gave them credit for, both here and on the mainland."

"Oh my God!" exclaimed Meg.

Duff looked at her. "Oh no!"

Meg nodded. "I think so."

"Think what," Charlie asked.

"Mary Keogh, that's who it is, Mary Keogh."

Charlie asked, "What about her?"

"She's the girl who is our receptionist – or was." Meg explained. "Applied for the job about nine months ago. I took pity on her."

"Is she by any chance Conor Keogh's daughter?"

"That's what she told me."

"You took a risk."

"Never liked her," mumbled Duff.

"Do you know her?" Meg asked.

"Not personally," replied Charlie. "She was interviewed after her father and mother's death."

"I'm afraid she had access to the reservation book. She would have seen James's name there. I have a terrible feeling about this."

Charlie gave Meg a sympathetic smile. "Did she tell you anything more about herself, like where was she living now? Her house was repossessed after her mother's death. Since then we've had no reason to watch her."

Meg looked apologetic. "She didn't give me an address. Mistake. I had made up my mind to employ her even before I interviewed her. I felt so sorry for her. She seemed so sad and she was very presentable. That was good enough for me."

"She's always trying to help lost souls," Duff grumbled.

Charlie rubbed his chin. "Well I think we have our spy in the camp you might say."

"What a fool I've been," Meg sobbed

"You couldn't have known," Charlie said.

Meg dried her tears. "Why would they kidnap James?"

Charlie said, "I think I better fill you in."

"You mustn't blame yourself Inspector, how could you have known a Fitzpatrick was coming to Ireland," Meg said once Charlie had finished speaking.

Charlie hunched his shoulders. "You're right, but it sticks in my gullet that I have been out-manoeuvred."

"If this is Flanagan what will he do?" Duff questioned.

"Almost certainly money to buy explosives and arms," Charlie replied. "Since the decommissioning of weapons his group will be short of hardware. They are a fanatical bunch – mad and definitely delusional. They really believe they can change the course of Irish history. Totally wrong, but mad men have no logic. They refuse to see the advantages of peace – they ignore the smiles on peoples' faces. They don't want people to live in peace. They were born into violence – it's ingrained in their souls. They only see what they want to see. They will fight until they die."

"That is crazy," Duff said. "If they are after money they might as well whistle in the wind. Surely London won't negotiate with terrorists?"

"But the father might pay," Charlie added. "Wouldn't you do anything to get your son back? And Richard Fitzpatrick will have the money."

Meg, felt tears well up in her eyes again. She said in a quiet voice, "So if the father doesn't pay up those two young men are as good as dead."

Charlie didn't waste his breath trying to convince her otherwise.

Twenty-Two

Murphy was cold, dreading another night sleeping rough. He'd left his flat a soon as he'd got back to Belfast and jacked in his job at the Lansdowne. They were the two places that Seamus would certainly have someone watching. Nor did he dare to ask for shelter from the pub landlords who would have normally come to his rescue. He smelt danger everywhere. He was also very hungry and, although he kept trying to kid himself it wasn't the case, he was very scared. But another half-hour and he'd be in sight of safety – well at least temporary safety. His information could earn him protection. The thought of money was no longer on his list of priorities. He weaved his way through the crowds on Knock Road. Not far to go now. Surely not even Seamus would try anything outside police HQ. Not with so many people about at any rate? But Seamus was not like any other man. Seamus had never left anything to chance, so why should things change now. *He will have eyes watching you Murphy. One wrong move and you're dead.* He lowered his head and walked on. He heard the whoosh, whoosh of the helicopter's rotors. The air support unit had been called out. Instinctively he ducked his head as the Eurocopter EC135 roared over his head. The hunt for Fitzpatrick was on. If he reached Mr O'Malley he would save the air support unit an expensive bill for fuel. Murphy managed a laugh. Getting to him alive was the problem, but with Seamus preoccupied he reckoned it was his best time to reach safety. Mr O'Malley would see him right – offer him twenty-four hour protection until he could be whisked out of the country on a plane to some far off place that not even Seamus could reach. "Murphy wants to live," he said out loud.

Michael Pakenham

The police car drew along side him – he gave it a glance – it gave him confidence – protection. "Murphy," a voice said from the patrol car. "You on your way to see me?" Murphy felt a wave of relief course through his body. O'Malley! He stopped and turned. "Ah Mr O'Malley, am I glad to see you." He rested his arms on the open window. The man was not O'Malley. "Jesus!" he exclaimed.

The long knife cut his throat from ear to ear.

*

Seamus took the call – grunted with satisfaction. His concern had been on the button. Murphy was a traitor. He smiled at Declan. "The piece of Irish shit has left us."

Declan returned the smile. He'd never liked Murphy.

Twenty-Three

Charlie looked at the Chief Constable in bewilderment. "Knifed not a hundred yards from here! And according to eye witnesses from a police car. If this is Flanagan, and I'm pretty sure it is, he's certainly covering his tracks. At least we know it wasn't a rogue policeman. The patrol car has been found abandoned a mile out of Belfast. It was a paint job – not a very good one but enough to fool poor old Murphy. He must have been coming here with more information."

The Chief Constable shook his head and waved at a chair. But Charlie was too much on edge to accept the offer. "We seem to be losing control," continued the Chief Constable. "Four mystery shootings of men that I admit are better dead and no leads on that. A kidnapping in front of our eyes and now a man killed right outside our door. We could become a laughing stock."

"It's a disaster," Charlie admitted. "Though there was no way we could be expected to know Fitzpatrick was coming over here."

"Do you know how this man Flanagan found out?" asked the Chief Constable.

"Well if it is him, and as yet we can't be sure, it looks as if he had a spy in the camp called Mary Keogh."

"Explain."

Charlie filled him in."

The Chief Constable asked, "And no sign of her?"

"None. Gone to ground with Flanagan I suspect, or given a ticket out of the country having served her purpose."

"Or maybe in a grave."

"Very possible I agree. Whatever, we have a very clever adversary. So far he's been one move ahead of us and I don't like that."

"That makes two of us," the chief Constable confirmed. "But if the girl is alive can we find her?"

"It seems unlikely. But Interpol have been alerted and every officer in Ireland is looking for her."

"Well I know you won't give up trying Charlie. But given that her trail may already be cold what are you going to do?"

"Wait for the kidnappers to get in touch. Then we will know their demands and hopefully put a face to the voice. Perhaps from that we can find something positive. Apart from finding the girl it is our best chance."

"That almost sounds like an admission of defeat. Most unlike you Charlie."

"I refuse to be defeated – a break will come."

"Well I really hope so. We need some answers Charlie, and pretty damn fast. This kidnap of the ex Secretary of State's son will be high profile. The media will soon be crawling all over us."

"You don't need to tell me that sir."

"I don't suppose I do." The Chief Constable fiddled with the papers on his desk. "This man Murphy, could he have helped you?"

"He's been my contact for years – never let me down. Bit of a rogue mind you. He fed info to the IRA as well. Somehow he's stayed alive, but this time he underestimated someone. Probably Flanagan."

"So this all points to 'Freedom for Ireland'?"

"That's my guess."

"And the kidnap Charlie, are you thinking the same as me?"

"The money might be their prime target, but I suspect these mysterious killings drove them into action. No doubt they hope this will put an end to more losses."

"That sounds right."

Charlie's mobile rang.

"Take it," said the Chief Constable, you never know it might be the kidnappers offering to return Fitzpatrick."

Charlie didn't laugh. He took the call, nodding his head every now and then. He broke the connection after a few minutes. He took a deep breath. "Are you ready for this sir?"

"I am."

"We've found a Volvo half buried in a farmer's field not far from Brascome Manor. Not a very good job. We know the farmer has sympathies towards the dissidents. He also does some odd jobs with his JCB. He's been found shot in his farm house. Eliminated by the kidnappers no doubt. My guess is that the Volvo was used for the kidnapping and this is where the kidnappers switched cars, probably provided by the dead man."

The Chief Constable slammed his hands down on his desk. "God!"

Charlie shook his head. "This stinks of Seamus Flanagan."

"I don't suppose you have a clue where he is?"

"None. We raided his house this morning."

"Any clues?"

"Swept clean – not even a finger print."

"How about the Volvo?"

"Nothing."

"It seems that we are in the shit at the moment," the Chief Constable groaned.

"You could say that sir. But as you and I know over confidence can lead to a mistake. One will be made soon."

"Hopefully before we find young Fitzpatrick and his friend dumped somewhere in the city."

"I think Henry Walters is in grave danger. I suspect he's no use to the kidnappers. He's got no siblings, no rich parents. He was an orphan. He will just be a nuisance."

The Chief Constable went pale. "That would be a disaster. Get to work Charlie and keep me informed of events, even if you have to ring me in the middle of the night."

Charlie turned to leave. "I'll do that."

Richard had known deep, all consuming despair once before but it made it no easier to withstand the pain and fear that despair can give the second time round. He held Rachel tight as they fought to come to terms with James's disappearance. Her face – normally so beautiful was white and drawn. Richard could swear she'd aged years. She'd hardly eaten since he'd taken the telephone call from the Irish police two days earlier.

"If only we knew something," Rachel cried. "If only we knew he was alive. This silence is so cruel."

Richard suspected that this was exactly what the kidnappers wanted – to drive a knife into their hearts. He knew these kind of men – understood how their minds worked. They would be relishing the pain they were causing. It was something he was not going to share with Rachel. Speaking with a confidence he didn't feel he said, "I'm sure James is alive. And I'm just as sure that sooner rather than later a demand for money will be made. Then we can make decisions."

Rachel pulled away, her eyes radiating anger. "Don't lie to me Richard, I'm not a fool. I know the government won't deal with these sort of people, so our son is as good as DEAD!" Her voice rose to a scream – she slapped his face and ran weeping from the room.

Richard made no attempt to follow.

*

The Prime Minister was drumming his fingers on his desk as Tim Holroyd entered the room. "Sit down Holroyd. We have a lot to discuss and precious little time."

Tim lowered his lean body into the proffered chair. "Good morning Prime Minister."

"You could have fooled me Holroyd."

Tim gave a weak smile. "Not good news from Ireland I agree."

"I didn't envisage this happening. Bit of a bloody mess. This is the last thing we wanted."

Tim ran a hand through his hair and said, "Very unfortunate about Fitzpatrick, but how could anyone know he was going to Ireland?"

"The dissidents or 'Freedom for Ireland' did. Why didn't we?"

"The Irish police had been informed that a kidnap might take place and they informed us. With such little information there was not much we could do and there was no way James Fitzpatrick would be on our radar. We don't keep tabs on innocent civilians. We are not a police state -yet."

"He was a journalist – his father had been Secretary of State - he visited Ireland regularly. I suggest he should have been on your radar."

"I disagree."

"Well the damage is done, so I won't press the point. But sharpen up Holroyd. So back to my first question. How did the dissidents know?"

Holroyd took the rebuke in his stride and replied, "the police in Belfast think they know the answer to that."

"Fill me in Holroyd."

Tim told him.

"And why a kidnap now?"

Tim told him his theory.

"So this is in retaliation. And I suppose the government will soon get a ransom demand?"

"I should think you'll hear something within a few hours. Either a ransom demand or a demand that we stop killing people."

"They can't possible know about your operation."

"They're not fools Prime Minister, it's not difficult to put two and two together."

"I know. So does that mean the two young men will die?"

"If they want a ransom they have a chance. If it's an eye for an eye they are as good as dead." And you of course can't pay the ransom, but Richard Fitzpatrick will."

"I hate to say this, but he must be discouraged."

"And do you think you can persuade a man like Richard Fitzpatrick to abandon his only son?"

"Probably not. I think he'd be very determined to protect his family at all costs. But you must try Holroyd."

"I'll do my best," Tim lied.

The Prime Minister gave him a knowing look but decided not to press the matter. He didn't want Holroyd or Fitzpatrick blaming him for two young peoples' deaths. Instead he said, "what about your men – my feeling is we should pull them out now. They are a complication we could do without."

"Are you ordering me?"

"Unless you have a good reason to keep them there."

"I have."

"Tell me."

"Russell could be very useful. He will still have valuable contacts. Ones that the police most certainly will not."

"You're not thinking what I think you are?"

"I suspect I am. I know this is risky but I think Russell should offer to help the police. He could be of great use to them. He needn't tell them why he's in Belfast."

"They will ask questions. I'm not too sure about this – it sounds a bit hit and miss to me because I can't see how Russell will be able to explain away his presence convincingly enough."

"It's a gamble I agree, but if you want these two young men back alive I think it's a gamble you must let me take. I trust Russell. He'll work something out. I will leave it to him to decide how much to tell the police."

"I can see this all blowing up in our faces, but I don't think I have any option other than to support you. I have gone along with your plans up until now and I think you are the only one who can get us out of the shit. Can't say David Saunders will be too pleased. I can just see him waving a chubby finger at me and saying, "I told you so."

"It might be better if you kept The Secretary of State out of this. If he has a grudge against either of us this might be the time for him to blow the whistle."

"He's already fuming. I'm afraid he reads the papers and watches television just like us. I won't tell you what he says about you. So I will do my best to keep him on side and I won't inform him of our decision here this morning."

"Thank you."

The Prime Minister leant across his desk and stared at Tim. "We can't afford to fall out over this Holroyd, but I would like to remind you at this point that this operation was your brain child. Like all your past covert operations it had my support. As you know I'm uneasy with your methods and your total disregard of the law and frankly you lot turn my stomach. But in this turbulent world, that we unfortunately live in, we need people like you. I'm aware you do a good job in dangerous situations. Don't however expect a knighthood when you retire, that is if you are not killed first. Like all these operations if the shit hits the fan I will deny knowledge of this one. Only you will take the can. Is that clear?"

"Absolutely Prime Minister, I would expect nothing else."

"Good, then as the saying goes get your arse into gear and get this mess sorted. I would like to see the two young men back home alive and well."

*

George Russell put the telephone down, a rueful smile creasing his face. Ever since he'd learnt of the kidnap he'd been wondering how London would react. His guess had been wide of the mark. He blew out his cheeks and turned to face his companions.

"We won't be going home just yet. New orders."

"Which are?" asked Dan O'Connor.

"I offer the police my assistance and you stay to help if needed. In the meantime you keep a low profile. No more assassinations"

"How much do you plan to tell the police?" asked Phil Dashwood.

"Not sure yet. I need to give it some careful thought."

"I bet you do," said, Peter Carpenter. "You could be putting yourself at risk."

"I'm aware of that, but Holroyd thinks I might be able to help find the two young men and that's what matters. Not a prison cell."

The three men knew George well enough not to waste time arguing.

"So when are you going to walk into the lions den?" asked Phil Dashwood.

"As soon as I've finished this cup of tea."

"Which station will you go to?"

"The one where there is a certain Inspector, who already knows me, and whose reputation for fairness goes before him."

"Okay, and who is this Inspector?" Dan queried.

"Charlie O'Malley. He was the man assigned to look into my wife's murder. I don't think he ever truly believed that I was an innocent tourist. I will come clean about my time working under cover here."

"Nothing more?" Phil Dashwood asked

"I will see how the cookie crumbles."

Twenty-Four

An hour before dawn they dragged Henry out of the cottage and bundled him into the Subaru. He cried out – pain shot across his chest. Declan punched him in the stomach. "Shut up British filth. Not a sound or I will cut out your tongue."

Seamus knew this was no idle threat. He put a restraining hand on Declan's arm. "Easy now – we want to dump him alive – better that way – he needs to be able to tell his friends that Fitzpatrick is alive. Put this tape over his mouth – that will shut him up." He handed Declan a ball of white tape. Declan grunted, he couldn't understand Seamus's desire to keep the Englishman alive – he was nearly dead anyway. But he knew better than to argue.

Seamus slipped into the driver's seat and Declan dropped in beside him. Henry was lying across the back seat, his hands and feet tightly tied. The excruciating pain in his chest made breathing difficult. Escape was not an option.

*

Seamus drove carefully, his eyes on the speedometer. He didn't want to attract the attention of the police. Dawn was just breaking as they passed George Best City Airport. There was little traffic on the road, but they were running behind time. He resisted the temptation to put his foot down. Twenty minutes later Seamus pulled up outside Standtown Baptist Church. The road was still light on traffic and no pedestrians were in view. Satisfied that no eyes were watching he pulled over to the kerb and tapped Declan on the shoulder. "All clear – go!"

Declan needed no further encouragement. He jumped out of the car and pulled open a rear door. He grabbed hold of Henry and lifted him over his shoulders. He ran up the concrete path leading to the church and dumped him in the porch. He shoved Seamus's note into a trouser pocket – kicked Henry for good measure and ran back to the Subaru. Before he could shut the door Seamus sped away.

"Job done," Seamus said with satisfaction. He was confident that no one had seen them. Once he was out of sight from the church he drew into the side of the road. "Time to make two calls," he said. "Then we will dump this car and obtain" – he laughed at his choice of word –"another one. Should be easy. The good folk around here are far too trusting." He pulled out the mobile from his jacket pocket and dialled. First the police and then the newspapers. "Wouldn't want the fucking police keeping this under wraps would we?"

*

Charlie was talking to a constable when the phone rang. He picked up the receiver. "O'Malley?" the voice asked. Charlie stiffened, waving the constable away. "Yes."

"There's a package that might interest you in the porch of Standtown Baptist Church in Belmont road."

"How do I know this is not a hoax?"

The voice spoke again. Then the line went dead. Charlie slammed down the receiver and shouted, "Constable! Patrol car now. Get two more officers. We need to move fast. This is not a hoax – I know that voice."

The constable nodded and ran.

*

Henry tried to move – he gasped – the pain was excruciating. His hands and legs were numb. He knew his body had taken a fearful beating – he was dehydrated and disorientated. He'd fouled himself and he stank. He was freezing cold and shaking uncontrollably. He was scared. He wanted to shout, but the tape was tight over his mouth. He felt he was suffocating. His brain was scrambled. He had no fight left in him. He closed his eyes and waited for death.

*

Charlie was cursing. Rush hour traffic was hindering his progress in spite of his flashing lights. What to expect at the church was the question on his mind. A body or a package? He feared a body. God how he hated men like Flanagan and now he was sure. A man he'd despised for years, but like so many of the IRA command he'd kept a low profile directing operations, never taking part in the killings and bombings. He was a psychopath. A man with a reputation that would make anyone's blood turn cold. But it looked as if the peace and these killings had flushed him out. He was desperate to regain the initiative and the only way had been for him to put his head above the parapet. It made him vulnerable.

His mind distracted Charlie nearly hit a Mercedes. He swerved and bounced off the kerb. He struggled with the steering wheel, his heart in his mouth. He managed to regain control just as he reached a set of traffic lights. The yellow was just turning red. It was too late to brake. He slammed his foot hard on the accelerator and shot across the road. He heard the blast of a horn. "Fuck that," he shouted as he reached safety, and roared into Belmont Road.

The three officers in the car stopped praying.

*

Charlie found Henry Walters lying in the church porch. He fitted the photograph faxed to him. It was what he'd feared – Walters was of no use to Flanagan. His body was shaking from the cold. His eyes were half closed – his breathing erratic. Charlie suspected he was close to death and he didn't want to lose him. "Ambulance," he shouted at one of the officers before dropping down beside the man. "Walters," he whispered in the man's ear. Henry's eyes blinked. Charlie put his hand on the tape. "This is going to hurt." He pulled – the tape resisted for a second – Henry moaned, and then his mouth was free. Charlie repeated the question –"Walters?" There was a slight nod. Charlie realised he hadn't the strength to speak. *Christ he's dying, he's dying.* Charlie tore off his uniform jacket and wrapped it round the shaking body. Not much use, but it was better than nothing. Then he moved to the ropes around the legs and hands. In spite of Walter's awkward position Charlie decided not to move him. He'd no idea what the injuries were. *Don't fucking die on me. I need you.* "Did you ring for an ambulance?" he shouted at one of his officers.

"Yes sir, it's on its way."

It was then that Charlie saw an envelope sticking out of Walter's trouser pocket. He reached for it and tore it open. He read it – neat writing, short and to the point. He blew out his cheeks and handed the note to one of the officers. "Read that!" he said.

"Christ sir, whose going to pay that?"

"I suspect no one and that makes this situation even more serious."

Charlie dropped to his knees. "We will have you safe soon," he said into one of Henry's ears. Can you here me?"

Henry nodded again.

"Good. Nod again if your friend is still alive?" Charlie swore he could see tears in Henry's eyes. He nodded. Charlie breathed a little easier. He heard the siren. *About bloody time!* "You'll be in good hands soon," he said patting Henry's arm. There was no response. Alarmed he searched for a pulse – very weak. His hand moved to Henry's neck – same result. "Damn, damn damn," he shouted, jumping to his feet. He yelled at the two paramedics who were running up the church path, "get over here fast!" One paramedic put a hand on Henry's neck. He looked up at Charlie. "Pulse very weak." He turned to the other paramedic. "We're losing him. We must try and revive him here. There's no time to get him to the ambulance."

Charlie bit at a finger nail. "You can't lose him. I need him."

The two men fought to save Henry's life. Charlie stood a few feet away feeling superfluous. He bit at another nail – soon most of them would be bitten to the quick. Finally, after what seemed an age the paramedics stood. "Sorry Inspector we've lost him."

Charlie felt a surge of irrational anger. "For fuck sake!"

Used to being sworn at by distressed people, one of the paramedics shrugged his shoulders. "Sorry Inspector, we tried."

Feeling ashamed at his outburst, Charlie nodded. "I know you did your best. Any idea what killed him?"

"Shock I suspect. He's had a terrible beating and his ribs are shattered and I wouldn't be surprised if he hasn't got a fractured skull. The post mortem will tell us more. Whoever did this was an animal. Poor bloke."

"Thanks for trying anyway," Charlie assured them, taking one last look at the body. An animal was the right word. His blood boiled. He had never got used to the apparent desire of man to inflict pain on another man. It was abhorrent. How could there be people capable of such cruelty? He followed the paramedics back onto the road and walked thoughtfully back to the patrol car. "Let's go," he said to the driver. "Our works finished here, and I need to get the Chief Constable up to speed."

*

I need a million quid, no less. You have a week to deliver this at a time and a place of my choosing. Otherwise Fitzpatrick dies. Instructions will be sent shortly. There can be no negotiations. We will never be defeated.

*

"Ha!" Exclaimed the Chief Constable, brushing back his greying hair, his brown eyes flashing with anger. "Bastard!"

Charlie was full of suppressed rage. "I'm not thinking straight right this moment sir. I just want to get my hands round the neck of the man who killed Henry Walters."

"Flanagan?"

"Definitely. Over the years I've had the unpleasant task of interviewing him several times. He has a very distinctive lisp."

"You've spoken to him!"

"He rang. He told me where to find Walters."

The Chief Constable stared at Charlie. "So what do we do?"

"One advantage is that Flanagan's power has dwindled – there are not so many willing volunteers out there now. He's already put his head above the parapet. This is our only hope. Knowing the identity of your enemies is the first step towards defeating them."

"Is that all we have to go on? I can't say it fills me full of optimism."

"For the moment yes."

"But a young man's life hangs in the balance."

"And we can do very little about it, at least not until Flanagan contacts us again."

"We need a miracle."

"I couldn't agree more."

"Then I think it's time we started to pray."

Charlie said nothing.

The Chief Constable picked up the ransom note from his desk. "I'll keep this. No doubt I'll have to inform London."

"They will already know. The media are aware. Need I say more?"

"Then I will have London up my arse every bloody minute of the day saying they want to send a team over here. I'll do my best to put them off."

Charlie's heart sank. He gave the Chief Constable an agonised glance.

"I know Charlie, I know. Maybe you'll strike lucky before this happens. Any thing else we should discuss?"

"Yes, how are we going to deal with the media? They will be clambering for information."

The Chief Constable gave Charlie one of his *it's your problem* looks and said "you deal with it Charlie – have a quiet word with them – you have good relations. Explain that things are very tricky – a man's life is at stake here and a bit of space would be gratefully received."

"Will do." With that Charlie rose from his chair – picked up his case file and left the room. As he walked into the incident room a feeling of complete uselessness washed over him. He'd hoped that with the Good Friday agreement moments like this had gone, but he'd been wrong – so very wrong. "Damn," he shouted out loud, causing a few understanding heads to lift from their desks. They knew the pressure he was under.

Twenty-Five

James's wrists and ankles were raw from the ropes. When they had been removed the pain had been excruciating. His body ached. He'd had no food or water since being dragged into the cottage. His mouth was dry and his tongue was sticking to the roof of his mouth. He had lost all trace of time. He was bewildered, shit scared and his vision was blurred. A terrible feeling of despair was threatening to overwhelm him. He'd watched Henry being carried out of the cottage, convinced that it was the last he'd see of him. He had been in some tricky situations for his paper, even looked down the barrel of a shotgun once, but he'd never had any hostage training, like some of his fellow journalists who were going into a war zone, to prepare him for this hell.

He saw the girl come through a door on his left and walk towards him. She stood over him. He saw a pretty face and a trim figure. In normal circumstances he'd have found her attractive.

"It's just you and me Fitzpatrick."

James didn't need to ask where the others had gone.

"Water please," James rasped, looking up at Mary. He struggled to sit up but his limbs were numb. "Please," he pleaded.

"Why should I help you, you British bastard," Mary screamed at him. "No water."

"Please, I need a drink. It's not much to ask."

"You're joking."

James groaned. "Please." His voice hardly audible.

Mary looked down at his broken body, his ashen face contorted with pain – the stench of his body odour reaching her nostrils. Her hand flew to her nose and she rushed into the kitchen. She filled a glass of water and moved back into the room. "Here," she shouted. "Smells as if you need a fucking bath." Then she threw the contents of the glass over him and watched him desperately trying to suck the water off his filthy shirt.

"Thank you," he said gratefully.

That threw her. How could he say thanks when she'd behaved like an animal? She turned away in disgust and went back to the kitchen clasping the empty glass. As she was running another glass of water she caught sight of her face in the cracked mirror fixed to the wall. She hardly recognised the face staring back at her. She could see the likeness she bore to her mother. Holy Jesus, she was the last person she wanted to be reminded of. It was far too uncomfortable. But a seed was planted and suddenly she felt the first stirrings of guilt. She tore her eyes away from the mirror but it drew her back like a magnet. "Who are you?" she asked herself. "What have you become?" She gripped the side of the sink and shouted, "Fitzpatrick does not deserve my sympathy. Never, never!" Then she threw the glass. The mirror shattered. The spell was broken.

She heard James scream out in pain. Fuck. She fumbled in a cupboard above the sink and pulled out another glass. She filled it with water and burst through the door, telling herself the only reason for this act of compassion was to save him from dying. Seamus's anger would be uncontrollable. She dropped down on her knees. "Here, drink this. I'll hold the glass." She held it to James's lips. He drank greedily – his hands holding hers. "Thank you," he mumbled, his eyes radiating his gratitude. When the glass was half full she took it away. "Now let's see if we can get you into a sitting position and then you can finish the water on your own. After that I'll try and make you more comfortable."

"You're kind," James said.

"Don't delude yourself Fitzpatrick, there is nothing kind about me. I just need to keep you alive." She could have added that she was wasting her energy. Once Seamus got his hands on the money Fitzpatrick was dead anyway. Seamus was not a man to hold up his side of a bargain.

*

The Prime Minister spoke briefly to Holroyd. "Sorry no deal."

It was what he'd expected. The British Government did not negotiate with kidnappers.

"There it is Holroyd, nothing more to be said. I will inform Stormont and ring Richard Fitzpatrick. As I said at our last meeting, it's all up to you now."

"Did they give you a time limit to decide what to do?"

"It's immaterial how long. Hours, a day, a week, makes no difference. Minds won't be changed."

"I will leave for Thornbury immediately. I hate to think what state the Fitzpatrick family will be in once you've spoken to them."

"I would be inconsolable if it was my boy who'd been kidnapped. Hope and prayer is all we have left it seems, although maybe a hostage negotiator might help?"

"Unlikely in this case."

"Probably right."

"It's so frustrating," Tim added. "It seems that the Irish police are thrashing around in the dark trying to find a needle in a haystack."

"No leads?"

"None."

The Prime Minister decided to say nothing. What happened next would only be of passing interest. It was a sad fact that as Prime Minister he could not allow his heart to guide him.

*

Tim drove dangerously, cutting in and out of the traffic with little concern for his or anyone else's safety. He made it in just less than two hours. Probably a record. He threw himself out of his car and raced up the steps to the front door. It was flung open just as he was about to ring the bell. Richard looked drawn, unshaven, wearing a blue woollen shirt open at the neck and a pair of blue corduroy trousers. On his feet Tim noticed his favourite brown brogues. Richard gave a weak smile and ushered Tim into the hall. "We are in the drawing room, trying to come to terms with the news. Rachel is in a fearful state."

Tim followed, guilt already knawing at his brain. He braced himself for the outburst he knew was coming. Rachel was standing by the fireplace and swung round as she saw the two men enter the room. Tim was shocked by drawn face. She glared at him but said nothing. Richard waved at a chair before moving to stand close to Rachel. He took her hand.

The fire was crackling in the grate, the room comfortably warm, but the atmosphere was icy. Rachel held a mug of coffee in her free hand, which at that moment she was contemplating throwing the contents at Tim. Richard noticed the movement and quickly asked, "Is it correct Tim that you know of the kidnapper?"

"It's a man called Seamus Flanagan. Do...."

Richard cut in. "My God I know of him. He's still making trouble is he?"

"Yes."

"How he must be gloating at getting hold of my son. How on earth did he know James was going to Ireland, and why a kidnap now? What brought this on? Most unlike Flanagan to come out into the open."

Tim took a deep breath, made sure he kept his eye on the coffee mug and said, "I think I must fill you both in."

"I think that would be a very good idea Holroyd."

It was the first time Rachel had called him that for years.

*

An hour later silence fell over the room. The three of them stared at each other. Tim, bracing himself for a rebuke, Richard and Rachel gasping from shock. It was Rachel who broke the silence. "So this is Flanagan's revenge for the killings," she said in an unsteady voice.

"That's how it looks."

"Looks!" screamed Rachel as her blazing eyes turned on Tim. "Looks! Of course it is." Her voice was shaking with anger as she pointed a trembling finger at Tim. "If you hadn't done this or that or thought things through James would not be a prisoner and Henry would be alive. Didn't you just once stop and think that these men would retaliate and put innocent people in danger? Of course it was bad luck that they found out about James and Henry, but it seems to me they were one thought ahead of you. You have stooped to the terrorist's level. Killing these men might have seemed the right move, but killing always brings more killings. What right have you got to order a death squad to Ireland? What right have you got to sentence these men to death? You didn't think this through damn you Holroyd. I have always known there is a shady side to MI5 and MI6 but I never thought I'd be sitting here listening to you confessing to such a loathsome plan. Is this what we have become as a country – IS IT! You make me feel sick. Have I misjudged you over the years when you were head of our security? Maybe you have always been ruthless like most men and women in your chosen profession." Then with an angry toss of her head she walked towards Tim. When she was inches from his face she raised a hand and slapped him. "This is what you have turned me into. I have never struck anyone before. I never ever want to see your face in this house again, and if James dies I hope you will share the misery that will be with me for the rest of my life. You're reckless actions have torn me apart."

Before Tim had time to speak Rachel swung round and ran out of the room leaving both men speechless and Tim, realising that he'd probably lost a friend, felt devastated. He'd hurt a woman he had known and respected for years. A woman of great courage – a woman who had lived for so long under threat. Seen her husband cheat death once. And now, having hopefully seen the last of danger, one of her most trusted friends had driven a dagger into her heart. He coughed and stared at the closed door and turned to Richard. "I'm so sorry. I wish with all my heart that this hadn't happened, but intelligence told me that we had to act or anarchy would have broken out. I had no choice but to move."

"Look Tim, I'm not going to say things should have been done differently. You're the man on the ground and I know that you have to make instant decisions. Sometimes they're right other times they're wrong. Unfortunately the times we live in dictate that on occasions a violent response has to be made. You can't be blamed for James going to Ireland and Rachel will see that eventually. You're a good man Tim – I owe you my life. This incident will not break our friendship. It will be strained, but it will recover. Right now I think it best if you leave and let the dust settle, but be sure to keep in touch. I'd rather have bad news from you than from the Prime Minister."

Tim nodded. Without another word he walked slowly out of the room and out through the front door. He never thought he could feel so ashamed. As he was about to step into his car he felt a tap on his shoulder. He swung round. "Can't let you go like this Tim." Richard held out a hand. Tim took it. "I know you will do your best, old friend."

Tim smiled wearily. "Thanks Richard, that's a great help. I can assure you we will do everything to find James alive. This man Russell is my ace. If I play it at the right time James just might come home alive."

Richard patted Tim on a shoulder and watched him settle himself in the Jaguar - the car he'd always longed for. "A rotten old Ford is all I'm ever going to be able to afford," Richard remembered him saying. So after his election defeat he'd bought Tim his longed for Jaguar as a thank you present. A gleaming XJ 4.2 V8 midnight blue model. As he closed the front door he could still hear Tim's joyous shout as he'd stood with mouth open looking at the gleaming car. He'd been like a little boy getting the one present he'd always wanted but thought he'd never get. There was some similarity to the scenario that was unfolding now. He had a wish, but one he feared was unreachable. As he closed the front door and heard the Jaguar roar away he decided that he had to take action. He could not sit and watch the wish blow away. He ran into his office and dialled Tim's mobile.

Twenty-Six

Knock Road was heaving with humanity. People with heads bent against the icy wind were hurrying to work or taking children to school. No one in their right mind would be out for a stroll. George Russell wished he'd waited for the city to become less crowded. But he was impatient. His eyes continually darted from left to right and he constantly turned his neck to see behind him. He was nervous. He had been trained to be aware of crowded streets. "You never know when the enemy is going to make a move and a crowded street is perfect for a blade," his instructor had told him. And he was well aware that there were still those in Belfast who would love to stick a knife into his back, if they recognised him. He no longer cared how or when he died but he was not a quitter when a man's life was under threat, as the men who had followed him through countless hairy moments would testify. He had another motive that drove him on. He wanted to stare into Flanagan's face and watch him die. He walked on purposefully and breathed a sigh of relief as he saw the police HQ only a few yards away to his left. He was apprehensive, unsure of how the next few hours would pan out. He'd decided not to hold back. He needed O'Malley's trust. Truth was the best option, but it was also the most risky. He doubted if O'Malley had ever had a man walk into the police station and confess to four killings – let alone sanctioned by a British government. But this was an emergency and all he could hope for was that O'Malley would prove to be a pragmatic policeman for the sake of a young man's life. If he refused to cooperate? Well the consequences would be dire. He stopped and looked up at the sign.

He took a deep breath – nodded at two officers coming out of the building and walked into the station.

The die was caste.

A desk sergeant gave him a suspicious glare and said gruffly, "Hold on sir what might your business be?"

George walked over to the desk. "I would like to see Chief Inspector O'Malley if possible."

"Can I enquire what about? He's a busy man these days."

"It's very urgent. I need to discuss the kidnapping."

The sergeant was immediately alert. "Well you're in luck, he's here. Just finished a meeting with the Chief Constable. Can I have your name sir?"

This was it. He knew how O'Malley would react when given his name. "It's George Russell sergeant. The Chief Inspector knows me." *Though not looking like this.*

"Very well sir, take a seat over there and I will see if he is free."

George moved across to a line of hard uninviting green plastic chairs and sat down.

*

Charlie was sitting behind his desk shuffling with some papers, wondering what the day would bring. Most days recently had been shit. He needed a break and he was damned if he knew where that was going to come from. He looked up as the sergeant entered the room. "Sergeant, what can I do for you?"

"Sir, there is a man down stairs wanting to see you urgently. He says it's about the kidnapping."

Charlie was immediately alert. "Did you get a name?"

"A George Russell."

"Who?"

"George Russell. He says you know him."

Charlie took a deep breath. "Well I'll be…" he stared at George as he walked into the room.

"Sorry Inspector thought I'd save some time. Didn't see any point in hanging about downstairs."

Charlie stared at the man in amazement. "*You're* George Russell?"

George said, "That's me Inspector."

"Good God," Charlie exclaimed. "So it is, but what's with the beard and long hair?"

George gave a rueful chuckle. "You were not supposed to recognise me Inspector."

"So I imagined," said Charlie, feeling irritation growing.

"I'll explain the reason for my disguise in a minute Inspector. Could we talk in private?"

Charlie turned to the sergeant who was hanging about the open door. "Thank you sergeant, please leave us."

Once the office door was closed Charlie sat down behind his desk, waving George to an uninviting wooden chair. He slapped his hands down on the desk and said, "I think you have some explaining to do Russell."

"It's George."

"I prefer Russell."

George smiled. "Okay O'Malley."

Charlie returned the smile and a little of the tension eased. "Very well, George it will be. Though I normally reserve first names for my friends and close colleagues."

George smiled again. "Let me assure you Charlie by the time you and I have finished we will be close colleagues, even if not friends."

Charlie licked his lips – frowned at George and asked, "so are you saying we are about to be partners?"

"You could say that."

"Okay, tell me how and why."

George scratched an ear. It was not often he felt nervous, but boy this was one of those times. He cleared his throat. "You're not going to like what you hear Charlie. You might blow a fuse. In normal circumstances I would not be sitting here telling you any of this. But one man is dead and another one's life hangs by a thread and that has changed things dramatically. My appearance has been changed because I'm here on a covert operation and I don't want to risk certain people recognising me. I might die just like my poor Rose. And that wouldn't do at all. I have a job to do first."

Charlie slammed his fists onto the desk. "I have it! You're responsible for these killings!"

"Good guess Charlie."

"And you walk in here bold as brass to tell me this? I could arrest you on the spot. You're nothing but a cold blooded killer."

"But you won't arrest me."

"Why the hell not?"

"Because I'm carrying out orders."

"What the hell are you saying?"

"This operation is top secret and I am requesting you to keep it that way."

"Requesting or ordering?"

"I think you're a man who likes straight honest answers so it's ordering, but as you well know if you want to make waves I can't stop you. It depends how much you value your career."

"Do you have that sort of power?"

"One word to my superiors and you'd be out. I don't bluff."

"At least I know where I stand."

"That's good to hear. So to go on. This operation has the tacit approval of the Prime Minister. Though as I'm sure you know if it blows up and becomes public knowledge he will deny any involvement. That's how these things work. I and my small team of three men have been in Belfast for just over a year. Bedding in you might say. Mixing in the community. I have had to keep a very low profile."

"Seems you've done a good job."

"Practice makes perfect. Anyway, a few weeks ago we started weeding out the targets. Men who were threatening the stability of all Ireland. It was going well. Unfortunately we underestimated the counter attack."

"You should not have underestimated a man such as Seamus Flanagan."

"You know this man?"

"He has history."

"Indeed he has. I was close to him when I was undercover. You look surprised."

"Do you blame me?"

"I suppose not, and while I'm surprising you I might as well tell you that it was Flanagan who killed my wife. I can still see his grinning face staring at me out of the Range Rover window."

"I felt all along there was more to you than you were letting on."

"The story of my life Charlie. I'll tell you about it sometime. We hoped to eliminate the seven most dangerous men including Flanagan. It's four down. As soon as our operation was finished we'd disappear into the night and the deaths would remain a mystery. You wouldn't have a hope in hell of solving them. We are very good at covering our tracks. In the end you would give up and silently be very grateful to us for a job well done. But now we are buggered. That is why I'm here Charlie. Breaking cover to try and save one young man's life."

Charlie cleared his throat. "What help can you be?"

"I know more about these men than you ever will. I have lived with them – befriended them and been trusted until my cover was blown and I had to get out quick. But I took a lot of knowledge with me and I still have contacts who might be able to help you. Informers prepared to risk their lives for some cash."

"Like a man called Murphy?" Charlie asked.

"Ah Murphy yes. A fool. I'm surprised he's still alive."

"He's dead. Shot outside here. Must have been coming to me with information."

"Or to ask for protection. Well that's one of my contacts down the drain. He was always sailing close to the wind. But I know others, and that is one reason why I was chosen to lead this small group."

"But you can't just go around killing people."

"We can."

Charlie felt anger welling up inside him but didn't bother to argue, realising this man had the power to do anything. Instead he said, "Pity you didn't go for Flanagan first."

"He was our next target, but he's disappeared."

"With Fitzpatrick?"

"Looks like it."

"There is no doubt about that. I've spoken to him."

George blew out his cheeks. "He's a monster, a cold blooded killer."

Charlie was tempted to ask, "And what are you?" But he bit his tongue.

George dropped his eyes to the floor and said quietly, "I want that man Charlie. I have a score to settle."

"This sounds personal."

"It is, but it won't make me rash. I'm a soldier first George, a grieving husband second. Personal cannot come into it. I'm disciplined – my job is my top priority."

Charlie looked at the man and saw the distress in his eyes and wasn't too sure he'd spoken the truth.

"OK Charlie, let me fill you in a little about Flanagan. I know how he works, how he breathes, how he hates. He calls himself a soldier, but first and foremost he is a ruthless killer He also knows me; he trusted me and it's not easy for a man like him to trust anyone. I was on the verge of becoming his right-hand man when I was betrayed. I was lucky not to be disembowelled and cut into little pieces, but I don't walk into situations like that without an exit plan. So here I am telling you about a man as slippery as a snake, he likes to stay concealed and out of the limelight, but this time he will have to break cover. These executions will have riled him and he's got no love for the Fitzpatricks, which adds to our problems, as this could become a personal thing with him as well. It was incredibly bad luck that James Fitzpatrick chose this time to take his holiday here."

"Well if you hadn't decided to go on a killing spree..."

George said nothing.

"Anyway you're not telling me anything new, Flanagan was on our wanted list during the Troubles, but we could never pin anything on him. Maybe this is our chance."

"With my help you have a better chance."

"What if I don't want your help?"

"You've got me, like it or not."

Charlie was nothing but a realist, and his motto had always been if faced with a fait accompli give in gracefully. But he had never gone along with the theory that as long as the end justifies the means it was okay. He looked across the table at this man who was licensed to kill by the tacit agreement of a legitimately elected government and wondered what the world was coming to. Here he was being put in a position that didn't rest easy with his conscience, backed into a corner and he didn't like it, but by God he'd have his say. "Listen up Russell, I may have to work with you but I don't like the prospect, the men you have killed may well have been murderers, and as you say, almost certainly hell bent on trying to destabilise the political process, but they shouldn't have been gunned down in cold blood. You're stooping to their levels, all my working life as a policeman I have tried to be fair, never judging anyone until the facts have been proven. They should have had a trial, what on earth have we become as a nation?"

"No worse than any other," George stated. "When needs must, quick and decisive action has to be taken. Look at the American drones, did they wait to get Pakistan's permission to strike? No, because the terrorists would never have been brought to justice. Did they inform the same country that they were going to kill Osama bin Larden? Did Israel tell the world that they were going to try and eliminate the nuclear scientists in Iran? Why not you may ask, though I can't believe a man of your intelligence doesn't know the answer. But I'll spell it out for you; the world is full of woolly-minded liberals who think being nice to everyone will solve the world's problems. People who think that a good chat and everyone will get on swimmingly, what a load of crap! You can't talk to people who have no respect for life, they'll smile, drink tea with you and as soon as your back is turned kill you and go on fucking-up the world. So there have to be operations such as this one, to at least give nations a chance to live in peace. Can you sit there and tell me there is another way?"

Charlie glared at George. "I understand your analysis, but I don't agree with it. Operations like the ones you have just quoted only lead to more violence, more threats and more distrust. So call me a woolly-minded liberal if you wish and let's just agree to disagree and get on with the job of rescuing Fitzpatrick. But there is one question I need to ask. Why did you come to Belfast with your wife? Was it really for a holiday or for something else?"

"Like what?"

"I don't know maybe to plan something, your wife would have made good cover."

George half-rose from his chair and slammed his fists down hard on Charlie's desk. "How dare you? How dare you infer that I would have deliberately put Rose's life at risk. I loved her and would have never knowingly put her in danger. It was a planned holiday. And yes, it was a terrible mistake to come here, I should have known better. I'll live with the guilt for the rest of my life."

Charlie chose to ignore George's anger. "So you took this job to exact revenge."

George said, "The moment Rose died my life became meaningless and now I feel as if I exist on auto-pilot, but I have one burning ambition."

"And in-spite of what you said earlier you want to kill Flanagan," Charlie finished for him.

The telephone rang.

Twenty-Seven

Seamus was on edge and he glanced at the Subaru's clock, it was time, O'Malley would be waiting but he knew there would be no deal. "The British Government does not do deals with terrorists," he could hear O'Malley saying, not even if Fitzpatrick's life was in danger. Jesus, how that word terrorist made his blood boil, he was no terrorist, he was a soldier fighting for freedom – a hero in his lifetime and he would fight on. Although they had lost good men 'Freedom for Ireland' was not dead in the water but he had to admit it was close. Good men, committed to the Cause were dead. The total loyalty of those left could be questioned, but with new weapons and explosives fortunes could be resuscitated and then he'd find out who the true patriots really were. Seamus smiled, Richard Fitzpatrick wouldn't let his son die, he'd pay the money he was sure of that, Seamus Flanagan was never wrong. He also had a personal goal, one he owed to fallen comrades, who in one way or the other had lost their lives because of the meddling Fitzpatricks. It was bad enough that Dermot Fitzpatrick had spread the words *peace* and *harmony* all those years ago, it was the reason Declan's father had shot him. The IRA had seen him as a threat. Then along had come his fucking son as Secretary of State for Northern Ireland and pushed through the Good Friday agreement. Richard Fitzpatrick, like his father, deserved to die. Seamus rubbed his hands together as waves of excitement coursed through his body and an evil smile crossed his face. The Fitzpatricks were doomed, but first he needed to get his hands on the money.

Unlike many of his comrades, who could only think of killing he'd always studied his enemies, watched how they worked, how they spent their leisure time. He looked out for any weaknesses, and he'd spotted a weakness in Richard Fitzpatrick. He nurtured great love for his family and he made no attempt to hide it. His speeches had been good, his manner persuasive, aimed at people's hearts, making great play about the values of family life in a peaceful society. "It's time to forget old animosities and join together to make a better Ireland," he said many times, and his speeches had born fruit. Unfortunately an attempt on his life had failed but he was vulnerable, and when the pressure was applied Fitzpatrick would play into his hands. He scrolled up O'Malley's number and put the mobile to his ear. His hands were sweating as a voice answered, he took a deep breath. "O'Malley?"

"Hello Flanagan."

"You know who I am?"

"Not difficult. You should have had speech therapy Flanagan."

Seamus swallowed. *Keep calm, don't be diverted.* He sucked in his breath, clenched his fists and asked, "Has the government an answer to our demands?"

Charlie swallowed his anger, shouting at the vile man would get him nowhere, he gripped the receiver and replied as he'd been told. "We need more time Flanagan." He heard a sharp intake of breath and a moment's silence. Then, "No more time. I need an answer. Now! If not Fitzpatrick will be delivered to you in parts by the morning. Clear?"

"Perfectly. Wait." Charlie looked across at George and shook his head.

"Ask for forty- eight hours. He'll agree, he's desperate for the money."

"Forty-eight hours and I will have an answer," Charlie said.

There was silence on the line and Charlie feared Flanagan had cut the connection. "Are you there Flanagan?"

"Forty-eight it is O'Malley and not a second more, or your boy is dead."

"Very well." Charlie hung-up, as he put down the receiver his hands were shaking. "Bastard!" he spat.

From the other side of the room George said, "That didn't go well by the sounds of it."

Charlie shook his head. "It's money, or a dead man."

George said, "we have forty-eight hours to find Fitzpatrick."

"And the chances of doing that are almost nil," Charlie conceded.

"Exactly," George said. "And if Flanagan says he'll kill him, he means it."

"I know that," Charlie said, looking grim. "It seems that if Richard Fitzpatrick wants his son back alive he better cough up the money."

"Which I think he will, what would you do Charlie?"

"I'd pay up."

"That's where we're different."

"Are you telling me you'd allow your son to die?"

"In the end it would save lives."

"Dear god Russell, I don't understand you."

"I don't care what you think of me. But let me tell you something, Flanagan won't allow James Fitzpatrick to live if he gets the money and I suspect he'll try to kill his father. His hatred of that family goes deep. So where does that get you if his father pays up? Flanagan gets the money and two men are dead, think about that Charlie before you condemn me. However it's not my choice, so I'll get the news to Richard Fitzpatrick. Forty-eight hours or his son is dead."

Charlie said nothing.

*

By the time Seamus got back to Gartree Cottage he was pretty sure the money would be paid by the father. Okay, he didn't like the delay but forty-eight hours would give O'Malley little hope of finding him. However, it would give Richard Fitzpatrick the time to raise the money. He felt fucking good. He called Mary and Declan into the kitchen and closed the door, he didn't want their prisoner listening. There was a smug smile on his face. "Fitzpatrick will pay. He won't want his son to die."

"You seem very sure," Mary said.

"I'm never wrong. The next time I get back to O'Malley the father will have the money."

Mary dared to say, "You could be wrong. Every soldier, policeman in the whole of Ireland will be looking for you, in the end someone will talk. And you can't hide for ever."

"They'll never find us," boasted Seamus.

"And when the ransom has been paid?" asked Mary, suspecting she knew the answer already.

"I'll kill the boy anyway."

Declan slapped Seamus on the back.

Mary said nothing. She could hear her mother's words ringing in her ears.

*

"So where do we go from here, "Charlie asked. "You say you have contacts, you say that only you can find Fitzpatrick. Well if that's the case I suggest you do something about it pretty damn quick." He said tapping his watch. "We haven't got time to sit here drinking coffee. Let's see if your confidence gets you anywhere."

George said, "I'm not that confident Charlie. I'm as desperate as you, but I do have a man in mind who owes me one." He put a calming hand on Charlie's shoulder. "His name is Johnny O'Riordan, he was close to Flanagan and hopefully still is. I spent my time in Belfast boarding in his mother's house and I got to know him well. We struck up a friendship if that's what you can call it, he confided in me, I learnt a lot. But then my cover was blown and I had to make a swift exit. You might well say that I'm the last person he'll feed information to and you might be right. I suspect he isn't too pleased that I fooled him for so long and no doubt he got a painful rap on the knuckles from the IRA high command. However, his mother was a very sick woman and who, I gather, now needs an operation.

He's very short of money and I can offer him a large carrot, I think he'll bite."

"And I suppose this is a silly question, but no doubt you have clearance for this?"

"Of course."

Charlie shook his head. "You puzzle me George, I keep wondering what you'll pull out of your hat next."

George chuckled. "I'm running low on rabbits, and time."

Charlie gave a half-smile." Just one other thing before I have a meeting with the Chief Constable, after what you've just told me aren't you putting your life at risk getting in touch with O'Riodan? "

George put his hands on the desk and stared at Charlie. "As I said, my life ended when Rose died, I'm expendable. If I die saving a life, and seeing Flanagan behind bars or knowing he's dead, at least I will feel I have made some recompense for my catastrophic mistake in bringing Rose to Belfast."

Charlie said, "I understand." He looked at his watch. "Must go George, the Chief's waiting and he doesn't like people being late. Keep me informed."

"I'll do that, I presume you' re going to brief the Chief Constable on my involvement?"

"I have no option."

"I think that's right. This is too big to keep him in the dark, but try and persuade him not to create waves in Whitehall – at least not yet."

*

Chapel Lane was always quiet on a Sunday morning, as most of the residents were taking Mass inside St Mary's Church. George parked his Ford Escort opposite the church gate hoping that O'Riordan was still a devote Catholic. He instinctively patted his coat pocket where the pack of filter-tip camels used to lie. Damn it! "You'll go to an early grave if you go on smoking those filthy things," Rose had said. So he'd quit. But now the incentive had gone, and he'd never got rid of the craving when in a tight situation. Besides, he had no desire to live into old age any more, he'd buy a packet as soon as he got the chance. He got out of the car and walked towards the church gate, looking at his watch and swore under his breath; he really mustn't keep counting the hours. If things hadn't changed since his last visit the congregation would be spilling out in about five minutes, wrapped up in their religious fervour and thanking the dear Lord for His forgiveness, he thought irreverently.

"Good day," he said to a silver-haired old lady who looked as if a puff of wind would lift her into the sky. She rewarded him with a beaming smile and a nod of her head. "Waiting for someone?" he dared ask.

"My two grandsons. My husband and I are taking them home for lunch, we do it once a month. It's good for both of us and gives their parents a rest, though I'm not too sure how much the boys enjoy being with two old people anymore!"

"I think they should count themselves lucky to be lunching with such a lovely lady," George assured her, thinking how different her life must be to his. Contentment was written all over her face. How wonderful that there was still just enough room, in an ever disturbed world, for people like her; he felt a stab of envy.

The old woman touched his hand. "Are you here to pick up a friend?"

George gave her his best smile. "Yes, yes I am," he lied.

"Ah, here they come," said the old lady excitedly. "Have a good day young man."

Unlikely, thought George as he spotted O'Riordan limping out of the church – he was alone thank God. He hadn't worked out how to play it, if his mother had been with him. He'd have probably had to abort, as the sight of him would have been enough to give her a heart attack. He watched O'Riordan speak to a couple before walking through the gate onto the pavement. George took a deep breath, walked towards him and said, "Hello Johnny."

O'Riordan stopped and stared at George, a puzzled look creasing his face. "Do I know you?" he asked.

"Very well Johnny boy."

O'Riordan blinked. "I think I recognize your voice."

"I'm George Russell."

O'Riordan took a step backwards and nearly tripped over his cane. "Russell! What have you done to your face! That beard, the hair, the moustache!"

"A bit of disguise was necessary."

If O'Riordan had had two good legs he'd have turned and run but instead he swayed - visibly shocked – struck speechless."

"Not pleased to see me Johnny?"

O'Riordan found his voice. "What do you think? Christ Russell, what the fuck are you doing here?"

"Quite ruined your Sunday have I? I'm here to ask for your help."

"You are joking? You're bad news, do you think after dropping me in the shit I'd ever help you?"

"You might after I put a proposition to you, let's talk, in the car."

O'Riordan looked round nervously.

"Don't try and get away Johnny. That leg of yours is fucked."

"Damn you Russell. Why did you have to come back into my life?"

"I'll tell you, in the car."

*

"How did that go?" Phil Dashwood asked.

"So, so." George answered.

"How do you mean?"

"He needs the money, he loves his mother, but he seemed a little too eager for a man who minutes before had told me to fuck off. It made me uneasy I think he could be planning a double-cross."

"Like he'd tell Flanagan you're back."

"If he knows where he is, and we must assume he does."

"Dangerous ground."

"I know, but I need him. There's no way I'm going to walk away from this, there's far too much at stake. I'm meeting him at the Europa Hotel tomorrow at seven in the bar."

"The deadline will be getting pretty close by then, what happens if he disappoints you? Have you got another plan, another informant who might know of Flanagan's whereabouts? "

"Sadly no one comes to mind."

"So you just hope your hunch is right?"

"That's about the size of it Phil, and if I'm wrong young Fitzpatrick is as good as dead. But I think O'Riordan will either throw his hand in with me, or try to be clever and hope he can get money out of both myself and Flanagan."

"As you say, a double cross."

"I reckon so, I think he'll tell me where Flanagan is, in the hope of getting his money and then run like hell and inform on me. I know he lost Flanagan's trust when I ran, and this is his chance to get it back. Right now I bet Johnny boy is chewing his fingernails working out how to put this little double-cross into action."

"And if he doesn't know where Flanagan is holding Fitzpatrick he won't show?"

"Wrong, I think he'll show, he'll try and dupe me in the hope of getting his hands on the money I've promised him."

"Or he could bring Flanagan and his cohorts along with him," Peter Carpenter suggested.

"It's a possibility."

Peter Carpenter gave George a disapproving look. "So you'll be risking your life? I really don't like the sound of this Johnny O'Riordan, and to my way of thinking, if you dumped him in the shit, he'll be keen to show Flanagan where his allegiance lies,"

"That's why we must make a plan. As soon as I walk into the Europa Hotel this will be the setup; one of you will be in the bar, one on the street outside and one in a car, I'm sure you know what you might have to do."

All three men nodded.

"How will we know O'Riordan?" And what if Flanagan is with him? Dashwood asked.

"Flanagan will be elsewhere, he'd never kill me in a packed bar, Johnny will draw me out. And you won't have any problem in recognising Johnny, he had his right leg badly injured after a bomb blew up unexpectedly while he was planting it by a roadside. He was lucky not to be killed."

"Ah poor bastard," Dashwood said.

George laughed and continued. "He's small – just around five foot four - thin and in bad health, with long, straggly ginger hair. This will probably be irrelevant unless you get close enough under the lights in Great Victoria Street. What you can't miss is his limp, and the silver cane, it's always a silver cane, he can't help but show-off."

"Should be easy enough to pick that out," Carpenter confirmed.

"This all sounds far too iffy, frankly it stinks," Dashwood commented. "You know what we were taught George – the percentage thing?"

"And I would say it's fifty- fifty."

"And what were we told when learning this trade?" Carpenter asked.

"Fifty- fifty's not good enough," George conceded. "But also we were taught that if things got tough we had to make our own judgement. Well things are bloody tough – a man's life hangs in the balance and the hours are ticking by. So I've made my judgement."

O'Connor yawned. "Fair enough George, we were getting a bit bored anyway."

George looked at the three men and said, "thank you gentlemen for your vote of confidence."

*

Richard Fitzpatrick picked up the telephone and dialled Tim Holroyd's landline. He answered immediately. "Tim, it's me again."

Love Thine Enemy

"Good morning."

"I want to see you urgently, I'm in London tomorrow for Henry Walter's funeral, could I stay with you tonight?"

"Of course, will Rachel be coming?"

"I'm not too sure but I'll let you know. Are you going to the funeral?"

"Definitely."

"Good."

"Rachel and I still hold firm to what we said to you the other day."

"I thought you would, I'd do the same."

"You're on my side then?"

"One hundred percent."

"I suggest we talk this evening, there's no time to waste."

"No none at all Richard, we've been given a deadline and there's precious little time left."

"How long?"

"About forty three hours."

"Christ! That's not long. I'll see you around eight then."

"Look forward to it."

Richard put the telephone down and reluctantly turned away from the drawing room windows as Rachel walked into the room, the sight of the Highland cows contentedly munching away at their winter feed of silage in the park was particularly comforting, but Rachel looked more drawn than ever - all the sparkle gone from her eyes. He hated seeing her like this, hated the feeling of helplessness that it created inside him. He hurried over to her and tried to comfort her. Wrapping his arms around her he could feel her shaking and feared she was nearing a breakdown. He had to be strong for her. Rachel reluctantly pulled away and gave him a weak smile. "Have you rung Tim?" she asked.

"I just put the phone down from him now, I'm going up to stay with him tonight and we'll finalise our decision then, and go on to Henry's funeral in the morning. Will you come, I'd like you to."

Rachel played nervously with a string of pearls round her neck. "I don't think so Richard, it might seem pathetic, but I'll never stop thinking that the next funeral we go to will be James."

"Oh my darling, I quite understand."

Rachel flushed, "I don't know what I would have done without you to support me, you're so composed and on a different wave length to me. I expect you see the danger as clearly as I do and I'm sure you spend every second of every day worrying about James, wondering what terrible things are happening to him and how we will cope if he never comes back. I know you can't sleep at nights but, outwardly you're so calm. I'm quite jealous Richard, but I thank God for making you so strong. I don't understand how you do it, how do you keep your composure?"

Richard put his hands over his face and said quietly, "I do it because of you Rachel, and I need to keep it together for you. It's not easy." He dropped his hands and stared at her. He'd never imagined he would have to see such distress in anyone. And there was no way he was going to tell her that the chance of seeing James again was getting less likely by the hour.

*

He walked out of the front door with the distinct feeling that he was failing Rachel when she most needed him. But what more could he do? Short of conjuring up a miracle he had nothing to offer. It was bewildering, like being lost in a dark forest, the canopy of trees and thick undergrowth hiding the path he was searching for. As Rachel reluctantly released his hand and watched him get into his car she whispered, "I love you. I'll miss you."

"I'll only be away a night and ring me any time you want."

"Go," she said urgently.

He turned the key, raised a hand and headed down the drive.

Rachel didn't move until the car disappeared round a bend in the drive, stumbling back into the house she ran to the library. She lowered herself into Richard's favourite chair, she could smell him on the upholstery, and stared at the bookshelves. Would she would ever stop crying. "Resolve," she shouted to the walls, but before the word died on her lips she knew it was unobtainable, for the moment. She curled herself up in the chair and thought of James.

*

"Richard is going to raise the money," Tim informed the Prime Minister as dusk was settling over London. It was one of their regular meetings since what the Prime Minister liked to call "this small Irish problem," had arisen. "He'll be with me tonight, so we'll finalise the details."

"It's going to be a tight-run thing isn't it?"

"Very, but we'll make it."

"I still think he's a fool." stated the PM.

"Maybe, but what would you do Prime Minister?"

"I'd be a fool as well. But what about one more attempt to talk him out of it?"

"Already tried."

"You're a bad liar Holroyd, but given the circumstances I completely understand. My worry is that his actions may well set a precedent that will encourage others to kidnap."

Tim shook his head. "Short of putting him under house arrest and blocking his bank accounts I think there is little we can do."

The PM shifted uneasily in his chair. "I don't mean to sound heartless. I have two children of my own and love them both, but a question Holroyd. Do you honestly think that James Fitzpatrick is going to come out of this alive?"

Tim said nothing.

The Prime Minister nodded and held out a hand. "Wish Richard luck, he's going to need it."

Twenty-Eight

At three minutes past seven George spotted Johnny O'Riordan limping into the bar, it wasn't busy and O'Riordan was quick to make him out. His eyes darted round the room furtively as he walked towards George. George towered over him and offered his hand in greeting, which was duly ignored. Please yourself, thought George, amused.

"Evening Russell."

George fixed him with an icy stare. "Good evening Johnny. Forgotten my first name?"

O'Riordan broke eye contact and looked down at his polished shoes. "Just thought we ought to keep this business-like," he mumbled.

"Suit yourself."

O'Riordan said nothing, his eyes still twitched nervously. He'd already made a plan, but he wanted the money, it would be tricky. But he was Johnny O'Riordan and he could magic anything out of a hat, Russell's offer was too tempting to walk away from. So he'd decided to gamble, to tempt Russell and please Flanagan. His first task was to convince Russell that he knew where Flanagan was hiding, which wouldn't be easy, as he knew from experience that Russell was no fool.

"Drink," offered George.

O'Riordan was parched and nodded enthusiastically. "Pint of Guinness please."

Two pints ordered, George slipped off his bar stool and pointed to an alcove. "Let's move it's more private over there."

O'Riordan hobbled behind George, rested his silver cane against his chair and sat down. He placed the pint glass in front of

O'Riordan and said, "I've got no time to waste, have you thought over my offer?"

O'Riordan swept the room with his eyes once more, before saying, "I have."

"Good, let's have the information."

"O'Riordan licked his lips. "Flanagan has gone to ground."

"Yeah, I know that, but where? Come on Johnny, where for Christ sake?"

"East of Belfast."

"You're wasting my time."

"No I'm not but, I'll have more information in the next twenty-four hours. The word is out. Twenty-four carat-gold info, you have to realise this is very dangerous for me."

"I don't care if it's dangerous, that's too long."

"You're a hard man to please, okay what about twelve hours."

"Ten."

O'Riordan fiddled with his beer glass. "I'll do my best."

"Are you on the level, Johnny boy?"

"Would I lie when my mother's life depends on the money?"

George lent back in his chair and stared at O'Riordan. "Knowing you the answer is in the affirmative, but I'll give you a chance. We meet again in ten hours, here. If you have the information I will pay for your mother's operation."

"How did you know about that?"

"I know a lot of things Johnny."

O'Riordan shook his head. "You always were a cunning bastard. Okay, back here in ten hours."

"You promise?"

"You have my word."

"Worth shit."

"I'm hurt, very hurt George."

"Tough."

O'Riordan drained his glass and felt for his stick. He'd spent too long in Russell's company for his own good, Flanagan had eyes everywhere and as he hadn't made contact with him yet Flanagan just might get the wrong impression. He struggled to stand. "Can't say it was a pleasure meeting you again."

"Likewise."

O'Riordan pushed himself off the chair - stretched and limped towards the hotel lobby.

George watched him disappear, desperately disappointed. He'd placed a lot of hope in the meeting but Johnny-boy was lying through his teeth. He could smell treachery a mile off, he was planning to play him like a fish, and then deliver him to Flanagan. *You're a double-crossing little turd O'Riordan. Right now you'll be planning to get word to Flanagan that I'm back.* He could read O'Riordan like a book, he was banking on two sources of income; one for false information and one from tipping-off Flanagan. It made sense, cash and revenge. *No way Johnny boy, no way.* He looked across to the bar and raised a hand as if in greeting. Phil Dashwood didn't bother to acknowledge the signal. He dropped off his stool and followed O'Riordan out of the bar.

O'Riordan stepped out onto the street congratulating himself on pulling off his master plan. He had Russell hooked and a message to Flanagan would be well-rewarded, he longed to hear of Russell's demise, the thought gave him cause for a rare smile. A new house, a bungalow preferably, his mother's operation and money to burn. Russell had frightened the shit out of him turning up at the church like that, but now he wondered why? The God he worshipped had indeed sent him a gift. *Fuck you Russell, you've met your match at last!* He risked swinging his cane in the air and began to laugh, ah how good was the sweet smell of revenge.

He was far too occupied thinking of his invincibility to hear footsteps getting closer. Not until he felt the hard muzzled of a Walther PPK pressed into the small of his back did he realise he was in trouble.

"Keep walking," said the voice behind him. "Don't look round and don't try to run."

O'Riordan's heart sank. "Russell," he croaked.

"Wrong – a friend. Keep walking."

"Where am I going?" There was fear in O'Riordan's voice now.

"You'll find out soon enough."

The Walther was pressed a little harder. O'Riordan felt like shitting himself.

"Stop," the voice commanded. "Turn left here."

The side street was quieter than Victoria road and the shops were closed, there was no convenience store still open, no filling station. A few pedestrians hurried past the two men without a glance. They walked on. O'Riordan's leg began to hurt – he slowed – the Walther jabbed in the back. "Keep going," the voice said. O'Riordan limped on. At the top of the street was an empty shop. It had been a small haberdashery, but had given up the struggle to survive in the recession, there was no one walking past them any more.

No one would have heard the shot.

A car pulled up to the kerb. "Want a lift soldier?" asked Peter Carpenter.

Thanks," Phil Dashwood acknowledged.

*

George walked out of the hotel an hour later, he'd thought it better to let things settle down. He'd heard the police sirens and listened to three men excitedly telling the young man behind the bar that a man had been shot down. "Almost in front of our eyes," one of them said. "Blood everywhere."

George smiled at the confirmation and raised his half empty glass. "God rest your rotten soul Johnny," he said, allowing himself to feel a little sorry for the fate that now awaited O'Riordan's mother. And then it went out of his mind, Rose had seen him as a kind gentle man.

"Soft as butter" she'd say. Thank God she'd never seen the other side of him. As he walked slowly back the way he'd come it dawned on him that he was an embittered middle-aged man, intent on seeking out and killing Rose's murderer. It was personal as O'Malley had accused him. He glanced up the side street where O'Riordan had met his fate and saw the street cleaners still washing the last of O'Riordan's blood off the pavement.

Job done.

*

Charlie was puce with rage, his hand shaking as he pointed a finger at George. He'd wasted no time in bursting into George's flat as soon as he learned of O'Riordan's demise, bugger the lateness of the hour. "This has your doing stamped all over it Russell! I should charge you with murder. You can't just roam the streets picking off any one you like, you're despicable. He glared at the other three men and waved a hand at them. "All of you!"

George said, "You shouldn't jump to conclusions Charlie, you've no proof."

"Ah but I have," said Charlie. "I know you were drinking in the bar of the Europa with O'Riordan just before he was killed."

"That's not proof and you know it. There nothing wrong with me having a drink," George said calmly. "And I was the last person who wanted him dead, tomorrow he was going to give me information as to Flanagan's whereabouts. I'm sure you'll understand that I am bitterly disappointed. He was my best bet, you're pointing the finger at the wrong man."

Charlie refused to back down. "You're a bare-faced liar. Look at you all smirking at me. I might not be able to prove anything but don't take me for a fool. I don't know what went on between you and O'Riordan in the bar Russell, but as sure as hell one of you in this room killed him."

"No way," George said firmly. "If you want a suspect look no further than one of the 'Freedom for Ireland' group. I suspect they found out O'Riordan was going to feed me information. Anyway, believe what you like, it's irrelevant, O'Riordan is dead and I'm no wiser as to where Fitzpatrick is being held, don't waste my time by your unfounded accusations. I've got work to do." Charlie stared at the four men and shook his head. "I don't trust any of you, you're all as bad as each other. But I need you, I wish I didn't, I guess I have no choice, but to go along with you, for now."

George said, "Right then, now that's out of the way, let's get back to business, and may I remind you Inspector, no one will ever admit to our existence – and you do as I say. As I said to you in your office when we first met, we're above the law."

"Christ," exclaimed Charlie. "What is this fucking world coming to?"

"You don't have to like us."

"When this is over I don't ever want to set eyes on any of you again. If I do I'll take great pleasure in throwing you all in jail."

George smiled. "You haven't a hope in hell."

Twenty-Nine

Mary was sitting on the bed in the small attic room which smelt of mice droppings and damp. Her legs were curled up under her and she rocked from side-to-side, gently moaning. She was cold and felt used, a weak sun filtered through the window, which had stubbornly refused to close. She'd lain with Seamus a few hours earlier and as usual he was rough – almost savage; she had bites and bruises to show for it. She'd fled to the relative safety of the attic room and left him snoring, knowing he'd come looking for her when he woke but she couldn't bear to be next to him for a moment longer, farting and grunting like a pig. Once she'd fed off his violence, it had excited her and she'd enjoyed the pain, but no more. She was learning a lot about herself and discovering things about Seamus that she'd been blind to. He was sadistic, a loose cannon out of control, not a soldier fighting for Irish independence. She suspected that the kidnap of Fitzpatrick had become personal and the real reason it had taken second place. He'd once told her about the Fitzpatrick family and to this day she remembered the bitterness in his voice. Looking up at the ceiling, she noticed a small cobweb swinging gently from the bare bulb and silently asked God for guidance. Had Seamus changed that much, or had she? She'd been too much in awe of him, maybe even, brainwashed. There was no doubt in her mind that she'd loved him and truly believed that he was fighting for a just cause, that the resolve of the British government would weaken and then collapse but events had proved him wrong. Then it dawned on her, that she'd never made a decision on her own. Ever since she'd reached fourteen she'd been under the spell of her father, or Seamus, and had followed their way without question. Perversely, she wished she could still be the same person, with hate churning in her heart, with the desire to kill the hated Brits fermenting in her soul, it would make her life so much easier, but it was not to be. However dangerous her life might become, her eyes had been opened and she'd run out of hate. The callous killing of Walters and now the slow torture of the man downstairs was a step too far. No longer could Seamus claim to be fighting a war, he was a monstrous human being consumed by hate, and hatred, like love, must be regularly fed and watered; he'd lost her respect and forfeited their love.

She swung her legs onto the wooden floor, being as careful as she could to avoid the mice shit and walked to the window that looked out on Lough Neagh. She pulled back the thin curtains and watched them shifting slightly in the cool morning breeze. The mist was rising over Belfast as the sun was still struggling to break through the layer of cloud, she opened the window and breathed in the fresh air. She was trapped, a mess, and then the tears started to flow. Was she crying for Fitzpatrick or was it self-pity? She thought of the young man downstairs, suffering, lying half-conscious on the fouled sofa, short of water, food and dignity. How much longer could he withstand such deprivation? It didn't worry Seamus, but it was disturbing her.

Then she made her first ever solo decision. Wow! She had a brain of her own after all. She hastily pulled on pants and shrugged into her T-shirt, making a mental note to wash it later, and opened the door. She had to get to Fitzpatrick before Seamus woke. She threw herself downstairs and burst into the front room, hurrying over to where James lay, his eyes were open. She could see his desperation, leaning over she touched his face and gasped. His skin was cold and clammy, she pulled her hand away. Jesus! How could she hate this defenceless, pathetic figure lying on the sofa? At that moment her life changed forever and she knew exactly what she had to do.

Through misty eyes James stared at her, preparing himself for the usual onslaught of invectives, followed by a blow on some part of his bruised body. Anguish rocked him and he saw nothing but days of more misery. Death, which he thought was inevitable, couldn't come soon enough.

But the invectives didn't come, nor the blow, instead her face moved closer to him and she smiled. She could smell his sweat, rancid breath, the strong smell of urine and was close to throwing up but she swallowed the bile that was threatening to choke her and said, "listen up, you need to move – to get the blood flowing. We are going to the kitchen, hear me?"

James nodded.

"Good. Listen, we haven't got much time, Seamus will be awake soon. Come on I'll give you a hand."

"You will have to lift me," James croaked."

"I can't lift you, I'm not strong enough, try and get into a sitting position and then I can help you swing your legs onto the floor and we can work things out from there."

"I can't do it."

"You fucking can!"

James gritted his teeth and suddenly he found some inner strength – this girl was not playing mind games – he dared to think she wanted to help. He felt tears burning his eyes at this first sign of kindness since he'd been kidnapped. As his bare feet touched the ground he struggled to stand, the room spun, his legs went from under him and he crashed to the floor. Mary moved like lightening, she put her hands under his armpits and managed to get him into a sitting position. She said, "No giving up Fitzpatrick – let's try again." She moved over to the only armchair in the room and pulled it towards him. "Okay, put your hands on this and stand. I'll try to hold you."

"I can't do it."

"No! Don't say that, grab the chair, come on - one last try eh?"

"Why?"

"You can't live without food and water."

"I don't care if I die."

"No, don't say that! You have a chance, believe me. Get your hands on that chair and show some guts, for Christ fucking sake! I'm putting my life on the line for you."

James wiped away the sweat from his forehead and reached out for the chair. With both hands gripping the chair arms he heaved himself off the floor and managed to stand, he swayed but didn't fall. He felt Mary's arms pushing against his back and it gave him confidence. He risked a shuffle, his legs were like blocks of concrete, but he managed a few steps forward.

"Fuck that!" exclaimed Mary triumphantly. "It's not far to the kitchen."

At that moment Seamus burst into the room – naked. "What the fuck!" He flew at Mary and grabbed her arm, pulling her away from James who collapsed in a heap on the floor. Seamus laughed, before turning his anger on Mary. "Fraternising with the enemy eh Mary, rather than being in my bed?" He pulled her close and she could feel his hardness, he pushed her to the floor and tore down her pants forcing open her legs and fell on her. Mary stared boldly into his eyes and said nothing, she knew it would be over quickly – Seamus never wasted time. He rolled off her and laughed, before cuffing her face. "Never, ever help Fitzpatrick, do you hear? He's filth. Let him starve. If I find you helping him again you'll feel my fists. I don't like disloyalty. Now I'll deal with Fitzpatrick, you get to the kitchen and make me a cup of tea."

Mary didn't move and braced herself for another blow, but Seamus was already moving towards James, so confident that he would be obeyed. He aimed a kick at James's back.

"Leave him Seamus," screamed Mary, throwing herself between the two men.

It was an unequal contest. Seamus grabbed Mary by the hair and dragged her away, aiming a blow to her head she cried out, he kicked her legs from under her and she fell to the ground. Rubbing his knuckles he spat at her. "Maybe that will teach you not to interfere with Seamus Flanagan."

Mary was too stunned to say anything and Seamus swiftly moved back to James, who was desperately trying to get to his feet. When he saw Seamus coming he gave up and braced himself for the inevitable. Seamus bent down and grabbed both his legs. Then he dragged him face down back to the sofa. "Bad boy," he hissed, "no fucking water for you today."

James closed his eyes, a day before he would have felt the all too familiar prickling of fear, humiliation and utter hopelessness, but through the pain that wracked his body, and his desperate need for water, he felt that something had changed. It was the girl. He opened his eyes and watched her slowly get up off the floor – stagger past Seamus and make for the stairs. Did he dare hope?

*

By six am Rachel had given up on sleep, it had been her worst night so far, images of James's broken body kept floating in front of her. There was no Richard to comfort her, no warm body to wrap her arms around and cry onto his bare shoulders, the room seemed threatening, claustrophobic and unfriendly. She kicked the duvet onto the floor and with a sob of anguish went towards the bathroom. She hadn't needed to be on her own, her torment was self-inflicted, she could have been with Richard. "My own stupid fault," she shouted as she threw open the bathroom door.

*

Richard and Tim left St Bride's Church in Fleet Street, feeling thoroughly depressed. Richard was glad Rachel hadn't come. "The service was slow torture Tim. By the end I was imagining that it was James's body in the coffin."

Tim rested a hand on his friend's shoulder as he guided him away from the crowd of mourners. There was only so much unhappiness he could expect Richard to take, and there had been plenty of that on show. "Come on, I'll take you to lunch at the Savoy Grill. It's just reopened and I've heard very good things about it."

"I don't think so but thanks Tim it's a kind thought, but I'm not in the mood. Some other time eh, like when we are celebrating James's safe return. Right now a large whisky in the nearest pub will do."

Sensing the turmoil churning within his friend, Tim didn't press him further. "Okay a pub it is and I know a decent one not far from here."

A few minutes later they walked into The Old Bell and stared at the packed bar. The place was humming. "Lunchtime," said Tim. "We could try another one."

"It'll be the same everywhere," Richard said, "look, there's a table by the window, you order, I'll grab the seats." Once seated with two double whiskies in front of them Richard leant across the table and said, "It's urgent we make our move soon, I've got the money."

"How the hell have you managed to get your hands on that so quickly?"

"A very helpful bank and I mortgaged Thornbury."

"Christ. Does Rachel know?"

"Yes, it was the only way we could get that amount of cash quickly and losing Thornbury is the least of our worries. What value has money got in a situation like this? It's worth nothing if the worst happens. So I pay the ransom and pray. I know I can still lose him, but I'm damned if I'm going to stand back and allow him to die without making an effort to save him. You don't need to tell me that paying the money to that murderous man will guarantee James's safe return, because I'm well aware that it doesn't."

Tim drained his glass. "I won't."

Richard put his elbows on the table, he felt exhausted. "Come on Tim, the hours are ticking by too fast for comfort."

"I spoke to the Prime Minister this morning and told him we would go to Belfast immediately."

"What did he say?"

"He understood, let's put it like that."

"I would have expected nothing else, at heart he's a decent man. We've had our disagreements in the past but he was always honest and straightforward, rare qualities these days."

"He's hoping that this stays out of the press."

Richard laughed. "There's not a chance, even if we keep *our* mouths shut you can be sure as hell that Flanagan will shout it from the roof tops."

"That's just the type of thing I'd expect from him."

"Okay, just one more question before we move, how do you rate my chances?"

"It's hard to read, we still have Russell on the ground and knowing the man as I do he will bust a gut to find out where James is but if that fails then we're in the hands of ruthless men who have little regard for human life, especially your son's. In some quarters your name is still reviled. What ever you do, you mustn't hand over the money until James is free. That would spell certain death."

"So it's not even fifty- fifty?"

Tim reluctantly nodded. "That's about the size of it."

Richard stared at his untouched glass, the desire for a drink had passed. "It all seems so depressing – so utterly futile."

"You must hang on," begged Tim. "For Rachel's sake if nothing else. How is she?"

"Not good, but she's halfway to forgiving you. What she can't understand is my composure, as she calls it. I left her in a state of bewilderment. She can't comprehend why I don't cry all day – why I can sleep at night. I tell her it is because one of us has to stay sane to help the other. I don't tell her that I pop sleeping pills like sweats. Christ Tim I could cry all day, scream at the heavens, asking God what the hell he thinks he's doing. I could lie awake all night imagining the most terrible things about James, but I don't, I have to stay strong for her."

"She'll thank you when this is over."

"I don't want thanks, I just want to see her smile and hear her laugh. If James dies I hate to think what will happen to her." Richard glanced at his watch. "We better go, I've left Rachel long enough, are you coming with me or will you follow?"

"I'll come with you, and as soon you've spoken to Rachel we must head for Southampton."

"Southampton? Will we get tickets?"

"I have a Britain-Norman Islander standing by."

"My God you can still pull strings Tim."

"Only in an emergency and this is certainly an emergency."

"I'm glad you've persuaded someone of that."

Tim shrugged. "One thing I've learnt after all these years, is that you need to know the right people and then you can get almost anything." Tim pushed his chair back. "Time to go."

They walked away from the table and pushed their way through the young crowd, laughing at each others' jokes, blind to the desperation of the two men weaving their way towards the door.

Suddenly Tim felt terribly sad.

*

They sat round the fire in the drawing room, with a plate of cold chicken salad on their laps, the food was a necessity no one was hungry. Rachel was the first move. "I must go and throw a few things into a suitcase. How long have we got Tim?"

Richard mouth fell open. "You're coming with us?"

"I'm surprised you asked that."

Richard didn't bother to argue, he just looked at his watch – how many times had he stared at the bloody thing? He turned to Tim, "how long?"

"We must leave here in an hour."

"I'll be ready," Rachel promised over her shoulder as she left the room.

Once she'd gone Tim asked. "Is this wise?"
"You try and stop her."
"I don't think I'll waste my breath."

*

It was dark as they drove up to the airport, and in the car lights Richard could see mist floating in the air. Fog! Richard heard a gasp from Rachel and knew she was thinking the same as him. *Fog will seal our son's death.* He almost laughed at the irony of the situation. All the planning, raising the money, driving to Southampton as if the devil himself was pursuing them and then fog, a natural phenomenon that no one could do a thing about. "Shit," he said out loud.

"It' ll be okay," Tim assured him as they turned into the covered car park and drove to the area that was reserved for departures. "Not yet thick enough and we're not tied to departure times so once we've gone through the necessary formalities we'll be on our way. The fog is not expected to thicken until the early hours."

"Thank God for that," Rachel said, breathing a little easier.

As they exited the car Richard took Rachel's hand. "At last we're on our way, nothing can stop us now. We're within the time limit and do you know something?"

Rachel squeezed his hand and looked up at him. "What do you know Richard?"

"That all's going to be well."

Thirty

Mary had again slept in the attic room, anywhere was better then having to share a bed with Seamus, but she was well aware she mustn't antagonise him too much, she needed his trust. She'd confessed to her period and he'd bought it but it had been another miserable sleepless night. The cold had eaten into her body and the smell of mice shit seemed more over-powering than the night before, fear for her future was never far from her mind. She stared at the door frightened that Seamus might take it into his mind to pay her a visit, morning was his horny time. But the forty-eight hour deadline expired today, so hopefully he would have things other than sex on his mind.

Now, as dawn at last raised its head she rolled off the bed. Fitzpatrick's fate would be decided before the end of the day, free or dead? Free! Jesus, what were the odds? The futility of her intention had been growing on her like a slow developing cancer. What was she doing? Trying to save a Brit! She'd never imagined that one day she'd find herself in such a position. It was treason for fuck sake! It was abandoning all that she had been brought up to believe, that the only good Brit was a dead one. And yet here she was questioning that very thinking and wracking her brain for a solution. She banged her forehead with a hand in bewilderment as she finally realised she cared for the young man downstairs. Shit! Enough to risk her life? Enough to kill Seamus if she had to? Could she bring herself to commit the ultimate sinful act of being a traitor to the Cause? She moved to the window and watched the early morning flight of mallard circling over the Lough and made her decision.

Michael Pakenham

*

Eileen looked across their front room at her daughter. The rain was beating against the windows, making the room as dark as her thoughts. She would have liked to have been proud of her progeny, but she couldn't help thinking that she had given birth to something corrupt. Conor's genes must have been strong. Mary looked up from reading her book – a violent thriller – her usual read. "Love stories are for the weak," she'd once told her mother, who visibly shrank back into her chair under her stare. Mary smiled with satisfaction – she enjoyed putting the frighteners on her mother – the weak useless religious woman. Why couldn't she support her husband – why couldn't she be proud of her family? Eileen braced herself and drawing on the last remnants of her dwindling courage she forced herself to return her daughter's stare. She was determined to have her say. "Mary, can I say something?"

"If you have to."

Eileen fought back the tears. She had long since learnt that tears got her nowhere with her daughter. "You're sixteen now Mary. Old enough to make up your own mind about things and I accept that you have decided to follow in your father's footsteps." She was tempted to say 'evil' but knew that would be unwise. She didn't want Mary to flounce out in a rage – at least not until she'd had her say. "One day you may want to turn from that path, so remember that God is always there for you – to guide you away from evil. He will forgive. I know what you think of me and I have given up trying to change that, but please listen to my words – drink them in and never forget them."

Mary snorted with derision and rose from her chair. "You're pathetic mother. Your God is the same as mine, and He is on my side, not yours."

*

"One day you may want to turn off that path." Mary gave an audible sigh. That day had come. She looked up into the sky and mouthed, "Sorry."

The door flew open and Seamus, naked to the waist, his eyes blazing and a thin smile on his face stood there. "Sleep well?" he taunted.

"Better without you," was on the tip of her tongue, but that would send him wild. Instead she shook her head and put a hand on her stomach. "No. it's the pain."

Seamus just shrugged, he'd never had any sympathy for womanly problems. He said, "This is the day – by its end 'Freedom for Ireland' will be a million quid richer. Think what we could do with that."

"And Fitzpatrick?"

"No change, he dies."

She gave a sharp intake of breath but said nothing. Seamus must think she was on board – committed. "In that case I better go down and see that our prisoner is still alive." She pushed past him onto the landing and headed down the stairs, moving to the sofa she felt Fitzpatrick's forehead, he was burning up. His eyes flicked open and then closed, Mary knew he was close to death. There would be no need for Seamus or Declan to kill him – the job was nearly done. She noticed his swollen lips, Declan had no doubt been amusing himself. Mary wanted to run from the cottage and scream for help, to see Seamus and Declan shot down, she wanted to tell Fitzpatrick that his hell was over. In her mind she shouted, "Live, you must live!" But that was a dream, the cottage was isolated and she wouldn't stand a chance. With a shrug of her shoulders she rushed to the kitchen and brought back a glass of water. She put a hand under James's neck and gently lifted his head. "Water," she whispered one eye on the stairs, "it might help. Sip some slowly." She put the glass to James's lips. She could feel him trembling but he managed to a few sips before closing his eyes. "Enough" His voice was just audible.

"I'm sorry," she whispered, moving away as she heard footsteps on the stairs. She hurried back to the kitchen and put the glass in the sink.

"Breakfast," grunted Seamus as he walked into the kitchen, "get us some fucking breakfast."

Mary refused to look at him as she moved to the fridge, it was nearly empty. She moved to the freezer, same result, then she had an idea. They needed food if they were going to stay at the cottage any longer. She turned towards Seamus. "Just enough food for this morning and after that we starve."

Seamus rifled in his trouser pocket and threw a twenty pound note down on the table. "Shop," he said, "just bare necessities, we won't be here long."

Mary reached for the note. "Will Declan drive?"

"No, I want him to stay here you go on your own, then when you're back I'm off to see a friend. You and Declan will stay here and keep an eye on Fitzpatrick. I'll ring O'Malley at midday. Take the Rover, I won't be needing it for a couple of hours but don't waste time, remember I need the car later. The keys are on the table by the door."

Mary hid a smile, on her own! He still trusted her, she couldn't believe her luck. This could be her chance, excitement coursed through her body. If she moved quickly she'd have time.

*

She drove away from the cottage thinking her first stop was going to be the nearest public phone, to call the police and put an end to this horror. It might mean prison, but if it saved a man's life that was a penalty she was prepared to pay. Her hands were shaking so violently that she could hardly hold the steering wheel, but as she drove doubt started to creep into her head, of course she wasn't alone. How foolish to ever think she would be, Seamus never trusted anyone. She reckoned that as soon as they'd arrived at the cottage he would have made sure that at least one of his comrades was always watching the road, either to alert him to on coming danger or to follow anyone, but himself, who left the cottage. It would be his insurance. She cursed loudly and decided to drive straight to the supermarket to give herself thinking time, as she hit the road at the end of the lane her suspicions were confirmed; a green Audi tucked in behind her. She began to sweat. *Do I abort or carry on?* She decided to carry on, determination coursing through her veins.

Dashing around the supermarket Mary threw basic provisions into her trolley, milk, eggs, bacon, sausages, bread and a small bunch of daffodils. £20 did not go far. As she left the shop the Audi was parked two cars away from her. The driver was making no attempt to hide, Seamus wanted her to know she had a companion. Bastard! It was no good trying to lose the Audi, her first idea was dead in the water, but she'd had time to think of another plan. Starting the engine she drove slowly and carefully towards St Mary's Church in Chapel Lane, her plan was a gamble, but the only option she could come up with in the short time she had available. She'd never had time for priests and praying but this was an emergency. She parked and pulled out a biro from her bag – found a dirty piece of paper lying in the passenger foot-well and wrote a short note. Then, with a quick glance in her rear mirror to make sure her follower could see her, she left the car. She opened the boot and took out the daffodils. She was tempted to wave them at the Audi.

Once inside the church yard she walked towards the two graves. She knew a pair of eyes was watching her, but she didn't care. There was nothing wrong with paying her parents a quick visit. The churchyard was deserted. *Where the fuck is father Paul when I need him?* She placed the flowers on her mother's grave and wiped away a tear. What a fucking bitch she'd been. Her mother's grave was neatly tended. On the other hand her father's was covered in dying weeds. The kindness of the church ladies obviously only went so far. She knelt down next to her mother's grave, remembering how she'd spat on the coffin once it had been lowered into the hole. She looked across at her father's grave, thinking of the tears she'd shed for him. How different it would be if the funeral was today. Her tears fell on the wet grass. She had never been able to love her mother as a daughter should - never listened to her wise words – just worshipped the two men she thought she loved. She knew she could not alter the past – her mother would not suddenly spring back to life – she would never be able to say sorry to her face. If she'd had any lingering doubts about what she was doing they vanished like a puff of smoke. She shook her head. She'd wasted enough time. "Come on Father Paul," she said under her breath, "where the hell are you?" She looked at her watch – she had to go. Seamus would be getting edgy. She pushed the note into the daffodils. It was her last throw. She felt heavy with disappointment. She blessed herself, got off her knees and began weaving her way through the gravestones back to the church gate. As she reached the gate she heard a shout. "Can I help you?"

She whirled round and saw Father Paul walking towards her. Would he recognise her? Better if not. She was certain he had her marked down as a disciple of the devil. He would be aware of her past. She smiled nervously as he reached her. "Father, please listen well. I need your help desperately. Can't explain as I'm being watched. Don't say a word – don't look surprised. Smile and do as I ask. Please go to Eileen Keogh's grave. A note in the daffodils. Please, please do something. A man's life is at stake." Without another word she opened the gate and headed for the Rover. She'd done her best.

*

Father Paul stared at her back. There was something familiar about her. Eileen Keogh? That name rang a bell. He walked slowly towards the grave yard deep in thought. It didn't take him long to find the two headstones. He clicked his fingers. Of course, Conor and Eileen Keogh. A brave man and a deeply religious woman who had attended church every Sunday. There had been a daughter, Mary. He remembered the rumour. Mary Keogh was instrumental in her mother's death. He shrugged. What did he care? He'd long since decided to ignore rumours. He saw the note tucked into the bunch of daffodils – thought of leaving it there, but his curiosity got the better of him. He bent down and pulled it out of the flowers. As he read it he wished he'd left it where it had been put. Mary Keogh! He shoved it into his cassock pocket and walked reflectively back to the church. He had some serious thinking to do. He moved up the aisle and dropped into the front pew – buried his head in his hands and thought of the note. He pulled it out of his pocket and read it again. But his loyalties had always lain with the IRA. And at times he'd covertly helped the likes of Seamus Flanagan. It had kept him alive. As far as he was concerned there was no need to change the status quo. "You've come to the wrong person Mary Keogh," he said to himself as he rose painfully from the pew – age was catching up with him. He limped towards the vestry. There was a bottle of rum in a drawer. He cursed Mary – she'd quite upset his day. Once in the vestry he threw the scrap of paper into his rubbish bin, never giving it a second thought.

*

Seamus was standing by the cottage door as Mary pulled up. There was a cynical smile on his face. "Thought you never went to church."

"I felt like taking my father some flowers."

"How commendable."

"No fucking need for sarcasm, and you didn't have to have me followed Seamus. You should know I'm loyal."

"Spotted your tail did you?"

"You meant me to."

"Just my insurance and I never take chances."

Mary shook her head. "You're a distrustful bastard."

"That's why I'm still alive"

Mary smiled at him and handed him the car keys. "I'll take these bags inside. I'm sorry I gave you trouble."

"No trouble, just a precaution."

As she walked into the house it occurred to her how ironic life could be. Her father might well have just saved her life.

*

Meg Healy gripped Duff's arm and stared at Charlie O'Malley. "They are coming to stay here? Thanks for asking! Oh my God Inspector I'm really not too sure about that. I have other guest's safety to think of and you're not going to look me in the eye and tell me there's no danger to any of us if the Fitzpatrick's come here. Because if you did I would tell you that you are a liar. You know perfectly well that this man behind the kidnap has eyes and ears everywhere. I don't think you should have asked me."

Charlie was braced for the outburst and wondered what Meg's reaction was going to be when he gave her the *really* bad news. "I'm afraid you have no choice. When they land at Aldergrove they will come here."

Meg drew in her breath. "No choice, oh really?"

"Afraid so."

Meg fiddled with her mug of tea. "Tell me why."

"A question first Meg. When do this lot of guests leave?"

Meg threw a questioning look at Duff.

"Today."

"No problem about having room then. When do the next lot arrive?"

"What's it to you?" spat Meg.

"Just answer the question please."

"They are arriving in two days time."

"From where?"

"France."

Charlie took a deep breath. "Cancel them."

"What!" screamed the Healys in unison. "No way," Meg added.

"I'm sorry but that is not a request, it's an order."

"An order, an order Inspector? Well I tell you what you can do with your order, you can shove it right up your arse," Duff shouted.

Visibly shaking Meg said, "Well tell us Inspector why you want to ruin our business?"

"That will not happen," Charlie assured her. "You will be well compensated and for a time moved to other accommodation. We will provide temporary staff to look after the Fitzpatricks. Once this dreadful business is over you will be free to come back here and carry on as before. It will all be over in three days max."

Meg heaved her bulk off her chair and walked towards Charlie. "You're going to kick Duff, my small loyal staff, and myself out?"

"For your own safety."

"This better be good," Meg said.

"If you'll sit down I'll put you fully in the picture."

Meg retreated back to her chair and drained her mug of cold tea. "We're all ears Inspector."

Charlie began. "I don't think I need go over the appalling events of the last ten days and the refusal of the British Government to deal with the kidnappers. However there has been a new development."

"James's father is going to pay the ransom," Duff guessed.

"Exactly," Charlie continued. "That is why we need your hotel. We feel that there may be an attempt on Richard Fitzpatrick's life. We can guard them better here."

"Them?" asked Meg.

"Rachel Fitzpatrick and a man called Tim Holroyd. MI6. So I've been informed. This area is sparsely populated and those that do live around here know everyone. Very difficult for a stranger to go unnoticed and that goes for cars as well. I think I can provide better cover for the Fitzpatricks here rather than in Belfast where strange people do not stand out like they would here. Finally, if the threat is for real and there is a fire fight there is less chance of innocent people getting hurt or worse killed."

"So we have no choice? Can you really do this?"

"Yes."

"And what of poor James?" Meg asked.

Charlie decided not to lie. "His chances are slim, but we must hope."

"Hope! Is that all you can say."

"I'm afraid so. These men have no compassion. They cannot be trusted to do as they promise."

"So with only hope as your ally you blindly move on and hope God is on your side."

"That's about it."

"Poor James."

Charlie did not correct her. He felt impotent. He spoke without much conviction. "However if we can locate your girl Mary Keogh…."

"Not much chance of that," Meg said.

"Perhaps not, but we do have contacts that might be able to help."

"Well good luck to you inspector."

"'I'll need it. So, I beg of you not to be difficult about moving."

Meg planted her large hands on her hips and defiantly stared at Charlie. "We will cooperate in any way we can, but we are not moving are we Duff?"

Duff nodded vigorously. "No way. You may be able to take over the house but you can't forcible move us. That clear Inspector?"

Charlie thought for a moment. "It is against my better judgement, but if that's the way you…."

"It is Inspector," Meg said. "The only way we leave here is in handcuffs. These poor people will need someone better than your lot to look after them and that's going to be me and Duff." Then she added acidly, "I would have liked to think that you didn't feel it might be necessary to threaten us."

Charlie looked suitably contrite. "My apologies to you both – I look forward to your cooperation. Though I think…"

Meg gave a half-smile and wagged a finger. "No, Inspector we will not move."

Thirty-One

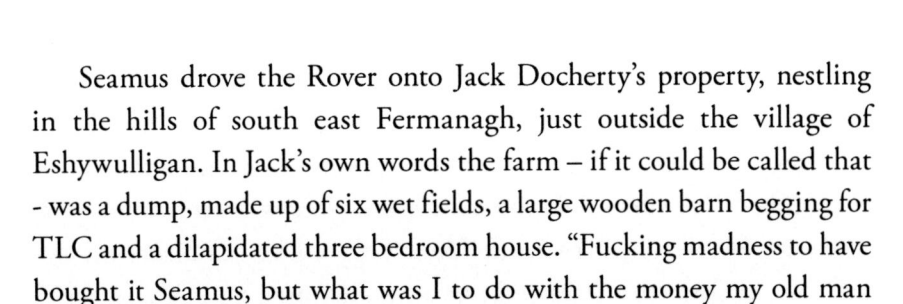

Seamus drove the Rover onto Jack Docherty's property, nestling in the hills of south east Fermanagh, just outside the village of Eshywulligan. In Jack's own words the farm – if it could be called that – was a dump, made up of six wet fields, a large wooden barn begging for TLC and a dilapidated three bedroom house. "Fucking madness to have bought it Seamus, but what was I to do with the money my old man left me? Spend it on drink, horses, or buy something Daisy and I could enjoy for the rest of our lives?" And then he'd added, "The remoteness makes it a bloody good place for our meetings."

Well he'd been right about that Seamus thought, as he nearly ran over one of several scrawny chickens hopefully scratching at the dirt in the yard. They'd plotted bombings and deaths, sitting comfortably in Jack's armchairs knowing that they were relatively safe. But he was a city man and had never envied Jack his way of life. He skidded to a halt and stepped out into one of many dung infested puddles. He shook his leg. *Fucking farmers.* Jack was standing at the entrance to the house, one arm draped round his loving Daisy. A fine looking woman Seamus thought, not for the first time. At times he'd been tempted to take up her offer of a 'little fun,' as she was prone to say to most men in the area. How Jack had put up with such infidelity over the years puzzled him.

He waved at the couple and threaded his way through the muck and puddles towards the house. As he looked at Daisy he knew there would be no offer of a 'little fun' this time. Their relationship had nose dived since the Good Friday Agreement. Her face was puce with anger.

"Good to see you Daisy, looking so well." He held out a hand to Jack. "Good morning comrade."

Seamus was the last person Jack wanted to see, but when the telephone call had come the day before he had little choice but to agree to his visit. "Morning Seamus," he said ushering him into the house. "We can talk in the front room."

"And then you'll leave Seamus. You're not welcome here," Daisy ordered.

"Something wrong?" Seamus asked, as he settled into one the armchairs.

"You know very well there is. There's peace now Seamus and I want my Jack to settle down. No more violence – it was getting on my tits. And here you are, chest stuck out, like a randy cockerel, no doubt to ask Jack for help over this kidnap. I repeat, want you to go away."

Seamus gave her a withering look. "I'm sorry to disappoint you Daisy but Jack owes me and I'm calling in the debt."

"Owes you! Jesus Seamus, he's followed you around like a fucking puppy for years. Done your bidding, risked his life for you and you come here and have the nerve to say he owes you."

"*I* saved his life you stupid woman. And that means he will owe me for the rest of his days," Seamus shot back.

Jack held up a hand. "Easy Daisy please. Let's hear what Seamus has to say."

Seamus allowed himself to smile. "Thank you Jack. I want you to help me get the ransom that is all. After that I won't bother you again."

"Promise."

"As God is my witness."

"Since when have you believed in God Seamus?" Daisy asked. "And I've heard your promises before – they are worthless."

Seamus ignored her. "Well Jack, are you going to let your long standing friend down in his hour of need? We've fought together too long to give up now. We will destroy this fucking agreement."

"You delude yourself Seamus," Daisy said in a quiet voice. "Most of Ireland wants peace. You fought hard but you've lost."

Seamus moved close to her and wagged a finger in her face. "Never!"

Jack looked at Daisy. "I can't refuse him."

"Coward. You're frightened of this man. He can't hurt you now."

Oh but he can, thought Jack as he looked into Seamus's eyes and saw the familiar look of a man who killed without a thought for his victim. And a riled Seamus wouldn't hesitate to pull a gun on him and Daisy. Not for the first time Jack wished he'd never set eyes on Seamus. "I'm in," he said quietly.

Daisy stared at both men. "You're a bastard Seamus. You knew Jack wouldn't have the balls to refuse you. Well I've had enough of you both. Get out before I puke on your shoes." Then turning to Jack she gave him a sad look and said, "You've made your bed Jack. I love you, but I can't live with you while you are still tied to this man. When you come back you will have to make a choice. I don't think I need to spell out what that choice is. Now get out of here."

Seamus grabbed hold of Daisy's hand. "Don't try anything Daisy my love will you. Jack will not be coming back if you do." Before she could answer he turned to Jack. "Come on Jack, time is of the essence."

The two men hurried towards the front door. Once outside Seamus said, "You've made a good choice Jack."

"There was no need to threaten her."

"You know me, never take a risk. Your little wife is a loose cannon. Now, no more time to waste. Get that old car of yours started and follow me. We will need it later."

As Jack pulled out of the yard he saw Daisy watching from a window. His heart lurched. He was under no illusions that he might have lost her.

Above Lisnaskea Seamus braked to a halt. Jack stopped his old Honda behind him and got out as he saw Seamus leave the Rover. "I will get a signal here," Seamus said thrusting his mobile at Jack. "You make the call. It will make O'Malley realise he's not just up against me. After that I will dump the mobile and the Rover and we will carry on in that rust bucket of yours. We're about to land a blow that the British Government won't forget."

Jack reluctantly dialled the number Seamus gave him. He thought of something Daisy had once said to him. "You're getting yourself in too deep you fool. Men like Seamus Flanagan will drag you to your death."

And Jack felt that Seamus had just made the first step.

*

Declan paced up and down in the front room of the cottage. He was fuming that Seamus had left him behind. It had not been the original plan but suddenly Seamus had grown nervous of Mary. "I don't want her trying anything with Fitzpatrick. So you must stay here," he'd said earlier. *Well fuck that* was Declan's thought, but he was far too frightened of Seamus to object. "Is Mary going soft?" he'd asked.

"She's changed," said Seamus. "Can't put a finger on it. Watch her."

Looking at the half-dead man lying on the sofa Declan didn't think there was any danger of Mary getting him out of the cottage to safety. He stared at Mary, the silly bitch, holding a glass of water to Fitzpatrick's mouth. Why feed a dead man? "You trying to save his life?" He sneered.

Mary looked up at him in disgust. Much as she'd have liked to have kicked him in the groin she knew she'd be dead within minutes. She had to play along with him. She said, "We need to keep him alive. He's no good dead until we have the money. After that you can kill him Declan."

Declan said, "I can't wait."

Mary felt sick. He was an animal like Seamus. She swallowed the bile and turned back to James, whispering. "Don't believe what you hear - don't give up hope." The look he gave her said it all. She was just like Seamus and Declan. She felt like shit.

*

The telephone rang. "He's a punctual bastard," murmured Charlie, picking up the phone. You could have heard a pin drop in the room as Charlie said, "Hello."

"That you O'Malley?" came the question.

"Good afternoon Flanagan."

"Wrong."

Charlie threw a look at George Russell who was standing next to him and covered the receiver with a hand. "It's not Flanagan."

"We must still talk," George said.

"How do I know you are one of the kidnappers, not a hoax?" Charlie asked.

Jack put his hand over the mouth piece. "Thinks I'm a fucking hoaxer or something."

Seamus grabbed the mobile. "Don't fuck me about O'Malley."

"Ah Flanagan, sorry I doubted your accomplice. Can't be too careful when dealing with scum." He heard something like a growl. "Raw nerve Flanagan?"

George was waving violently. Caught Charlie's eye. "Unprofessional, stick to the point." he whispered.

Charlie nodded, but he'd enjoyed the moment. He could imagine Flanagan seething with rage. "You still there Flanagan?"

He heard a loud intake of breath – he *had* riled the bastard.

"Don't play games with me O'Malley. I hold all the aces. Is that piece of British shit going to pay up? No prevaricating – one word will do."

"He's willing to negotiate."

Seamus laughed. "I gave you forty-eight hours. No change. The full million or the young man dies."

Charlie did not doubt him. But he decided to have one last throw of the dice. "The money is not yet ready. It takes time to raise that much cash."

"Balls O'Malley. We both know that the money will soon be here. My informant on the mainland is sound, so don't waste your breath trying to tell me otherwise."

Charlie sucked in his breath. Dear God the man seemed to have informants everywhere- worryingly it seemed even in a bank. On the mainland – Jesus! Did he know what time he took a shit each morning! It was unnerving. Flanagan was pissing him off something rotten. The man always seemed one step ahead of him.

"Now listen up O'Malley, as soon as the money lands here I will be in touch. I have eyes everywhere so no stonewalling."

Charlie had no choice but to say, "Okay."

"Good, that's more like it. Cooperation is your only choice. When we next speak I will tell you where we will rendezvous. And a warning O'Malley, no funny business. No armed response team lurking nearby. Just Fitzpatrick with a case full of money. I will have eyes everywhere. I will hand over his son unharmed."

Charlie nearly choked on his anger and frustration. "Your instructions are clear. I will do as you say."

"Good." Then the phone went dead.

Charlie turned and threw a rueful smile at George. "By God I hope I catch the bastard."

"Not if I get there first."

*

Jack looked across at Seamus and asked, "Everything okay?"

Seamus cracked a smile. "Going to plan and I surprised that detective – felt good. The money is on its way. We'll soon have a million quid."

"And what of your prisoner?"

"He'll be a piece of dead meat."

"And how do you think you'll get the money if he's dead?"

Seamus slapped Docherty on the back. "It's fucking simple Jack. We will hand over our prisoner – take the money and then as they leave kill both father and son."

"And if they have back up?"

"They won't. At least not near. They want our prisoner alive. I will have men everywhere. They know if I see anything suspicious he will die. Don't get into a stew Jack. This will be a piece of cake."

Jack said nothing. He'd always hated killing, but had accepted that at times it was necessary. But this? It was just gratuitous killing for killings sake. It was personal. He knew of Seamus's hatred of the Fitzpatrick family. But if he spoke up – threatened to withdraw his support he'd be a dead man.

"Speechless eh Jack?" Seamus laughed. "Well stay that way and do as I say, like getting away from here. We'll dump the Rover and mobile and head back to the cottage."

"And where is the cottage?"

"Gartree Point."

Jack blew out his cheeks. Gartree Cottage. How could he forget the cottage. It was a place of death. The execution cottage, he'd called it. How many men had he watched Seamus kill there?

Seamus's voice cut into his thoughts. "Come on Jack, no time to dream, let's go. As I said there is work to do. Trust me Jack I know what I'm doing."

Jack slipped into the driving seat and turned the ignition key. He didn't want to go the Gartree cottage. He'd rather be at home with his mangy chickens and a warm Daisy.

Too fucking late.

*

Mary heard a car pull up outside the cottage. She rushed to a window. No patrol car, just a beaten up old blue Honda. Her heart sank. She recognised the car - Jack Docherty. Seamus was gathering his most trusted lieutenants around him. She heard their footsteps on the gravel path and braced herself.

Seamus was the first through the door. His look told her everything. "They've agreed to pay the ransom," she said, forcing a smile.

"That they have." He moved into the room followed by Docherty.

Docherty smiled at Mary. She hadn't changed since he'd last seen her – still beautiful. If he'd been the sort he'd have lusted after her, but Daisy was good enough for him. "Hello me lovely," he said, giving her a gentle peck on a cheek "You look as stunning as ever."

Mary thought he was exaggerating a bit. She wore no makeup and she hadn't brushed her hair. Her clothes were showing signs of needing a wash and thank the Lord he couldn't see her underwear! "Thanks Jack, but I think I've looked better."

There was a roar from the sofa. "What the fuck!" Seamus was pointing at Fitzpatrick "What have you done?" He shouted at Mary.

Mary had prepared herself for the outburst – rehearsed her reply. There was no way Seamus was going to intimidate her – "those days are over," she'd told herself. She put her hands on her hips and walked towards Seamus until she was inches from his face. She could see the anger in his eyes, but she didn't flinch. "All I've done is given him water, washed his face and tried to comb his hair, poor sod. And unless I'm a complete fucking idiot you want him alive don't you? He can't live on air." Mary was warming to her task. "I'll tell you something. If you don't look after him better he'll be dead before you know it. I don't give a shit what happens to him after you get the money, but sure as hell you won't get a fucking penny if you deliver him dead. Use your brain Seamus – control your hatred – look after him for Christ fucking sake! You're looking at a package worth a million."

Seamus took a step back. He was not used to women talking to him like that. This was a Mary he had never seen and he didn't like it. He wanted to knock her to the ground – hurt her – make sure she knew she couldn't fuck with Seamus Flanagan. But it wasn't the time – that could come later. He glared at her – ran a hand through his hair and pointed at James. "I knew you were going soft woman. He'll live long enough. How dare you interfere and try to tell me what to do. I'm in control here – I make the decisions, and don't you forget it."

Mary gave him a stare which even made Seamus flinch as she poked his stomach with a finger. "Listen up. I don't care a stuff for this man. The sooner he dies after you get the money the better, and if you want me to pull the trigger that's fine by me, but he's dying Seamus and I won't stand by and watch our million quid disappear just because of your stupidity."

"No one calls me stupid," Seamus bellowed, clenching his fists.

Docherty stepped between the two. "No, Seamus leave it be. Mary talks sense. We must have Fitzpatrick alive for a little longer and by the look of him, lying on that stinking sofa, I'd say it was about fifty-fifty. The rest of us won't be too happy if you fuck this up."

Seamus glared at Docherty, but unclenched his fists. "I won't forget this," he shot at Mary, shoving her aside. She knew he was fighting his demons. She also knew she'd won a small, but significant victory.

Seamus walked up to Docherty and lightly boxed an ear. "It's not for you to tell me what to do Jack, but this time I will go along with you." He turned to Mary. "Okay, keep the little shit alive, but don't expect any help from me. If he dies before we get the money then I know who to blame."

Mary exchanged a glance with Docherty. It was not the look of a man who hung on every word Seamus uttered. It surprised her. She watched the three men walk into the kitchen and some of her tension eased. With luck James would live a few more hours. That would give her valuable time. But could she really save his life? Would it be kinder to end his life now? A cushion over his face and his agony would be over and Seamus would not get his million. No! She mustn't be so negative – any thoughts like that must be banished from her mind. There had to be hope and the thought was growing on her that there might be an ally in the camp. Why she thought this she wasn't too sure, but there had been a sign and she had little else to hang on to. The police had not arrived. "Never ever expect help from a Priest," her father had advised her. For once he'd been right. She angrily wiped away the threat of a tear and turned to look at James.

*

Mary was kneeling beside James. The three men were in the kitchen, no doubt swilling back Guinness. She heard laughter and shivered. Were they laughing at Fitzpatrick's suffering? Were they already celebrating the death of two men? Fucking psychopaths. Not for the first time she wondered how she'd been sucked into their way of life. *Animals the lot of you*. She fought to close her ears to the laughter and reached for one of James's hands. It was cold and clammy. *Like, when you're dead*. "James," she said urgently, squeezing his hand. She was rewarded by a weak smile. "Thank God," she exclaimed reaching for the glass of water on the floor. She put the glass to his lips. "I'm still your friend whatever you might have just heard. We have a chance. You must believe me and always do as I say. It's a shit of a mess, but have hope. Please have hope. I will not let you die." It was a lie. And by the look that spread across James's ravaged face he did not believe her. He struggled to sit up. "No, stay as you are. Don't waste the last of your energy. You might soon need it."

"Thank you," croaked James, forcing a smile through his cracked lips.

Mary said nothing. She heard the kitchen door open and turned to see Docherty. Was that a frown on his face? Could she dare hope that perhaps he was sick of the gloating at the impending death of an innocent man? His closeness to Seamus over the years said otherwise. He moved towards her, patted her shoulder. "Need fresh air. Not too sure about any of this," he confided through clenched teeth. He threw a weak smile and headed towards the front door.

Mary took a deep breath. *I'm not deluding myself.*

Thirty-Two

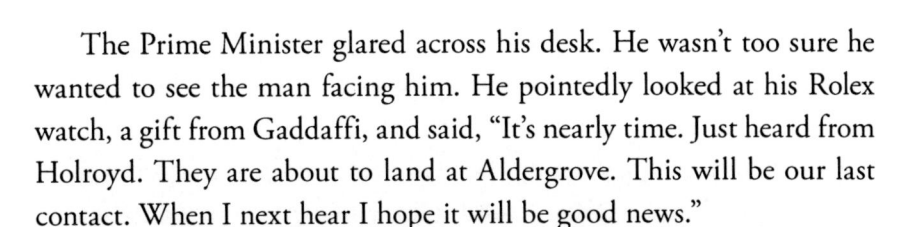

The Prime Minister glared across his desk. He wasn't too sure he wanted to see the man facing him. He pointedly looked at his Rolex watch, a gift from Gaddaffi, and said, "It's nearly time. Just heard from Holroyd. They are about to land at Aldergrove. This will be our last contact. When I next hear I hope it will be good news."

The Secretary of State for Northern Ireland made no attempt to hide his anger. "And if not what are you going to do about it? You know this is a hidden time bomb for our government. You should never have given the green light to the operation in the first place. I told you it would blow up in our faces, but did you listen, did you fuck! "No, no David I know what I'm doing. I have built a fire-wall around us," you confidently assured me. What rubbish. Has there ever been a fire-wall that the media can't get through? Do you not think that somewhere in a department there is a turd just waiting to take money for information? You may well say that no one, apart from a few select people, who you trust, have any idea of this operation. You delude yourself man. Somewhere someone, who you call a trustworthy friend, can smell money. Then the dam will burst and the media will dig and dig until there snotty little noses find out about your covert operation which has led to the kidnap. And if my hunch is right, the likely death of at least two men. You won't survive Prime Minister and I will be the first to laugh."

"And hope to step into my shoes David," The Prime Minister said to his erstwhile friend.

The Secretary of State leant across the walnut desk and laughed.

The Britain-Norman Islander dropped through the low cloud and landed at Aldergrove. It was directed to an isolated spot where Charlie O'Malley and George Russell sat in a Grand Cherokee Jeep. Both men were nervous – both were strung like a piano wire. They waited until the fuselage door swung open before exiting the warmth of the car. The cold air hit them. They hunkered down in their overcoats and walked in trepidation towards the plane. From whatever angle they had looked at it they knew they would probably be in for a rough ride. Tim had alerted them that Rachel Fitzpatrick would not be easy. As soon as the steps were in place they ran up them and entered the warm cabin. Tim met them, looking anxious. "Good to see you. Let me introduce you to Mr and Mrs Fitzpatrick."

Richard stepped forward and shook hands. Rachel kept her hands by her side.

"I think we should get away from here as quickly as possible," Charlie advised, breaking eye contact with Rachel. "All formalities have been dealt with and hopefully no one knows it's you who have landed. We don't want to risk alerting our enemies."

"You mean Flanagan," Rachel said tersely.

Charlie nodded and quickly moved on. "I have arranged for you to stay with the Healys at Brascome."

"Where James and Henry were going to stay?" Rachel asked.

"Yes. It's away from Belfast. You will be safer there."

"Safer Inspector? What are you suggesting?"

"I'm covering all angles. I don't want to put you in any more danger than necessary."

Rachel gave a bitter laugh. "Come on Inspector of course we're in danger. We are under no illusions that Richard is about to risk his life, and I'm sure this man Flanagan would love to see us both dead. He has reason as we all know. It's personal."

"You're a very switched on lady," George said, immediately regretting opening his mouth.

"And I think you are being patronising," Rachel spat back.

Richard moved swiftly, taking her hand and leading her towards the door. "I think we should be on our way darling, like the Inspector says."

Rachel gave him a weak smile and said quietly, "I don't like that man."

"No need to like me Mrs Fitzpatrick," George said, having over heard her. "But I'm doing my best to make amends for being part of something that has led to this dreadful situation. I will do everything to get your son back alive."

"Well that's something I suppose," Rachel conceded. "But I can't forgive you."

Once their luggage and the brief case, which contained the money, were locked into the boot Charlie opened the rear door. The interior had grown cold and Rachel moved close to Richard as they slid into the back. George road shotgun with O'Malley and Tim squeezed in beside Richard. An uneasy silence settled on them.

Rachel reached for Richard's hand. It was not how she thought they would be returning to Northern Ireland. She fought back the tears – something she was getting good at and squeezed his hand hard. She knew how he was feeling – like her, desperate. Their store of hope needed replenishing and it seemed that the bucket was nearly empty.

Tim broke the silence, turning to the couple and saying, "The Healy's are ready for us and security is tight. Everything has been done that can be done."

For a second no one said a word and then Rachel erupted. "This man," she pointed at George's back, "is the one I want to hear more from."

George cleared his throat – this was what he had dreaded from the moment he'd got into the Jeep and been driven to the airport. The truth was it was all very well glibly saying he was doing his best to get James Fitzpatrick back alive but he had no leads. His dilemma was whether he told the Fitzpatrick's this or lied. He decided to lie would raise false hopes and he reckoned the Fitzpatrick's would prefer to hear the truth, however painful. He half turned and said, "I'm afraid we have no leads as to the whereabouts of your son. I don't know whether Tim has told you a bit about me?"

"I know you're trouble and a man without compassion," Rachel said.

"Not true!" George wanted to shout but said, "Very well. For two years I was undercover at the height of the Troubles. Before my cover was blown I built up a chain of very reliable informants. I had hoped that a few of them were still around and could find out the location where James was being held. To my dismay I have drawn a blank. Either there is no word about or fear has stopped anyone coming forward. It seems lips are sealed. The one person I thought might help is dead. He had become a risk. I think his loyalties were elsewhere." George heard Rachel's sharp intake of breath and quickly carried on. If he explained O'Riordan's demise she would only think he was a butcher as well as lacking compassion. "One thing we do know is that a group calling themselves 'Freedom for Ireland' are behind the kidnap."

"We know that already. So what you're saying is that you haven't a hope in hell of finding my son," Rachel stated.

"We are leaving no stone unturned," Charlie promised her. "The whole Irish police force is on the alert."

"And this group are led by Seamus Flanagan," interrupted Richard.

"Yes, and I believe you know of him" said George.

"He featured in several reports that I received from MI6 when I was in office. They had him down as a psychopath."

George said," He might well be, but his aides are not so violent. Their main aim will be to get the money, not to kill your son. They may be able to exert some restraint. If lucky there might be a falling out. They don't want to put themselves in any more danger than they are already, because they have plans. They want to purchase arms from Iran and cause mayhem, hopefully leading to the collapse of Stormont.

They won't like this personal side that has crept in. Your son does stand a chance."

"A chance!" cried Rachel, burying her head in her hands.

George said nothing.

A tense silence returned, wrapping its arms around the four occupants of the car. Rachael stared out of her window at the wet tarmac and Richard bit at a finger nail. There was nothing more to be said.

*

George's hope that they had landed in Belfast unnoticed was a dream. No sooner had the plane's wheels touched the wet tarmac than one of the ground crew on duty was speaking on his mobile. Within half-an-hour Seamus was delivered a message. An hour later it was confirmed that the party had arrived at Brascome. In a few days the ground crewman would receive a wad of notes. There was nothing like money to keep people loyal.

"The mother has come as well," Seamus informed Declan. "And do you fucking know something boy? It's a chance to eliminate the whole family."

Declan smiled and reached for the glass of Bushmills, which these days was never far from his lips. "Good; looks as if I might be useful again and not just a fucking nanny."

Seamus was not slow to notice the slurred voice. Drunken comrades were a risk. And Docherty gave an inner smile. Just maybe Declan wasn't as dangerous as he first thought. He'd make sure there was a regular supply of Bushmills available. An inebriated thug was no different to any other drunkard. Slow reflexes and a scrambled brain. Not the best scenario if you needed to pull a gun and aim straight. He gave Mary a meaningful stare.

*

They were sitting around the oak table in Brascome's rather austere dining room. A large fire was burning in the grate – the only means of warming the room – Duff did not believe in turning on the central heating until his guests' teeth were chattering. On the table was a large steaming hot chicken pie and in spite of the mood everyone was eating – they hadn't had a meal since leaving Southampton and Meg's pie was something to be savoured.

Charlie ate slowly, studying the Fitzpatricks from under his large eyebrows. He wondered how they were bearing up – wondered if they had already accepted that the chance of their son living was about nil. He'd come into contact with Richard Fitzpatrick when he'd been Secretary of State and although he did not know him well his reputation as a fair man went before him. He didn't deserve to be in this situation. He would be hurting – ghosts from the past would be dancing in front of his eyes. Charlie knew how much his father's death had shaped his future. And Rachel? Well for sure she was a fighter and she would not just sit back and allow him or George to run the agenda without wanting her say. Devastation was written all over her face and from experience Charlie knew desperate people could do desperate things. He wondered how much influence she had over her husband. He waited a few minutes until everyone's plate was cleared and said, "I think it is time for me to carry on where George left off."

"That's sounds a good idea," said Rachel, a note of sarcasm in her voice.

He's not going to find it any easier than I did, thought George.

Charlie took a sip of water – his throat was dry and when he spoke it wasn't the usual confident Charlie O'Malley. He addressed himself direct to Rachel. "We have" – he glanced at his watch – "still a few hours before we are contacted with orders as to where to drop the money. I have to tell you Mrs Fitzpatrick that this is the tricky bit. We have no way of knowing if your son is still alive, but it is a reasonable assumption that he is. Flanagan knows he won't get the money if he kills your son. But that doesn't mean he hasn't got evil plans. I'm sorry to have to say

Love Thine Enemy

this, but I don't want to lie to you. We are going into the swap blind. Not a situation I'm happy with but we have no other option. I'm afraid Flanagan holds all the aces. We cannot risk having backup or have myself or George with your husband. He will have to do this alone. And just to make matters worse Flanagan is not the sort of person to keep his word."

"So he might have plans to kill both my son and husband. Is that what you're saying?" Rachel asked.

Charlie looked down at his empty plate. "That is a possibility."

"Look at me inspector," Rachel demanded. "How likely is this?"

Charlie looked into her eyes. "I can't answer that, but we must be prepared for anything."

When Rachel next spoke her voice was firm. There were no tears. "I think Inspector we are all realists in this room. James's chances are small; as I fear are my husband's. But thank you for your frankness and I know you will try and save their lives. That's all I can expect."

This woman is strong and brave. Charlie was sure he'd have completely broken up if it was one of his children in such terrible danger. One of the reasons I have never married, he reminded himself.

"So how do we precede Inspector?" Richard asked.

"For the moment we have to wait. There is still a faint hope that Russell may yet turn up something, but time is running out. You will have to trust me sir. I'm the one negotiating."

"Knowing you as I do Inspector I have confidence that you will do your best."

"And we all better start praying now," Rachel added.

*

Flanagan munched on an egg sandwich made by Mary. Egg yoke was running down his chin. Mary watched him in disgust. Declan was fiddling with a piece of buttered toast and gazing at the bottle of Bushmills that Seamus had removed from his grasp. Docherty was staring at Fitzpatrick. Mary wished she could read his thoughts. She moved to James's side feeling Seamus's eyes burning a hole in her back – but sod him.

"Feel like shit?" she asked.

James nodded.

"This is the day James – don't give up hope now. I'm going to get you out of this," she whispered.

His look said it all. He didn't believe a word she said. He was going to die.

Mary's heart missed a beat. It was odds on he'd be dead before the sun went down. Not for the first time she wished she could castrate Father Paul, the spineless little weasel. But she wasn't about to give up.

"I'm so tired," the voice croaked from the sofa.

Mary realised James was almost at the end of his tether, but there was nothing more she could say. But she could hope. She reached for one of James's hands and forced a smile. Don't give up."

"How can I believe you?" James managed to ask through cracked lips. He started to cough. His whole body shook. He closed his eyes. He hadn't the strength to say any more.

"I'm sorry, so sorry," Mary said, turning away with a heavy heart. She saw Seamus glaring at Docherty. Mary knew immediately the look spelt trouble. Declan was grinning from ear to ear. But Docherty was shaking his head. "No Seamus, we cannot go bursting into the hotel spraying bullets all over the fucking place. You might well kill the Fitzpatricks, but there is no guarantee you will find the money. Do you honestly believe that you will meet no opposition – there will be armed men everywhere. Don't underestimate the police. You don't stand a chance man. Come to your senses. And are you expecting to do this foolish raid with just your drunken friend here, myself and Mary as back-up?" He turned to look at Mary "What about you lovey – are you for or against Seamus on this one?"

Mary went to stand close to Docherty where she reckoned Seamus would be less likely to hit her. "You're daft Seamus. You're close to getting a million quid and you want to barge into Brascome and kill the Fitzpatricks. Jack is right; you're putting everything at risk just because of your hatred for these people. Come to your senses – get the money – buy your fucking arms and one day die a hero."

For a moment Seamus said nothing. Mary held her breath, and then his reaction surprised her. He nodded and said, "You're right girl, I'll get to kill two Fitzpatricks anyway. The woman will suffer for the rest of her life."

Mary swallowed. She wanted to throw herself at him – call him names – spit in his grinning face. But she knew she'd die. *Careful Mary, play along.* She forced a smile. "You'll kill them after you have the money?"

"That's my plan."

Mary wanted to shout, "Why Seamus, why? You will have got what you want. Why kill? Let them go Seamus. You just might live a little longer if you do." But that would have proved fatal. Instead she said, "Have it your own way."

Seamus shook his head. "That I will. They will die and that's the end of it."

"I think you're a fool," Docherty said.

Seamus walked towards him shaking with fury. He was not used to being talked to like this, not least by the man who he'd sculptured into an acolyte. He kicked at a chair and stabbed a finger in Docherty's chest. Docherty moved swiftly. "If you as much as lay a finger on me I will be tempted to kill you."

"Kill me Jack, kill me?" laughed Seamus.

By way of a reply Docherty pulled out his SIG 9mm from his waist band and saw surprise register on Seamus's face. "I always carry a gun, you should know that. And if your side kick makes one more move behind me I'll kill him as well."

Seamus didn't want to die and he knew enough about Docherty to know he wasn't bluffing. For the moment he had to accept defeat.

Docherty had the upper hand. This was a changed Docherty. He waved Declan away.

He stepped back – breathed in – felt his rage subside and raised his arms in surrender. "Okay we stick to the original plan. We can't fall out now. We are so close to success. So let's get moving."

Docherty lowered his gun. "Glad you've seen sense Seamus. No hard feelings?"

"None."

Mary knew he lied. Docherty had just signed his death warrant. Where and when was the only question.

Thirty-Three

The tension was getting to them all. Time was dragging. Charlie had left Brascome promising to ring as soon as he'd spoken to Flanagan. Rain lashed the windows. Duff was half way through a bottle of malt and Rachel was staring at the telephone. Richard was playing with the handle of the briefcase.

"Tea anyone?" asked Meg.

Three heads shook in unison. All minds were on one thing. When would the call come through?

Outside on the drive Tim was briefing Paul Carpenter and Phil Dashwood. Dan O'Connor sat behind the wheel of George's car cleaning his gun and waiting to get the order to move.

From inside Tim heard the telephone ring. He rushed back into the house. Richard was holding the receiver to his ear. Everyone was holding their breath. This was crunch time.

After what seemed an age Richard lowered the telephone back onto its stand and moved to Rachel's side. "It's time to move."

"Where to," asked Rachel.

"Police HQ. I'm to go there with Russell. O'Malley suggests that you and Tim stay here." He sensed Rachel was about to object. "No, darling, you must stay here. Please."

Rachel hunched her shoulders resignedly and nodded. There was an audible sigh of relief in the room. The tension eased a little.

*

In 10 Downing Street the Prime Minister sat alone in his office. It was going to be a trying day - one that would test his skills and he wasn't the most patient person in the world. He was due to meet the German chancellor just at the time that events could unravel in Belfast. Somehow he'd have to push thoughts of Fitzpatrick to the back of his mind. Not easy when the whole bloody thing could implode in his face. He had never been a man to take risks but sure as hell he'd taken one this time, and in spite of Holroyd's assurances that the flack would never touch him, he was wracked with doubt.

He heard a telephone ring in the adjoining room– he jumped – looked at his watch and relaxed. Stupid fool, there was three hours to go before any news would come through. He would really have to pull himself together. The meeting was far more important for the country than a kidnapping, although not so newsworthy. The whole financial structure of Europe was at stake. He gave a rueful smile. "Get your priorities right," he said out loud. "Saving the nation from bankruptcy is a vote winner. But wasn't that a bit callous? Sure it was, but sadly that was how things worked out every now and then. He gave a long sigh and gave up the struggle. James Fitzpatrick must be firmly pushed to the back of his mind.

*

Seamus felt surprisingly uneasy. Whether it was because of Docherty's shitty behaviour he wasn't too sure, but something was worrying him and when that happened he needed to take action. The telephone call had gone well, maybe too well? Was it that that was bothering him? There was still time for things to unravel. Like some rat at this final hour informing the police where he was holding Fitzpatrick. *You're becoming paranoiac* he told himself, but still the scent of danger was tickling his nostrils. Time to move – now! Not far to go. An ideal spot. He could have men hidden in every corner. If Fitzpatrick didn't come alone he'd know within seconds. But he was pretty sure Fitzpatrick wouldn't take any risks. And once the money had been handed over and the son produced? Bang! His men would open fire. No one would leave alive. *So Jack fucking Docherty enjoy your last few hours on earth.* Who was that prick Docherty to question his motives? Freedom for Ireland' would have money to buy arms and explosives and there would be no more male Fitzpatricks to carry on the line. He held the upper hand, no doubt about it. Yet something was bugging him. He shook his head, what fucking nonsense, he'd planned meticulously and it was far too late for anything to go wrong. It was just nerves. This was the biggest operation he'd undertaken in his glorious career and if it went according to plan he'd be the toast of the dissident movement. He smiled. He'd like that. He wanted his name to be on everyone's lips after he died - the man who single handily had wrecked the peace accord. He slapped his thighs and kicked at the sofa where James lay. "Time to go British bastard." He shouted for Mary and Docherty. "We're on our way."

"Where to?" Mary asked.

Seamus beamed at her. "We're going to the old Langford Lodge airbase. The owners seldom come there. There are two model flying clubs that use it at weekends so we are safe there for the moment and there are open spaces. We will use the old Control Tower – a good place to see any enemy activity. My men will be with us ready to kill the Fitzpatricks."

Mary gasped.

Seamus fixed her with an icy stare. "You have a problem with that?"

"No, no of course not."

"Good. As soon as the money is in my hands and I have handed back the little shit they will open fire. End of the Fitzpatricks!"

Mary could swear he was salivating.

"What a plan," slurred Declan, already well lubricated.

Seamus pointed a finger at Docherty. "Well Jack, what are you going to say to that?"

Jack knew he was on dangerous ground and it was not the time to disagree. In this mood Seamus was like a cobra. Strike fast. Kill. And although Jack suspected that Seamus had already decided his fate he at least wanted a chance to survive. So he clapped his hands – made a vow never to have his SIG 9mm far from his side and said, "You're a rare one Seamus, I would never have thought of that. I take back what I said earlier – You're a genius."

"And you girl?" Seamus asked, with what had become his familiar smirk whenever he asked her a question.

Mary said, "You're the leader."

"So that's settled. Let's make a move. Take your personal belongings. We won't be coming back here. We'll be bedded down in a safe house before O'Malley knows what has happened. No time to alert the Air Support Unit and no time to put up road blocks. We will disappear for as long as it takes for the flack to die down."

"That could take a long time," Mary pointed out.

"The price of success."

"I've never been to the old airbase," Jack said.

"It's about twenty minutes from here on the eastern shores of Lough Neagh," Seamus said. "There is a small lane that will take us there. At this time of the year there is hardly a soul about. The only attraction is the Lough and in weather like this it is pretty inhospitable. The one problem is that it is a dead area for mobiles, but I will go to just outside Crumlin where there is no problem and ring from there."

Mary turned cold. Her options were fast running out. Not that she'd had many in the first place. It was beginning to look very bad for James. She gritted her teeth, determined not to lose all hope. She said, "We will have to carry Fitzpatrick to the car."

"We'll drag him if necessary," laughed Seamus. "Now, no time for a Florence Nightingale act girl, just get your arse into gear." Then adding, "Time to kiss your boy friend good bye."

Mary said nothing, but if she'd ever had any doubt left about the choice she was making Seamus had just eliminated it.

*

Dan O'Connor screeched to a halt outside police HQ. Traffic had been heavy and they were running late. He leapt out of the car, shouting to the other two occupants to follow him. He ignored the desk sergeant's shout and ran up the stairs. Charlie was standing at the top. He clasped Richard's hand in a vice-like grip. He nodded a welcome at George. He pointed to a door. "We can talk in there."

They moved into a small office – no window and no heating turned on. Charlie pointed to two chairs. "I prefer to stand," Richard said George nodded in agreement. O'Connor did the same.

"Very well. As I told you on the telephone we are waiting for Flanagan to contact us about the location where you must take the money." Charlie didn't add that the time was already up and he was getting nervous. "I've been told that you must go on your own sir," said reluctantly. "But it's what we expected. However, I will have an unmarked car standing by in the hope that I can follow you undetected. It's dangerous, but I think worth the risk."

"Not worth the risk Inspector," Richard advised. "If the boot was on the other foot I would have someone watching this station for just such a move. My best chance of survival is for you to do nothing. It stinks I know, but as you said back at Brascome Flanagan has us by the throat. The worse thing we can do is to antagonise him further."

Charlie shrugged in agreement. He didn't like it but he had to admit Fitzpatrick was right.

"Well at least take a mobile."

"No mobile."

Charlie raised a hand in frustration, but before he could speak George interrupted. Charlie and Richard turned to look at him. "You have something to say? Charlie asked.

"I have an idea. Carpenter and Dashwood could travel in the car."

"Are you saying they will be invisible?"

"They will be in the boot."

"Locked in it" Charlie said with a touch of sarcasm.

"No, one of them will hold the boot open – done it before – a piece of string works wonders. They will stay there if everything goes to plan." He pointed at Richard. "But if things go badly at least you sir, will stand a chance."

Richard said, "I'm grateful to you both for thinking of my safety, but sorry, as I've just said I'm going to insist I go in alone. We can't risk James's life any more than it is already. If we both die that is a gamble I must take, but I don't think a load of you skulking around will in anyway help us to survive."

George raised an eyebrow towards Dan O'Connor. He was tempted to say that his men were not skulkers; they were well trained for just this sort of operation. He looked across at Charlie and shrugged. "I must accept your decision sir. It's your life on the line."

But Charlie decided to try again. "We could put an electronic tag in the briefcase. That way we would at least be able to track them after the swap."

"Okay, do that, if you think it won't be found," Richard agreed.

"You could wear a bullet proof vest," Charlie advised.

"If that's what you would like I agree, though if they start shooting I suspect my head will be the target."

Charlie nodded. "Probably, but some sort of protection. So let's get you fitted up and we'll see if we can hide the bug. Not much time left." He looked at O'Connor – his face was blank. Charlie suspected that like him, he already had decided that the day was going to turn out to be a disaster. A colleague had once said to him, "You're the most pessimistic person I've ever come across."

*

Mary stepped out of the cottage door and stared at the black Range Rover. Where the hell had that come from?

Jack saw her surprise. "Declan nicked it last night."

"I wanted something fast and reliable," Seamus added.

"Bit obvious though," Mary stated.

"Once we've made our getaway and arrived at our destination Declan will dump it. And the police have no idea what type of car I will be driving. I'm confident that we will be one step ahead of them and been long gone before they have time to set up road blocks and alert the airports and ports."

"Gone where?" Mary asked.

"You'll soon find out."

Mary said nothing. But she felt a cold hand running down her spine.

*Sea*mus rubbed his hands together. "Come on then let's get a fucking move on. I've a call to make to O'Malley. Everything loaded?"

"All except our cargo," Declan said.

"Mustn't leave him behind must we," laughed Seamus. "Blindfold the fucking shit and bring him out."

"I'll get him," Mary said quickly.

Seamus glared at her. "No you won't girl. You go Declan."

The atmosphere was electric as they waited for Declan. Mary stared at the front door wondering if she could get past Seamus before he stopped her. Seamus seemed to sense this and moved to block her way. He shook his head at her but said nothing. He didn't need to. She turned to Jack, her eyes begging for help, but Jack shook his head. *Fuck you!* She was shaking, hyperventilating – she thought she was going to faint. She swayed, shook her head to clear it and was about to launch herself at Seamus when Declan appeared dragging James by his feet. "No!" she screamed, but some invisible force anchored her to the ground. It was as if her feet were buried in concrete. All she could do was stare in horror, hearing James groan as his back scrapped along the gravel path. His eyes caught hers and the look said it all. *I knew I couldn't trust you.*

"You can, you can," she wanted to shout. But she knew he wouldn't believe her. She felt the bile rise in her throat, but somehow she managed not to vomit. It would give Seamus pleasure and he was already enjoying watching a man suffer. She heard a voice behind her – it was Jack saying in a voice meant only for her ears, "bastard."

Declan threw a questioning look at Seamus, who pointed to the Range Rover. "On the back seat."

Declan bent down and heaved James onto his shoulders – carried him the few yards to the Range Rover and said to Mary, "open a door."

Jack moved quickly. "I'll do it," he said. Declan dumped James onto the back seat and slammed the door. "Fucking stinks," he said rubbing his hands on his trousers.

Mary threw a look of thanks at Jack and chose to say nothing.

"Right then," Seamus said. "Job done. You follow us Jack."

Jack made for the Honda. He gunned the engine which groaned, but as usual started without a second turn of the ignition key. He had a soft spot for the old car, it had served him well and he had resisted the temptation to put it on the scrap heap and buy a new one. He didn't go far these days. He waited until Seamus was on the move and then tucked himself in behind the Range Rover. "Don't let me down," he said, tapping the steering wheel lovingly, and pressing down on the accelerator. The Honda coughed - Jack smiled – it was a sign that all was well – for the moment at least.

As he drove he had time to reflect on the events in the cottage and in particular Seamus. The man had changed for sure. His veracious appetite for violence had escalated. What did he expect? Seamus had always been a killer, and had never shown any respect for other people's lives. Maybe I'm growing soft in my old age, thought Jack. "You're no bloody saint yourself," Seamus had reminded him. But that was when we were at war, he thought. To Seamus the war was not over and that was the difference between the two of them. He'd always hated indiscriminate killing. To kill James Fitzpatrick could not be justified. He gave a rueful smile. For fuck sake what was he becoming, a man with a conscience? Pull the other one mate. *Jack Docherty, my old friend, you're just looking for absolution.* But of one thing he was sure, he no longer wanted anything to do with Seamus. Daisy was right; the man was out of control. But if Seamus knew what was going through his mind he'd be a dead before he could blink.

The Honda coughed again – he was pushing it too hard, but he had no choice. If he slowed he'd lose the Range Rover. If he kept up this speed he might break down. He raised his eyes to the heavens and sent up a silent prayer. The engine changed tone and Jack knew there was still life in the old bucket. He saw the brake lights of the Rover and watched Seamus turn right. He followed into the lane, nearly running into the back of the Rover as it slowed to make sure he was still behind. His hands were clammy on the wheel – he knew what he had to do. He was pretty sure he'd have Mary on his side, but that made it no less dangerous. He shook his head in amazement. What on earth was Jack Docherty becoming? Willing to risk his life to save a Brit? He swallowed – spat onto the floor and burst out laughing. His old friends would think he was joking.

Thirty-Four

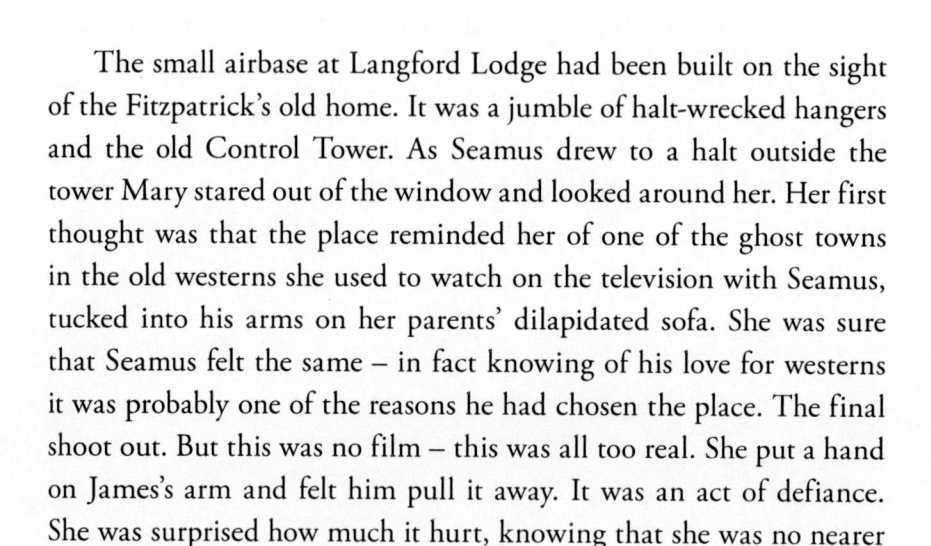

The small airbase at Langford Lodge had been built on the sight of the Fitzpatrick's old home. It was a jumble of halt-wrecked hangers and the old Control Tower. As Seamus drew to a halt outside the tower Mary stared out of the window and looked around her. Her first thought was that the place reminded her of one of the ghost towns in the old westerns she used to watch on the television with Seamus, tucked into his arms on her parents' dilapidated sofa. She was sure that Seamus felt the same – in fact knowing of his love for westerns it was probably one of the reasons he had chosen the place. The final shoot out. But this was no film – this was all too real. She put a hand on James's arm and felt him pull it away. It was an act of defiance. She was surprised how much it hurt, knowing that she was no nearer being trusted. She tried to smile at him – he blinked and turned his head away.

"Out," Seamus ordered, turning to look at Declan. "Get the body into the tower. Dump him on the ground floor. The second floor we will use as a look-out post. I'll drive the Rover around the back. You follow me Jack."

Declan took James by the feet and was about to drag him out of the Rover when Mary leapt forward. "No!" said urgently. "He'll die if his head hits the ground. You take his legs I'll take his shoulders."

Declan didn't bother to argue. "Please yourself Mary, but the bastards going to die anyway."

Mary gritted her teeth. "But he must be alive when his father gets here you idiot."

Declan glared at her – grunted in his usual way and ignored her, thinking that Seamus should get rid of her. She was getting an uppity cow. He tried to move James before Mary could put her arms under his shoulders, but she was quick and although she couldn't hold him, she at least managed to break his fall. Declan started to pull James along the tarmac. Mary did her best to put her hands under his head, just managing to keep it from scraping along the hard surface. Declan saw what she was doing and increased his pace but Mary was up to the move and kept her hands under James's head. It was painful – her arms ached – her head felt as if it was going to burst – she was bent almost double and her shoes slid on the wet surface. But she made it. Once inside Declan dropped James's legs and grinned at Mary. "Enjoy that did you? Saved him for me later."

Mary glared back. Declan was trash – a drunk piece of trash. "Go piss yourself," she shouted after him as he shuffled away, leaving James lying on the concrete floor. Declan gave her two fingers and kept walking.

Immediately Mary dropped down beside James. He was already shivering – the control tower was damp and cold. The windows were open to the elements and a cold wind was whistling through them. There were signs that the flying clubs used the tower. A ping-pong table sat in one corner. A small white ball lay against the net. Three trestle tables lined one wall. An old rusty kettle rested on one of them, along with several multi-coloured mugs. Two waste bins were upturned on the floor and a pair of dirty trainers lay beside them. None of these items were any use for keeping out the biting cold and Mary knew she needed something to cover James's shaking body.

She put her mouth close to James's ear. "I know what you're thinking, but you are wrong. Please, please believe that. I'm on your side I swear, but my options are very limited. I'm your only hope James, so don't try and fight me."

But James didn't seem to be listening. He started to cough violently, a moist chesty cough, and Mary feared he was close to pneumonia, if he wasn't afflicted already. She gripped his arm and this time he made no attempt to pull away. She put both hands on his head and tried again. "I still have hope. You must hang in there James. We are not beaten yet."

James's eyes closed and for one terrible moment Mary once again thought he'd died, but he coughed and she let out a sigh of relief. And then the thought that she'd had back in the cottage returned. Kill him now – put him out of his misery and Seamus would not get his hands on the money. She shook her head, shit where was she coming from - what was she thinking? If there was only the smallest hope this man had to be given it. He deserved to get another chance at life – a life full of happiness with a wife, children and no Seamus – especially no arsehole Seamus. Despite the cold eating into her body she took off her thick coat and put it over James's shoulders – inadequate but the best she could do. His eyes flicked open and he raised a hand. Mary took it and squeezed. She would have liked to have lifted him off the concrete, but there was nowhere soft or warmer to take him.

"Thank you," she heard him whisper and tears filled her eyes. He'd heard her. Perhaps he believed her. *Oh you soft stupid cunt.*

She heard Seamus and Docherty walk into the hanger and stood up not wishing to give Seamus the opportunity to aim another arrow at her – she might well flip and the consequences would not help James. She said, "I thought you'd gone Seamus. You better be quick. This man won't live much longer." It gave her some pleasure to see a flicker of panic in his eyes.

Jack said, "There's a flask of tea in the Rover Seamus. Mary's right. Must keep this piece of shit alive for a while longer. I'll go and get it."

Seamus frowned, but made no move to stop him. He turned to Mary. "I'm on my way. Make sure you give a warm welcome to my men when they arrive. Declan knows what my orders are."

"How many are you expecting?"

"Four of the best."

Mary's heart sank. The odds were stacking up against her. She swore under her breath. She nodded and said, "That should be enough to kill Richard Fitzpatrick and anyone who comes with him."

Seamus said, "He will come alone. No doubt about it."

Mary feared he was right. What a man will do to save a son, she thought, wondering how she would react in the same situation. She watched Docherty walk back into the room and moved to take the thermos off him. As she reached for it Docherty grabbed her hand and pulled her close, "Be ready," he whispered, and then quickly dropped her hand.

Her eyes widened but she said nothing. Excitement coursed through her veins. Her gut feeling had been right. She did have an ally. She walked towards James with a little piece of hope knocking at her heart. She dared to dream.

Seamus watched Mary putting the mug of tea to Fitzpatrick's lips. "No!" he shouted as he lunged at the mug, knocking it out of Mary's hand, the tea spilling onto the floor. Mary reeled back. Seamus laughed. "Let him lick the liquid off the floor."

Mary swung round, fists clenched, ready to launch herself at Seamus, but a voice in her head was saying, *leave it, leave it.* "I should have thought of that," she managed to say and to reinforce the remark she kicked the mug across the floor and stood over James. "Did you hear that scum? If you want a drink lick it off the floor." She stepped away and stared at Seamus. He was laughing. Mary breathed easier.

Seamus turned to Jack. His voice was menacing as he spoke. "Guard Fitzpatrick well Jack until I return. Your life depends on it. My men will be here soon." He moved to kiss Mary. She had a split second to decide what to do. She moved into the kiss. A man's life depended on her. Seamus licked his lips, leered at Mary and turned to walk out of the Control Tower.

Mary watched him go, wiping her mouth with a sleeve. She felt sick. "Jesus!" she exploded. "I was so tempted to kick the shit out of him. What now?"

"It means it's now or never," Docherty said.

*

Rachel thought she was close to screaming. The ticking of the carriage clock, sitting on the mantle piece of the Brascome drawing room, and the constant tap-tap of Meg's nails on a table were getting on her nerves. Every second that passed was taking her closer to the climax of her suffering. She wasn't sure she could take much more of the suspense. It would have been easy to collapse into a heap, gibbering with fear, but she was determined to be strong for Richard. Nevertheless, it didn't make the approaching scenario any less terrifying. Was Richard going to see his son killed and then shot down himself? Was she about to lose the men most close to her heart? She felt trapped in this large rather depressing house, staring at the three other occupants sitting around her, casting sympathetic glances at her every now and then. She wanted to be alone but hadn't the heart to shout, "Get out!" It was not their fault – they were all under the same pressure, and they thought they were being kind. She tried to put her hands over her ears to cut out the noise. She tried to take slow deep breaths, but to no avail. She finally leapt out of her chair and announced, "I'm going for a walk."

"I would rather you didn't," Tim said.

"Why on earth not?"

"Because we can't be sure we are not being watched."

"Oh for God sake Tim, don't be so melodramatic. Who on earth would be watching us?"

Tim looked at her – he felt her pain but…"I'm sorry."

Rachel collapsed back in her chair. The reality of the situation dawning on her. These people would no doubt like to kill her as well. "Of course, silly of me," she said. Then adding, "Christ Tim, are these people everywhere?"

"We can't be sure Rachel, that's what I'm saying. So, having taken all these precautions to keep you out of danger, I would much rather you didn't go outside for the time being."

"Even with your two men outside?"

"Yes."

Rachel once again looked at the clock. It was taking on demonic features. "I think I'm going mad, "she said in an unsteady voice.

*

Seamus turned the ignition key of the Range Rover engine. His hands were shaking. He was not happy at leaving the air base, but he had no choice. No signal on his mobile meant he had to go where there was one. But he felt uneasy and he couldn't put a finger on it. Was it doubt about Mary, Docherty, maybe even Declan? Before driving off he took a few moments to consider the possibility that one of them had turned. Declan? No way. Docherty? It might be on his mind, but he hadn't the balls. Mary? Ah maybe. She'd changed no doubt. Become bolder, argumentative and less receptive in bed. Was it possible that she had formed feelings for the English turd? *No, no Seamus, she's loyal to you.* But maybe it was time to wipe the slate clean. No one was indispensable. There were plenty of young women out there to amuse himself with. What woman would not willingly go to his bed? He was Seamus Flanagan for fuck sake. There were still sober men, though he had to admit not as many as there had been, still happy to serve him without asking questions. He allowed himself a smile. The solution was staring him in the face. He'd see to it just as soon as he had the money in his hands. He hunched his shoulders and gripped the steering wheel. He pulled away from the back of the Control Tower noticing that the clock on the dashboard was showing ten minutes to twelve. It was nearly time. He pulled out onto the lane and increased his speed. A surge of excitement hit him. All his planning was falling into place like a jigsaw puzzle. Only the final piece had to be slotted in and then he could sit back and admire his work. He slammed his hands on the steering wheel, started to hum the British National Anthem. No one could accuse Seamus Flanagan of not having a sense of humour, even in moments of stress.

As he reached the outskirts of Crumlin he slowed down, his eyes darting every now and then to the rear view mirror. He wanted to make sure he was not being followed. Unlikely, but he never took chances. He didn't have far to go now. Through Crumlin, up the high street and out into open country. There was a lay-by not far out. The call would not take long. Then he'd wait for confirmation from his man outside the police station that Fitzpatrick was on the move alone or not. It would be a nerve wracking wait.

Thirty-Five

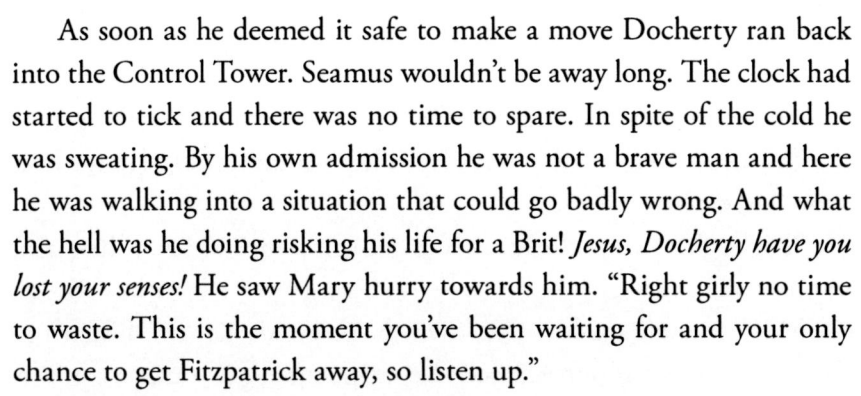

As soon as he deemed it safe to make a move Docherty ran back into the Control Tower. Seamus wouldn't be away long. The clock had started to tick and there was no time to spare. In spite of the cold he was sweating. By his own admission he was not a brave man and here he was walking into a situation that could go badly wrong. And what the hell was he doing risking his life for a Brit! *Jesus, Docherty have you lost your senses!* He saw Mary hurry towards him. "Right girly no time to waste. This is the moment you've been waiting for and your only chance to get Fitzpatrick away, so listen up."

Mary froze, every nerve sizzling. "Do you mean…"

Jack cut her short. "If we're lucky, yes."

"I'm listening."

"This is what you do. Once you're away from here and you have a signal on my mobile you ring Brascome – I'm assuming you still know the number?"

"I do."

"Tell them what has happened. At first they may not believe you, but Richard Fitzpatrick's life depends on you somehow persuading them. One problem is we don't know where he is. He could be at Brascome - with O'Malley at police HQ or on his way here alone. I just hope you can alert Fitzpatrick before it is too late. If not things might get messy. Then drive as fast as the Honda will allow to the Mater Hospital. This young man needs urgent attention and you will be safe there. After that no doubt all hell will break loose."

"Are you not coming with me?"

Docherty shook his head. "I need to create a diversion to make sure you are well away from here. Besides, I have some unfinished business to attend to with Seamus."

"You will be in grave danger."

"I can look after myself. Now come on, there's no time for arguing. Let's get a move on. Declan could appear at any moment." Docherty held out his keys and mobile to Mary. "Take these now and if Declan appears I will kill him. He'll be drunk for sure so I will have the advantage. Whatever you do don't stop – get away. Don't look back – I'll be fine."

Mary did not argue. She took the keys and the mobile and together they hurried to where Fitzpatrick lay. They could hear Declan moving about above them.

"Right girly," said Docherty, let's get this poor sod out of here and into my car."

Mary reacted quickly. She knelt down beside James. "Listen up. This is it, this is our only chance. We are going to get you to a car. But you can't walk and we can't carry you. Dragging is our only option. It will hurt but you must try not to make a sound. If you do it will alert that thug above us and then all will be lost. Understand?"

James struggled to roll away. "Oh shit," shouted Mary. "We are here to help you. For Christ sake understand!"

Whether he understood or not the exertion proved too much and he lay still, coughing and breathing heavily. He wasn't going anywhere.

"Good," exclaimed Mary. "Okay Jack, you ready?"

"As I ever will be," replied Docherty sliding his hands under James's shoulders. "Let's go."

By the time they got to the Control Tower doors Mary was struggling and she could hear Docherty fighting for breath. She stopped. "We need a break Jack – my arms are killing me. Do you think we could get James onto his feet? Then with one of us on either side of him we could get him to the car."

"Let's give it a try."

Mary looked down at James – he was deathly white, pain written all over his haggard face. Waste of breath to ask him if he was alright. "Somehow James, we are going to get you on your feet and with one of us on each side we will get to the car. If we can't make it we're dead."

He said nothing.

"Can you help us at all?" asked Docherty.

Through the pain it registered that perhaps these two people wanted to help him. What did it matter anyway? He gathered every last ounce of his strength and croaked, "I'll do my best." If Docherty had any doubt about what he was doing it vanished. No man or woman deserved to suffer this way. "I don't think he's going to be able to help us much, so let's get him sitting up Mary, and then hopefully we can heave him onto his feet. Holding him up is going to be our problem."

But it didn't prove as difficult as Docherty feared, because as Docherty was about to learn James was a fighter. "He's got guts," he said to Mary as they made painful progress.

"You don't need to tell me that Jack. Where's the fucking car?"

"Round the corner. Not far to go."

"I think I'm going to faint," James gasped.

Mary tightened her grip around his waist. "NO! You can't! We're nearly there. Jack, Jack hold him tight, he's close to passing out." She felt James sag against her arms. "Jesus Christ man, hold in there – we're doing our fucking best. Don't you let us down." Her words seemed to galvanise him. "Good, that's fucking good, not far now." She saw the car. It looked more like a rust-bucket than a car. Would she get to the hospital in *that*?

At that moment James slipped to the ground. "Shit, shit," Mary cried. "What now Jack?"

"Drag him. If it kills him too bad. If we give up now he's dead anyway." Docherty took hold of one leg. "You take the other one girly, only a few feet now."

They dragged – they swore – they used every ounce of strength they had left.

"Made it!" cried Mary fumbling with the keys to unlock the Honda. To her surprise she heard a welcome click. She almost fell as she lunged for a back door. "Easier to get him into the back," she said, seeing a questioning look on Docherty's face. "Front will be too cramped."

Sweating and breathing heavily they man-handled James onto the back seat. There was no question of him helping them – the pain was biting too deep and he was floating in and out of consciousness.

"We've done it," Mary whispered in his ear, taking hold of one of his hands. "You must believe we are here to help you please. She felt slight pressure. He understood – he wasn't dead. She straightened up and smiled at Docherty. "Come with us Jack, please come with us."

She never knew what Docherty's reply might have been for at that moment they both heard a loud roar and Declan hurtled round the corner of the Control Tower waving a gun. Mary thought he looked remarkably sober.

"What the fuck..."

Docherty moved like lightening. He withdrew his SIG 9mm from his waist band and without shouting a word to Declan, he fired – missed. Declan retreated behind the Control Tower. "Go girly, go!" shouted Docherty.

Adrenalin pumping through her veins Mary fell into the Honda. Her hands were shaking so badly that she couldn't get the key into the ignition. "Come on," she shouted trying again. "Bingo!" she screamed, as the key slid into the ignition. Then with heart thumping she sent up a prayer to the Lord and turned the key. The Honda started.

"Told you she wouldn't let you down," shouted Docherty firing another shot in Declan's direction. "Now get!"

Mary released the hand brake and shoved her foot hard down on the accelerator pedal – she nearly stalled.

"Easy, easy," shouted Docherty.

Gripping the wheel she started to move away from the Control Tower. She heard a fusillade of shots – felt a thump at the back of the car and knew Declan was shooting at her. Where was Jack? She slowed and looked in the cracked rear view mirror. Her heart sank – she could see Jack lying on the tarmac. If he wasn't dead he soon would be. She knew Declan seldom took prisoners and he was mad – very mad and unfortunately sober. Docherty's fate was sealed. As she focused on the air field gates she had a feeling that Jack had always known that this was the day he was going to die. She heard another shot. It galvanised her. Choking back the tears she risked increasing the pressure on the accelerator peddle. The old car responded. The back window shattered, sending shards of glass all over the prone body of James. Was he hurt? She forced herself not to look round. She couldn't do a fucking thing if he was and she knew Declan would be running after her. She drove through the gate onto the lane and out of sight of Declan. For the time being she was safe. Declan had no wheels. She beat her hands on the wheel. – she'd made it!! Jesus fucking Christ she'd made it! A sigh of relief escaped from her mouth and she sent up a silent prayer asking God to forgive her for her shouted profanities.

As she turned left round the second corner of the lane she narrowly avoided a car coming towards her. As it passed she saw there were four men in the car. Wow, she'd had a close call. But did this present a new danger? Once the men had talked to Declan would they set off in pursuit? Probably. But she had a start, and Declan had no idea where she was heading. Once she got to the main road she should be safe. If the old bucket didn't conk out she stood a good chance of getting to the hospital. If they caught her….well at least she'd done her best. Now she had to get a message to James's father, and that meant losing valuable time stopping somewhere. She shook her head. Not good, but she had no option. Driving without hands on the steering wheel caused certain problems. She laughed mirthlessly. With one hand she fumbled for the mobile in her pocket – wrapped a hand round it and pulled it out. She drew into the side of the road, casting a nervous glance into the rear view mirror. With engine still running she switched the mobile on. A signal! "Yes!" She shouted. She punched in the numbers and pressed the send button. Once she heard the dialing sound she accelerated away, held her breath and waited.

A voice! Meg Healy's. She hit the verge –gripped the steering wheel with her free hand and swung back onto the tarmac. "Hello, hello," Meg was saying.

Mary found her voice. "Don't hang up; please don't hang up Mrs Healy. It's Mary Keogh. This is urgent."

*

Seamus drove into the lay-by. His watch said five minutes past the hour. He reached for his mobile and dialled.

O'Malley jumped as the phone rang – Richard moved to be beside him – George didn't move. He'd know soon enough what Flanagan's demands were.

"O'Malley?"

Charlie flicked on the audio and said, "Let's not waste time Flanagan."

"Okay. Do you know the old airport at Langford Lodge?"

"By Lough Neagh?"

"That's the one, and Fitzpatrick knows the area well. He'll be going back to his place of birth. Rather symbolic don't you think?"

Charlie swore down the telephone.

"No need to get worked up O'Malley. Just listen. I want Fitzpatrick by the old Control Tower in half-an-hour. Needless to say alone with the money."

"Understood. And what about his son?"

"As agreed, we will hand him over once we have the money."

Charlie wanted to ask, "Alive or dead," but that was not on the cards with Richard listening. Instead he asked, "How can I trust you?"

"Listen up policeman all we want is the money. We are not interested in the Fitzpatricks. Understand?"

You're a liar, thought Charlie, but again he bit his tongue. He looked at Richard, who nodded.

"Very well Flanagan. Fitzpatrick will do as you say."

"A sensible man," Seamus said and broke the connection. Then he sat back – lit a cigarette and waited.

Fifteen minutes later the old man propped up on a lamp post opposite Police HQ reading the Irish Telegraph and with a photo of Fitzpatrick clasped between his fingers saw two men come out of the police station. One had a hand round the other one's shoulder; the other man was holding a black briefcase. He tucked the newspaper under his arm and looked at the photo. He had no doubt that the one holding the briefcase was Fitzpatrick. He allowed himself a satisfied smile. It was the easiest fifty he'd ever earned. He watched Fitzpatrick shake the other man's hand and get into an unmarked car. He watched it move onto the road. He waited another five minutes – no tail. Flanagan's orders were being followed to the letter. He pulled out his mobile and dialled.

Seamus answered on the first ring. "Yes Bill?"

"Subject matter on his way. No companion, no followers as far as I can see."

Seamus didn't reply. He broke the connection – opened the passenger window and hurled the mobile into the bushes. Then he turned the ignition and headed back to the airfield. He felt drunk with excitement. Nothing could go wrong now. The Fitzpatricks would be dead within the hour.

Seamus Flanagan had triumphed again.

Thirty-Six

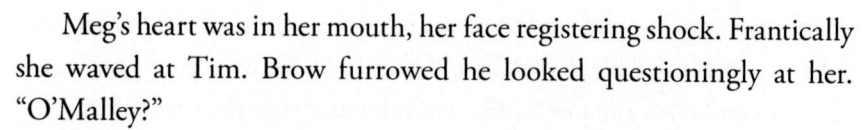

Meg's heart was in her mouth, her face registering shock. Frantically she waved at Tim. Brow furrowed he looked questioningly at her. "O'Malley?"

Meg put her hand over the mouth piece and whispered, "No, Mary Keogh!"

"The girl?"

Meg nodded vigorously. She could hear the panic in the Mary's voice. No time to talk to Tim. Meg's first reaction was to let rip at the girl who she now suspected of treachery. But an inner voice was warning her to back off and stay calm. "Mary I can hear you. What is it?" Meg mouthed at Tim, "Urgent."

Mary blurted out, "I have James – James Fitzpatrick."

Meg's mouth fell open. "You have James!"

Rachel flew towards Meg, shouting "James is free? Oh my God!"

Meg urgently waved her to silence.

Mary was swearing loudly. "For fuck sake woman shut your mouth and listen. This is a desperate situation and I only have a few minutes. My life and James's depend on you. James is in a very bad way. I'm taking him to the Mater hospital. Do you understand?"

"Yes," Meg croaked.

"Good. You must also put his father off going to the drop zone. You have not got much time. If you fail to stop him he will die."

"Is this some cruel game you're playing?" Meg asked.

"Shit no! You have to believe me, you have to. Please, please."

Meg heard the hysteria in the young voice and made an instant decision. "I believe you Mary. But Mr Fitzpatrick is not here, He's in Belfast at police HQ."

"Then he's probably about to leave. Oh Christ! You must try and stop him. You may only have a few minutes."

The line went dead.

Meg blurted out to the room. "James is free! He's alive! Mary Keogh, the girl who worked here has him. Don't ask me to explain, because I haven't a clue what's going on but I believe her." She turned to Tim holding out the telephone. "According to the girl you only have a few minutes to stop Richard from leaving the police station."

Rachel sank to her knees sobbing. Meg rushed to her side.

Before Tim could ring Charlie the phone rang. It was Charlie.

"Charlie! I was about to ring you."

"Richard's left."

"How long ago?"

"Five minutes."

"You must stop him."

Charlie flicked on the audio so that George could hear. "What the hell are you saying?"

"Mary Keogh has got James. No, don't interrupt. She's on her way to the Mater with him. He's in a bad way. This changes everything. You must somehow reach Richard and stop him. Flanagan won't be too happy that his prize has escaped."

"You believe the girl?"

"We have no choice."

"You're right." Never one to be slow in an emergency Charlie said, "Right I'm on the move. I'll alert the air support unit. They should get to Richard in time. I'll instruct them to pick him up. I will tell them to wait until I arrive. I don't want them flying off until I've spoken to him. I just hope he hasn't had too much of a start. God knows what awaits him if he reaches the air field."

"Surely Richard's got a mobile?"

"He refused to take one. And anyway the signal is very iffy."

"Not good."

"Not good as you say. Now get to the Mater. George will be on his way in a minute. Make sure the girl doesn't do another disappearing act. I want to talk to that young lady."

"And if this is a hoax?"

"We're in the shit Tim."

"Good luck Charlie."

"I'll need it. Stay in touch if you can."

"I'll do my best."

Charlie broke the connection. He turned to George. "You heard that?"

"Every word. I'm on my way."

"I'll contact the Chief Constable. Get him to alert the air support team and send an armed response team direct to the airfield. I hope this is on the level, not just Flanagan playing with us again."

"You have to gamble sometimes Charlie."

"I know, but not with two lives."

"Being a policeman is a bitch sometimes," George said, grabbing his overcoat and making for the door.

Thirty-Seven

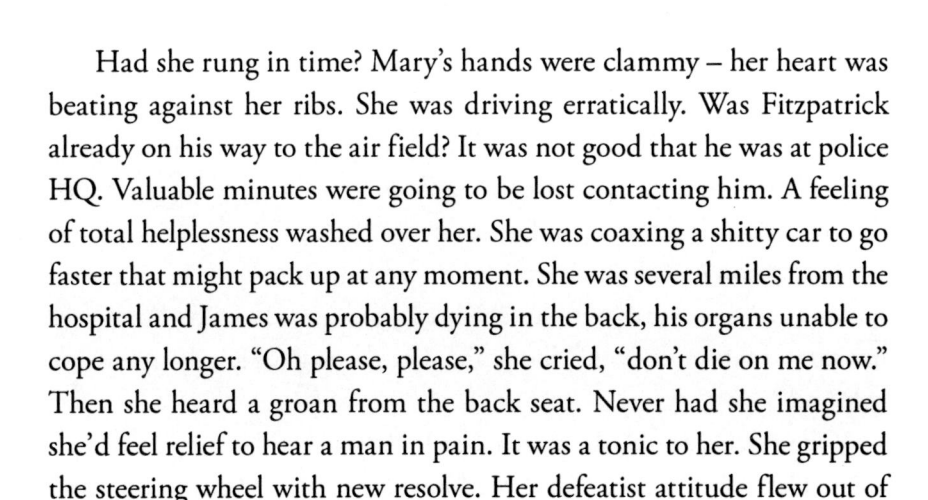

Had she rung in time? Mary's hands were clammy – her heart was beating against her ribs. She was driving erratically. Was Fitzpatrick already on his way to the air field? It was not good that he was at police HQ. Valuable minutes were going to be lost contacting him. A feeling of total helplessness washed over her. She was coaxing a shitty car to go faster that might pack up at any moment. She was several miles from the hospital and James was probably dying in the back, his organs unable to cope any longer. "Oh please, please," she cried, "don't die on me now." Then she heard a groan from the back seat. Never had she imagined she'd feel relief to hear a man in pain. It was a tonic to her. She gripped the steering wheel with new resolve. Her defeatist attitude flew out of the window. She took another look in the rear view mirror. The road was empty. Would her luck hold? Or would she soon hear a roar of a powerful engine behind her? If Seamus's thugs caught up with her there was nothing she could do about it. She had no gun and anyway one woman against four large armed thugs was no contest. Within seconds she'd be dead. "But I have a feeling luck is on my side," she said out loud.

She dared to press a little harder on the accelerator and the old car responded. It filled her with hope. *Mary Keogh, you're going to win this one.*

*

Mary eased off the accelerator as she swung into Crumlin Road. Towering over most of the other buildings was Bedeque House, the home of the Mater as it was commonly known. It was where she'd been born and it crossed her mind it might be the place she died. She had no illusions that Seamus's tentacles spread far and wide and he'd be as mad as hell. She had made a dangerous enemy. She roared up to the entrance to A&E, making a middle-aged couple jump for their lives. She swore at them as the man shook his fist. She cut the engine – leapt out of the Honda, leaving the driver's door open and ran into the hospital. She had already decided that the best way to get urgent attention was to start screaming the moment she reached the reception desk. When she saw the queue she knew it was her only hope.

She screamed.

A startled nurse looked up - saw a filthy dirty young woman – hair everywhere and with tears streaming down her face making a terrible wailing sound and tearing at her scalp.

Mary soon had all the attention she needed. She gulped in air as two nurses tried to restrain her, but she broke free and shouted, "A man in my car, a man in my car." She pointed at the exit. "He's dying! Please help me!"

One of the nurses shook her head. "Come on darling, too much alcohol last night was it? Your friend not able to walk? I've a good mind to get you thrown out. The likes of you are menaces to us working all hours to save lives. Now shut up, either get out or join the queue and be sure not to vomit or I'll make you clean up your own filth. And if you don't shut that gob of yours I'll call security."

It dawned on Mary that security was just what she wanted. So she folded her arms and refused to budge. "No," Mary shouted. "I'm telling the truth. I'm not drunk, nor is the man in the car. Go and look for yourself you idiot. For fuck sake do something."

That was enough for the nurse to call up security on her radio. "Right you little trouble maker now you're going to be in real shit."

A small crowd had gathered round Mary. A few were showing concern, but the majority were supporting the nurse for giving Mary a piece of her mind. They were grumbling loudly that they *really* needed urgent attention. Mary decided her screaming had had the desired effect and addressed her next remark to three women who were looking at her sympathetically. She shook off the nurse's grip and took a deep breath. "I have a very sick man in the car outside. Why doesn't this stupid woman believe me? All she has to do is go through that door over there. This man has been beaten and starved of food for several days. He's in need of urgent help."

The three women's eyes widened in shock and one of them took a step towards the nurse. "Do something," one of them ordered.

But the nurse was not in the mood to budge. She knew she had the majority of the queue supporting her. She'd also had a long night on duty and all she needed, half an hour before going off duty, was a drunken girl causing mayhem. She put her hands on her large hips and said, "We will wait for security."

At that moment a middle aged man, struggling with two sticks, limped into A&E shouting, "There's a car outside with a man lying in the back covered in glass! He looks in a bad way. Anyone going to help!"

"Told you so, you bloody idiot!" shouted Mary.

We're on our way." shouted two security men, who had just burst into the reception area and thought this was the reason for the nurse's call. The nurse looked aghast and taking Mary by the arm stammered out an apology. "I'm, I'm so terribly sorry love. Bad night."

"Not half as bed as mine," mumbled Mary, giving the nurse a look which plainly said she didn't care how bad her night had been. Not waiting for her reaction she forced herself through the crowd and raced after the security men.

"His name is James Fitzpatrick," Mary said breathlessly as they reached the Honda. "He's been kidnapped. I've rescued him. *God, that sounds trite*. You've got to believe me."

But it had an instant effect on one of the security men. He turned to look at Mary. "I don't know who the hell you are but I know about the kidnap of James Fitzpatrick. It's been all over the papers and on the telly. Is this really him?"

Mary nodded.

How the hell have *you* got him?"

"Tell you later," Mary promised. "Right now helping this man is more important."

The security men opened the rear door. "Jesus! Look at this!" One of them gasped as he stared at the blooded man lying in a blanket of glass. He turned to his companion. "Shit! Get help Pat – now! I'll check the pulse."

"Is he alive?" Mary dared to ask.

"He's breathing lady. And I'm going to call the police. Don't have any ideas of running for it."

It had crossed Mary's mind, but the danger outside was far more threatening than anything the police could throw at her. "You must be joking mate," she cried. "I'm in grave danger."

"Are you now?" The security man said, wondering if at any moment this bedraggled young woman would pull a gun on him. He felt a lot safer when two male nurses rushed out of the hospital doors carrying a stretcher, followed by a man who Mary soon discovered was a doctor. They gently lifted James off the back seat, out of the car and onto the stretcher. "You with this man?" asked the doctor, looking at Mary.

"Yes."

The security officer who had stayed by the car interrupted. "This looks a very serious business doctor. I've called the police. I think this woman has a few questions to answer. She says this is the Fitzpatrick who was kidnapped. No doubt you've read about it."

The doctor looked at Mary with renewed interest. "Please tell me anything that could help me."

"He's dehydrated, suffering from beatings, lack of food and sleep. And before you jump to any conclusions, no I am not responsible. I have tried to keep the poor fucking man alive."

"But by your own admission you have been with him throughout his ordeal." said the doctor, letting his deep set green eyes wash over Mary. "But that's not my concern. Mine is to save this man's life." With that he signalled to the nurses to follow him. "We will do our best," he assured Mary over his shoulder. "It seems to me you care."

Mary felt her composure crack. She ran after the stretcher and stared down at James's emaciated body. She stared at him for several moments – she was scared for him. She touched him tenderly, feeling his hot skin. Tears rolled uncontrollably down her face. "I care doctor. More than I ever thought was possible. I'm gambling with my life for this man. So don't let him die please."

The doctor gave her a wary smile, not sure how to read this young woman. "I will do my best I promise."

"Thank you," whispered Mary. She watched the stretcher disappear through the hospital doors thinking that this would probably be the last time she would ever see James again.

*

Seamus drove off the lane onto the air field's tarmac, singing at the top of his voice. He was feeling well pleased the way things had worked out and soon he'd be a million richer and two Fitzpatricks would be dead. He'd celebrate later. He swung round the side of the Control Tower and slammed on the brakes, a cold hand gripping his heart.

In front of him lay Docherty, blood congealing on the tarmac. Declan was standing over him. Of the four men he'd expected to be waiting for him there was no sign. "What the fuck!" he shouted as he nearly fell out of the Range Rover.

Declan, pointed his Glock at Docherty and exclaimed, "It was Docherty, Seamus, Docherty helped Mary escape with Fitzpatrick!"

Seamus took a very deep breath. "Fitzpatrick's gone?"

Declan nodded.

"And where were you Declan while Docherty and Mary struggled to get Fitzpatrick to the Honda and Mary drove away."

Declan was visibly shaking – he knew it looked bad – knew Seamus would not be impressed with his explanation. "I was up there," he said pointing to the upper floor of the Control Tower. "Watching for your men as you told me to do."

"And you never heard a thing. Never heard Fitzpatrick being moved – never heard voices – never heard Fitzpatrick cry out in pain – never heard the engine start – never thought something was wrong. Jesus Declan."

"I heard a car start and ran down and onto the tarmac. Docherty fired at me."

"Pity he missed," Seamus growled. "What did you do, run back into the Control Tower shaking like a baby? I must admit I never had you down as a coward."

"No! I returned Docherty's fire – killed him. Then I fired at the car – hit it several times."

"But not enough to stop it," Seamus shouted. "Why didn't my men give chase?"

"They arrived several minutes after Mary had left."

"But it would have been easy for them to catch that clapped out Honda, especially as the lane is the only way out to the main road, unless you take to the fields and the Honda wouldn't get a yard. So what happened, as I presume by what I see here, they have not caught Mary?"

"They did a runner."

"They what!"

"Said they wanted no part in a botched operation. Sent their love and drove off."

Seamus felt the anger boil inside him and once it was out it would not subside until he'd taken action. The anger was like hundreds of little demons flicking their tongues and waiting to strike. He stood staring at Declan, as the demons danced around his heart. But Declan knew the signs and wasn't prepared to allow the demons to have their way with him. He was close to death.

He raised the Glock.

His eyes took on a brief look of total bewilderment as he looked down at the blood staining his shirt. His hand dropped the pistol and he sank to the ground. His last thought, as his blood drained from his body and mixed with the congealed blood of Docherty's, was how the hell had he ever thought he could outdraw Seamus.

Seamus moved and kicked him – Declan said nothing. He was dead.

"You were a good man once," Seamus conceded, walking away without another glance at the two bodies. They had failed. Mary had destroyed a dream. He would no longer be talked about in the bars of Belfast with awe. The man who had condemned the peace agreement to the dustbin. "Arseholes the lot of you," he yelled in frustration. He looked round the air field, its wet tarmac, its broken buildings, adding to his feeling of despair. His life was fucked. He ran into the Control Tower and threw a few items into his bag and then made for the Range Rover. Valuable minutes were ticking by. No doubt that bitch Mary has sung like a bird. It was time to get out. He wasn't ready to be captured or shot down by some fucking policeman. Richard Fitzpatrick would not be coming, so why risk his life. He got into the Range Rover and turned the ignition. "Jesus this hurts," he mouthed. He'd lost. It was a strange feeling.

He drove up the tarmac- took one last look in his rear-view mirror at the two bodies and hit the lane at speed. He heard the sound of a helicopter overhead. His reasoning was correct. He did not have much time. The man-hunt would be on. He would have to disappear for some time, but he was still young. He knew where he was heading. Escape had been planned a long time ago. He never left anything to chance. He gave a self-satisfied smile and scratched his chin. He'd surprise his enemies. In a few years time he imagined himself in a well fitting blue suit – light blue tie and polished black shoes as he strutted through the gates of Stormont smiling happily at the reporters eager to get the first picture of Seamus Flanagan, ex IRA commander, entering Parliament. And that will stick in your gullet O'Malley, he thought. But first there were urgent things to do, like getting away and reinventing himself. And of course planning his revenge on Mary.

Thirty-Eight

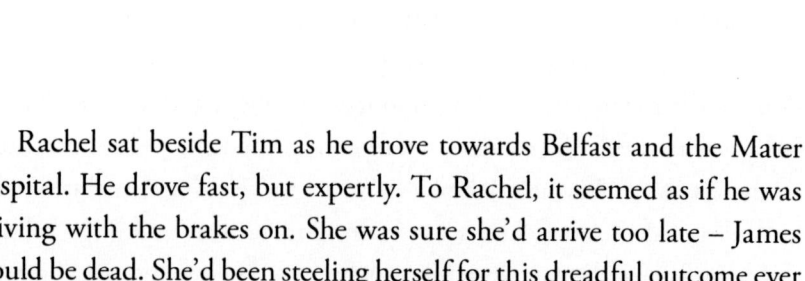

Rachel sat beside Tim as he drove towards Belfast and the Mater hospital. He drove fast, but expertly. To Rachel, it seemed as if he was driving with the brakes on. She was sure she'd arrive too late – James would be dead. She'd been steeling herself for this dreadful outcome ever since the news of his kidnap had reached her, but now all her control was rushing out of her like water from a leaking bucket. To make matters even worse Richard was in danger as well. She wondered what she'd done to be so ignored by God. She was living in a nightmare and it was one she feared she might never wake up from. She looked out of the window as the countryside flew past chewing at the remnants of her once manicured nails. She knew Tim would have to slow down as he hit the outskirts of Belfast and that meant more time to fret. She wondered if she could ever be the same woman again. The one who friends called a quiet, well organised person, not prone to panic, always with a smile on her face, always ready to see the best of everyone and ready for a laugh. It was why Richard had fallen in love with her as he still enjoyed telling her. She'd managed to stay that same woman all through his political career, even when he'd become Secretary of State for Northern Ireland. But this was so different, so scary and so utterly desperate. She looked across at Tim and asked, "Richard will be okay won't he?"

That was worrying Tim. He hesitated, before saying, "The police will catch up with him for sure."

But Rachel was quick to hear the doubt in his voice. She said nothing more. She would only cry. She bit her lip and slumped down in her seat. She was in God's hands now and she wasn't too sure He cared.

*

Charlie's guts were churning, but outwardly he managed to look calm. As he drove he kept glancing out of the window, his eyes searching for the Eurocopter EC 135. It was the best chance of catching up with Fitzpatrick before he reached the airfield. Then he heard the roar. "They're in the air," he shouted, feeling the first spasm of hope hit his body. Surely it would only be a few minutes before they spotted the car.

Charlie allowed himself a rare smile. Maybe things were turning in his favour. He crossed his fingers. The next few minutes would be agony.

*

At Brascome Manor all they could do was wait. Meg was making the interminable cup of English breakfast tea for Peter Carpenter and Phil Dashwood who had come into the house for a few minutes to warm their frozen limbs. They drank quickly, all too well aware of Tim's last words. "Be vigilant lads, you never know what might happen now. Once Flanagan knows he's beaten he might just be tempted to pay this place a visit."

Meg was wondering if she should have opened her doors to Richard. "Too big hearted," Duff answered, as she broached the subject once the two men had returned to the biting cold. "But we had no option my love. We couldn't turn James's father and mother away."

Meg was grateful for his support. She shrugged. "You're right Duff, but maybe we should have given it more thought."

"Waste of time old thing. You would never have turned them away. And that policeman's mind was made up. He was not going to take no for an answer."

"Right again, but I'm frightened as to how this is going to end."

"We will soon find out," Duff said before pointing at the window. "I'm glad it's not me out there half freezing to death."

"They're tough and they will guard us well, frozen or not," Meg said. "I don't think they're the sort to leave their post. I suspect they would be long dead if they were inclined to do that."

Duff nodded. "I find it hard to believe that those two young men are trained to kill."

"It's the world today Duff – we just live in a vacuum here."

"Well I'm bloody glad we do."

"But no longer. Our lives will change whatever happens. We will not be the same old married couple, able to ignore what terrible things are going on in the world today. We will never be able to forget the last few days or the despair on Rachel's face, nor the obvious pain coursing through Richard's body. We have had a shock, the outcome of which will never leave us."

Duff was not going to argue with that.

*

Richard was driving like a man possessed. He turned off the main road into the lane which led to the airfield, a lane he knew well. He'd bicycled along it many times as a boy – the wild hedges on either side giving him the opportunity, when the season was right, to pick blackberries, other times to gather chestnuts that had fallen from the chestnut trees that lined the left hand side of the lane. He'd laughed at the rabbits as they had scurried for cover and smiled up at the sky whatever the weather. He'd been innocent then, thinking his life was one great glorious adventure. And then when he'd visited Belfast as Secretary of State he'd taken this route to Gartree church to visit his father's grave. By then it was much changed. Most of the chestnut trees had died of disease, the hedges were neatly trimmed, the road surface replaced with shinny new tarmac and no rabbits. It was no longer a boy's paradise.

The black briefcase with the money was lying on the front passenger seat and every now and then he'd glance at it as if he was terrified it would fly out of the window. To his surprise he was not frightened, even though his heart told him he was probably driving to his death. Men like Flanagan thought nothing of killing and Richard suspected that this man was also on a personal crusade. There were several factions still active in Northern Ireland who would not shed a tear at the death of a Fitzpatrick. Memories were long in Ireland. But he'd never had any choice other than the one he'd chosen. It was his only hope of getting James back alive. He slowed – there were several blind bends. And then he heard the sound of a helicopter above him. He'd visited Ireland too many times not to recognise the noise.

His brow furrowed. Had O'Malley broken his word? He didn't think he was a man to break a promise. He lowered his window and glanced up. There it was, the helicopter hovering over him, quite low and one of the crewmen waving frantically at him. What was going on? His first thought was to ignore it, but then why was it flying so low, so obviously trying to attract his attention? It dawned on him that something was wrong and he felt a cold hand touch his heart. Was he too late? Was James dead? He stuck his head out of the window, taking his eyes off the road.

The horse box coming round the ninety degree bend slammed into him head on.

There was a great whoosh. Richard's car was enveloped in a fire ball. His scream was choked off by the flames – the briefcase was ashes in seconds – his flesh roasted and fell off his bones. The driver of the horse box, a young woman, died instantly as the flames fried her. Her daughter was thrown out of the cab, but broke her neck as she hit the tarmac. Two horses in the back died more slowly. The crew of the helicopter could only look on in horror.

Ten minutes later Charlie came on the scene. He braked violently; threw himself out of the car and hit the tarmac running. Flames were still licking the car and the horsebox. He saw the helicopter in a field and the two crewmen running towards him, waving frantically.

"There was nothing we could do, nothing," gasped one of he crewmen, as he reached Charlie's side. His face had drained of all colour and he was visibly shaken. The other crewman was vomiting onto the grass. "There was a fireball," the man blurted out. "No one can have survived. We were trying to stop him sir, trying to stop him. He must have taken his eyes off the road."

Charlie felt sick as he walked slowly towards the two wrecks shielding his face from the heat with a hand. There was no stench. Burnt bodies don't give off much odour. The flesh and bodily gasses, the twin engines of forensic malodour, had been burnt off. Charred remains carried a scent, but it was not a disagreeable one. Charlie had smelt it before. He managed to get near enough to the car to see a form still smouldering in the driver's seat. He shook his head in disbelief. The gods were certainly conspiring against him. The shock wave that hit him nearly forced him to his knees. It was not meant to end this way.

*

Seamus saw the fireball as he came over the hill. He slammed on his brakes – saw the helicopter flying low. He let out a sigh of relief as he watched it land – it was not tracking him. His luck was still holding. Something was seriously wrong. He didn't waste time wondering what – he had to get off the lane. To go on would be foolish – his freedom threatened. He swung the steering wheel hard to the left and ploughed through the hedge. He knew the route he would take. The Range Rover would manage the terrain. Then once back on the road he'd turn away from the smoke and take a detour to his destination. It would take longer and there were a few risks, like road blocks, but Seamus had no doubt he'd make it. The good Lord took care of Irishmen like him. He smiled, fought the steering wheel as the wheels bumped over the rough ground. A herd of cows took off in panic. So far it had not been the best of days, and that was making his blood boil.

*

Tim manoeuvred his car into a parking space and jumped out to open Rachel's door and put a reassuring hand around her waist. "Don't panic," he said knowing how inadequate his words were. In Rachel's shoes he would already be flying through the hospital doors. But they would get a lot further if Rachel could stay calm. And as she gave him a weak smile he knew she understood. "Well done," he said by way of encouragement. "Now let's go and find James."

*

Charlie tried his mobile – no signal. He ran into the field and tried again. He dialled emergency. Heard the ringing tone and breathed a little easier. He spoke rapidly. Then he rang HQ. The desk sergeant answered. "Bad news here," Charlie said. "Serious accident – no survivors – Fitzpatrick is dead."

"Christ," came back the voice. "What happened?"

"A horse box ploughed into him. Big explosion. Emergency services on the way. No need for any action your end." And then Charlie asked, "Any news from the Mater?"

"None yet, but I've been trying to get hold of you."

Network is terrible here. Anything important?"

"You could say so."

"Spit it out sergeant."

"Flanagan has left you a message. It says, "Today I was unlucky. But remember I only have to be unlucky once. You will have to be lucky always."

Charlie nearly chocked. "Bastard," he said quietly, and then said. "Get road blocks set up and airports and ports notified. Hurry sergeant, no time to waste."

"I'm on it now."

"Good. But I have a feeling Flanagan will outwit us again."

"Our luck will change sir."

"I'm not too optimistic sergeant. Keep in touch. I'll be at the Mater." Charlie broke the connection. It was not his way to wish anyone dead but right now he'd give anything to see Flanagan in a coffin.

He tried George's mobile. He answered immediately.

Charlie quickly filled him in, ending by giving him Flanagan's message.

George said, "I've just reached the Mater. Trying to find somewhere to park. Rachel and Tim have arrived."

"Don't say a word to Mrs Fitzpatrick George. I'll do that."

"Very well, if that's the way you want it. What a disaster Charlie."

"I know. I'll keep in touch."

George didn't reply immediately. He needed to control his heart beat. If he got to Flanagan first he'd kill him. His conscience was undisturbed. He didn't care about the consequences. It was a price he was prepared to pay. After all what value did he put on his life since Rose's death? *And a man who cares little about living makes a dangerous adversary Flanagan.* He found his voice. "What now Charlie?"

Charlie said, "I'm leaving for the Mater when I've finished here. I'll have to break the new as soon as possible to Mrs Fitzpatrick or she might hear it on the radio or see it on television."

"What about the airfield?"

Charlie said, "an armed team are there by now. I should hear any minute if Flanagan is still around, but I doubt it. He won't have wasted any time in getting away once he found James gone, but others might still be there."

"I'll not hold you up any longer Charlie. See you at the Mater."

"Yep, see you there."

Charlie blew out his cheeks. He heard the sirens. He ran back to the carnage just as an ambulance and a fire crew screeched to a halt. Two paramedics and four firemen were quickly on the tarmac, running.

"Christ!" exclaimed the first paramedic to reach Charlie. "What the hell…"

Charlie interrupted him. "Head on collision. No survivors. Bit of a grisly mess I'm afraid. I know the identity of the man in the car, but no idea of the other occupants in the horse box. One body in the cab and one dead woman on the road. Two dead horses in the back. Apart from the woman on the road identification may prove difficult for the forensic team but the unburned body might have some identity on her, which might also help us learn the name of the driver. My second-in-command will be here any minute now and he can start enquiries. He's going to take over from me. I've got to get to the Mater as quickly as I can."

A touch on Charlie's shoulder a few minutes later made him turn away from the grisly sight. Jack Speedwell, a reliable Inspector. He was an experienced policeman – seen it all. "Which is why I'm grey haired at fifty," he explained to any one who bothered to ask. He was several years older than Charlie but did not resent that he'd been promoted over him. He was content where he was in the pecking order, unlike some of his more ambitious colleagues. Charlie sighed with relief. He was just the man he'd have chosen.

Speedwell looked at the smouldering wreckage for a few moments before asking, "You ok Charlie?"

"Not really Jack. This is a terrible tragedy. Fitzpatrick is dead. You take charge here while I go to the Mater."

"Rather you than me," Speedwell replied with relief. He'd visited many families with the news that a loved one was dead and it had never got any easier. "In fact it gets worse," he'd once said to Charlie.

"Part of the job Jack, part of the job as you well know. Now let me give you all the details as I know them."

Once Speedwell had been briefed Charlie raised a hand to the paramedics and fire crew and hurried to his car. "Good luck," Speedwell said.

Charlie gave a wry smile. "I think I might need more than that. I'm not going to enjoy the next few hours. Let me know if you find out who the two women are."

"Will do. What about the airfield?"

"Armed response should be there by now. I've warned them to be careful even if Flanagan is not there. I wouldn't put it past him not to have booby trapped the place. He will be a very angry man. He's lost a million quid and as far as he is aware both Fitzpatrick's are still alive."

"Won't he bloody laugh when he hears what has happened!"

"He will gloat," Charlie added as he turned the ignition key. Without another word he did a u-turn and accelerated away.

*

James lay in intensive care, his eyes staring unseeingly at Rachel. She stared horrified at all the tubes attached to him and was certain it was only a matter of time before he died. She rested her head on Tim's shoulder and cried. Tim put an arm around her waist and allowed the grief to flow. A nurse, with short red hair, wearing glasses which hid caring eyes, stood beside Rachel holding her hand. Like Tim, she made no effort to try and stop Rachel from crying. From experience she knew it was best to get some of the grief out of the system. Apart from the crying the only other sound in the room was the noise of several machines working hard to give James the support he needed.

"Will he live?" Rachel choked, after a few minutes.

The nurse, never one to raise hopes at such an early stage replied, "It's too early to tell love. But he's in good hands. Give it a few more hours and then we will know more. All I can say is that his breathing is level and heart beat okay. X-rays show two broken ribs and internal bruising, but no damage to his head."

"He looks terrible," Rachel cried.

"He's badly dehydrated – he's been beaten, there are cigarette burns on the soles of his feet and certainly he's been deprived of any worthwhile food."

"So not life threatening?"

"As I said I really can't say love. What I suggest is that you and this man go away, find a cup of tea and wait for the doctor to see you."

"I think that sounds a good plan," Tim confirmed, looking questioningly at Rachel.

"I would prefer to stay here," Rachel stated. "But maybe you're right nurse." She gave one more look at James – took a deep breath and grabbed Tim's hand. "Let's go."

As they walked out into the corridor, all white and impersonal and smelling of disinfectant Rachel shuddered. "God, Tim I hope he doesn't die in such a sterile place."

"He's not going to die Rachel," Tim assured her. "You must believe that."

"Do you Tim, do really think that? No lying this time."

Tim took hold of her and stared into her eyes. "My heart tells me he will live."

*

George Russell slipped into a parking space and locked the car. "Don't want someone stealing a police car do we George," he said to himself. He looked up at the hospital building and thought of the last time he'd walked through its doors. Rose's bloodied body lying on a stretcher, before being rushed into emergency. There had been little point – she was dead before the ambulance had arrived at the scene.

He nearly turned away. But then he reminded himself that he wasn't the only poor sod to lose a loved one in violent circumstances. Right now there was a woman in there, suffering as he did, and her pain was only just beginning. And if his long drawn out suffering was anything to go by she would be facing a nightmare that he wished on no one. He had long since accepted that he'd never fully recover. Perhaps, with the support of a family, he might have dealt with the trauma better. He wondered where Rachel was going to get that support.

He walked through the doors, noting a gathering crowd of reporters no doubt waiting for Charlie. He hurried to the reception desk and asked for Intensive Care. At the end of the corridor he saw Rachel and

Tim. Before he could turn back he heard Rachel shout, "Oh God it's that man! I don't want him around me."

George wheeled around and hurried away. He didn't blame Rachel for not wanting him around. He was still the bad boy in her eyes and he understood grief. He acknowledged Tim with a smile. He would find security, check that they were still holding Keogh and break the bad news to the Healys. After that he'd wait for O'Malley.

*

George heaved a sigh of relief when Duff's voice came down the telephone. He'd been dreading having to break the news to Meg. "Duff, its George Russell."

Duff's voice was gruff. "Wondered if you'd forgotten about us Russell. Any news?"

"I wouldn't do that Duff, but events have been moving very swiftly."

"Good or bad news?"

George cleared his throat. "Bit of both."

"Well go on then man."

"James is free and alive. In a pretty bad way but the news is encouraging. Mary Keogh's call was not a hoax. She took him to the Mater as she said she would. Charlie O'Malley will be interviewing her shortly."

"Wonderful news. So what's so bad?"

"Richard Fitzpatrick has been killed."

There was a moments silence on the line before Duff spoke. "Shit! Flanagan got to him then?"

"No. He was killed in a car crash."

"I don't believe it. Tell me how it happened."

George related the terrible events.

Thirty-Nine

The adrenaline rush had died and in its place came despair. Mary sat on a very hard chair in a small office leading off from the main reception area. "A consulting room," the security man had told her. She held a mug of tea in her hands and stared at the blank walls. They made her think she was already in prison. Her mind was in turmoil and all she could think of was that she was alone and very vulnerable. She'd heard the turn of the key in the lock as the security man had left the room. *Consulting room, my arse.*

She looked at her watch. Nearly two hours had passed since the key had turned and no one had come near her. Bastards! She was dying for a pee and desperate to hear how James was. Would she ever hear? Would he want to see her? Would she be shut out now, just a suspect to a kidnap who'd had a change of heart to save her skin? "Fuck you all!" she screamed and hurled her mug onto the floor. It bounced but did not break, just leaving a dark stain on the green carpet. She knew she could be in deep shit. But that wasn't her main worry – prison might give her some protection from Seamus. Otherwise she was on her own. No home. Even if she had one she would never dare go there. Seamus would get her for sure. She had no friends, no family – in fact she was fucked. From now on she'd be looking over a shoulder for the grinning face of Seamus. How had she got herself into such a hopeless situation? She'd allowed her head to over ride the easy way. So simple. Stick with Seamus whatever he did and too bad if innocent people died. Her head dropped into her hands. No! Whatever lay ahead she knew she'd done the right thing. She could not have sat by and watched James die. But never had she felt so alone. Her compassion had come at a price. No one cared about her, no one loved her. She faced an unknown future and right now it looked as if it would be pretty fucking bleak. She jumped up from the chair – ran to the door and started beating it with her fists and shouting. "If someone doesn't come soon I'm going to piss all over the fucking floor."

*

The officer of the armed response unit stared at the two bodies lying on the cracked airfield tarmac. They were already gathering a crowd of curious ants and flies. He looked at their faces, and then signalled for his men to move cautiously towards the Control Tower. "Might be booby-trapped." His voice urgent. They held their weapons cocked as they advanced, ready to return any enemy fire, but none came. "Leave it," the officer commanded. "This has the makings of an execution and the executioner or executioners have obviously fled. No need to risk being blown up." He pulled out his mobile – swore loudly when he saw 'no network coverage' on the screen. He ran up towards the lane. Half way he got a signal. He rang Charlie. He got his voice mail. He explained what they had found. "Two dead. Neither face matches Flanagan. We have not entered the Control Tower as you advised. We'll wait until the bomb disposal team and the medics arrive." He broke the connection and waved his men back to their vehicle. "Get the tea out Osgood. We may have a bit of a wait."

*

Charlie's worse fears were confirmed as soon as he drove up to the entrance of the hospital. A wall of journalists was waiting for him. With luck news of the explosion and the fatalities had not filtered through just yet. He prayed that this would be about James's rescue. It wouldn't take long for the media to get wind of the crash but it would give him time to see Rachel first. He jumped from the car and was immediately surrounded. There was no way he was going to get inside the hospital without saying something. He thought quickly. Don't mention the crash. He did his best to smile. "Gentlemen. James Fitzpatrick has been rescued – details will come later. He is now in Intensive Care. His condition is critical. No questions please until I call a press conference."

"And when will that be?" asked a reporter who had always irritated him with his probing questions. This time he wasn't going to be given the chance.

Charlie glanced at his watch and glared at the questioner. "You heard what I said."

"Then give us a time," persisted this thorn in his flesh.

"Three hours from now gentlemen, unless you plan to block my way much longer. I will organise a room here. "Now please gentlemen, some of us have urgent work to do."

A path opened and Charlie smiled his thanks and ran into the building. At times like these he hated being a policeman and this time it was going to be very tough.

Forty

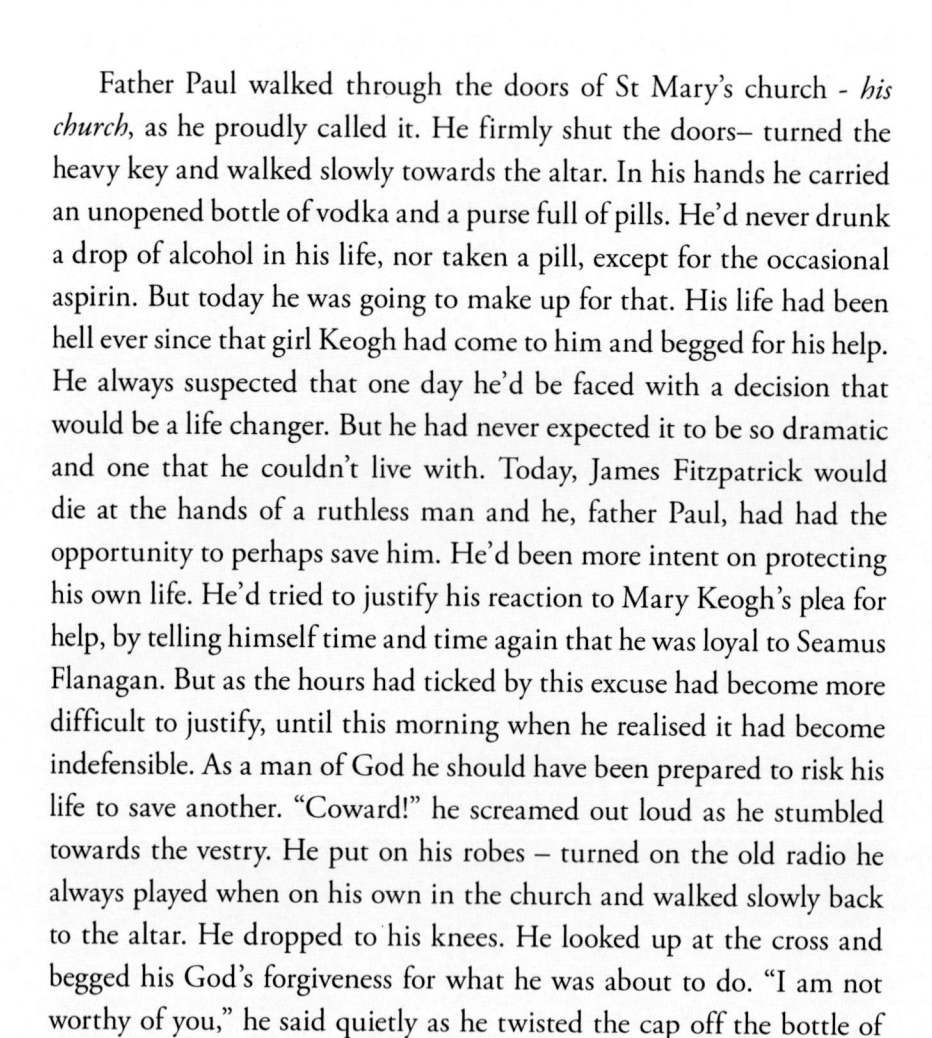

Father Paul walked through the doors of St Mary's church - *his church*, as he proudly called it. He firmly shut the doors– turned the heavy key and walked slowly towards the altar. In his hands he carried an unopened bottle of vodka and a purse full of pills. He'd never drunk a drop of alcohol in his life, nor taken a pill, except for the occasional aspirin. But today he was going to make up for that. His life had been hell ever since that girl Keogh had come to him and begged for his help. He always suspected that one day he'd be faced with a decision that would be a life changer. But he had never expected it to be so dramatic and one that he couldn't live with. Today, James Fitzpatrick would die at the hands of a ruthless man and he, father Paul, had had the opportunity to perhaps save him. He'd been more intent on protecting his own life. He'd tried to justify his reaction to Mary Keogh's plea for help, by telling himself time and time again that he was loyal to Seamus Flanagan. But as the hours had ticked by this excuse had become more difficult to justify, until this morning when he realised it had become indefensible. As a man of God he should have been prepared to risk his life to save another. "Coward!" he screamed out loud as he stumbled towards the vestry. He put on his robes – turned on the old radio he always played when on his own in the church and walked slowly back to the altar. He dropped to his knees. He looked up at the cross and begged his God's forgiveness for what he was about to do. "I am not worthy of you," he said quietly as he twisted the cap off the bottle of vodka. Then he tipped the pills out of his purse onto the wooden floor. Methodically he placed one in his mouth, followed by a swig of vodka.

Then another and another. Always followed by a swig of vodka. His fear was that he'd vomit, so he took his time. He found the music coming from the vestry strangely comforting. Gradually the pile of pills got smaller and the bottle was three-quarters empty. He began to feel light headed – his eyes became dilated and he had a job to keep them open. His body began to sweat and he knew his task was nearly done. Only six more pills to go and a few drops of vodka left. Soon his guilt – his disgust at himself would be no more. He wouldn't be at peace though, the devil would see to that. As he popped the last pill he rolled onto his side and curled up into the foetal position. The altar was swaying – the cross seemed to be moving towards him. The walls of the church were closing in on him. The stained glass windows were shattering all around him. He was aware of the music coming from the vestry. And then it stopped. A man's voice replaced the music. "We interrupt this programme of Mozart's best known works to let you know that we have just heard from the police that the kidnap of James Fitzpatrick, that has caused all of those who live in Belfast great concern, is over. He is safe. We will try and give you more details as they come into us. Now back to Mozart."

Father Paul let out a gurgling noise as his life drained away.

*

Rachel saw Charlie coming along the corridor. "Inspector," she said, rushing towards him and taking his hand. "Thank you, thank you for what you have done. The news of my son is good. The doctors have told me he should make a full recovery. How did you manage it?"

Charlie forced a smile. "I didn't manage it Mrs Fitzpatrick. The girl, Mary Keogh is the one to thank. I haven't been able to interview her yet, but certainly, whatever the circumstances, she has saved his life."

Rachel gave him a bewildered look. "Why would she rescue him?"

"No idea at the moment."

Rachel turned to Tim. "Did you hear that?"

Tim nodded.

"Can I see her?"

"I will need to interview her first. She has a lot of questions to answer."

"I understand, but please keep me informed. I would like to thank her, though I might not be able to forgive her." She looked at Tim. "Now I'm going back to sit with James. I want to be by his side when he regains consciousness."

Charlie took a deep breath. "Before you do that Mrs Fitzpatrick I have some bad news for you."

Rachel visibly paled. "Oh God!"

"There is an empty room along the corridor. I suggest we go there," Charlie advised.

"Tell me here Inspector."

"Are you sure?"

Rachel reached for Tim's hand. "I am."

Charlie sighed. There was no gentle way to break the news. He'd learnt from many scenes like this that it was best to come straight to the point. "Your husband has had a fatal accident. A car crash, a fire. He must have died instantly."

Rachel swayed and Tim caught her. She screamed. The noise echoing down the corridor. She tore at her hair – her eyes filled with tears – she pulled away from Tim and collapsed onto the floor. "No, no!" she yelled. "It can't be! You're mistaken, you must be mistaken."

"I'm afraid not," Charlie said quietly. "There is no mistake."

For a moment there was silence and then Rachel staggered to her feet. She wiped away the tears, brushed down her beige trousers and stood straight. "Can I see Richard Inspector?"

Charlie's silence said it all.

Rachel took an unsteady step forward. "Then I think I'd better go and see James. At least he is alive. Please let me know when I can bury Richard. It will of course be at Gartree church."

Charlie deemed it not the right time to tell her that it might be some time before they released what was left of the body.

"You're continued silence Inspector tells me all I need to know. Come Tim let's go and see the living."

Charlie watched the two of them walk away. Rachel's recovery took him by surprise. Some might have said she seemed indifferent to her husband's death. But Charlie suspected otherwise. She'd bravely pulled herself together. It was no more than he would expect from a woman he admired. But he knew her calmness was only skin deep. Inside despair would be ripping her apart. It would only be a matter of time before her torment came to the surface. He was drained. He felt that he'd failed the family. This was not how he'd hoped things would work out. He turned away. Unfortunately at the moment there could be no place in his life for sympathy. His job was to find the man responsible for all the mayhem of the last few days. Right this moment he had no idea how that was going to come about. He saw he had a text on his mobile. It was from the officer at the air field. He read it. No sign of Flanagan. A moment later Jack Speedwell rang. "So far nothing to report from the road blocks or the airports or ports. Nothing from the border. It seems he's just vanished."

"Thanks Jack, that's all I need to know. Bugger."

*

Seamus drove with exaggerated care. He had no desire to catch the eye of some cruising copper. Although he was fairly confident he was far enough away from the accident he felt uneasy in the Range Rover. He had no doubt that every policeman in Northern Ireland and on the other side of the border would be looking for him and road blocks would have been swiftly set up. The sooner he dumped the Range Rover the better. He was entering dangerous territory. Mary would have told the police what he'd be driving. "Fuck you Mary," he shouted as he turned back the way he'd come. Belfast would not be safe. After a few miles he spotted a lay-bye. He drove in and braked, turned off the engine and jumped out of the car – threw the keys into the undergrowth – pulled out his knapsack from the boot and started to walk. His plan was about to be activated. Of course he'd hoped he'd never have to press the button. His dream of becoming a hero of Ireland would have to be put on hold. He swore loudly. Mary had fucked with him. His plan had been blown out of the water, but he wasn't ready to die yet. In less than an hour he'd be with a loyal friend. The plan was to lie low for as long as it took for the flack to die down. Then, as planned, he'd flee to America where three Irish Americans, who viewed the peace accord with as much hatred as himself, would be waiting. And then he'd re-invent himself. Seamus Flanagan would return to Belfast. He was about to cheat Charlie fucking O'Malley out of what must be his most cherished dream. To see him, Seamus Flanagan, behind bars for the rest of his life.

He left the road and headed off across the fields confident that he would reach his destination. A little later than expected, but still a free man. As he trudged along, climbing gates, getting a good soaking from the incessant rain and water sloshing around in his shoes his thoughts turned to Mary. He barred his teeth. How he'd like to get his hands on her. She'd have to die - pay for her treachery. He realised that could be his undoing. Had he the inner strength to sit back and let someone else do his dirty work? Somehow he must try to control his basic desire to put his hands round Mary's neck and squeeze the life out of her. The only thing that cheered him up was the satisfying thought that she'd be shit scared. "And you'll stay like that until I get you," he shouted to the sky.

He reached Belfast two hours later. He was tired and foot-sore, but he was almost there. In another half-hour he turned into a familiar road. Many a plot had been hatched in the house he was heading for. He blew out his cheeks as he saw it. He'd reached his first destination safely. He would have loved to see O'Malley's face if he knew how close he was. He walked up the drive and knocked on the door. It was immediately thrown open by a small, ferret like man christened Joseph, but known as Jo to his friends. He looked at Seamus in amazement. "I thought they'd got you," he blurted out.

"Seamus Flanagan does not get caught," Seamus boasted, casting an eye towards the sky as he walked, with some trepidation, through the front door. It might be a long time before he saw daylight again.

Forty-One

Charlie wasted no time in contacting the Chief Constable to brief him.
"Not good Charlie."
Charlie gripped his mobile. "You can say that again sir, but we have the girl."
"Ah yes the girl."
"I'm about to talk to her. She is our only hope. If she was prepared to save James Fitzpatrick she might be prepared to give us information as to Flanagan's whereabouts."
He heard the Chief Constable grunt. "Well keep me informed Charlie. The media will be all over us soon."
"Already are, but I've stalled them. I want to talk to Keogh first."

*

Charlie decided to let George sit in on the interview. "Just keep your mouth shut unless I say otherwise." He took the key off the security man standing outside the door – waved him away. "I won't be needing you for a while." He turned the key in the lock and walked into the room. A young woman was standing by a desk, her large red-rimmed eyes staring at him suspiciously. He walked towards her and held out a hand. She refused to take it. He shrugged. "Hello Mary, I'm Chief Inspector Charlie O'Malley and this is my colleague George Russell. I have some questions to ask you. Why don't you sit down?" Without waiting for her to move he dropped into one of the chairs, George following suit.

For a moment Mary didn't move. She screwed up her eyes and bit her lip. Charlie waited patiently. From experience he knew the next few moments would decide how the interview would proceed. With relief he watched her drop into the chair.

"Well detective, what do you want to know."

"Chief Inspector actually."

"Whatever detective."

Charlie couldn't stop himself from smiling. She was going to be full of lip. He had no doubt her guts were churning, but she was obviously strong. No one fucked with Flanagan, as she had done, unless they were full of bottle. Charlie crossed his legs – rubbed his hands together and asked, "Ready Mary?"

"Ready detective." She held Charlie's eyes. *Kindness is going to be their first move.* And she wanted it kept that way. Aggressive questioning she would not be able to handle in her fragile condition. She had decided to hide nothing – to tell the truth. She knew it was the only way.

Charlie asked, "Your name is Mary Keogh?"

"You already fucking know that detective."

Charlie nodded. "Okay, why not tell us a bit about yourself for starters. You know, some background stuff just so that I can understand better what you're about. You see you're a bit of a mystery to us. You have never been on our radar and that seems surprising as you knew Seamus Flanagan so well."

"I was his lover."

Charlie felt a bolt of excitement flow through him. This woman must know a lot. He glanced at George.

"So why did you rescue James Fitzpatrick? A lover's tiff?"

"No!"

"Then what?" asked Charlie.

"Could I have a glass of water please?"

"Of course. George?"

With George gone Charlie said, "This interview is off the record. Our next one in the police station will be different."

"Okay. So you're not arresting me or cautioning me?"

"Not at the moment."

Mary shrugged. "Makes no difference to me." Then she gave Charlie a smile. "This will take a bit of time."

Even though Mary was dishevelled and quite obviously in need of a shower Charlie was looking at a strikingly beautiful young woman. How on earth did she get involved with a psychopath such as Flanagan? It was easier to imagine her singing in a band or walking down a catwalk showing off expensive clothes. But then he'd long ago learnt that he could not judge people by their outward looks. He said, "We have all day Mary. Your information is very important to us."

"Oh I bet it is," Mary said.

Charlie gave her an encouraging smile. He felt the next hour, or maybe longer, was going to prove very enlightening.

George returned with a glass of water – slammed it down on the desk in front of Mary and then went back to his seat.

"Ready?" asked Charlie.

Mary took a sip of the water. "This might take some time detective."

"I have all day if necessary," Charlie assured her. He asked his first question.

*

James was aware of moments that came and went like the sun appearing from a cloud-broken sky. A man, a vicious man. Pain, thirst, cold, a young woman's face. He felt the warmth of a hand on his forehead. Then finally emerging from darkness. The world seemed somehow to becoming solid again. The pain was still there, like a distant echo in the recess of his brain. He knew he was in a bed – tubular metal at each end. He was in a hospital and he was aware of someone leaning over him. A woman. She seemed vaguely familiar but his eyes were not yet focusing. The room was spinning like a top. He was aware of a hand on his arm. It felt soft. He heard her voice.

"Don't try and move darling."

His mind cleared. He knew the voice. "Mother," he croaked. "Where am I?"

"In hospital. You have been unconscious."

He looked at her puzzled. "In hospital, why?"

Rachel was worried now. "Can't you remember anything?"

He shook his head. "I'm trying."

"You were kidnapped."

He nodded. "Yes, yes. Give me a moment." He closed his eyes and shook his head. Rachel looked at Tim. They waited; every second stoking Rachel's growing panic.

At last James spoke. He struggled to sit up. "It's coming back to me." His eyes grew wide. "I remember the pain – a man – a woman. Yes a woman - I think she…." The effort exhausted him. "I can't…" His eyes closed – lay back, defeated.

Rachel bent to kiss him, relief coursing through her. "You sleep now darling." She ran a hand across his brow. "He's okay Tim, thank God he's okay. His memory will come back. Now I think we should let him sleep. She heard his regular breathing and said, "At least I haven't lost both of them."

Tim said nothing. Just held out his arms and Rachel ran into them. She felt the tears hot on her skin. She rested her chin on Tim's shoulder and silently thanked the God she thought had deserted her.

*

Mary drained her water. She'd been talking for an hour. The two men had remained silent. *You bet you have – didn't expect anything like this did you?* She looked at their eager faces – noted that one of them was sweating. Russell, she thought his name was. She didn't care if he was called Bonzo! He was just one of the many policeman she knew she'd come face to face with in the next few days and probably months. She had no illusions – she was heading for prison. And what did she care?

At least she'd have a roof over her head and some protection. She cleared her throat – put down the water glass and continued. "I discovered lots of things about myself after we'd kidnapped James. I began to doubt Seamus. His fanatical hatred of the peace agreement didn't rest easy with me. Maybe peace was better than a war I was beginning to think. A war I was coming to believe we couldn't win. But what eventually made up my mind to rescue James was Seamus's cruelty. Kidnap for the Cause was one thing but to torture your victim – well it made me feel sick and I saw a vicious man with no heart. Maybe God sent me a massage – one last try to redeem a rotten soul, though I doubt it. I suspect He has given up on me a long time ago." She wrinkled her face. "I don't believe in Him anyway."

"I have my doubts as well," Charlie replied.

Mary gave him a defiant look. "Don't get me wrong detective, I'm not sorry for what I have done in the past, so don't think you're going to get me begging your forgiveness. My father was in the IRA, fighting for what he believed in and I was the same. I hated you Brits."

"Just for the record I'm Irish," interrupted Charlie. "And let me ask you this. Was your father Conor Keogh?"

"Aye that he was." Said with pride.

"He was a vicious murderer."

He watched Mary's cheeks redden. "You're entitled to your opinion detective but my Dad died a hero. And let me tell you something. Not long ago I wouldn't have given you the time of day. So let's keep my dad out of it, okay? Look detective, I know I did wrong, know I'm in the shit. Know the whole thing sucks, but I discovered I had a conscience. I couldn't let a man die. That doesn't make me a better woman I know. How is he?"

"Why should that bother you," spat George, feeling the anger rising inside him. "I suspect you only rescued him in the hope of saving your skin."

Mary glared at the man. He had begun to get to her and she didn't want that. She had too much on her plate to start a fight with a fucking macho detective. She took a deep breath – clenched her hands and made eye contact with George. Neither of them blinked. "Think what you like sweating man, but I saved him….*oh shit I'm going to start crying…* because, because," she stammered, "I, I cared for him. Yes, you might well look surprised, but he was an innocent caught up in something he had nothing to do with. His treatment was sadistic – horrible. And he was brave, so fucking brave." She pointed a shaking finger at George. "Have you ever seen a man tortured? Watched his eyes fill with terror? Smelt his fear? Watched him shit himself, aware that he is slowly dying? Praying for a quick death. Well let me tell you it's not nice, it made my stomach churn – made me hate myself – made me realise that killing was wrong. Oh yes, you may well raise your eyebrows, but I realised for the first time that life *did* matter, and that I had no right to judge whether a person should live or die."

"Bit late," said George quietly. "How many deaths have you been responsible for? Tell me Keogh. Henry Walters, your mother, Jack Docherty, and no doubt many more. You're no better than Flanagan."

Mary rose from the table trembling. She made no attempt to stop her tears. She slammed her hands down on the wooden table and sobbed, "I'm no fucking saint I know, but I've changed. I really care – yes really care for James."

George stood and laughed in her face. Then adding, "Well let me tell you something Keogh, if you hadn't taken part in the kidnap, Richard Fitzpatrick wouldn't be dead."

Mary's hand flew to her mouth. "Dead! Jesus how did that happen?"

"An accident," said Charlie, thinking that George had said quite enough, but George wasn't finished. "I hope his death will be on your conscience, if you have one, which I doubt, for the rest of your miserable life."

Charlie put a restraining hand on his arm. "That will do George."

George knocked his hand away and moved within inches of Mary's face. She could smell his breath. "I've heard it all now. And do you know something Keogh, I have never heard so much shit come out of a person's mouth in my life. You tell me you care. Well I say you're lying through your teeth young lady."

Mary sank back onto her chair. "Life can suck sometimes," she said quietly, her eyes staring at Charlie.

Charlie put a hand on one of hers. "Yes it can Mary."

George exclaimed, "For Christ sake Charlie, don't waste your sympathy on this woman – she's evil."

"I'm not, I'm not," Mary cried.

George turned away shaking his head. He wanted to hit her. "I've had enough of this," he shouted as he walked towards the door, slamming it behind him.

Mary said nothing for several minutes and Charlie made no attempt to break the silence. He guessed she needed time to recoup her damaged faculties. When she spoke she asked, "What's the matter with him?"

Charlie said, "he's not a detective. He's Special Forces and when in Kuwait he saw the result of a man tortured. He was still alive but begged Russell to kill him. He also knows Seamus Flanagan killed his wife."

Mary's mouth fell open. She tried to speak but no noise came out. She wondered if her life could get any shittier.

*

The press conference was the last thing Charlie wanted at the moment, but there were at least fifty journalists fidgeting in their chairs growing ever more impatient for his appearance. As he stood outside the room, which was far too small for the gathered company, he pulled at his blue tie and checked that his flies were zipped. Beside him stood the Chief Constable who had thought his presence was required. "It's not fair to put such heavy responsibility on your shoulders Charlie. This whole incident has gone global. You will need my support."

Charlie thought 'incident' was utterly the wrong word. The day had been a disaster, one big fuck up. He couldn't even claim credit for the rescue of James Fitzpatrick. However soothing the Chief Constable words Charlie knew that the buck stopped with him. "Ready sir?" he asked.

"Let's do it Charlie. Buy you a drink afterwards."

"Thanks."

"Listen Charlie, I know what you're thinking, but rest assured I'm right behind you. You are a good copper. There is nothing you could have done. Just thank your lucky stars that the girl saved James Fitzpatrick's life. Be positive. With her help we will catch Flanagan."

"Thank you sir and I need to talk to you about her after this conference – that is if we come out in one piece."

The Chief Constable patted Charlie on the back. "We will. Now here we go."

The conference room was stiflingly hot. It was not designed to hold fifty of the world's media. Flash bulbs added to the warmth and within five minutes Charlie was sweating profusely. He glanced at the Chief Constable and derived a little comfort from the fact that he was also over heating.

"Good morning gentlemen, sorry to have kept you waiting but I'm sure you will understand this is a very busy morning for the Chief Inspector," started the Chief Constable.

There were understanding nods. The last I'll get today, thought Charlie, forcing a smile as he fidgeted nervously with his papers. "I think it best if I give you a resume of events first," he said. "Then the questions." He looked at his watch. "I will give you ten minutes for those."

There was a resigned sigh from the room.

*

The pressure had not been as bad as Charlie had feared. Yes, doubts as to how the whole episode had been handled were to the fore, but they were polite. Most of the journalists in the room knew Charlie well and respected him. They understood the complexities of the case

– the twists, the surprises, the unexpected deaths. At Charlie's request they had held back asking too many questions about the girl. Content for the moment to hear about the tragic circumstances that had lead to the death of Richard Fitzpatrick and the expected arrest of Seamus Flanagan. Charlie had not let on that the girl had not been able to shed any light as to his whereabouts. Many of the gathered company had got to know Richard Fitzpatrick when he was Secretary of State and none of them wanted to exasperate an already delicate situation. The Chief Constable was profuse in his thanks and Charlie had promised another conference in twenty-four hours. This time back in police HQ.

As the two men walked out of the room they both let out a relieved sigh. They had been given time, but it would not be such plain sailing the next time if they didn't have some concrete answers to feed to the hungry. Like where the hell was Flanagan.

"Well done," said the Chief Constable. "Very well handled Charlie."

Charlie knew he meant it. The Chief Constable was not a man to butter up his officers. Frank speaking was his way.

"And now that well earned drink eh?" suggested the Chief Constable.

Charlie hesitated. "It's tempting, but wherever we go we will have a hoard of journalist following us."

The Chief Constable beamed at Charlie. "Thought of that. So I came prepared. I have a bottle of Scotch in my brief case but perhaps it might be a bad idea to be seen drinking in a hospital. Let's get out of here."

Charlie laughed.

*

Back at police HQ and with the Chief Constable's door firmly shut the bottle was produced. Two plastic glasses were half-filled with the scotch. The Chief Constable waved to a chair. "Sit Charlie. Water?"

Charlie shook his head and sat, crossed his legs and took a sip from his glass. He felt the warmth of the liquid travel down to his stomach. It felt wonderful.

"Can I talk to you about the girl?" asked the Chief Constable.

Charlie lent back in his chair and said, "I can't quite make Mary Keogh out. She's got a terrible history for one so young. She was Flanagan's lover and admitted to helping him with the kidnapping. Her father, Conor Keogh, was a well known IRA man and was executed for want of a better word by Russell. At least there has been no leak from Whitehall about the covert operation."

"Well we can thank our lucky stars on that one Charlie." The Chief Constable grunted. He didn't want to delve too deep. The less he knew the better.

Charlie realised this and quickly continued. "Mary is convinced she's the cause of her mother's murder. She was a bit vague. As I read it she told Flanagan that her mother was likely to be a threat to him now Conor was dead. She says it was probably Flanagan who killed her."

"And she stuck with Flanagan?"

"Yes."

"Wow, she's a tough one Charlie."

"Seems so, but it is my opinion that she's in love with James Fitzpatrick."

The Chief Constable made no effort to hide his scepticism. "Oh come on Charlie."

"It's happened before. The kidnapper forming a close relationship with the victim."

"And you honestly expect me to believe this has happened in this case?"

Charlie nodded. "All I'm saying is that it might be a possibility."

"Well you're entitled to your opinion. So Charlie, what now? Charge this girl or encourage a romance?"

Charlie didn't laugh at the Chief Constable's attempt at humour. He said, "I haven't charged her yet."

"Why the hell not?"

"I'd like to offer her a deal."

The Chief Constable held up his hands. "Wait a minute Charlie, have you thought this through?"

"I have."

"Go on then."

"I'm not saying she doesn't deserve to go to prison."

"She got to you Charlie? I hear she's a real looker."

"I've seen bad ones just as beautiful, seen ones younger than her throwing Molotov cocktails at our troops, brainwashed by their relatives. And this is what I see here. A young woman brainwashed, first by her father, and then Flanagan. She was fed hatred on a regular basis. She grew to loath the British and Flanagan became her hero. She knew no other life."

"What of her mother?"

"According to Mary she was a devout Catholic but beaten into the ground by the father. Mary says she had no time for her. 'Despised' was the word she used. Something she bitterly regrets now."

"So?"

"I don't think we've a chance of finding Flanagan without her."

"But she's already told you she doesn't know where he is."

"I know, but if he's still in the country we might be able to tempt him to break cover."

"How?"

"Use Mary as bait."

"Good God man!" The Chief Constable took a deep breath. "You know what I think of risky moves that threaten anyone's life."

"Do you want Flanagan sir? Because I think that if he's still in Ireland this is the only way we'll get our hands on him."

"And this Mary girl, have you spoken to her about this?"

"Not yet, but if you agree with this plan I will."

"And you think she will help you because she's fallen for Fitzpatrick?"

"I think it could be one reason, but I also strongly suspect that she deeply regrets the pain she caused her mother and if I play on this she might see it as a way to making some amends. And one other thing that makes me optimistic, is that she went to her priest Father Paul, and asked him for his help. Now it seems to me she wouldn't have done that unless she wanted to get away from Flanagan's clutches."

"She did what?"

"Told him of the whereabouts of James Fitzpatrick – hoped he might go to the police."

"But he didn't go."

"Obviously not, which isn't surprising."

"How so?"

"I've done some research on this Father Paul. He had strong IRA sympathies."

"I see."

"It sounds as if he should be paid a visit."

"He's topped himself. Found in his church."

The Chief Constable blew out his cheeks. "How many more are going to die Charlie?"

"I can't answer that. But if we get Flanagan I'll wager things will quieten down."

"And the covert operation we know nothing about?"

"Aborted."

"Brushed under the carpet?"

"Yes."

The Chief Constable scratched his chin – took a long pull at his scotch and stared over the rim of the plastic cup at Charlie. "If I was Flanagan I'd be long gone. A man like him would have made plans to flee if things got too hot for him. How do you know he's not already on a boat planning a new life? And would he be so stupid to try to get to Keogh knowing that you will have a ring of steel around her?"

"I'm afraid I don't have any of the answers," confessed Charlie. "And maybe you're right. He's slipped through the net already. The road blocks have seen nothing and all the ports and airports on both sides of the border report no sightings. But my gut feeling is that he's still in Belfast. I can't believe he's that clever to have boarded a boat or an aeroplane without being spotted. Also we've found a Range Rover in a lay-bye outside Belfast. When I gave the girl a description she was pretty sure it was Flanagan's. She thinks he's holed-up somewhere not far from here waiting for the man-hunt to die down before making a move."

"He might have a long wait."

"And that could be to our advantage. The girl says he's not the patient type. He'll be boiling inside, she said, he doesn't like being defeated. He might well be prepared to do something rash, like trying to get to her, his hatred for her will consume him. "He'll want to kill me with his own hands," were her words. It's our best hope; we can't stay on high alert for ever."

"Okay you've got my permission to go ahead but I don't like it, however, I want Flanagan. Don't make any deals with her Charlie. It strikes me that girl is bad, and a leopard never changes its spots. She deserves to spend the rest of her life in prison if you ask me."

Charlie wasn't asking.

Forty-Two

The day after Richard's death Meg Healey stepped out of the door of Brascome and looked up at the sky. It was a beautiful November morning, the frost still on the trees and the sun shining brightly, in stark contrast to her feelings. She could hardly believe that Richard Fitzpatrick was dead just when everything had seemed so positive. It did no good her endlessly telling herself that at least James was alive. A man had died a violent death, and she'd never been any good at handling painful news, and this was as painful as it could get. Poor Rachel, poor James. Had God lost all compassion? She thought of Duff sitting alone in his office, locked in with only several bottles of malt as his companions. He'd retreated with only a grunt as soon as he'd put down the telephone and told her the news of the death. By now he'd be dead drunk, no use to her, no bloody use to anyone. "Damn you Duff," she shouted at the sky. "I need you!"

She hunched her shoulders against the cold and started to walk up the drive, Scruff running on ahead. It had always been her favourite walk, especially in the spring when all the daffodils that she and Duff had lovingly planted burst into bloom. She pulled cold air into her lungs and increased her pace. It took her seven minutes to reach the road – it used to take her five, she noted with a resigned smile. From the road she looked down across the valley that she loved so much and was shocked to find herself wondering if it was time to sell and return to England. "That's what this whole dreadful affair has done to me," she advised a tail wagging Scruff. "Put doubt in my mind and turned Duff into a drunk." She shook herself vigorously, this wasn't the time to make such a momentous decision. And no doubt Duff would eventually come out of his study full of remorse and throw his arms around her. She allowed herself a smile. He knew how to win her back. A hug and one of his lingering kisses still, after all the years, made her knees go weak and set her heart pounding.

She heard the sound of a car approaching at speed and moved to where she could see down the road; a police car. A minute later it skidded to a halt beside her. It was a police constable. "What's happened now?" she asked, her voice full of dread.

"Nothing Mrs Healy. I'm to replace the two men who are with you, they're needed elsewhere. Things are warming up."

*

The Prime Minister's PPS was concerned. The PM's mind was not on the job. It was the disturbing news from Belfast the day before and since then silence from Holroyd. But he had yet another futile meeting with one of Europe's leaders to discuss the crisis in the euro zone. The talks would take the same route as they had done with the German chancellor and to the PPS's mind the French president would be far more hostile than the German chancellor. Therefore the PM needed his mind to be free of other clutter. The PPS silently cursed Tim Holroyd – he should have been in touch long before the story of Richard's Fitzpatrick's death hit the television screens. What was the bastard doing! He shuffled some files on his desk and tucked them under his arm ready to go to the meeting. And then the telephone rang. Tutting with annoyance the PPS picked up the receiver.

"It's Tim Holroyd," came the voice down the line. "Sorry I didn't ring last night."

"I don't think sorry will placate the Prime Minister," The PPS spat. "He's furious. Saw the news on the television this morning and I have been fielding calls from the media since dawn. What's held you up?" He listened to the man at the other end, heard the fatigue in his voice. But what did he care. "No. you can't talk to the PM. He's in a meeting with the French President. No doubt he'll contact you when the meeting is over. And don't swear at me man, I'm only doing my job. I suggest when you've simmered down you text your report to me. What? No, I've told you already you bloody well can't speak to him now. And when you do you better have a good explanation as to why you have made such an utter balls up. It's time some of you MI6 morons realise you don't run the country. What's that you say? Well the same to you Holroyd, but it won't be me who losses his job."

"Jumped up little prick," shouted Tim to Charlie. "But he's right damn him – I should have contacted the PM immediately. Very bad judgement."

"You had other things on your mind – Rachel for instance."

"Our Prime Minister thinks he's the most important man in the world Charlie. No one, absolutely no one is more important than him."

*

"There is no easy way to tell you this James," confessed his mother as she sat on the side of the bed. She was shaking; fighting the desire to bury her head on her son's chest and pour out her grief. But she couldn't. The doctors had deemed that James was now strong enough to take the news. "Of course we can have no idea how he will react," she'd been told, "but it won't kill him." She looked at James's bruised face, his split lips, one tube still pumping liquid into his body and the strapping around his bare chest and wondered if James really was strong enough to hear the devastating news. She felt Tim's hand on her shoulder. She turned to look up at him. He'd read her thoughts. "Tell him," he whispered. She blurted out, "Dad is dead." At first there was no reaction and she wondered if he'd heard her. She cleared her throat. "There is no...."

"I heard you," James interrupted. "I'm so sorry."

Rachel stared at her son – shocked by his apparent indifference. She'd expected tears – even screams, not this. She reached for one of James's hands and squeezed it. "Do you understand James, your father is dead."

He nodded, but said nothing.

Rachel felt a bolt of panic. Had the doctors missed something, like brain damage? Was he unable to take in the dreadful news? Could he remember his father? Or was it shock? Yes, yes, that must be it. He was still in shock, the reaction would come later. She stared at Tim.

*

"You're right Mrs Fitzpatrick, its shock," the consultant confirmed. "He can't take your news on board just yet, his brain is still struggling to cope. But let me assure you it will sink in. He is not brain-damaged. He's just had enough for a while."

"You make it sound so bloody simple."

"Let me tell you that I take this seriously, but I see it all the time. Right now the most important thing is to never leave him alone for a moment. When this news hits him the result will be explosive. There's no other way I can put it. And the best person to be beside him is you. It's a tough call. Can you deal with it?"

"For my son I can deal with anything doctor."

That evening James became hysterical and had to be sedated.

*

Mary was escorted into the interview room. It was larger than the room at the hospital and more intimidating; blank walls, a small high window with bars, two hard chairs and one worn table with stains on it. This was going to be the business – this was going to be the end of her freedom, though what sort of freedom she was thinking of she wasn't sure. Her police escort pointed to a chair. "Sit there young lady, someone will be with you shortly."

She dropped down into a chair on one side of the table - closed her eyes and waited.

"Good morning Mary," said a familiar voice.

She opened her eyes. It was O'Malley.

"You look better," he said.

"Had a shower and some clean clothes." She tugged at the blue T-shirt. "Bit big and a bra would have helped."

Charlie felt embarrassed. "Sorry, best we could do. Food any better than the clothes?"

"Pretty shitty. And where is the sweating one?"

"Only me today Mary. We have some things to discuss."

"No caution yet?"

"I want to talk to you first."

"Oh a deal eh?"

"We'll see."

Mary said nothing.

Charlie shuffled his papers. This was the moment he hoped he'd find out what was really going on in Mary's mind. The moment his plan got off the ground or to be met by shouted invectives and a firm "you fucking mad detective!" He leant across the table and stared into her eyes. Such beautiful dark green eyes, seemingly wide with innocence, but it was an illusion. By her own admission, she'd willingly thrown Molotov cocktails at the army and been involved in her mother's death and then taken part in a vicious kidnap. Had he read her wrong? Was Russell right that she was just trying to save her own skin? But he was not about to admit that his judgement was flawed.

She held his gaze and it gave him no clue to her thoughts. It was as though some vital piece of the human machinery had broken deep inside of her, and it made it impossible for him to decide whether she was cold and calculating, or a deeply remorseful young woman who was keen to help him.

He began. "I want to catch Flanagan. I want to see him on trial. Frankly I would like to watch the rope tighten around his neck if we still had capital punishment. He's evil Mary and I think you know that. However, if he isn't already out of the country, I need your help. And you've just told me that you think he's still around. Whatever, I suspect time is short." Charlie took a deep breath. "Will you help me?"

"How?"

"I want to use you as bait."

Mary didn't blink.

"How do you feel?"

Mary didn't blink.

"I need an answer."

"You can have one."

Charlie was fighting to keep the frustration out of his voice. "What is it?"

"I'll do it, but on one condition."

Charlie didn't like conditions, but he had no choice but to ask, "What is the condition?"

"That I get to see James. Not tomorrow or the next day or the next – today. If not throw me in jail and find Flanagan on your own."

This was not what Charlie expected. It took a few seconds for him to think of how he should reply.

"Well?" Mary asked impatiently.

"I can't promise anything. Have you considered that he might not want to see you?"

"He'll see me."

"How can you be so sure?"

"Because I saved his life."

"But you were a willing partner in his kidnap."

"I had no idea that Seamus was planning to kill him and his father. If I had I would never have gone along with it, though it would probably have cost me my life. James knows this. I told him many times. He knows I risked my life to save him, he'll see me detective. Just go and ask him."

"Let me ask you this Mary. "Do you think you two have bonded?" Charlie swore he saw her blush.

"Bonded detective – bonded! Tell me how you bond with a man who is semi-conscious most of the time – can't speak and once his gratitude for saving him has passed he'll probably hate my guts. Don't make me fucking laugh."

But as Charlie had told the Chief Inspector it was quite possible. And as he stared into Mary's eyes he suspected she was not being straight with him. He hadn't interviewed suspects for the best part of thirty years without being able to see in their eyes if they were lying. But he decided not to press the point. Instead he asked. "Alright, so why do you want to see him?"

"I want to apologise."

He thought quickly. "Okay, I promise I will see him after our talk is over. That's all I can do. I don't think it will be a good time just after learning his father is dead."

Mary's eyes filled with tears. "How much more suffering has he got to endure?"

"I can't answer that."

"No, you can't."

"So where do we go from here Mary?"

"There are two options open to me; if I refuse, I face trial for kidnapping, if I say yes I risk being killed by Seamus if you can't catch him or by one of his followers. Wow detective what a choice! But I prefer the latter, only because it gives me a chance to see Seamus locked up for life. And believe it or not I trust you detective, so I will co-operate. Tell me what you want me to do."

"I was hoping you'd tell me."

Mary smiled. "Oh you really do need me don't you. Perhaps it's time to bargain."

Charlie looked at his watch. "We're wasting valuable time here."

"Okay, okay you're offering me nothing, is that it?"

"Maybe later."

Mary shrugged. "Your hands are tied aren't they? But it doesn't really interest me anyway. Whatever you come up with my life will be shit. I have no home, no job and no money. Prison would be like a five star hotel compared to the alternative."

"What about your parent's house?"

"That's a big fucking joke! "Dad had it mortgaged up to the hilt. He hadn't paid for months, apparently we were about to be thrown out and the house repossessed. Its gone detective, like a puff of smoke. So shall we move onto how you are going to hang me up like some bait for a hungry animal? And let me tell you if Seamus is still around he will be very, very hungry."

"Good."

"You bastard, you're just like the sweaty one. You don't care a damn what happens to me."

"That's not true Mary. I do care, and you'll be well protected."

"Save your breath."

Charlie felt he'd slipped up and that at any minute Mary would change her mind. He said, "Have you any idea how to catch the man?"

"I have an idea, yes. Want to hear it now."

"After some coffee?"

"No booze?"

"Afraid not."

"Okay coffee – black."

*

They drank their coffee in silence, neither of them wishing to say something they might later regret. But Mary's eyes never left Charlie's as they stared at each other like a pair of prize fighters trying to work out each others moves. Eventually Mary spoke. "Thanks for that – I feel better now. Do you want to hear my idea?"

Charlie felt the adrenaline begin to rise. "Go ahead."

"From what Seamus said to me back at the cottage I strongly believe that he'll still be in the country. And as I said, if he is he'll be very angry and dying to get his hands on me. If he thinks I'm reachable I'll bet all his planning of lying low will go out the window. He doesn't like to be double-crossed and that's how he will see this. He doesn't want to die, but his desire for revenge will be very strong. But don't make the mistake of taking him for a fool, however you wrap this up he'll smell a trap."

"But he's out of control?" Charlie suggested.

"My bet is yes, he's out of control. So mad that he will ignore all the warning signals. But make no mistake detective you're up against a very cunning man," Mary laughed mirthlessly. "There is no way you can guarantee my safety, and as we are talking frankly I don't suppose you care too much. After all you are a policeman first and as the saying goes you want your man. I'm just a piece of useful fodder, I'm expendable and you won't be shedding too many tears if I die. But first Seamus has to take your bait."

Charlie said, "I know, so tell me how I'm going to do that."

Mary knew she had about ten seconds to change her mind. Tell this detective to go fuck himself and take the consequences which, given the present state of play, prison looked a lot more attractive than being gunned down by a grinning Seamus.

But then she thought of James and cleared her throat.

*

"Well funny you should call," said the consultant down the line to Charlie. "I was about to ring you."

"About what?"

"Fitzpatrick is asking to see Mary Keogh."

"That's what I was ringing about. She *wants* to see him."

"Well God knows why he wants to see her, but he's getting quite agitated. I'm not sure he's thinking straight. He took the death of his father very badly and as I see it this woman is partly to blame for his death."

"Have you suggested that to him?"

"To the mother."

"And her reaction?"

"She agrees with me but still thinks it might be a good idea for the two to meet. Partly I suspect because she wants to meet the girl."

"To thank her?"

"It seems that way."

"Bizarre, but okay, let's arrange it."

"Can you be here in about an hour? I don't want him to get too tired before he sees her."

"Let me ask you something doctor."

"Go ahead."

"Do you think seeing her might make him worse?"

There was a pause on the line. "I think that's a risk I've got to take."

"Okay, I'll be over within the hour."

Charlie put the receiver down – stood up from his desk and headed back to the interview room. He hadn't expected this part to be so easy. But then he'd learnt over the years never to be surprised by anything.

Forty-Three

Rachel sat by James's bed doing her best to control her feelings, she didn't know what to expect. She was curious, nervous and coiled like a spring; part of her wanted to hug the girl and thank her, the other part wanted to scream invectives in her face. "I need to see her," she told Tim. "just as much as James, though I'm not quite sure why. George Russell thinks she's just another nasty little terrorist trying to save her skin. But both James and I need closure on this and the only way to get that is to talk to her. I know James won't rest until he's seen her. What's he going to say Tim, what should he say? *Thank you for saving my life, but you've killed my father!* I doubt that. He talks about her as if they were friends. Its weird isn't? So bloody weird, and I'm so confused. I just wish I could be anywhere else but here in this ghastly hospital. I wish I was at home, at ease, loving Richard, looking forward to seeing James at weekends. If only I could wake from this nightmare. But I'm not going to am I? This is real Tim and I don't know how to deal with it. Help me."

"I'm not sure I'm the right person," Tim ventured. "But I feel I'm responsible for this mess. If I hadn't sent Russell into Belfast, Richard might still be alive. No, that's wrong. He would be alive. I'm devastated by the turn of events, and I think you need someone with a clearer head to advise you."

Rachel reached for his hand and said quietly, "You mustn't beat yourself up anymore. It will change nothing and I forgive you and right now I need you. Any minute now the girl is going to walk through that door and I have no idea how I'm going to react. You must help me."

The tension was tangible as O'Malley and Mary entered the room. Three pairs of eyes were turned on Mary. He whispered, "You'll be okay," as Rachel leapt up from her chair and stared at Mary, a questioning look on her face. In front of her stood a beautiful young woman, it unnerved her. "You're not what I expected, not at all," she blurted out."

Mary gave her a nervous smile, twining and untwining her fingers. She saw anger in the eyes and braced herself.

The attack was not long in coming. "You," Rachel, exclaimed, as she took a few steps towards Mary. Her voice rose, and all the bitterness that had been building up inside her cascaded out like a breached dam. She just couldn't smile and say thank you. "You bitch! You bloody killer! You've ruined my life. I hope you rot in hell." Then just as suddenly as the bitterness had erupted it dried up and the dam was empty. She lurched away from Mary. She would have fallen if Tim hadn't caught her. She sobbed uncontrollably. "I didn't mean that I promise – I don't know what I'm doing. I don't know what I mean. I'm so, so sorry." She looked at the girl and saw the distress on her face. "Are you really that cruel? Convince me you're not."

Mary was speechless.

O'Malley was stunned. He had not expected this. He looked at Mary. "I think we'd better go."

Mary tore her hand away. "No!" She moved swiftly to Rachel's side. "Don't apologise to me lady. I'm shit. You're right, I will rot in hell. Of course you hate me. I don't know what I can say to you that might convince you that I'm not all bad. I have felt compassion, if that is the right word. Oh fuck it I don't know. But I'll say this, I'm not into brutality lady, and your son suffered because of me. I'll never forgive myself for that, but, believe it or not I care for your son. Yes, you may well look at me like that but I didn't rescue him to save my skin. It would have been much easier to go along with that murdering bastard Seamus and watch your son die. I'm in far more danger now." She looked across at the bed and pointed a finger at James. "But he didn't deserve to die. He's suffered untold hardship and humiliation and he's fucking brave."

Rachel moved to within an inch of Mary's face. She could see the tears seeping out from her eyes – she could see she was trembling. This was genuine remorse, not acting.

She could forgive her.

Suddenly she felt a great load lift from her shoulders. She kissed Mary lightly on a cheek. "Thank you," she whispered to the startled girl. "Whatever you were before, I don't care. You risked your life and that's good enough for me." She gave a weak smile and said, "Now James wants to talk to you." She turned away and beckoned to the two men. "Come on, let's leave them alone."

"Is that wise," Charlie asked?

Rachel turned to him. "Yes, Inspector, it is."

*

Mary stood at the end of the bed. She looked down at James propped up on three white pillows, which matched the colour of his face. His eyes were closed. She could hear his breathing and she wondered if he'd heard the exchanges. Then panic hit her. *Run!* She was not needed, nor wanted. This had been a mistake. She flew towards the door, but as her hand touched the handle she heard a weak voice say, "Mary."

Her hand dropped from the handle and she whirled round. "You're awake. I'm told you are going to recover, that's really good. That's why I came but there's no need to stay. I just wanted to see for myself that you're better." She almost laughed at her inept words.

"Stay, please."

"No James. I'm not wanted here."

"I owe you Mary."

"No, please don't say that."

"I mean it. Please come and sit down."

Mary reluctantly dropped into the chair by the side of the bed. She had the most fatuous urge to reach out and take this tortured man into her arms, which she quickly dismissed. *Leave, leave* a small voice was saying. But the moment passed. "Oh James I'm so sorry about your father. I can't find the words to describe how I feel, I thought he was going to be safe."

James struggled into a sitting position, and without thinking Mary moved to plump up his pillows. "Thanks. And a little water as well?" He asked.

As Mary reached for the glass they both remembered the times he'd laid on the sofa and begged her with those words. They looked into each others eyes and said nothing.

Mary broke the awkward silence. "I came to apologise James for all the terrible things that were done to you. I don't ask for your forgiveness. I'm as guilty as Seamus, simple as that. I'll never see you again, but out of all this mayhem you've taught me something of great importance; there's more to life than living with hatred washing around in your guts. There's no place for such a word, I'll never hate anyone again. Oh actually that's not quite true, I'll never stop hating Seamus Flanagan. Well enjoy the rest of your life James. Goodbye." Mary reached out and took his hand. "You're a brave man."

As she moved to go James held on to her hand. "No, you can't go just yet. You've said your bit now it's my turn." He coughed and winced with the pain, sweat breaking out on his brow.

"I must go. You're tiring yourself."

But James held on to her hand. "This may sound like the ramblings of a man gone mad but you must believe it, you're important to me." He saw disbelief in Mary's eyes. "Just let me finish. I will walk away from here knowing I have met a brave young woman. Okay you made mistakes but you saved my life and risked your own. My father's death was a terrible accident. You did your best and if he was alive he'd thank you for saving mine. You're not evil Mary. I know you face the threat of a prison sentence but that won't be because of me. I'll say nothing

Love Thine Enemy

that might make matters worse for you. It is time for us both to move on, what's done is done and I bear no malice towards you. Oh God this sounds so trite."

"No it doesn't."

"Well I'm not putting it very well, but I hope you understand how I feel?"

Mary pulled her hand away. "I think I do." Then leaning forward she kissed his damp forehead. "Have luck James. I'll certainly never forget you." She straightened her back and walked towards the door, the conversation had unnerved her. It didn't seem real. James had shown no anger. How was this? She shrugged her shoulders and turned for one last look at James. Even with all his battle wounds he was beautiful. He'd told her she was important to him – that she wasn't evil. She had saved him - put his safety before her own. Why was he so forgiving? Had she missed something? And then it struck her. She had and big, fat tears filled her eyes. She turned the door handle and walked out into the corridor where Charlie was waiting. Let's go," she said.

Forty-Four

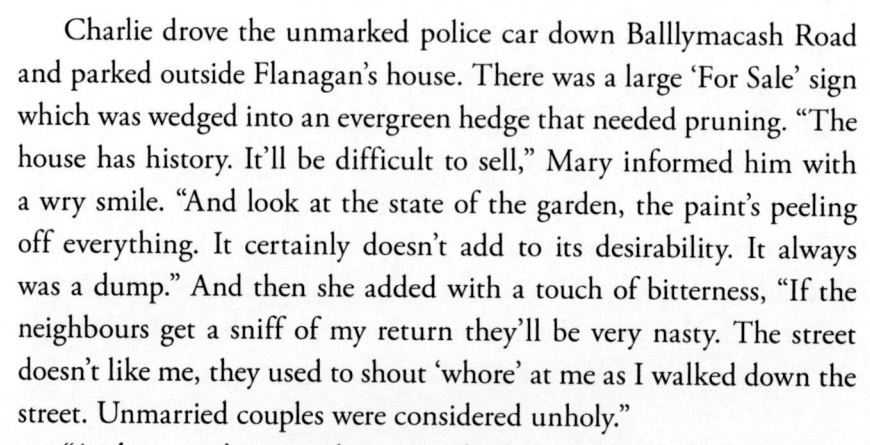

Charlie drove the unmarked police car down Balllymacash Road and parked outside Flanagan's house. There was a large 'For Sale' sign which was wedged into an evergreen hedge that needed pruning. "The house has history. It'll be difficult to sell," Mary informed him with a wry smile. "And look at the state of the garden, the paint's peeling off everything. It certainly doesn't add to its desirability. It always was a dump." And then she added with a touch of bitterness, "If the neighbours get a sniff of my return they'll be very nasty. The street doesn't like me, they used to shout 'whore' at me as I walked down the street. Unmarried couples were considered unholy."

"And yet you've agreed to come back," Charlie said, hoping that there were no prying eyes watching the car.

"Concerned detective?"

Her bouts of sarcasm were annoying Charlie, but he suspected that was her aim. He was beginning to read her mind. So he bit his tongue and said, "Yes, I am."

"Well don't waste your time. I want Seamus dead. End of story, okay?"

"Okay, so here's what we do."

"We?"

"Yes we Mary, this is a combined operation."

"You could have fooled me."

Charlie's patience broke down. "Now listen hear young lady, this was your idea, I'm not dumping you here to be killed. I'll protect you as much as I can. Day and night we'll be watching the house and one of Russell's men will be with you all the time."

"Hope he's good looking."

Charlie ignored the remark. "Please Mary listen. This is important."

"I'm listening, for what it's worth."

"You're getting on my nerves."

Mary looked across at Charlie and thought she saw real concern in his eyes. Why couldn't she believe that he was on her side? Whatever, she was behaving like a bitch. It came naturally, but this wasn't the time, she needed Charlie as much as he needed her. "I'm sorry. I owe you a lot. I'll try not to be so bitchy. I'm just struggling a bit with our relationship, for want of a better word. So just ignore the smart arse remarks detective; sometimes I can't control my mouth. The truth is I'm scared shitless. It's like walking into a trap."

"I understand. But if Flanagan tries a full frontal assault he won't have a hope of getting near you. There'll be a ring of steel around you. You will come out of this alive and Seamus Flanagan will be out of your life."

"That'll never happen, not even when he's dead. You have no idea what influence he still commands, even from the grave my life will be in danger. It doesn't need to be him to pull the trigger."

"I think you're exaggerating."

"Think what you like detective, but I know Seamus better than you ever will. His tentacles will stretch beyond the grave."

Charlie said nothing.

Mary shrugged, opened the car door and stepped out. "Come on detective let's get out of sight before some nosy bitch rushes over to see what is going on. And there's no point taking this conversation further, I know what I know and you can believe what you like."

Charlie nodded in agreement and joined her on the pavement, handing her a small duffle bag that she'd packed with a few items she and Charlie had bought on the way. A hair brush, some hair spray, tooth paste and soap. Then they'd gone to a clothes shop and she'd bought a bra, smiling at Charlie as she'd swung it in front of him. "Next time you buy a woman clothes don't forget most of us need one of these," she'd joked. She took the duffle bag off him. "And how do we get in? I don't have fucking keys."

Charlie dangled a set of keys in front of her. "All taken care of. New doors."

"Bullet-proof no doubt."

Charlie smiled. "As a matter of fact, yes."

"Wow detective!"

"Okay let's go. We're vulnerable standing on the pavement and as you've said, it's better no one knows that you're back."

"Quick then. Are you coming in, or just dumping me here?"

"I'll wait until I'm satisfied everything is in place."

"And until my good looking companion has arrived?"

"He won't be long."

Once inside the house, they moved into the kitchen which, although Charlie had had it cleaned, still smelt of stale cigarette smoke and damp. "No wonder no one wants to buy it," Mary commented eyeing the cigarette burns on the formica table and remembering the last time she'd sat around it listening to Seamus and Declan plotting Fitzpatrick's kidnap. "It's till a dump. Makes your poxy cells look like luxury accommodation"

"We try to please."

Mary laughed. "Okay, what now detective?"

Charlie looked at his watch. "Earlier today I held a press conference. The two most asked questions were if I had any information as to the whereabouts of Flanagan and what was going to happen to you. I had to admit that I had no information about Flanagan but that you were still helping me with my enquiries. I said that you weren't under arrest, but that you had asked for protection and that I'd agreed to keep you in custody. I don't want the whole of Ireland knowing that you're free – the media will never stop following you and that will mean our plan is a non-starter. I also said that you were being very helpful and had risked your life to rescue James Fitzpatrick."

Mary stared out of a filthy window. "You might have cleaned these, detective."

"Are you listening to me Mary?" he said irritably.

"Yeah, yeah, I'm listening. So I'm a prisoner here then?"

"It would be wiser not to show your face."

"Okay, I'm a prisoner. I suppose I might as well get used to it."

Charlie chose his words carefully. "You can think what you like Mary, but at the moment I'm undecided about what I'm going to do with you."

"You sound like my fucking maths teacher. She used to say that, and then make me stay in and do extra work while everyone else was in the playground. Prison bares a resemblance. So tell me teacher what are you planning to do with me?"

"I can help you."

"Like asking the judge for leniency?"

Charlie said. "If it gets to that."

Mary threw him a questioning look, but he avoided eye contact. "Hey detective don't ignore me okay. So you haven't a clue. Okay, well here is another question. If the media think I'm still in custody how is Seamus going to know that I'm free and squatting in his fucking house?"

"That is up to your friend Russell."

"Jesus detective you're a clever boy."

"It goes with the job."

"And how long do we wait to find out if Seamus has fled the country?"

"I was going to ask you that. Any ideas?"

Mary ran a hand through her hair. "I think he's still around. All his possible escape routes were blocked too quickly. I've got to hand it to you detective you were very efficient. He had another plan for just such an outcome but I don't know what it was. Seamus kept his own council.

But he's in Belfast detective, he's mad, he's vengeful and he's very, very angry and when he's angry, he does things against his better judgement. He'll be totally out of control and there are very few people about who'll be able to rein him in. And that is what will give you your chance, he'll come after me. He won't want anyone else to pull the trigger or slit my throat. Give him a week at most detective."

"Or he's more patient than you give him credit for."

"Mary shook her head. "Never."

*

George Russell dropped himself into Charlie's chair and smiled his thanks to the station sergeant as a mug of steaming hot coffee was put on the desk in front of him. He needed the caffeine to keep him awake. He blew loudly on the liquid and sipped – it tasted good. He had a man to call, Paddy, he'd never known his other name. Everyone called him 'Big Paddy." He was a great bear of a man, with a huge smile and jet black hair down to his shoulders, a plumber by trade and a good one by all accounts, but his income fell short of his needs. Paddy was a compulsive gambler and not a very shrewd one. "Cards and the horses, have been my downfall," he cheerfully told George. Debt was a word he knew well and George had used this to good advantage. Whilst undercover Paddy soon became his ears, he was trusted by the IRA, played cards in the same pubs and was treated with good humour wherever he chose to play. George had paid him well and his information had lead to several attacks being nipped in the bud. George had never lost touch, checking up that he was okay from time to time and every now and then sending him money. It was unusual for a man in his position to do this, and he had no doubt his superiors would disapprove. *"Once out of an operation make sure you cut all ties. Never ever keep in touch with any of your informers; you could be putting yourself and them at unnecessary risk."* But Paddy had saved his life when his cover was blown and that deserved reward. So he'd ignored the advice, besides he had a soft spot for the big man, he pulled his mobile out of his trouser pocket and dialled. It was pay back time.

He held his breath. One ring, two, four, then seven. Would it be voicemail?

"Hello, Paddy here."

George's heart turned a somersault. "Ah Paddy, a friend here." He was careful to disguise his voice, it wouldn't do for Paddy to know he was back in Belfast. George wasted no time with pleasantries. "Mary Keogh is free and living in Seamus Flanagan's old house. She's not in protective custody as the media are saying. I thought this might be worth a bob or too for you."

"Who the fuck are you?"

George hung up.

"Don't let me down Paddy old son," George said to himself as he drained his mug. If Paddy had recognised his voice he was in trouble. So now he had to wait and see how the next few hours unravelled. If Flanagan was still in the country and Paddy had not recognised his voice, he was as sure as he could be that it would not be long before Flanagan made a move.

George dialled Charlie. "Job done, I got my man. I'm confident the message will be passed on if Flanagan hasn't already evaded you. Although it might take a few days as my contact won't go direct." He put the mobile back in his pocket and felt the stirrings of excitement, danger always made him this way, and whichever way you looked at it he was facing danger. Was he at last going to have the opportunity of coming face to face with Rose's killer? He had no doubt that given the chance he'd kill Flanagan and fuck the consequences. If he hadn't still got some humanity left in his body he knew he'd like to torture him first – hear him beg for mercy – a chance that Rose never got. His thoughts made him realise that he was no longer the professional soldier he'd once been. Trusted by his men and aware that killing should always be the last option. By his own admission he'd become a loose cannon, nursing revenge in his bosom. The pain of loss would never go until he'd looked Flanagan in the eyes and pulled the trigger.

He walked out of the station, hunching his shoulders against the biting north wind and slipped into his car. He was heading for Ballymacash Road and a meeting with someone who would not be pleased to see him.

*

The news reached Seamus two days after Russell's phone call. Joe Cassidy, a distant cousin of Seamus, took the call and his legs began to shake. The call was dynamite. Over the years of their friendship Joe had witnessed Seamus's rage many times, but it would be nothing to the rage that would erupt once the message was passed on. Joe took a deep breath wishing he hadn't, in a moment of cousinly love, agreed to hide Seamus if his freedom was ever threatened.

He watched Seamus's face redden, then the mug of tea he was holding flew across the room and smashed into fragments against a wall. "Keogh, you fucking bitch!" he yelled. "In my house! You're living in *my* house! Eating sleeping and shitting in my house! Laughing at me! Well I'll jam your laugh down your throat Mary Keogh, and that's not all I'll do with you, you fucking traitor! You'll die a slow painful death."

Joe saw the signs. This was all that was needed to push Seamus over the edge. Already he was becoming like a caged animal and this was only days into what might well be a long incarceration before he could get out of Ireland. "Keep calm Seamus, for Christ sake" Joe advised.

His advice fell on deaf ears. "I'll get the bitch," Seamus shouted. The chair he was sitting on crashed to the floor and broke into several pieces. It would take a skilled carpenter to mend it. "What's she doing in my house? Why isn't she in prison?"

Joe deemed it better to say nothing.

And then Seamus tapped his head. "Of course, of course, the bastards are using her as bait just in case I haven't fled the country.

They hope to draw me out. Fuck you Mary Keogh! I'm holed up in a house, where I am a virtual prisoner for fuck knows how long. All because of you." He pointed a finger, Joe shivered. "No one plays with me, I've got news for you, I don't give a fuck that you're bait – I don't care how many filthy Brits are guarding you. You'll soon die!" His rage was organic, like a tumour growing in his body, a cocktail of diseased bodily fluids, fusing together until they erupted. And the explosion was about to make him reckless.

"I'm out of here Joe. I can't stay. I want that girl to myself."

"Let me take care of her," suggested Joe nervously.

"You, Joe, you! For fuck sake you couldn't kill a cat. You could never pull a trigger."

"Then someone else, you still have loyal friends."

Seamus glared at Joe. "Are you listening? I'll kill her, okay? She's mine Joe. Do you hear that, she's mine. Get that into your thick skull."

Joe made one last try. "If you break cover now you're risking all our forward planning. You' re as good as dead and your future plans will die with you."

Seamus shook his head. "I'll survive – you'll help me. Let me think. Then we'll make a move."

And that was just what Charlie O'Malley was hoping.

Joe thought it might be time to quit.

Forty-Five

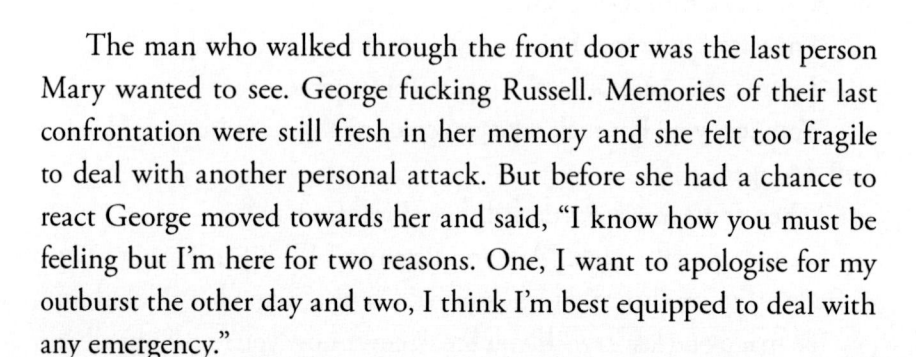

The man who walked through the front door was the last person Mary wanted to see. George fucking Russell. Memories of their last confrontation were still fresh in her memory and she felt too fragile to deal with another personal attack. But before she had a chance to react George moved towards her and said, "I know how you must be feeling but I'm here for two reasons. One, I want to apologise for my outburst the other day and two, I think I'm best equipped to deal with any emergency."

Mary glared at him and turned to Charlie. "Jesus Charlie, I could do without this man guarding me. I thought it was going to be one of his men."

"So did I," Charlie said, scowling at George. He suspected there was only one reason why George had come and it wasn't to apologise. Seamus Flanagan.

George ignored Charlie and said to Mary, "My lads will be here soon."

Charlie shook his head. "Yeah, I'm sure."

Mary blew out her cheeks and did her best to control her voice. "I'm not looking for a fight with you soldier. The detective has told me about your wife and I know my reactions would have been the same, had our roles been reversed. But let's do away with the apology crap shall we, and accept that we don't like each other? I suspect you're here because I'm your ticket to getting your hands on Seamus. So be honest with me. Right now we need each other, okay?"

"I couldn't have put it better myself," George conceded.

And Charlie agreed, which made him all the more uneasy about George's presence. Revenge could make you careless, and that to his way of thinking, made George unreliable. He'd be glad to see Peter Carpenter and his two mates walk through the door. "Tea anyone?" he asked weakly.

Mary said, "I think I need to go for a walk."

"No."

She glared at Charlie. "Why the fuck not?"

"I would've thought that was obvious after what I just said to you. Added to that Flanagan may well know where you are by now."

Mary gave an audible sigh. "Ah well, my mother once said to me that when God punches your ticket, he does so with authority. Whatever plans you make, whatever you decide to do it's not going to change the Man's decision to pull your string. But have it your way detective, let's have that tea."

*

"Just some fucking girl, some girl?" Seamus roared. "Keogh is an enemy of Ireland, a traitor to our Cause. Let her live? Walk away as if she's done nothing worse than cheat on me with another man?" He stabbed a finger in Joe's face, who was now convinced he'd have more of chance of staying alive if he went to the police. He'd survived through the Troubles and no longer wanted to die for a cause that he accepted was lost. It was out of loyalty that he had agreed to help Seamus – mind you the money he was being paid had helped as well. But now the thought of being dragged into a fight that Seamus could not possibly survive, did not look appealing – shit no! Did the man think he was invincible?

Seamus sensed Jo's reluctance, he could see it in his eyes, he'd seen that look before. He glared at him and started pacing the room. "You're not going to tell me that you want no part of this?"

Joe was dumb enough to speak out, after all Seamus was a mate, he didn't want to drag him to a certain death, he told himself. "For godsake Seamus, you're a dead man if you walk out of here. Do you think the police are going to let you get within striking distance of the girl? You're throwing away your life for nothing, can you not see reason?" And then he added more in hope than anything else. "You'll get your chance one day."

Seamus moved like lightening and hit him hard in the stomach. Joe went down fighting for breath. "You arsehole. I'm Seamus Flanagan, invincible. No one can kill me. Do you hear that you lily-livered coward? No one shits on me without paying the ultimate price. Wait. Why should I wait? I want to kill that girl now."

Joe finally knew that Seamus had flipped over the edge and there would be no stopping him. He rose painfully to his feet, gasping, "That does it Seamus, you're out of control. You might as well slit your throat here and now. Do you want me to get a knife?" He laughed mirthlessly. "Sorry, but as far as I'm concerned you're on your own. I wish you luck." Holding his stomach he made for the door. "See you again, I hope" he mumbled.

The bullet from Seamus's SIG 9mm slammed into his back.

Seamus tucked the gun back into his waist band, not at all worried that the shot might alert the neighbours. The house was detached at the end of the road, fields to the back and the nearest house empty, besides, it was a road where gun shots had been the norm and memories were long.

He moved to Joe's body, grabbed his feet and pulled him towards the cellar steps, he pushed and heard the thump as Joe hit the ground. "That's better," he said. He shoved his hands into his trouser pockets. *Count your days Mary, count your days.* But he needed help, like wheels and more fire-power, like a decoy to replace Joe the lily-livered shit. He smiled, as he thought of the perfect man, a man whose loyalty was beyond question. A man that would die for him; well he had thought that of Joe. Sinking ship! He'd show his doubters, he'd prove to them that he was the man to follow. He reached for his mobile – the landline was too risky.

*

The young man who answered was Patrick, in his late-twenties, both parents dead and living with an aunt who hated him. He was a real hothead, a man you did not willingly pick an argument with. He stood nearly six-five in his socks, his arms tattooed with the Republican flag. He wanted everyone to know where his loyalties lay. He was in constant trouble with the police and had served one spell in a young offender institution, Seamus Flanagan was his hero. "I'm family," he enjoyed boasting. He felt a rush of excitement as Flanagan spoke. "Patrick, I need your help. I need weapons, a car and a driver, you up for a bit of excitement?"

"Shit Seamus what a surprise, I didn't expect to hear from you. The word about is that you're long gone. But I'm up for anything – getting a bit bored. No action."

"Do the drums tell you where I'm hiding?"

"No."

"Listen then."

Patrick whistled in admiration. "Right under the police noses, only you would do that!"

"It's the best place to be wanted for something?"

"No, I'm clean."

"Good, then get over here fast, there's no time to waste and I'm fed up with waiting. I'll fill you in when I see you."

Patrick put the phone down with a shaking hand, the adrenalin pumping. He was tired of going straight and he'd never let Seamus down. Throwing on his thick black coat he shouted to his aunt that he'd be back sometime, there was no need for an explanation, the old bat would be glad to see the back of him, and she'd learnt it was better never to enquire into her nephew's business. He ran out of the house and jumped into his battered, old Land Rover. He'd a visit to make before joining Seamus, he never kept guns in his aunt's house.

Forty-Six

Mary was sleeping fitfully, her waking haunted by fear, her sleep punctuated by nightmares. She's in bed with Seamus, she's kissing him, his face stares down at her and suddenly turns into a snake's head dripping blood from its mouth. She wakes, her armpits are sweaty, her clothes stick to her body. She'd not dared undress. She hears a strange sound and leaps out of bed. She glances at her watch – it's four in the morning. She cannot bear her own company any longer, the room spooks her. She hurls herself down the stairs and burst into the kitchen. George Russell is sitting at the table drinking coffee. "Oh shit. It had to be you didn't it?" She turns on her heels. "Hold it," George says. "There's room for us both. No need for us to speak."

Mary hesitates. She's feeling very vulnerable and she knows the soldier won't hurt her. She takes a tentative step back into the kitchen. She doesn't need to like the man sitting at the table but he's company, and she knows she'll feel safer. She moves to the table and sits down. "Do you mind sharing a few hours with this piece of trash?" she asks in a quiet voice. "I don't think I want to be alone."

*

Charlie was collapsed in an arm chair in the front room, also wide awake, he's dog-tired but sleep is proving elusive. He'd always been a worrier but there shouldn't be any need. The house is well-guarded, George and his three lads are capable of covering every inch, but has he missed anything? Surely not. It's the waiting that is getting to him.

Two days now and no movement, no sighting of Flanagan, absolutely fucking nothing. Had George's news got to him? Or was he laughing his head off, probably in America? Intuition was telling Charlie that Mary was right, that Flanagan was out there somewhere, waiting, waiting, choosing his moment. The early hours when men's eyes grew heavy, this was the time to be alert. Charlie knew this man. Relax for a second and you'd regret it. He runs over his plans, is every avenue covered? Has he enough men out on the streets? Yes, yes, he couldn't have done more. He gets out of the chair, stretches his weary body and makes for the kitchen, the smell of freshly made coffee tickling his nostrils.

"Morning Charlie," says George, as he appears in the kitchen. Couldn't sleep? Bit like Mary here?"

"Too many things to think about."

"You're not the only one," Mary says. I've had Seamus in my bed, turning into a monster. I've heard strange noises which turned out only to be the soldier here making coffee. Jesus, the dreams get worse. When will this end? Soon there'll be no need for Seamus to kill me. I'll be dead from lack of sleep. How much longer are you going to wait before we have to admit that I was wrong and Seamus has slipped through your net?"

Charlie rubs his chin. "It's something that's bothering me," he confesses. "but I still think your hunch is right, I'm not dropping the operation yet. I just can't believe he got out of the country. I was so quick, he would have been spotted. He's here Mary, I can smell him."

"But he *has* slipped through your net detective. So why not to a ship or a plane?"

"Because every likely route out of here was sealed tight. No, he's somewhere in Belfast. I'd stake my life on it, he could easily have avoided the road blocks and got to a safe house. We know he walked, we couldn't cover every street and Flanagan knows Belfast better than anyone. So we wait. Keep alert. He wants us to get frustrated, to begin doubting that he's around."

"Well he's doing a fucking good job of making me nervous detective."

*

Meg Healey shifts her plump body on the chair and wonders how many hours in the last week she's spent sitting in the same chair waiting for news. Duff is sitting opposite her sipping tea, not a bottle of malt in sight. A headache is pounding in his head, but it's no good asking for sympathy - he knows the reply he'll get. He looks at his watch, five in the morning. Like Meg he hasn't even moved to go to bed. Like Charlie O'Malley he and Meg are waiting.

*

Tim Holroyd paces up and down. He wonders how many miles he's covered in the last two days, walking up and down the same corridor. He reaches James's room and risks pushing open the door. He sees James asleep in the bed, no doubt knocked out with sleeping pills. He almost feels envious. His eyes shift to Rachel sitting bolt upright in the chair by James's bed. Her eyes are wide open, rimmed with black shadows. He thinks she's aged years and wonders when she last slept. She looks up at him. "Any news?" she asks hopefully. He shakes his head. "I'm still waiting."

*

At six James is brought his first morning cup of tea. As usual the nurse is smiling, asking him how he's feeling. "Okay I think," he says, still half asleep. "The pain in my chest feels better this morning."
"And your bruises are turning yellow."
James takes a troubled breath. He does his best to smile. "I'll live."
The nurse pats his hand, she knows how much he's suffering inside. She knows what it's like to lose someone close to you, and no one comes much closer then one of your parents. "You're doing well James. You'll soon be out of here and on your way back to London."

"Without my father."

The nurse has no answer to that and she turns to Rachel. "Cuppa Mrs Fitzpatrick?"

Rachel yawns. "Oh that would be lovely nurse."

"You sleep Mum?"

"On and off. But right now I feel like dropping to the floor and sleeping for the next ten years. I think my body is reacting to all the strain of the last few days, but I'm fine James," Rachel lies. "And you?"

"As good as can be expected I suppose." James takes a sip of his tea. "Do you know what's worrying me?"

"No."

"It's the thought of Mary hung out as bait for Flanagan. I know you can't understand, but it doesn't sit well on my conscience."

Rachel is puzzled by these words. "Why do you say that? You don't owe her anything, she was part of the kidnap gang, just remember that. She doesn't deserve your concern. We've both said thanks, now forget her. You won't ever see her again."

"I'll never forget her. She kept me alive."

"James, for goodness sake listen to me; she kept you alive so they could get the money, you were no use to them dead. You know they had no intention of letting you live after they got what they wanted."

James shakes his head. "But Mary had nothing to do with that. You didn't hear her telling me not to give up, that she was on my side. You didn't see the concern in her face every time she gave me water. If it hadn't been for her I wouldn't have survived. And she saved me didn't she? You can't tar her with the same brush as Flanagan. Look at her now – prepared to risk her life, so that the police can get their hands on him. Is that the sign of a wicked woman?"

"She's just saving her own skin."

"Maybe at times I doubted her, I thought she was playing games with me, but I was wrong."

"Darling believe what you like, it doesn't make any difference. Mary Keogh is history."

"You don't get it do you Mum?"

Rachel shakes her head. "You're right, I don't understand and I never will."

*

George's mobile rings, he puts down his mug and answers, he listens – smiles and ends the call. He turns to Charlie. "The waiting is over. Flanagan will move tonight."

A pulse of excitement shoots through Charlie's body. "You're sure of this?"

"As sure as I can be, my source never let me down."

"Does your source know where he is? Perhaps we could move on him. Then we wouldn't be putting Mary Keogh or any of our men in danger."

George shakes his head. "My source has his life to think of. Just telling me that Flanagan is going to move tonight could have put him in severe danger. Telling me where he's hiding would almost certainly be a death sentence."

"But he knows?"

"Probably."

"Perhaps we could persuade him."

"Not a chance. He's survived all these years by being elusive and I don't know where he is, be content with what you've got. You're lucky I still have a contact like this. You've plenty of time to organise a welcoming party for Flanagan and as for this young lady's safety I think you both know my views on that already."

Charlie throws an apologetic smile at Mary. "Okay, you've done well George. Let's put everyone on red alert, and then I must make a couple of calls; one to the Chief Constable and one to Tim Holroyd."

Forty-Seven

Seamus was like a tiger waiting to pounce; every sinew taut, his eyes blazing. He'd been in some dangerous situations before but he was under no illusions that this was going to be the most difficult to get out of alive. He imagined his house would be guarded by half the Belfast constabulary. *But I'm Seamus Flanagan*, he kept telling himself, and he had Patrick – his ace. He felt no guilt that he might be sending a man to his death. Why change now? This was war and men had to be sacrificed. He looked across at his cousin, gripping the wheel of the clapped out Land Rover, and wondered if the motor would get them to Ballymacash road. "Is this thing road worthy?" he asked Patrick.

"Sure it is Seamus. It'll get me anywhere, it's just a wee bit slow."

"Well it's a bit late to doubt you," Seamus said through gritted teeth. He fingered the Smith and Wesson double action auto pistol with a fifteen round magazine, chambering 9mm Parabellums, which Patrick had brought along. Several of these weapons had come from the United States at the height of the Troubles. They didn't fire bursts, but they loaded a new round each time you pulled the trigger. Seamus had used them to good effect before.

He thought of O'Malley, he'd set the bait and made sure that the news would get to him; he was a shrewd policeman. Confident that he'd blocked his escape he reckoned that to hang Mary out to dry would prove too much for him. Too much for him! Didn't O'Malley know who he was taking on? If anyone died it would be O'Malley. He laughed out loud, slapping Patrick on an arm. "This is going to be fun."

Patrick wasn't too sure about that, he was beginning to think that Seamus was deluding himself, in fact he was wishing he'd never picked up the telephone but he said nothing.

Seamus sat back and ran his hand over the Smith and Wesson thinking of how he was going to kill Mary. Slowly. First, he'd mash her legs and then as she screamed he'd pump a bullet into her stomach. Finally, he'd walk up to her, grab her by the hair and blow her head away. It never entered his head that he might be dead before he got to her. His brain was awash with anger, nothing was going to stop him. He would never find peace until she was dead. *No one gets the better of Seamus Flanagan.*

*

There was no moon, it was pitch black. A north east wind howled around the Land Rover, their progress painfully slow. They still had a few miles to go to Lisburn and the time was ticking by, not that Seamus was worried too much as it was only half-past midnight and he didn't plan to make his move for at least another hour. But would they make it at all in this bucket that called itself a car? He needed time to reconnoitre. Seamus broke open his second packet of chewing gum wishing that he'd told Patrick to go out and steal a car. He was freezing cold. The Land Rover's heating had long given up pumping out warm air and the cold wind blew through dozens of cracks. He blew hard on his fingers – he would need them fairly soon. He looked across at Patrick staring out of the cracked windscreen, seemingly oblivious to the draughts. He'd make sure he had a decent burial.

*

Charlie skirted the river Lagan and made his way to a spot where he could watch the rear of the house, George was already in position watching the front. He'd wanted to stay in the house but Charlie had refused him – he knew what George had in mind. George had grumbled and glared angrily but could say nothing. "I want to be here to kill him," wouldn't go down well. So in the house with Mary was Phil Dashwood and Peter Carpenter, along with two armed officers, was with Charlie. Dan O'Connor had gone with George. The rest of the armed response unit were spread around Ballymacash Road. No way could Flanagan get through to Mary but what worried him was a fire-fight breaking out in the road. He didn't want innocent casualties and there was always the possibility that Flanagan wouldn't come alone. There was no doubt he still had a following of disgruntled republicans, but were they willing to kill? He pulled his mobile out of his jacket pocket and dialled police HQ. The Chief Constable answered immediately. "All's in place sir. If Russell's information is right we can expect Flanagan any time now."

Charlie could hear the nervousness in his boss's voice. "What about the girl Charlie? Are you moving her out?"

"No, she's staying."

"Is that wise?"

"I'm not sure to be honest, but I'm guessing Flanagan will have eyes everywhere. So I can't take the risk. This is how Keogh feels as well and she knows a lot more about Flanagan's chain of communication than we do. And we really want to get the son of a bitch."

"Okay, understood. But what about the neighbours? Is there a risk of innocent casualties? "

"There's always that possibility, but I think Flanagan will move in the early hours. Hopefully most of the occupants will be asleep and I'm banking on stopping him before he gets too far. The alternative is to evacuate the whole road which will lead to awkward questions and frantic media activity. We'd never manage to evacuate the road quietly."

"So you gamble."

"I prefer to think I have all angles covered."

"Do you honestly think that Flanagan will risk arrest or death when he's disappeared successfully and only has to bide his time before he sneaks out of the country?"

"I think he's been driven over the edge and won't be thinking straight. He wants Keogh."

"He must want her dead really badly."

"Keogh says that he'll see her actions as betrayal and that will have hit him hard. For Flanagan betrayal is unforgivable. Punishable by death, were her words. And he's lost – he'll lose face, so he's mad as hell, and mad men take risks. He'll want to kill Keogh by his own hand."

"He'll almost certainly die."

"He thinks he's invincible, and I guess he's past caring. You and I can't understand men like that sir, but they exist and they're very dangerous."

"To true Charlie, I'll leave it up to you. Good luck, may God be with you."

"I don't think he'd approve."

A dog barked somewhere and Charlie jumped. Jesus, he was getting paranoid!

*

George moved quietly into position – he'd reconnoitred the empty house the day before. "We can hide in the garden Dan. There's a good view of the road both ways"

"Which way will Flanagan be coming from?"

"From the right, from Belfast."

"You sure George?"

"Yes."

Dan felt no need to question him. He had complete trust in George.

"Now we settle down," George said. "Let's have that flask Dan – could be a long wait."

*

Patrick drew to a halt at the top of Ballymacash Road – killed the engine and looked across at Seamus. "What now?" he asked. His body was shaking and it wasn't from the cold.

Seamus spat his chewing gum onto the floor and stared out of the window. Not a sign of any movement. That didn't surprise him, O'Malley was no fool. "Ah Patrick my son this is the moment I test your metal. You're going to become me; put on my cap, wear my coat, take the shotgun and walk down this street. You're about my build and you'll attract all the attention; guns will be pointed at you from all angles. And while the bastards make up their minds whether to pump you full of lead I'll walk down the other side of the road towards my house. I'll have reached the house before they've either shot you, or arrested you and realised they've got the wrong man. And I'll be long gone before they have time to refocus their shattered nerves and Mary will be dead. It'll be a piece of cake."

"I'm going to be a decoy?" Patrick was incredulous.

"You've got it in one."

"I might die."

"Indeed you might, but you have a chance Patrick. And if you die you will be a hero. Let me tell you something, when I was a young man like you, cutting my teeth in the IRA, my commander told me always to do as I was told and if necessary die a brave man. So look at it this way. I'm your commander and you do as you're told, clear? Besides, O'Malley would like to take me alive. So you have a chance."

"And if I tell you that I don't want to go to prison, or die what will you do? Think of another plan?"

"No, *I* will kill you."

"Jesus, Seamus you joke."

"No Patrick my son, I never joke. So come on let's swap."

Patrick's shaking grew worse. "I…" He looked down the barrel of the Smith and Wesson.

"Make up your mind boy. Take a chance on living or definitely die in the next few seconds. I'll count to ten."

"You're mad."

Seamus shook his head. "Oh you shouldn't have said that, five, you'd better be quick, seven." Seamus clicked the safety off.

Patrick threw himself out of his door.

*

"There's a Land Rover at the top of the road," whispered Dan urgently, adjusting his night-vision glasses. "Shit, someone's just fallen out of it. He's up and running."

George swung his night-vision glasses up the road. "There's another man getting out. He's pointing a gun at the man!"

A shot rang out. "Jesus Dan he's shot him! He's down, quick, alert Charlie. We've an incident on our hands. Tell him I think it must be Flanagan and something has gone badly wrong. This isn't a diversion. Tell him not to move."

Dan did as he was told. "He says he can see the top of the road. He's staying where he is. He says hold hard and wait."

"Okay." George raised his night vision-glasses again just as another shot rang out. "Fuck this. I think he's making sure the man is dead. This has got to be Flanagan!"

Several lights were turned on in some houses. "Oh shit!" George exclaimed. "Bang goes our silent operation. Here, give me the mobile. I want to speak to Charlie. Hello Charlie, lights are going on. What? Okay." George turned to Dan. "Charlie says to still hang on and wait to see how this unravels. But I'm not waiting, Flanagan isn't getting away from me. I'm on the move, it's up to you if you follow me. I'll understand if you stay here."

Dan said, "I'm with you boss."

George and Dan broke cover running. George had a red mist floating in front of his eyes, at last revenge was close. Oblivious of danger he charged up the street. Dan followed – radio to his mouth shouting to Charlie. "For Christ sake sir, get out here quick. I don't think I can control Russell, he's on a mission."

Charlie, Peter Carpenter and the two officers hit the road running. To Charlie's dismay more lights were being turned on and doors were flying open. "Stay inside, stay inside," Charlie shouted. "Police! We have a dangerous situation. Close your doors!" He could make out George running up the street followed by O'Connor. He sprinted and was almost by George's shoulder when he saw, without a doubt, that the man standing by the Land Rover under a street light was Flanagan. He was waving a weapon, his legs were spread. He yelled, "Come and get me you police bastards."

Charlie heard George shout. "You're dead Flanagan."

"George no," bellowed Charlie. "No, no, no!"

Flanagan charged like a raging bull down the street, yelling obscenities and firing wildly. Dan O'Conner grunted and fell, George raised his pistol. Charlie smacked it down. "No! I want him alive!"

"He'll kill us all you damn fool," George shouted. "He's out of control."

Charlie grabbed George's arm. "We wait for backup." A bullet whistled past. George wrenched his arm away from Charlie's grip and fired. "Murderous bastard. See if you like that" George yelled. Flanagan let out a howl of rage and fell groaning. His Smith and Wesson clattered onto the road. There were screams behind Charlie. "Someone's been hit," he shouted at the two officers. "For Christ sake go and see what's happening. Get people back in their houses if you can, I'll stay with Russell."

Pandemonium was breaking out. Armed officers were running up the street, shouting at people to stay inside their houses. Paramedics, who had been waiting close to Ballymacash road, came running and the Air Support unit's Eurocopter EC 35 was hovering overhead, a searchlight playing on the scene below. Charlie turned his full attention to Russell and he stared in horror. Oh bloody shit!" he exclaimed.

George was kicking at Flanagan's legs. Flanagan was yelling. George shouted, "You murdering scum, you killed my wife." He kicked Flanagan again. "Do you recognise me Flanagan? I'm George Russell."

Recognition spread across Flanagan's pain–ridden face. "Russell!"

George bent down until he was only a few inches away from Flanagan's face. "Yes, George Russell, the man who fooled you – the man who's been topping your murderous colleagues. Now it's your turn." George put his gun against Flanagan's temple. Flanagan rolled away – tried to stand – let out a cry of agony and collapsed. "Looks as if you've the upper-hand Russell," he said through clenched teeth. "Go on then kill me, pull the trigger. I don't think you've the guts."

"Bravado won't save your life you murderous bastard!"

"No!" shouted Charlie. "Don't do it George!"

George pulled the trigger and Flanagan's face exploded in a mass of blood and shattered bones. "It's done," said George quietly, handing his pistol to Charlie. "Self-defence." He touched Charlie on a shoulder, turned and walked away.

Charlie watched him disappear into the dark and felt a hand on his shoulder. "You okay Charlie? Carpenter asked.

Charlie straightened up. "Yeah, I'm okay. Any casualties?"

'Fraid so. Dan's dead. One civilian severely wounded."

Charlie shook his head. "Shit."

"And our boss sir?"

"Got his revenge poor man. I don't think it will do him any good."

"Will you arrest him?"

"Self-defence Peter, it was self-defence. You can vouch for that can't you?"

"Indeed I can sir."

"Then let's get back to the house."

They were halfway down the road when the overhead searchlight picked out Mary running towards them. Charlie cursed loudly. "That's just what I didn't want." He spread both arms out in front of him as Mary came to a stop. "That's as far as you're going."

"Fuck off detective, he's dead isn't he? I want to see him."

"Yes, he's dead, so there's nothing to be gained by seeing him."

"How can you say that? You can't begin to understand what that man nearly did to me. I need to see him"

"To gloat."

"Oh detective, you're on the ball. I need to move on and I can't do that until I see he's dead with my own eyes. So, either you have to shoot me or let me pass."

"I could just restrain you."

"I'd kick the shit out of you."

Charlie swallowed a laugh, and gave in. She had the right.

Mary walked slowly towards where the medics were kneeling by Seamus's body. She wanted the chance to spit on his face. But as she moved closer she was surprised to feel a tear trickle down her cheek. It confused her. "Jees, am I crying because I've lost him?" she asked out loud. She stopped, trying to work out what her emotions were up to. "Miss him?" she shouted at the medics. "Miss the bastard?" They looked at her questioningly. "How could I miss that fucking bastard?"

The medics looked away, some crazy girl being a nuisance. One of them moved towards Mary. "Look lady, could you just make yourself scarce. We have work to do here."

Mary raised two fingers. "I'll go when I'm ready."

"Then we will have to forcibly move you."

Mary raised a hand. "Okay, okay, just give me a minute. This man wanted to kill me."

The medic tapped his watch. "You're on borrowed time."

Mary squeezed past the medics. She gasped when she saw Seamus's shattered face, her hand flew to her mouth and suddenly she realised why she was crying. She was crying for Seamus. He'd lived a life of violence, hatred and bitterness. His whole life had been one fucking big fight, he'd never loved her. She had been a means to an end. He'd never had children, never enjoyed a holiday – never been at ease with himself. He trusted no one. He'd thought he was a hero but in fact he'd turned out to be a loser. She doubted if Seamus knew the word happiness and that was why she was crying. No man deserved to have such a bad hand passed down to him by God. She wiped away a tear – took one last look at the mutilated face and walked away.

*

Meg Healey poured tea for the gathered company. Duff had wanted to offer champagne, but Meg had told him it was inappropriate. "Not when we're about to bury Richard." She finished pouring. "Help yourselves to sugar and milk and there are homemade biscuits on the table." She was feeling particularly tearful. The events of the last few weeks had tested her resolve and now that the curtain was about to fall she felt like breaking up and 'having a damned good weep,' she'd told Duff before everyone had arrived. She looked across at Rachel, white faced, dressed in black and wondered how she was copping. She'd been so brave. James stood by her side supporting his weight with a stick. He looked weak, he was only just out of hospital. She'd been told that physically he was making a good recovery, but she guessed that mentally he was struggling. Charlie O'Malley, Phil Dashwood and Peter Carpenter were talking quietly amongst themselves, no doubt mourning the loss of Dan O'Connor and discussing their futures. Tomorrow they would be flying back to England with his body. Meg could see O'Malley rising to the top of his profession and no doubt the two younger men would go on plying their trade until some well aimed bullet or well placed booby trap put an end to their lives; so many dead and all because of one man. Meg fervently hoped Seamus Flanagan was in hell. How could someone be so evil? George Russell had done everyone a favour. How was he coping, she wondered, where had he gone? Was he now at last able to live with himself? She'd probably never know. Hearing tyres on the gravel drive and looking out of the window she saw the hearse and two other cars pull up. "I think it's time to go," she said, turning to Rachel.

*

The little churchyard at Gartree was bathed in late November sun. There was still a chill in the air and Rachel shivered under her thick overcoat. She was carrying out Richard's wishes to be buried next to his father and grandfather. "If I can't go back in life at least I can go back in death," he'd once said to Rachel and she wasn't going to let him down, even though she would have liked to bury him at home. But then in a way this had always been Richard's home. His heart had never quite left Langford Lodge. She knew he'd be at peace lying beside his father – the man who unintentionally had mapped out his life. She gripped James's hand as the coffin was lowered into the ground. The service had been brief – the attendance, just those who had come with her from Brascome. She hadn't wanted a crowd of strangers. Charlie had worked miracles to keep the press away. The vicar said the last prayer and then there was silence, she turned away. She did not want to throw a handful of earth onto the coffin, nor her wedding ring. It had been precious and even more so now, it was all she had left of Richard. She shook the vicar's hand – smiled and looked at James. "Let's go," she said.

James held onto her hand as they walked back to the cars, he could feel her shaking and knew she was fighting to keep the tears back. "Richard wouldn't want me to cry," she'd said on the way to the church. He understood how his father felt, he was never a man to want sympathy, nor a man who would ever want people to cry for him. He was a man full of life, generous to a fault and ironically that had been his downfall. James choked back a tear and squeezed his mother's hand hard. She asked, "You okay?"

He couldn't speak, just nodded.

As they went through the gate onto the road he turned to look at the church, thinking that he'd be visiting it again fairly soon. He had no intention of letting his father lie in a grave, a forgotten man. He gasped as he saw a familiar figure standing alone by the church porch, Mary.

He let go of his mother's hand and walked back through the gate not sure how to react. Mary saved him making a decision, she shook her head. He stopped – half-waved in welcome and threw her a smile. Mary raised one of her delicate hands and mouthed something he couldn't catch. He watched her walk over to the fresh grave and place a small bunch of flowers on the earth. Then she turned and walked towards him, he froze, when she was close enough she touched his arm. "I'm so very sorry James." But before he could reply she hurried away, he watched her until she was out of sight. He would have liked to have got to know the real Mary.

Forty-Eight

One year later.

George Russell walked along Turkey Road in Bexhill-on-Sea into the Rose and Crown and ordered a pint of his favourite bitter. "You're early today George," commented the landlord.

George smiled. "I'm a bit thirsty."

The landlord chuckled. "Good a reason as any."

George paid, and took the beer over to the window seat where he and Rose had always sat, even when the sun shone, she'd never liked sitting outside. He took a long pull of beer and smacked his lips, it tasted good. He leant back in the chair and imagined Rose holding his hand and looking out of the window at people passing by. They'd never said much to each other on these occasions, they were simply happy with each others company and enjoyed just being together, drinking their favourite tipple and eating their favourite salt and vinegar crisps in harmony. How he missed those moments. He hated his own company – loathed the lonely nights in the bungalow where he and Rose had hoped to spend the rest of their lives. And the days were no better, eating on his own sitting in front of a blank television screen pining for Rose. He'd hoped that with the death of Flanagan some of the pain and anger would have seeped from his veins, but it hadn't happened. For a man who had spent a lot of his life facing danger it surprised him how hopeless he felt at reconstructing his life. On the first night of returning from Belfast, he'd knelt down by the side of the bed he'd shared with

Michael Pakenham

Rose, and promised her to give it a year. Now time was up and nothing had changed.

Yesterday he'd made the decision.

He'd walked into an estate agent and put the bungalow up for sale. It was the first step towards what he hoped would be a happier future. Then, this morning, he'd walked to the pub and was now drinking a pint of his favourite beer. When the tankard was drained he left the pub with a wave to the landlord. He lit a cigarette and sucked in the nicotine – the one habit he'd taken up after Rose's death. At least there wouldn't be time for cancer to get him. He headed for the beach, taking the familiar route that he and Rose often took for their Sunday stroll. He thought he might be in time to meet Rose for lunch and smiling at the thought he increased his pace. He felt no fear, in fact the opposite. At last his suffering was about to end and a strange aura of peace enveloped him. He looked at the sea, so calm, so friendly. The winter sun casting shadows on the waves, it was almost hypnotic. He listened to the water lapping at the sand and throwing off his jacket, he started to walk towards the water. He imagined Rose looking down on him – waiting.

*

Tim Holroyd sat back in the large spring broken arm chair that his father refused to have mended and equally strongly refused to throw on the tip. He heard him clattering around in the next room, probably trying to find the third pair of glasses he'd mislaid already that morning. Tim's mother had always said that if she died before him he'd have to have six of everything important for the day, especially glasses and keys. Sadly she'd died four years back, but she'd never spoken a truer word. Holroyd sighed contentedly and looked out of the window as a light snow fell on the surrounding Perthshire countryside. Never for one moment had he regretted his decision to leave all the skulduggery and political intrigue behind him. His father's farm had proved the ideal place to unwind and once settled he had no intention of leaving. He heard a grunt of satisfaction from the next room, at last his father had found the Range Rover keys. He heard the front door open and felt a cold draught. "I'm off to see the sheep," his father shouted, remembering that he now had a partner. "Okay with you Tim?"

"That's fine Dad. Don't lose your way coming home." He heard a chuckle and then the door shut. Alone, Holroyd stretched out his long legs – held his breath as the springs sank a little further towards the ground. He raised the glass of Glenlivet whisky to his lips and thought back to the day he'd walked into Number 10. It was a morning he'd never forget.

*

The Prime Minister clasped Holroyd's hand and waved at a chair. "Have a seat Holroyd. I have an interesting morning laid on for you, but before the show begins let me say it's good to see you back alive. Bit of a hairy time I know and not completely the outcome you and I wanted, but a few dangerous men are dead and not a word has got to the press. Not yet at any rate. Of course I'm devastated by Richard Fitzpatrick's death and I have written to his wife. One concern however is the girl. What's her name?"

"Mary Keogh."

"Yes of course. Her trial might open a can of worms. Is there anything you can do about that?"

"You have nothing to worry about Prime Minister. There will be no trial. Mary Keogh has no case to answer. She's free."

"How on earth…"

"There is no one to testify against her. They're all dead and James Fitzpatrick has refused to help the investigation. So the Chief Constable and Chief Inspector O'Malley see no reason to pursue a lost cause and waste money and time."

"I'm sure it's not quite as simple as that, but I'm grateful to men like the Chief Constable. They put the safety of the nation first."

Tim smiled. "And saved our bacon."

The Prime Minister returned the smile. "Indeed he probably has. So, Holroyd what's your plan now? Back to the dangerous world?"

"I'm off to Scotland."

"What on earth is going on in Scotland? Not a terrorist cell I hope?"

"I'm going to run my father's estate in Perthshire. He's an old man now and my mother's dead. He needs some help and I'm sick of my profession, I can't stomach seeing good men die any longer, and you politicians are only interested in saving your skins. So it's time to go and live in peace, even if not with my conscience."

The Prime Minister reached out across his desk and shook Tim's hand. "I'll miss you commander and your frank speaking. I know you don't hold us politicians in much regard, but you have served us well and with honour. And now for the show I promised you, I think you'll enjoy this."

As if on cue the door opened and The PM's PPS put his head round the door. "The Secretary of State has arrived."

"Show him in."

David Saunders strutted through the door with a smile on his face. It rapidly turned to a scowl when he saw Holroyd. "What are you doing here?"

Tim gave him a broad smile. "Just saying my farewells."

Saunder's features brightened considerably. "Getting rid of you at last is he?"

"No, David it's not like that," The PM said. "Yes, he's leaving the Service but only because he wants to. He's going to Scotland."

Saunders stepped away from the door. "I can't say I'll be sorry. Good bye Holroyd. Have a good day."

"I think he'll have a good day," the PM said. "But he's not leaving just yet. I want him to hear what I've got to say to you."

"Is that wise?"

"I think so. Now gentlemen I haven't got all day, so please can you both take a seat."

Both men lowered themselves into chairs, looking puzzled.

"Now then," the PM began. "Can I ask you David where you will be going? Not Scotland I suspect." His look froze David's guts.

Love Thine Enemy

"What, what do you mean?"

The Prime Minister was beginning to enjoy himself. "It's come to my attention that you have had a mistress for the last two years." The PM watched his erstwhile friend squirm in his chair. "Not only that, but my information tells me she's an illegal immigrant. Tut-tut David. I have also been told that you have been fiddling your expense account. What a naughty boy you are David. Now I'm sure you don't want that darling little Welsh wife of yours to hear of your infidelity, or for the public to hear of your dishonesty. And if you have it in your head to blow the whistle on this last operation, which by the way my informant tells me is on your mind, I will make sure that the media know about your little misdemeanours.... . However I'm going to throw you a lifeline, which I suspect you wouldn't do to me if our rolls were reversed. I promise you I will keep this entirely between you and me, just as long as I have your resignation letter on my desk by six this evening and the young woman out of your bed for good."

Saunders face was puce. He was speechless and glared at Holroyd.

"Well?" asked the Prime Minister tapping his desk impatiently.

Saunders found his voice. "How did you find out?" was all he could think of asking.

"Like you David I have friends, in fact a good deal more than you, once you began plotting against me your fate was sealed. I'm hurt that a close friend can have been so vindictive."

Saunders shook his head. "How do I know Holroyd won't blow the whistle on me?"

"Ah well David that's my insurance you see. You'll never know. It's something you'll have to live with. Of course you can walk out of here and blab to the press and hope to take me down with you. But both I and Holroyd will deny everything. And who do you think the media will listen to? A pompous Welshman who is cheating on his wife and keeping his mistress in a flat paid for by the public, or a Prime Minister who is running high in the polls and a man who has served his country with distinction?"

Saunders rose from his chair feeling a defeated man. "And what reason shall I give for this sudden resignation?"

"I think you will come up with one, but personal matters sounds good eh David? That way you won't have to tell a lie."

*

Tim allowed himself a smile, as the PM had said, it had been a good day and one he'd never forget. As he sipped the last of the Glenlivet the telephone rang, he moved across the room and picked up the receiver, his features grew sad; "God, how awful. Thanks for letting me know. Drowned you say? Could it have been an accident? Yes, I understand. Let me know the date of the funeral will you? Thanks, bye." Hanging up he thought, poor George, even after death, Flanagan had managed to kill.

*

Meg stood at the door of Brascome swathed in a new dress, bought the day before from The Large Shop in Belfast. It was bright red, not a colour she normally chose, but this was a day when everything was going to change, so why not change her clothes? It had taken a lot of soul searching and long hours of discussion before she and Duff had come to a decision. They would stay and reopen, and they would do as the nice Chief inspector had asked and help Mary Keogh. "But we won't go as far as having her back here but I'll find her a job I promise," she'd told Charlie. Now Duff stood beside her, clean shaven, sober and deeply in love with his forgiving wife, he didn't deserve her, which she'd told him many times. He ran a hand down her side and smiled. She playfully pushed him away. "There's a time and place for that sort of thing Duff Healy and it certainly isn't now." She gave a loud laugh. Duff smiled back. It was good to hear her laugh again.

"I hear a car," he said excitedly.

Meg cocked an ear. "You're right. Get ready to welcome our first guests, we're back in business!"

Duff sighed happily – life was getting on an even keel again. He'd learnt a lot about himself since the day Mary Keogh had walked into the house – some good, some bad, but above all else he'd learnt that Meg was his life, not the bottle. If it was possible he loved her more now than on the day, thirty years ago, when he'd stood by the altar and said, "I do."

*

James jumped out of his hired Audi outside Gartree Church, and walked hesitantly towards the wicket gate. He wasn't sure how his emotions were going to react, would he be overwhelmed with grief? Would his anger surface again? Would he be able to stand over the grave and talk to his father, or would he turn and run back to the Audi? Three possibilities that had been on his mind since catching the plane to Belfast. He would've liked his mother to be with him, and he'd struggled to understand why she refused. He acknowledged that she'd gone through a terrible time this last year and it had tested her resolve to the limit, but no more than him. She was now just beginning to put some sort of life together. But as he pointed out to her, so was he. He'd begged – he'd shouted, but she'd stood firm. "If I put a foot on Irish soil ever again, all the terrible memories will flood back and drown me. It may sound callous James darling but I will never go back. Your father would understand. Say hello to him for me though won't you?"

So here he was, alone. As he lifted the rusty old latch on the gate he would rather have been anywhere else in the world, and that filled him with disgust. How could he not want to say hello to the man who'd died trying to save him? The father he'd loved.

The psychiatrist had warned him he would feel like this – questioned if he needed more time before he went back to Ireland. "I need to say goodbye and it's been all of a year now," had been his answer. But right this minute he felt the psychiatrist might have been right. The sun was breaking through scattered clouds and the cemetery was bathed in its weak winter rays, lighting up the rather bleak surroundings. For some inexplicable reason it lifted his spirit and gave him a new resolve. He clenched his fists and moved up the path. The first thing he saw when he got near the grave was a small blue vase of fresh flowers. It was obvious whoever had placed them there made it a regular visits. He wondered who cared enough, Meg Healy perhaps, or an unknown friend from when his father had been Secretary of State? Whoever, it didn't really matter, but it eased his feeling of being alone. He dropped down on his knees – touched the marble head stone and smiled. "Hello Dad."

He wasn't sure how long he remained on his knees, just thinking about the man cut off in his prime; he didn't speak, time stood still. But he felt the anger, the grief, slowly drip from him, the psychiatrist had been wrong. This is what he should have done months ago. The huge black cloud that had hovered over him ever since he'd been flown back to England, a mental wreck, evaporated. As he looked up at the sun he could imagine his father looking down on him, willing him to move on. He rose slowly to his feet – made a silent promise that it would not be too long before he returned and this time *he'd* also bring flowers. He smiled for the first time for many months and moved back to the gate. He looked at his watch, and on the spur of the moment decided he wanted to visit one more place before catching his plane. He hurried towards the Audi – jumped in and turned the key.

*

The sun, now reflecting from a cloudless sky made Lough Neagh look tranquil as James walked slowly along the shore line. He was making for the old boathouse and quay, which his grandmother had told him had been built in 1885; "A quiet place where your grandfather and I liked to unwind at the end of a hectic day." Well it had proved far from quiet on the day the sniper had pulled the trigger. James had never had a chance to visit the boathouse but today he felt a compelling urge to do so. He walked on until he came to what remained of the building but there was no sign of the quay. He guessed it had long since slipped into the water. Several mallard rose in alarm at his presence and he could see the tell-tale ripples on the water where fish were rising. He understood why his grandparents had loved the Lough so much. He could imagine them walking hand in hand from the house to share a few minutes of peace with nature. How could they ever have imagined the evil that was watching them? The noise of an aeroplane passing over shook him out of his reverie and he realised it was no longer a place of tranquillity. Some remnants of the boathouse walls were still standing and he picked up a piece of stone that was lying in the reeds, he'd take it home. The shingled roof had completely collapsed. How different it looked to the photograph in his father's photograph album He looked up towards where the old house had stood over looking the Lough. All that was visible now was the airfield Control Tower where he'd been dragged by Declan. He shivered. It was time to leave, bad memories were still floating in the recesses of his brain and suddenly he wanted to be a long, long way away. He would never be tempted to come back.

As he turned to walk away he was aware of someone else walking on the Lough side. He screwed up his eyes and waited as the figure grew closer, a minute later he saw it was a woman wrapped up in a black coat, her hair was tucked into a baker boy cap, she waved. His heart leapt into his mouth. It was Mary!

"James."

"Mary!"

She stared at the ground, frightened she might see anger in his eye. "Yes, it's me," she mumbled.

James fought to recover his composure. He asked, "What are you doing here?"

"I followed you from the church. I shouldn't have done, I'll go."

"No! You just gave me a shock, stay."

Mary kicked nervously at the reeds. "If you really want me to, but you don't have to be polite."

James laughed. "I want you to stay. I've never thanked you enough for saving my life."

"You did, in hospital."

"I can't remember."

"But I killed your father."

"No, no you mustn't think that. It was an accident. As I said in the hospital nothing you did led to his death."

"You still lie nicely James."

James changed the subject. "Is it you who's put flowers on my father's grave?"

"Every week, it's my pathetic way of saying sorry. I was walking away when you arrived but I stayed and watched you."

"You should have called to me."

A flash of anger lit up Mary's eyes. "Why are you being so fucking nice? I don't deserve this. I'd rather you swore at me, even hit me. I'd understand that better."

"I don't blame you for anything. The truth is I think of you a lot – hope that Flanagan's thugs haven't hurt you. I often wonder what you're doing, you risked your life for me Mary. How can I possibly hate you?"

"Is that why you saved me from prison?"

"How could I testify against you?"

Mary shook her head violently and her hair flew out behind her. "I don't understand you, or the detective. He knew the danger I might be in when I was released from custody. So what does the man do? Let's me have a room in his house. He said. "Just until you find somewhere to go that is safe.""

"He's a compassionate man and he admires bravery. Whatever you did before you rescued me didn't deserve a prison sentence. Beside, there was no one else to testify against you. Flanagan unwittingly saved you, he killed all the witnesses."

"He must be turning in his grave."

James kicked at the ground. "Whatever, I'm glad you're here – really glad Mary. Tell me how are things with you?"

"I think you could say I've been lucky. My life could have been a lot worse. I'm not on the streets, though that was an option, I had no home, no friends."

James nodded.

"But apart from the detective, a good woman came to my rescue." Mary stared at James. "Do you know something, I can't understand why everyone who I'd hurt and despised is so nice to me."

"Meg Healy helped you?"

"Yes, she found me a job at a hotel in Belfast and lodgings nearby. She explained, very nicely, that they didn't want me back at Branscome, which I can quite understand but they wanted me to have a chance to make a fresh start. And next week I'm off to New York, Meg understands that I'd be safer out of Belfast. She has somehow persuaded a friend of hers who runs a hotel to take me on. She spoke very highly of me I'm told. Jesus, some people are mad. It's for the best. The detective thinks I could still be in danger even after a year. And now he's leaving the police force and returning to the mainland. To retire he says."

"So you're on you're way to a new life?"

"Yep. I want to go somewhere where I don't have the past sitting on the back of my neck like a dead weight and constantly in fear of being killed. I see Seamus round every corner. So I can't help but to agree with the detective."

"I understand your concern – I'd feel the same."

"And you James, what have you been doing?"

"I gave up my job as a journalist. The doctors said I needed time to rest and get my head back in order. So I went home, my mother needed me. I was told I needed peace and quiet and I'm still at home – don't think I'll ever leave. My mother has never fully recovered and I've fallen in love with farming."

"So like a good upper-class Englishman you'll look after your castle and your mother – marry a suitable woman who she approves of – raise children, and once they have left the nest you'll sit by the fire at nights smoking your pipe, watching your midriff grow, and reading the Racing Post."

James chuckled. "I don't think that's me."

"No, I think not, I'm just teasing."

James said, "I'm sure you'll be very happy in New York, it's probably for the best."

"Why did you say that?"

"Not sure."

Mary smiled. "So it's really goodbye this time James."

James returned the smile. "It looks like it."

"You seem flustered."

"No, no, oh I don't know. Perhaps I was hoping…it doesn't matter."

"Explain."

"I can't."

Mary searched his eyes. Surely that wasn't a tear she saw? She wondered if he felt the same, was he sad that they would never see each other again? Did he feel there had been a bond which was now about to be broken? *Crazy idea.* She was beginning to regret that she'd followed him, her emotions were not in check as she'd fervently hoped, and time had not dulled her feelings. *You stupid idiot, forget him.* She pulled her coat tightly round her and stepped away. "It's time I went, but one last thing before I go. I saved you because I knew that what I had done was *so* fucking wrong. I discovered that I wasn't the person Seamus had made me think I was. You changed me James – suddenly the hatred that was embedded in my soul evaporated. There have been times when I wish you hadn't."

"Oh Mary I'm so sorry."

"Oh for fuck sake James, stop being so English." She leant forward and kissed him lightly on a cheek. "There, probably the only kiss you'll ever get from a bad Irish girl. It marks the end of the book James. Soon I'll be thousands of miles away and you'll go back to your mother and your farming and maybe one day tell your wife about the little Irish girl who saved your life. Goodbye James – take care."

"You're very beautiful you know."

That completely threw her and all her intentions to walk away without showing any regret collapsed. "I've missed you," she choked.

Before James could think of a reply she turned and splashed away through the reeds. He smiled at her back; a strange feeling of loss came over him. He stood still. Was he thinking the ridiculous? He gave a little laugh and tore his eyes off Mary's back, looking at the Lough. He'd let her get out of sight before he moved. Out of sight out of mind? No! This wasn't how he wanted it, the feeling was so strong that it took his breath away, there was no way he was going to ignore it. He swung back round and shouted, "Mary! Mary! Stop!"

She carried on. He shouted again. "Please Mary stop!"

She heard the urgency in his voice, the desire to stop was so strong, for a moment she fought it with all the willpower she could muster, but her heart won. She stopped and turned to face him. He was running towards her. "Idiot," she shouted. "Leave me alone."

But he didn't stop, and as he got closer her limbs seemed frozen to the spot. Her legs refused to move, she waited.

"I don't want to close the book," he said breathlessly. "I think there are a few more chapters to write."

"You're crazy, or something?" Mary asked.

"Probably, but I can't write the chapters without you."

Mary felt her legs go weak. "You want me to be your co-author?"

"That's what I'm saying."

"Okay, as long as I get half the royalties."

His heart turned a somersault as he saw the twinkle in her eyes. "On one condition."

"That is?"

"That not every other word you write is fuck."

"Okay, it's a deal. But this shouldn't be happening."

"You really feel that?"

She whispered, "No."

"Then let's agree on one thing then, that we both want it."

"But we come from different worlds."

"Oh for God's sake Mary, stop trying to find reasons for us to walk away."

"This isn't real, it can't be happening to me."

"It is real, and at this moment I want it more than anything else in the world." James held out a hand.

Mary hesitated and shook her head. "I give in." She reached out and took his hand.

The End

Acknowledgments

My thanks to Jeannie, my wife, for all the hours she spent giving me advice, sometimes not too well received. To my daughter Caroline, Nina Kenyon and Ian Hutchinson for reading and editing the book. To all those at AuthorHouse UK for their support and help. And finally to my band of loyal readers for buying the book. But your pain is not yet over as another one is on the way.